W9-CJC-823

DREAMS LIE BENEATH

ALSO BY REBECCA ROSS

The Queen's Rising
The Queen's Resistance
Sisters of Sword and Song

REBECCA ROSS

DREAMS LIE BENEATH

Quill Tree Books
An Imprint of HarperCollinsPublishers

Quill Tree Books is an imprint of HarperCollins Publishers.

Dreams Lie Beneath
Copyright © 2021 by Rebecca Ross LLC
Map illustration © 2021 by Virginia Allyn

Library of Congress Control Number: 2021936685
ISBN 978-0-06-301592-0 — ISBN 978-0-06-322241-0 (special edition)

Typography by Molly Fehr
21 22 23 24 25   PC/LSCH   10 9 8 7 6 5 4 3 2 1

First Edition

To my parents, who first taught me how to dream

THE REALM

THE
SEREN DUCHY

THE FORTRESS
IN THE CLOUDS

ULLA

THE
MOUNTAIN DOORS

STARLING RIVER

HERESWITH

THE
BARDYLLIS DUCHY

N

W   E

S

... OF AZENOR

THE WYNTROUGH DUCHY

MARKSWORTH

CATRINE RIVER

ENDELLION

THE MERROW SEA

AMARYS

THE BOOK OF NIGHTMARES

PART 1

Magic of Old

September's new moon waited for the sun to set, and I found myself trapped in Mazarine's library, drawing her twelfth portrait by candlelight. For as long as I had known her, she had never left her house during the day, and she kept her curtains closed while the sun reigned. She liked to summon me every few months for various things, the foremost to commit her face to paper with my charcoal stick as if she forgot what she looked like, the second to read to her from one of her leather-bound books. I was eager to do both because she paid me well, and I liked the stories I could sometimes coax from her. Stories that came from the mountains. Stories that were nearly forgotten, turning into dust.

"Do I look the same as I did the last time you drew me?" she asked from where she sat in a chair, its armrests carved as roaring lions. She was wearing her usual raiment: an elegant velvet gown the shade of blood with a diamond necklace anchored at her neck.

The stone caught the firelight every time she breathed, winking with secrets.

"You look unchanged," I replied, thinking that I'd drawn her only three months ago, and I continued with my sketch of her.

She was proud, even with her multitude of wrinkles and her age spots and her strange beady eyes. I liked her confidence, and I drew it in the tilt of her chin, the hint of her knowing smile, and the waves of her long quicksilver hair. I wondered how old she was, but I didn't dare ask.

Sometimes I feared her, although I couldn't explain why. She was ancient. I had rarely seen her move from the furniture scattered about this gilded, shadowed room. And yet something pulsed from her. Something I couldn't identify but all the same cautioned me to keep my eyes open in her presence.

"Your father does not like when I summon you here," she drawled in a smoky voice. "He does not like you alone with me, does he?"

Her words unsettled me, but I concealed my feelings. The dimness of the room was like a cloak, and while it seemed impossible to draw a portrait in such poor light, I did it well.

"My father simply needs me home on time today," I said, and she knew what I implied.

"Ah, a new moon awaits you tonight," said Mazarine. "Tell me, Clementine . . . have you read one of my nightmares recorded in your father's book?"

I had not, because there were no recordings of her nightmares in the book my father filled and guarded. I didn't want to confess such to her, for fear it might upset her.

And so I lied.

"My father doesn't let me read all his recordings. I'm only an apprentice, Ms. Thimble."

"Ah," she said, drinking from a sparkling glass of wine. "You are an apprentice, but you wage war beside him on new moon nights. And you are just as strong and skilled as him. I have watched you fight in the streets on the darkest nights. You will surpass him, Clementine. Your magic shines brighter than his."

I finished with her portrait at last. Partly because her words fed a hungry spirit within me that I strove to keep hidden.

"Your portrait is done." I set down my charcoal, wiped my fingers on my skirt, and walked the paper to her. She studied it by the candlelight that burned from iron stands around her, wax dripping like stalactites.

She was quiet for a long moment. A bead of perspiration began to trace my back, and I felt anxious until she grinned, her yellow teeth gleaming in the firelight.

"Yes, I am unchanged. What a relief." She laughed, but the sound was far from reassuring.

My blood hummed with warning.

I gathered my supplies, tucking them into my leather satchel, eager to be gone. I couldn't judge the time of day, since Mazarine had the curtains drawn, but I sensed that afternoon was waning.

I needed to get home.

"A magician and an artist," Mazarine mused, admiring my sketch of her. "An artist and a magician. Which one do you desire to be more? Or perhaps you dream of learning *deviah* magic and combining the two. I would indeed like to see an enchanted drawing of yours someday, Clementine."

I hefted the satchel strap onto my shoulder, standing halfway between her chair and the double doors. I didn't want to say that she was right, but she had an uncanny sense of reading people. She had also watched me grow up in this town.

Since I was eight, my father had instructed me in *avertana* magic, a defensive magic that lent its strength to spars and duels. We often faced spells bent by malicious intent, which made for dangerous and unpredictable situations, such as the new moon nights. And I liked *avertana* more for those things, but I also had started thinking of the other two studies of magic, *metamara* and *deviah*—but *deviah* in particular. To take one's skill and create an enchanted object was no simple feat, and I had read of magicians who had devoted decades of their lives to reach such achievement.

I needed more time. More time to hone my craft of art before I tried to layer magic within it. I had taught myself how to draw and had gradually become proficient with charcoal, as art supplies were hard to come by in this rustic town, but I knew my experience was lacking, and there were many other branches of art, waiting for me to explore.

"Perhaps one day," I replied.

"Hmm" was all Mazarine said.

She at last rose from her chair with a slight grunt, as if her bones ached. I always forgot how tall she was, and I waited while she crossed to the other side of the room, where a bureau sat in a darkened corner. I listened to her open the drawers; I listened to the chime of coins as she gathered them in her hand.

"You claim I am unchanged," she said, coming to meet me where I stood. "And yet you are not, Clementine. Your skill is improving, in magic as well as art." And she extended her fist—knuckles like hills, veins like rivers beneath her papery skin, fingers full of coins.

I turned up my palm, and she paid me double. More than she had ever bestowed upon me before.

"This is very generous, Ms. Thimble."

"Your father and that housekeeper of his who looks after you may not like me. But you are the only one in this town who does not fear me. And I reward such valor."

I held her gaze, hoping my wariness wasn't shining like ice within me.

"Let me walk you out," Mazarine said with a sweep of her arm. "The day grows old, and you must prepare for tonight."

But she didn't move, and I sensed she wanted me to precede her. I led the way to the double doors, and she remained two steps behind me. We passed a mirror hanging on the wall, which I had never noticed before. Its frame was golden and elaborate, fashioned as vines and oak leaves. I saw my reflection—a girl with a smudge of charcoal on her chin and thick copper hair that refused to be tamed by a braid. My gaze began to shift to the doors when I caught a glimpse of what walked behind me.

Not Mazarine. Not the elderly woman I had drawn multiple times.

She was something else, tall and broad shouldered, her face creased and jagged like rocks, with a long nose that hovered over a thin, crooked mouth. Her skin was pale and her hair was still silver, but it was long and wiry, and threaded with leaves and sticks and thorny vines, as if she had risen from a forest. Two horns crowned her head, small and pointed, gleaming like bone.

Her eyes, large and dark and glittering with glee, met mine in the mirror for a fleeting moment, and I knew that I had just beheld her true nature. She knew it, too, and yet I didn't react. I told myself to walk no faster, to breathe no deeper. To remain calm and poised. I swallowed the urge to bolt and I paused at the doors, to give her time to open them for me.

"You can find your way out from here?" she asked.

I smiled. My face felt strange, and I imagined I was grimacing. "Of course." Once more, she appeared as the elderly woman that I had always known. But her eyes . . . I saw a trace of the wild being that she truly was, flaring like embers.

"Good. Until next time, Clementine."

I slipped past her and made my way down the curling stairwell, my boots clicking on the marble in a measured pace, because I knew she was listening.

Her butler—an old, craggy man dressed in livery of a lord long dead—was sitting in a chair by the front door, snoring. I tried to sneak past him, but he startled and stood, fumbling for the door handle.

"A good day to you, Miss Clem," he said in a raspy voice. "And may you be victorious in battle tonight, with the new moon."

"Thank you, Mr. Wetherbee."

While his eyes were gentle and haunted by cataracts, the sort of eyes a grandfather might have, I couldn't help but wonder what reflection he cast in a mirror: if he was the old human man he appeared to be, or if he was something quite different.

I passed over the threshold, descending the steps to the gravel path that led to the road. Triangles of shrubs grew in perfect symmetry, and when I reached the iron gate, I dared to glance back at the house.

It was a grand manor, built of red brick and three stories high, with square windows that glistened like teeth. The first magician of Hereswith had dwelled here, and then her successor. This had always been the domain of the town magician, and one would think magic still lingered in the walls and had seeped into the floors. And yet Mazarine had lived here for many years, according to the town records, and she was no magician.

She was not even human.

I wondered how she had accomplished such a feat, hiding her true face. Fooling us all.

I hesitated, as if to turn my back on the mansion was foolish. But at last, I pivoted away from the gate and began the brisk walk home.

Hereswith was not a vast town. My father and I could walk the entirety of it in the span of an hour. It was quaint, if one forgot the curse of the adjacent mountains. Cottages were snug, two storied, and built of stone and cob, capped with thatched roofs. Some had little gardens with ivy that attempted to eat the house; others had brightly painted front doors and mullioned windows blown from an erstwhile era. And then there was Mazarine's mansion, which felt overwhelmingly out of place with its grandness, but still lent character to the town.

To me, Hereswith was home, beloved, even as it seemed to languish beneath summer's final days. By late afternoon, when the sun began to set, the shadows from the Seren Mountains would reach us, and the breeze would smell of cold grass and smoldering wood and damp stone. Like old magic.

I never wanted to leave this place.

With each step I took from Mazarine's demesne, the more my doubt began to simmer. By appearances, Hereswith felt idyllic and charming. But I began to wonder if the town was hiding something beneath its exterior.

I learned a vital lesson from Mazarine that day. One that made me vow that I would never trust appearances alone.

2

"What is Mazarine?" I asked Imonie the moment I returned home. She was exactly where I knew she would be—in the kitchen, preparing dinner. My father and I always ate well on new moon nights, just before the streets turned deadly. If it wasn't for Imonie, the two of us would have been shriveled-up magicians with threadbare clothes and wounds that never healed properly.

She stood at the counter, peeling a mountain of potatoes. She was like a grandmother to me, although she was too young to be such a thing. She had never confessed her age, but I guessed she was in her early fifties. She was tall and trim and had threads of silver in her corn-silk hair, and while she rarely smiled, a few wrinkles touched the corners of her eyes.

"What do you mean?" Imonie asked, her attention devoted to her task. "Mazarine is a grumpy old woman."

"No, she's not."

It must have been the tone in my voice.

Imonie stopped her peeling and met my gaze. "Did she threaten you, Clem?"

"No," I said, despite the fact that there *had* been a moment when I'd felt afraid of her. When her gaze had met mine in the mirror.

"I've told you for years now to stay away from her."

"She's lonely and she pays me well. She also feeds me stories from the mountains." I intently watched Imonie's face, and I noticed how her brow furrowed. She longed to return to her ancestors' home in the Seren Mountains.

"I could tell you the same stories," Imonie said, and resumed her paring, viciously.

"Then why don't you?"

"Because they fill me with sorrow, Clem."

I fell quiet, feeling a twinge of regret. But in that silence, I thought of the mountain story she had told me often when I had begged her as a girl.

The realm of Azenor had not always been beset with tangible nightmares, although it was difficult to imagine such a world. It was all I had ever known, but Imonie had told me the legend that had started it all: Once, the mountains held a prosperous duchy. Magic itself had been first born in the summits, where the clouds touched the earth. But when the Duke of Seren was assassinated by his closest friends, the mountain province had sundered. Well versed in magic, the duke had cast a curse as he lay dying. No death and no dreams for those in his court who had been touched by the betrayal. They would live endlessly, watching as those they loved grew old and perished without them. And without dreams . . . their own hearts would become dry and brittle.

One does not realize how powerful a dream is, in the sleeping world as well as the waking one, until it has been stolen from them.

The duke had died on a new moon, and that was when the mountains began to spin nightmares into reality, all across the other two duchies of Azenor—the valleys and forests and meadows of Bardyllis and Wyntrough. No one could escape it, and so magicians had risen to answer the danger, perfecting the *avertana* branch of magic and becoming wardens of intricately mapped territories. Like my father.

Imonie hefted a sigh, as if she knew the exact story I was imagining. It seemed fitting for a new moon day, though. And she set down her potato and knife, leaning on the counter to fix a firm gaze on me.

"I can smell her from the road when I pass that ugly manor," she said. "Moss and stone and cold winter nights."

I waited for Imonie to continue, eager to know the truth. Eager to know who I had been drawing over and over for months now.

But then Imonie smirked and asked, "What do you think Mazarine is, Clem?"

"I think she's a troll from the mountains."

"You're probably right, although I haven't gotten close enough to her to see for myself."

"Is she cursed?"

"Cursed? I think whatever guise she dons is one of her own making, how she wants to be perceived. For while Hereswith has warmly welcomed those such as me from the mountain duchy . . . do you think the mortals here would be delighted to know a troll dwelled among you?"

"Most people would be afraid of her," I confessed. "Although it seems people already are."

"And perhaps she likes the fear," Imonie said. "Just enough to keep people and their suspicions away. So she can live peacefully here." Her eyes narrowed at me. "And how did you come to know her true nature?"

"I caught her reflection in a mirror," I answered, and remembered seeing her two steps behind, crouching toward me with her bloodied teeth and fierce, dark eyes. Would she have harmed me? I wanted to believe that she wouldn't.

I began to consider a spell I might craft to protect myself, sharpen my senses when I was in her presence.

"A foolish blunder on her part, then," said Imonie.

"Actually, I think she planned it," I countered, tracing the bow of my lips. "She wanted me to see who she truly is."

"Why?"

I realized I still had charcoal on my fingertips, that I must have smudged a mustache on my face. My hand drifted away to hold the strap of my satchel.

"I think she wants me to draw her true self."

"Of course she does!" Imonie grumbled, returning to her task. "Trolls are insufferably vain."

"Is something burning?" I asked, sniffing the air.

Imonie went rigid, and then rushed to the oven. A thin plume of smoke rose when she cracked the oven door. "You've made me burn the galettes!"

"They look fine," I reassured her as she took a mitt and retrieved them from the oven.

"Clementine?" my father called from upstairs.

Both Imonie and I froze. When she looked at me, I saw the worry in her expression.

"Is he still sick?" I whispered.

"His fever has yet to break," Imonie said. "Best you go up and see what he needs. Here, take him this cup of tea. Make sure he drinks it."

She took the kettle from the stove and poured a cup of a pungent-smelling brew that made my nose crinkle. But I took it as she ordered, nearly burning my hand on the mug. I didn't realize it, not until I was on my way to the stairs. I set my art satchel down and glanced at the table and saw only one place was set with the fine china. My place. Imonie had not set a dinner plate at my father's chair, which meant she believed he was too ill to face the new moon.

I had never encountered a new moon night on my own. He and I were always together in the streets, fighting as one.

Dismayed, I climbed the stairs and stepped into his bedroom.

My father was sitting up in his bed, leaning against the headboard, waiting for me. He seemed to get sick every year, right around this time. When summer surrendered to autumn, my father inevitably fell prey to a fever and a cough, blaming it on a final bloom of some vengeful valley weed. And while he always recovered within a few days, I still didn't know what to do with him when he was like this.

"Papa?" I tried to hand him the tea mug, but he motioned for me to set it on the bedside table. "Did you need something?"

"I received word of a nightmare this morning," he said.

"Whose?"

"Spruce Fielding's youngest daughter."

"Elle?"

"The very one. She had a nightmare last night. According to Spruce . . . it frightened her so badly that she hasn't spoken a word today."

I quirked my mouth to the side, my heart aching with this news. Children's nightmares were always the worst. They were the recordings that kept me up at night when I read them. They were the dreams I dreaded to see stalking the streets on new moon nights.

"And you need me to go and record it," I surmised, and a quiet thrill went through me. I had never been the one to divine a nightmare, or to record it in my father's book. I accompanied him most of the time, and I observed, and I read his recordings afterward so I could prepare for the new moon. But never on my own.

"Yes, Clem," Papa said, and I could not discern if he was proud or nervous. "Don't use the divining spell unless you absolutely *must*. And if you must, please use my spell, word for word."

I nodded and felt his gaze as I moved about his cluttered bed-chamber, gathering supplies for the visitation.

"I will, Papa." I opened his cupboard, where a hoard of tiny blue vials waited within, gleaming in the light. Remedies. I selected two, the corked glass the size of my pinkie. The dark brew sloshed within them as I hesitated, thought better of it, and grabbed three more vials, slipping them into the deep pocket of my charcoal-streaked skirt.

"Divining," my father continued, as if he was about to impart a lecture. I inwardly braced myself. "Particularly done with . . . oh, how do I say this, with *precarious* intent, can open a door that you might not know how to close."

As if to prove a point, I shut the cupboard door, more forceful than necessary. I could hear the vials rattling in protest, and I met Papa's gaze, swallowing an impatient response. Sometimes he acted like I had no inkling how to cast a charm or divine a nightmare. This was a lesson I had heard countless times from him, before magic had even sparked at my fingertips.

"I haven't done anything precarious in *months*, Papa."

And by precarious, I meant *spontaneous*, when magic came to me in the moment. The sort of magic he was afraid of. That was why he was diligent in studying the nightmares, so he could prepare potential spells. His memory was immense and deep, and while I admired him for it . . . my strongest magic was forged from intuition.

I felt him watching me, thoughts churning. He was stern and imposing, even as he perspired from a fever, bedridden. I favored him in appearance, far more than I did my mother. My father and I were both tall and willow thin, with square jaws and large brown eyes and wiry auburn hair, lustrous as copper when it met the light. A stranger could tell we were kin from a mile away. But that was where our similarities ended. Our souls were two different points on a compass; the intent behind our magic flowed in opposite currents. He was cautious, reserved. Traditional. And I wasn't.

I knew what he saw in me. I was young and reckless. His one and only daughter, who favored the wilder, natural study of magic. My ideas and spells scared him sometimes, although he would never say such a thing aloud. Because without me, Papa would never take a risk.

"Pack what you need for the divination," he said.

Relieved that he believed me capable, I walked to his desk. A detailed map of Hereswith was spread over the wood, river rocks pinning down the four corners. It was a map I had memorized with its crooked, winding streets. Above the desk, shelves lined the wall, burdened with leather-bound spell books, stacks of paper, jars brimming with crushed flowers and salt crystals and swan quills, ornate ink pots, cast-iron spoons with jewels embedded in the handles, silver bowls nestled into each other, a potted fern whose wilting leaves dangled like unrequited love.

I gathered what I needed: a bowl that shone like a full moon, pink salt, dried gardenias, a spoon with an emerald chip, a pitcher full of water, a swan quill, a silver inkwell that was crafted as an octopus, its tentacles holding a vial of walnut ink. I charmed them all beneath my breath with a shrinking cantrip—a spell my mother had taught me—until the objects could sit cradled in my palm, and I slipped them into my pocket, where the remedies waited. The objects clinked like musical notes when they met, weightless as air.

My father made a noise of disapproval. Of course, he wasn't fond of any sort of *metamara* magic, which transformed and influenced objects.

"Why don't you pack a bag?" He indicated his worn leather satchel, sitting on the floor beside his writing chair, like a sad dog awaiting a walk.

"My pockets will do fine." My leather satchel was for my art supplies alone, and I didn't want it mixing with magical ones yet. "Now, then. Where is the book?"

"There will be absolutely *no* enchanting the book to make it fit in your pocket, Clementine."

"Very well. I'll carry it in my arms, like a good *avertana*."

Papa wasn't amused. But he relented, feeling the urgent pull of the afternoon, the slant of sunlight as it began to shift across the floor. I wouldn't have much time to fetch the nightmare. So he uttered a spell in his storytelling voice, smooth and polished like sanded oak. And the book of nightmares materialized. It had been sitting on the map of Hereswith, in the center of my father's desk, charmed invisible.

Clever, I thought. All these years, I had believed my father had simply hidden the prized ledger in a secret nook.

I took it reverently, surprised by how heavy it was. Seven magicians had kept detailed dream recordings before Papa had come to Hereswith, and I had always hoped to become the ninth magician, after my father retired. But I felt the weight of those inked dreams of people now dead and buried. I felt them as if I had embraced a millstone.

I met Papa's gaze, and he saw my shock. I hadn't realized it until now. The weight he carried as the town's magician. And suddenly . . . I didn't know if I was strong enough to bear it.

"Come here, daughter," he whispered.

I crossed the room, the book heavy in my arms, and sat on the edge of his bed. I could feel the feverish heat rolling off him in waves, and it made me worry.

"I've taught you all that I know," he said. "You'll do just fine recording this dream, as long as you stick to the rules and predetermined spells." He paused to study me with squinted eyes. "You know, it's not a bad thing to be fearful every now and then. The fear reminds you of limits, of what lines you should not cross. Of the doors you shouldn't open."

"Hmm."

"And what does that sound mean?"

I smiled. My dimples I had stolen from my mother, and I knew my father softened at the sight. "It means I hear you, Papa."

"Hear but do not heed?" he countered, but he was teasing. "Regardless, it's time for you to do a visitation on your own. Go to the Fieldings and come directly home. If you're not back before dusk, I will come searching for you. And we both don't want that."

"I will return with time to spare," I said, rising from the bed. "And if you're not feeling well by nightfall, then I can—"

"I will be more than fine when the new moon rises," Papa growled. "Tell Imonie to set me a place at the dinner table. We'll eat before we go, as we always do."

There was no sense in arguing with him, no sense in telling him that he might be more of a burden, that his fever would make him and his enchantments weak and frail.

"Drink your tea," I told him, and slipped from his bedroom.

I descended the curling stairwell of the cottage, scaring Dwindle, my old calico cat, on the way down.

"Did I hear your father say to set him a place at the table?" Imonie asked, her back angled to me as she tended to meat sizzling in a skillet.

I often forgot how sharp her hearing was. She could hear through walls, it seemed.

"You did, and I don't think he'll listen to reason." I stopped at the counter, where the pan of almost-burned cherry galettes was cooling. "And you should stop eavesdropping, by the way. One day you'll hear something you wish you hadn't."

"We'll see about that," Imonie said with a snort, seeming to answer both dilemmas—my father's stubbornness and her keen hearing. She glanced up at me, a rare smile warming her solemn face. "Now, are you going to help me fry this venison, or are you going to tend to that nightmare?"

"Ugh, I'm off, of course." I pushed away from the counter but swiped two cherry galettes.

"Clementine!" Imonie cried, but she wasn't surprised as I grinned and shoved one of the pastries in my mouth, bolting out the front door.

I lingered by the withering jasmine at the front gate, long enough to tuck the remaining pastry in my pocket and look up, to where the clouds were streaked like ribs across the sky, exposing a burning heart of sun.

What a strange day.

I glanced at the book of nightmares in my arms. It was a tome, the sort that could hold back an ironclad door. I had read only portions of it, and some accounts had made me laugh at their absurdity, while others had actually made me fall asleep, only to wake hours later with my cheek pressed against the caramel-tinged pages. But there were some recordings that made me shiver, dreams influenced by the mountains. They had sparked such fear in my bones that I hadn't slept for a week after reading them, although none of these nightmares belonged to me.

No. I studied nightmares, and I confronted them every new moon in the streets of Hereswith, when the magic flowed freely from the mountain fortress and dreams were cursed to materialize. But I didn't know what it was like to experience a nightmare. What it felt like to wake frightened from something that felt hauntingly real.

As a magician, I chose to never dream.

 3

I walked through town, holding the book of nightmares on my hip like it was a child, smiling and waving to the people I passed. All who I knew well, by name and by dream alike. I hurried when I reached the market, the heart of Hereswith, where both gossip and activity thrived. I didn't have time to be ensnared by either one, and I followed the eastern road to the lower edge of town, where the cottages became more distant from each other, melting into verdant patches of farms marked by low stone walls.

I smelled the Fieldings' sheep before I reached their gate. A black-and-white collie barked as I approached the front door, which sat ajar. I hesitated on the stoop; I could hear a faint argument, just within the cottage. . . .

"We can't afford it, Jane. Our daughters need bread more than they need dreamless sleep."

"Look at her, Spruce. Will you do nothing? She won't even speak!"

"The girls have brought this on themselves. I've said this time and time again, and those cards need to be—"

"Those were my *grandfather's* cards!"

Spruce sighed. "I've summoned the magician. If you won't see the cards burned . . . what more do you want me to do, woman?"

I didn't like Spruce Fielding's tone. I knocked on the door, and it creaked open farther, exposing the central room of the cottage. Jane Fielding, a woman whose blond hair was lank and streaked with gray, sat on a threadbare couch with a bundle of blankets—which was probably her youngest daughter—cradled on her lap. Spruce, a ruddy-faced man with a thick brown beard who was so tall he had to stoop to avoid banging his head on the timber beams, was pacing until he saw me.

"Miss Clem!" he said, surprised as he moved to greet me. "Thank you for coming. We were expecting—"

"My father," I concluded. "Yes, I know. But he's in bed fighting a fever. I've come in his stead."

"Oh, I'm sorry to hear that," Spruce said, removing his cap to twist it in his hands.

"Sorry that I'm here, or that my father is ill?" I jested, hoping to lighten the mood as well as the dread the Fieldings were expressing upon the realization that *I*, and not my esteemed father, had come to divine the nightmare.

Spruce was speechless. Sometimes the men of Hereswith didn't know how to take my wit. I stepped into the room, my eyes adjusting to the dim interior light.

All five of the Fielding daughters were present. Two were in the loft, peering down at me like roosted birds, and the other three were on the main level. The eldest was chopping carrots in the kitchen; the second-eldest, by the hearth, was trying to make a quilt out of scraps; and the youngest, the one whose dream I had come to glean, was indeed wrapped in her mother's arms. All the girls' names began with an *E*, to my distress. I could never keep any of them straight—Enya, Esther, Elizabeth, Edith—save for little Elle, who had a palindrome name, something I had always wanted.

Elle, who was around seven and far too thin and small for her age, blinked at me from the edge of her blanket.

"Hello, Elle," I greeted her. "May I come sit next to you?"

The little girl gave a curt nod, and I sat beside her and her mother on the lumpy couch, easing the book of nightmares down to rest on my thighs. I detested having an audience, how both parents watched me with wide, dubious eyes, and how the sisters froze like statues, soaking in my every move. Even the collie, who had snuck into the house, sat in a patch of sun, one blue eye and one brown eye pinned on me.

I hated resorting to stagecraft. The sort of magic my mother reveled in. The art of enchanted performance that provoked emotions in observers, whether it was horror, delight, or wonder.

But this was a moment for stagecraft if there ever was one. I could feel it call to me as the tension and worry began to overpower the room. And I was thankful for those early years, for my oldest memories. Memories I refrained from rousing too often, for fear they would crack me. A time long ago, when my parents had still been together in the city. All those evenings I had sat on my father's lap in the theater, watching Mama perform magic on the stage.

"I have something for you, Elle."

The little girl said nothing, only watched me with large, frightened eyes.

I held up my palms, to prove they were empty, before cupping my hands together. I silently called forth the cherry galette from my pocket, lifting one of my hands up in the air to reveal the pastry.

Jane Fielding gasped in delight—stagecraft *did* have its perks—and the wonder captured her youngest daughter. The blanket lowered a fraction, then a little more, until Elle's arms were free. She smiled and accepted the galette, and I suddenly wished I had brought more, to feed the four longing stares of the older girls.

The silence was awkward as Elle began to munch on the pastry. I decided this was a good time to prepare for the divination.

"Mr. Fielding? Do you mind bringing one of your kitchen chairs over here? I need to use it as a makeshift table."

He quickly obliged, shooing his daughter Elizabeth, who had been sewing by the hearth, out of the way.

Elizabeth left her scattering of quilt and stood near me. That was when I noticed one of the cards on the floor, nearly hidden beneath a square of fabric. Its illustration caught the light, even as the card itself was tattered. I discreetly studied it, unable to quell my interest as an artist.

The painting depicted a svelte man with a shock of long white hair, dressed in colorful, ornate raiment. A top hat sat on his head, spilling a shadow across his face. Only his crooked smile and his eyes could be discerned, glinting like two emeralds. His title was hand-lettered beneath his feet. *The Master of Coin.*

I wanted to reach for the card. I wanted to hold it and study its illustration, to learn from whoever had painted it, long ago. A story caught in time on paper.

And then I remembered myself. I was visiting as a magician, not a pining artist. But I now understood the conversation I had overheard on the stoop. The Fielding girls must have played a round of Seven Wraiths, and little Elle must have lost, ending up with one of the seven illustrated cards in her hand. While I had never played this game, as my father and Imonie both detested and forbade it, I knew there was great enchantment within its rules. To lose with one of the seven wraiths in your possession meant you would experience a nightmare the next time you lay down to sleep.

I withdrew my attention from the card and prepared for the divination. I called forth the trinkets from my pocket, speaking the reverse spell. They returned to their normal sizes without qualm: the silver bowl, which I filled with water from my pitcher, and the jars of salt and gardenia, the octopus inkstand and quill and the iron spoon with the emerald chip.

"Did you have to go to school to learn how to cast magic, Miss Clem?" Elizabeth asked.

"No. My father taught me most of what I know," I replied. "My mother also taught me a few spells."

Elle had finished devouring her galette. I took my time opening the book of nightmares, leafing through the fragile pages until I found the latest entry, which Papa had penned four days ago. One of Lucy Norrin's nightmares, which I often found to be ridiculous on the spectrum of dreams.

"Do you want to tell me your dream, Elle?" I asked.

Elle shook her head, her curls bobbing.

"She hasn't spoken one word today," Spruce said, hovering. "I've tried to get her to describe it, but it was that game . . . that bloody game!" He pointed upward, to the two daughters in the loft. "You should have known better than to let your little sister play."

"Mr. Fielding," I said coldly, drawing his attention. "It's paramount that the dreamer be calm when I cast a divination. If you can't be quiet, I'll have to ask you to step outside."

He was thunderstruck that I had spoken to him in such a way, but he swallowed his retort and silently stewed.

I smiled at Elle. "Then I must cast a spell, so I can see your dream. Is that okay, Elle?"

Elle clung to her mother, fearful.

"You won't have to see it again, Elle. Only I will. Okay?"

The child buried her face into Jane's chest, and Jane sighed. "Please do, Miss Clem. I know the evening is coming, and we mustn't keep you here much longer."

But I waited for Elle to glance at me again, more curious than afraid now.

I poured a few crystals of salt in one palm. Next, I gathered some dried gardenia petals in my other hand, extending my palms out to Elle.

"Which one do you like more?" I asked, coaxing the opposing fragrances to rise.

Elle studied them both but pointed to the clean rainstorm fragrance of the salt.

A girl after my own heart, I thought as I dropped the crystals into the bowl of water, returning the flowers to their jar. I took my spoon and began to hum my father's divination spell, stirring the water until the salt had dissolved and the emerald in the handle cast a green pallor on the surface.

The nightmare still lingered in the cottage.

As soon as I found the dream's door, etched in shadows in the center of the room, the Fielding family froze, as if I had stopped time. I knew they were experiencing the opposite from their vantage point; they were waiting with suspended breath, watching a glazed-eyed, entranced version of myself as I inwardly located the lurking threshold of the dream.

Focusing on the door, I rose and opened it.

I stepped into Elle's dream.

Elle is in the market of Hereswith, accompanied by two of her sisters and her father. Things feel normal but the light is gray, and distress ripples at the edges of the dream, like the pounding of a distant drum. The mountains are dark shadows in the distance, but fires burn along their slopes, marking the fortress in the clouds. Night falls, sudden and nonsensical, and the crowd in the market vanishes in a blink. Elle is alone, searching for her father, her sisters. A cold mountain wind blows, rattling shop signs and scattering loose papers on the street as Elle runs from door to door, knocking, begging to be let in. They are

all locked, the windows darkened, shuttered. And then comes a dif-
ferent noise. One that pierces Elle's heart with fear.

Heavy footsteps. They meet the cobblestones slowly, deliberately,
clinking like strange music.

At once, Elle's thoughts race.

Hide, hide. Whatever it is, don't let it find you. Hide . . .

She runs through the streets but there is nowhere to hide, and the
heavy footsteps faithfully follow her. They grow louder—closing the
distance between them—and Elle whimpers as she tumbles back into
the market green. She crawls toward a wagon and cowers beneath its
bed, crying, although no matter how hard she tries to scream for her
father, no sound emerges from her mouth.

She finally sees a glimpse of the one who is hounding her, whose
tread makes that strange music.

A knight is walking to her, as if he knows exactly where she hides.
She sees him from the knees down as he approaches the wagon in those
measured, heavy steps. His armored legs and feet gleam silver in the
darkness. Plated steel and rusted with blood.

He unsheathes a sword, but he lets the tip of it drag along the
cobblestones at his side, as if he wants to hear the tempered steel screech
and spark against the rock.

He comes to a stop, directly before the wagon. Elle trembles, stares
at his steel boots, the edge of his sword. And then she hears the creak of
his armor as he begins to bend, to crouch, reaching for her . . .

I jolted.

The dream had broken, spitting me back into reality, and I
drew in a deep breath.

I was sitting in the Fieldings' cottage. The afternoon was warm, the light golden as the family gazed at me, and yet I felt the chill of Elle's nightmare. I could still hear the echo of those strange, armored feet that had followed her. The ring of the sword dragging on the stones.

Who was he? I wondered, glancing at Elle.

But I couldn't ask the girl. Not now, with the dream lingering like smoke in the air, choking us both with fear.

I took up my quill and ink and recorded the nightmare swiftly in the book. My hand trembled; my penmanship was slanted and riddled with blots. Papa would no doubt notice later when he read it and asked me why this nightmare bothered me so badly.

"Well?" Spruce Fielding prodded when I had finished the recording, shutting the tome.

I looked up. "Well what?"

"What was the dream? Why won't she speak? Was it truly so frightening?"

I didn't reply. I began to gather my things, shrinking them back into my pocket until I remembered the remedies. I had brought five, and I withdrew the glass vials as I stood from the couch.

A swallowed remedy kept dreams at bay for an entire day. The good ones as well as the frightening ones. If drunk before bed, a person would experience a tranquil sleep. An inner fog, culled of dreams. Like my sleep, every single night.

I handed the first one to Elle. Then I moved to Elizabeth and gave her a vial. Next, the oldest sister in the kitchen. And lastly, I enchanted the remaining two remedies to float up to the loft, where the roosted sisters continued to observe. They reached out in awe when the vials hovered before them.

"I didn't ask for any remedies," Spruce said, wringing his hat again. "I can't pay for them. Why did you—"

"I know you didn't ask for them," I cut him off, weary. I smiled one last time at Elle and Jane Fielding before turning to leave. "I give them to your daughters freely, but I would like a word with you, sir."

Spruce followed me outside into the yard. The sun had already set behind the mountains and the shadows were long and cool. Dusk was coming, and I felt the urge to get home as quickly as I could.

"I know what you're going to say, Miss Clem," he said.

I arched a brow. "Oh? And what is that, Mr. Fielding?"

He raked his hands through his thin hair. "My daughters shouldn't be playing Seven Wraiths. I know your father disapproves of the game. I know it makes his work *that* much harder, with nightmares sprouting up like weeds, thanks to the cards being dealt. But I can't keep my daughters from playing it. They're of Seren ancestry; both my and Jane's families hail from the mountains. And so my daughters will continue to play the game, even with the threat of nightmares, just as Jane and I once did. Because we long for home, even as it lies in ruins, doomed. Even as we have never seen it with our own eyes. Only in dreams do we behold it."

Silent, I listened to his every word. I knew the Fieldings were of mountain descent, just as Imonie was. I knew they would not be able to return to the home of their ancestors until the new moon curse was ended. But I didn't think such a spell could be broken by playing a game of enchanted cards, which had ironically been inspired by the same curse. In particular, by the seven members of the mountain court who had each played a hand in the Duke of Seren's assassination.

"It's not my place to tell you whether or not your daughters should play the game," I said. "All I wanted to do is to remind you that the new moon comes tonight. Ensure your shutters are bolted, your doors are locked, your family and livestock are all safe inside tonight, Mr. Fielding."

"As I do every new moon, Miss Clem," he said, somewhat indignant. But then he seemed to realize what I was implying, because his scowl and voice mellowed. "You don't think . . . that my little Elle's nightmare will manifest tonight?"

I didn't know. But it inspired a tremor in me when I imagined coming face-to-face with the armored knight who reeked of violence, who had threatened a little girl. I had to confess that Elle's nightmare had felt alarmingly tangible. It had fooled me for a span of terrifying moments, when I had been her, believing everything was real and unfolding, as if I could have reached out and touched the cold glint of the knight's bloodied armor. And perhaps it was only due to my inexperience with divination, and perhaps it was only due to the fact that this nightmare had been spawned by a sinister card game. But it felt heavier than the others I had encountered.

I glanced at the mountains. If the new moon chose to spin Elle's nightmare when the stars began to burn . . . the knight wouldn't be a wisp in a dream. He would be flesh and blood encased in steel, and his sword would be ready to cut.

I wanted to know who he was, what he wanted. If he was inspired by someone.

I bade Spruce Fielding farewell and began to walk home, my gaze on the sunset. But I feared I wouldn't be able to find the answers I sought. Not until I challenged the knight in the streets of Hereswith.

4

"Miss Clem!"

I was just coming upon the market, which had become vacant as shops closed early for the evening, when I was intercepted by a frantic Lilac Westin, the revered baker in Hereswith. Flour dusted her face as she all but collided with me.

"Miss Clem, there are two men in the market!"

I blinked, wondering what this had to do with me. Whether she was attempting to play matchmaker, which she had woefully done with me in the past.

"Are men forbidden from the market these days, Miss Westin?"

"If only they could be," the baker countered, but then pondered on such a possibility, and her face creased with a frown. "Although my business would surely suffer for it. But no, there are two men—*strangers*—lurking about town, asking about your father."

"My father?" I echoed. "Why would they be asking after him?"

Lilac hesitated, and I saw the panic in her expression. Quickly, I moved around the baker and made for the market on quiet tread, hiding behind a stack of empty wire cages at the trader's stall. Lilac rushed behind me, and we stood in the shadows and watched the two men drift aimlessly about the market.

They were not what I expected. I had envisioned dignitaries sent by the Duke of Bardyllis to collect the town's dream tax, milling about with rings on every finger. Or perhaps delegates from the Luminous Society, visiting to ensure my father was adhering to all magical laws. Or perhaps descendants of the fallen mountain duchy, such as Imonie and the Fieldings, searching for a safe place to settle. But these two men were dressed in dark clothes, finely tailored, with silk-lined cloaks and rapiers belted at their sides. They were too young to be ranked members of the duke's court, too inexperienced to be delegates. Nor did they appear to be seeking sanctuary. But they boasted the air of ones who thought they were important, their posture stiff and proper.

They walked past a burning streetlamp, and I finally saw it. The men cast no shadows, and I sensed the illumination within them.

They were magicians.

"How long have they been in Hereswith?" I asked.

"For an hour now," Lilac said. "They've gone from shop to shop, asking where to find your father. None of us will tell them. And Mr. Jeffries—*bless* him—agreed to put their horses in his stable but closed the inn early, refusing to give them admittance,

34

so they've been wandering, seeking hospitality and answers."

I continued to watch the magicians. One was blond, his hair trimmed short, his face coldly handsome as he knocked on the Brambles's door. The other magician had dark hair bound with a ribbon, and his face was trapped in a scowl, as if he had smelled something foul. They looked related, one like day, the other like night. Brothers, most likely.

And they could not be here for anything good.

They were uninvited, trespassing on my father's territory.

"I bet they're vultures," I murmured, thinking of all the magicians who visited Hereswith to glean information about the doomed fortress in the clouds. *Vultures* was the word we used for such people, because they only wanted stories from us before traveling to the mountain doors—the sole passage to the summit, where Seren's abandoned stronghold waited for someone to arrive and break the curse. One could reach the fortress if they could merely open the mountain doors, which sounded quite simple until one realized the doors were enchanted and impossible to open since the curse first fell a hundred years ago. But it didn't deter ambitious magicians from trying, and using us along the way.

"Miss Clem," Lilac whispered. "If they're vultures . . . why are they asking for your father?"

Her question gave me pause. She was right; when vultures arrived, they wanted to speak to mountain descendants, not the town warden. My voice wavered when I said, "Then they must be here to challenge my father for Hereswith."

It had been a good while since such an event had occurred. So long, in fact, that I had almost forgotten it always hung as a possibility.

I was ten years old the first time it happened. Two older magicians had come to town on the heels of the southern wind, just before the new moon, and had challenged my father for the right to guard Hereswith from nightmares. A year after that, another set of them had arrived, keen to win the town that thrived in the foothills of the infamous mountains. In both instances, the magicians *at least* had the courtesy to write to my father a fortnight in advance, informing him of their intentions. And while it didn't seem fair, the newcomers could lawfully win the title to become warden of the town and displace my father, but only if they defeated the nightmare before Papa did.

He had vanquished the challengers in both instances. But my father was ill tonight. I would most likely face the new moon on my own, and I had never encountered competition when it came to a nightmare's defeat.

"Are you going to speak with them, Miss Clem?"

I glanced at the baker, who had crossed her arms and was glaring in the direction of the men. "No, I'm not," I said, relieved the Brambles had refused to open the door to them.

"Then I will." Before I could ask what she planned to say to them, Lilac marched out into the market and drew their attention with a sharp whistle.

I remained lurking in the stall, and while I couldn't hear what the baker said, I saw her point to the northern street. Point to where Mazarine's mansion sat visible on the hill, catching the last hue of the sunset.

I watched, mouth ajar in horror, as the magicians nodded and began to take the northern road, up to the troll's mansion. I had every intention to go directly home and avoid crossing paths with them. I had every intention to mind my own business and leave the strangers to their fate.

In fact, I made it halfway home before I stopped at the crossroads.

But I turned north and took a side street, rushing over the cobbles, cutting through a neighbor's garden, jumping a low rock fence, to catch the men before they became Mazarine's next unexpected meal. If I hadn't known what she truly was, I wouldn't have chased after them. Or so I told myself as I hurried to meet them on the road. They were almost at her gate. And I had a moment of hesitation, a moment of doubt. . . .

"The magician you seek doesn't live here," I announced.

My voice startled them.

The blond actually made a noise and jumped, to my immense satisfaction, but the dark-headed one only widened his eyes at the sight of me emerging from the dusk.

"Of course the magician lives here," the blond said with a sweep of his hand. He glanced back to the manor. "This is the finest house in town."

"The magician doesn't live here," I said again, sharper. "And I must say it's a terrible night to arrive, gentlemen."

The dark-headed one studied me with hooded eyes. I sensed

he was not at all impressed until his gaze drifted to the book of nightmares I held. He saw the flame within me, then, although the dusk made it difficult to measure my lack of shadow. But he said nothing, only brought his gaze back to mine.

The blond, however, was belligerent. His pride was bruised from being turned away and snubbed by every single resident of Hereswith. "We know which night we arrive, miss. And *you* are not the town magician."

He meant it as an insult. I only smiled.

"Indeed not. That would be my father."

The magicians exchanged a careful glance.

"Then you must be Clementine Madigan," said the dark-headed one.

I had to swallow the shock of that—to hear my name flow from a strange magician's mouth. I hoped that I didn't flinch, that my smile didn't falter. "I am. And you're both lucky that I've chosen to aid you this night, despite the fact that you've arrived *unannounced*. Come, you can sup with my father and me, and we'll put you up for the night, since the new moon is rising and you need to be off the streets."

I turned and began to walk home, listening as the magicians scrambled to follow me.

Imonie heard us coming, long before I even laid a hand on our gate. She heard me and the tread of unfamiliar boots in my wake, and she threw open the door with a murderous look on her face.

"You're late, Clementine."

I came to a stop on the stoop, narrowing my eyes at her. "Yes, well, I ran into these two magicians on the street."

She scrutinized them over my shoulder. A long, uncomfortable moment passed. "I see that." She brought her eyes back to mine and said, "Go and tell your father we have company."

I did just as she bade, and found my father still in bed, flushed from fever.

"Who did you bring home?" he croaked at me.

I stood in the center of his chamber and stared at him, realizing he was worse than before.

Dread unfurled within me, and I set the book of nightmares back on his desk.

"I found two magicians wandering the town, seeking you. I brought them here, so they're off the streets tonight."

"You *what*?" He was suddenly ripping the quilts away, stumbling to his feet. I reached out to steady him, because he looked like he was a breath from fainting, his eyes unfocused until they found me. "Who are they?"

"I don't know their names yet."

"Are they from the Luminous Society?"

"No, they're not."

Papa stared at me, but he was not seeing me. His gaze was very distant, and he was suddenly shaking.

"You need to lie down . . ." I tried to direct him back to bed, but he broke from my grip, lumbering to his wardrobe and drawing out fresh clothes. A long-sleeved linen shirt, a green waistcoat with golden embroidery, a white cravat, a black jacket . . .

"Papa."

"Go and change, Clementine, and then return to me here," he

said, pausing to lean on the wardrobe. "We both must look our best tonight."

He must sense it, then. He was being challenged by upstarts for his town, for our home.

I left his chamber and shut the door, tarrying in the upper hallway, listening. Imonie was setting two more places at the table; she set the china down with clinking intensity. The magicians were quiet, but I heard them walking in the room beneath me, the floor protesting their elegant steps.

I slipped into my bedroom.

A few candelabras were lit, casting uneven shadows on the walls. My window was closed and shuttered tonight, because of the new moon. The desk before it was messy, crowded with my journals of spells and illustrations, a tray of pastels and charcoal and half-drawn imaginings. Imonie had already laid out clothes: my favorite black-and-white striped skirt with pockets, my weapon belt, a stark white chemise with billowy sleeves, a velvet bodice that laced up the front.

But I chose not to wear any of it. I poured lavender-steeped water into my basin and washed my face and arms. And then I went to my wardrobe and found the dress I wanted. A long-sleeved gown made of black velvet. I had only worn it once before, to a winter solstice party that my father didn't attend, and the looks I had drawn made me so self-conscious that I decided I wouldn't wear it again.

But this night seemed to call for it.

I undressed, remembered I still had tiny trinkets in my pockets, and returned them to their proper size. I drew the black dress on, pulling the golden ribbon at the bodice tight.

I brushed my hair but left it down, and I fastened my leather weapon belt to my waist. Two small daggers gleamed at my hips as I walked back to Papa's room. The belt had been his gift to me on my fifteenth birthday two years ago, when he had at last allowed me to join him in fighting on the new moons. In my mind, it marked my coming of age.

He was sitting in his chair this time, dressed in his finest and out of breath from the effort. This was truly going to be a disastrous night, I thought, and watched him frown at my choice of clothes.

"Where did *that* come from?" he asked.

"It's one of Mama's old dresses," I said. "She sent it to me last year."

His frown deepened, but then he coughed, and it seemed he forgot about the gown. I poured him a cup of water, which he drained, and then he stood and motioned for me to come closer.

"How are your stores, Clem?"

I knew he was asking about my reserved magic, the amount I had available to burn. Magicians could fuel their spells in one of three ways: body, mind, or heart. Depending on what energy force the magicians preferred to cast with, we needed things like food, drink, sleep, good company, books, art, music, and solitude to refill, or risked burning ourselves into oblivion.

I often cast with my mind and my body, and while the dream divination had drained a portion of my reserves, I measured myself and found that I still had plenty to give.

"My stores are good."

"Then I need you to glamour me."

"*Glamour* you? This fever must truly be making you senseless."

"Yes, just a little. To hide that I'm ill."

He waited for me to do something. I merely gaped up at him.

"Papa . . . I don't think—"

"This *is* a good idea," he said, reading my mind. "Please, daughter. This night is important, and I must make an appearance with the arrival of these . . . visitors."

"But I don't think you should fight tonight," I said. "You're far too sick for it."

"We'll see. Perhaps I'll feel better after dinner."

Unlikely. But he was right; these magicians had come all the way to Hereswith to see him, and he looked terrible.

I drew in a deep breath and worked a gentle charm over him. Another spell of my mother's. One that brushed away his paleness, the perspiration on his brow, his glazed eyes, the lankness of his hair, the uneven tilt of his shoulders. But the glamour wavered, and I saw a much different version of him. There was no gray at his temples, no hollowed cheekbones, no furrows in his skin. It was like catching a glimpse of him from the past when he had been younger, before I had been born, and it rattled me a moment. As soon as it came, the vision was gone, and I thought it must have been influenced by my glamour. He now looked vibrant and hale, just as I knew him to be, and I exhaled a soft sigh.

My father rushed his palms over the front of his jacket, which was already pristine under Imonie's care. He was nervous, I realized, and I reached out to take his hand. The fever still burned beneath his skin. I felt a stab of fear for him.

"Whatever the reason they've come," I began, "I'm sure it's not as terrible as we both imagine."

He only smiled at me, tucking my hand into the crook of his elbow.

Together, we descended.

5

The blond magician was beside the hearth, where the shelves overflowed with books. The dark-headed one was standing on the threshold of the solarium, gazing into the small glass chamber, where Papa and I grew an array of plants. The magicians reeked of curiosity and judgment, as if our provincial lives were something they would later spin into a joke they told at court, and I stiffened the moment they both turned toward my father and me.

Imonie had already taken their cloaks, and I could see they were dressed in the latest fashion: cream cravats, waistcoats embroidered with moon phases and stars, black jackets with coat-tails, trousers with silver trim running up the sides, knee-high boots that only carried a hint of dust from the road, and belts with rapiers sheathed at their sides.

I sensed their weapons were not intended to keep them safe on their travels.

"Mr. Ambrose Madigan," the blond greeted Papa with a sharp smile. "It's an honor to meet you. Allow me to introduce us. I'm Lennox Vesper, and this is my brother, Phelan."

"You're the Countess of Amarys's sons," my father said, and while he sounded polite, I heard the cold shift in his voice. "You're also a long way from home and the luxuries of your court. What brings you to the border?"

Lennox was still smiling, but it was stretched far too wide, and he reminded me of a puppet in a child's nightmare. "We've come to see Hereswith. To go as far as we can before stepping into the mountain duchy."

"The mountain duchy is no more," Papa said. "And Hereswith would have been better prepared if we had known of your visit."

"Yes, well, it was a sudden change in plans," said Lennox, and he glanced at his brother. Phelan was silent, but his eyes were on me, dark and inscrutable. On the gleam of weapons I wore at my hips.

"Come, then," my father said, indicating the table, where Imonie had just finished setting down dinner platters. "Eat with us tonight. Refresh yourselves. You must indeed be weary from a long journey."

"And we thank you for your generous hospitality, Mr. Madigan," Lennox said, and unbuckled his belt, leaving his rapier by the door.

Phelan followed suit, but I was not about to shed my weapons, even if it went against all manners to partake in a meal armed. The four of us arrived at the table, and an awkward moment passed.

The guests were to take their seats first, to lower themselves in gratitude, but the magicians were not sitting.

No, Phelan was staring at the meal that was spread between us, and Lennox was staring at me.

"Forgive me for asking, Miss Clementine," Lennox drawled. "But do you always take part in a meal with weapons on your belt?"

"It depends on the night," I replied. "And the company."

Lennox laughed, a garish sound that instantly set me on edge. Like Mazarine's laughter had. I felt my hands gripping the back of my chair, my knuckles draining white, and I wished I had let them knock on her door.

Phelan finally broke the tension. He drew back his chair, sitting with an elegance that was reminiscent of a waltz. My father and I waited for his brother to also relent, and then we were gathered at the table, ready to eat.

My stomach was wound in a knot, but I put a proper amount of food on my plate. Venison with currant jelly, rosemary potatoes, glazed carrots and beets, boiled eggs, and a cold salad of fruit and toasted nuts.

Imonie was pouring ginger beer in our glasses when Lennox sniffed his napkin, studied the water stains on his fork, and then cleared his throat.

"Do you mind if I cast a cantrip, Mr. Madigan?"

My father sounded wary. "What sort of spell is necessary during dinner?"

"To see what ingredients are in the food. I have a delicate disposition."

I snorted, only to draw everyone's attention. I raised my glass to them and drank, to hide the curl of my lips.

"Just eat the food, Lee," Phelan murmured with a twinge of mortification.

"You should cast too, you know," Lennox whispered in return, and that was when I realized *why* the magician wanted to sift through the food. He thought we had poisoned it, which was irrational, since my father and I were also eating from the same platters.

Papa came to a similar conclusion. "If you fear an upset stomach, don't worry. We have plenty of herbs to calm it. If you fear poison . . . then let me reassure you, Mr. Lennox. It's bad fortune to harm a guest under one's roof, and I don't intend on bringing terrible luck upon my household."

"What a reassurance," Lennox said, and he continued with his cantrip, searching the food on his plate and the ginger beer in his cup.

Imonie stood beside the china cabinet and watched with a flat expression. But her eyes shone like obsidian.

I forced myself to eat. I was sitting across from Phelan, and I noticed how he cut his meat into proper bites, how he handled his fork and knife. I made a point to be his opposite. My cutlery screeched against my plate, provoking winces from the men, and I put a hunk of meat in my mouth, my fork upside down.

Phelan watched in shock, as if he couldn't believe my manners. Lennox looked disgusted.

I smiled as I chewed, close lipped and full of terrible thoughts.

My father cleared his throat. "May I ask how long the two of you plan to stay in Hereswith?"

"It could be a short visit," Lennox said, dragging his disbelieving gaze from me. "But then again, we might decide to stay for a while."

"Could you please provide me with the date you'll be departing, then?" Papa continued, and from the corner of my eye, I saw his hand was trembling as he speared a potato with his fork.

"We have no definite date as of yet." Lennox sounded smug. "But as it is the new moon . . . I was wondering what sort of nightmares haunt your town, Mr. Madigan. Are they indeed vicious, since you dwell so near the mountains and the accursed Seren Duchy? What sort of terrors stalk the streets on the darkest of nights?"

My father was silent. But he stared across the table at Lennox Vesper, and I felt the chill in the air. A chill that expressed how angry my father was, even as he secretly smoldered with a fever beneath the glamour.

"The nightmares are mine to keep, Mr. Lennox," Papa said. "I'm the warden of Hereswith. These streets are mine to guard, these people mine to honor and protect. Despite your education and polished upbringing, you seem to have forgotten the most basic of laws and respect when it comes to the magic of dreams and guardianship."

Lennox chuckled, reaching for his ginger beer. "I've not forgotten at all, Mr. Madigan. My memory is rather sharp, and I do nothing without thought."

"Then let's not dance around the bear," I said, impatient. "What do you want?"

Lennox glanced at me, fair brow arched. "I believe that is something I need to discuss with your father, since he is the magician of Hereswith."

Despite my confidence, I felt my cheeks flush from the way he made me sound of little consequence. As if I were no one and nothing important.

For one brief, terrifying moment, I imagined Lennox had come to ask my father for a partnership. To have the opportunity to be warden of Hereswith alongside Papa. To uproot and replace me. I knew from my brief upbringing in the capital that nearly all warden magicians took partners, because the collection of dreams was a cumbersome task and nightmares had the capability of being anything. It was always best to have someone guarding your back on the new moon, to grant you aid if a violent dream unfolded.

"My daughter is my partner and has vast knowledge of magic," my father replied, as if he shared the same worry. My posture softened, relieved. Although I was not his partner *yet*. Only his apprentice. "Whatever you have to say to me can also be said to her."

"Yes, of course, Mr. Madigan," said Lennox with a forced smile and a graceful motion of his hand. "I suppose there is no sense in delaying, since night has fallen." But he glanced at his brother, as if seeking reassurance. Phelan was silent, staring into his goblet. He eventually lifted his eyes and nodded, and my dread rose, threatening to drown me.

Lennox stood.

He set his gaze on my father, and it seemed like the firelight dimmed and the shadows deepened around us. He withdrew a red silk handkerchief from the inner pocket of his jacket and dropped it onto the table. I watched the fabric flutter down, resting on the wood like a patch of blood.

"*Sever occisio loredania*. I have come to challenge you, Mr. Madigan. I have come on this new moon in the month of September to win the right of guardianship and the title of warden for Hereswith."

Lennox's announcement rang in the chamber, reverberating off the walls and the windows and the roof of my childhood, sundering my peace. The challenge teemed about us, shimmered in the air like rain in sun. I breathed it in, felt the incantation lock about my heart like an iron cage.

Sever occisio loredania.

My father and I sat frozen, staring up at the young magician. Lennox waited, shifting his weight as the heavy silence continued.

"Did you hear me, Mr. Madigan? I said I challenge you—"

My father rose. The chair nearly overturned in his haste, and my heart was pounding, my hands shaking as I also stood. Papa had not won the wardenship of Hereswith; it had been passed down to him when the previous magician had retired, nine years ago. He had never stood in the place of Lennox Vesper. He had never stolen territory from another magician.

"I heard you, Mr. Lennox," said Papa, and his voice was hoarse, his distress making my glamour waver on him for a breath. "I accept your challenge. You have an hour to make it to the market green of Hereswith, where Clementine and I will meet you for the challenge of the new moon."

Lennox bowed. He left his red handkerchief on the table as a mark of contract, and retrieved his cloak and weapon, Phelan following him. I held my breath as I watched them depart. Even Imonie seemed unable to breathe as she stood in the kitchen, staring at the table, the dinner half eaten on the plates.

The cottage was quiet again. A quiet that wanted to crush my heart.

I turned to look at Papa, my glamour melting away from him. It should have held for at least another hour, but my magic turned brittle in that moment.

"Here, Papa. Sit."

He allowed me to ease him back into the chair, and he sat with a groan.

"Imonie?" I glanced at her. "Some warm wine with clove and honey for Papa?"

She began to move to the wine cupboard until my father spoke.

"No," he said. We never drank before battle because it dulled the senses, and I knelt at Papa's side, my thoughts whirling.

"You're too ill to accept this challenge, Papa. Let me answer it for you."

"I've no choice, Clem. And I won't let you face them alone." He looked at me, his eyes bloodshot. "I've no choice," he repeated in a whisper, and rubbed his brow. We didn't have much time, and I cracked my knuckles, anxious until Papa took my hand.

"We have the advantage," he said, and Imonie rushed to make him a warm cup of tea since he would not take the wine. "We know the nightmares that might appear tonight. The magicians of Amarys don't."

"Yes, but . . ."

"We'll treat this night no differently, daughter," my father said. "Let me rest for half an hour and then we'll go." He leaned his head back against the chair and closed his eyes.

Imonie set the cup of steaming tea down on the table. She looked at my father before she pinned her gaze on me.

"This is your night, Clementine," Imonie said. "Your father will accompany you, but you'll have to be his strength. You'll have to defeat this dream before that upstart does. Be patient. Be shrewd."

I nodded. She spoke those four words to me—*be patient, be shrewd*—every new moon, just before I went to battle. I think she worried about a nightmare getting the best of me; I had a tendency to rush through things, although I had never been badly wounded before.

My courage wavered, but only for a moment.

I met Imonie's stare and offered her a tilt of a smile.

"Any other words of advice, Imonie?"

She snorted, but it was impossible to decipher what she was thinking.

"Don't underestimate these magicians. Particularly the quiet one. He was watching you very closely tonight."

I remembered the way Phelan had regarded me, the way he had spoken my name.

And all I could think was, *I should have let the troll devour them both.*

6

The night was cool and quiet as my father and I walked to the market. Every door was bolted, every shutter closed. It never ceased to surprise me how different Hereswith felt on new moon nights. Desolate and achingly silent, menace chilling the air like fog. It felt abandoned.

I dwelled on the legend of Seren's fall, like I did every new moon, my gaze drawn to the dark shadow of the mountains. The fortress in the clouds had been abandoned when the curse had been set a century ago, and yet I wondered what phantoms walked those mountain passages. What joy and light and friendship had once crowned the summit, before the duke's assassination. Before everything fell apart.

Some legends claimed the duke had been a cruel man, passing harsh judgments on his people. His sadism had been the reason why the seven members of his court were driven to kill him. But other stories depicted him as a gentle ruler, claiming his court plotted his demise because of their own desire to rule.

I wondered which one was true as I slowed my pace to keep in stride with Papa. His breaths were labored, his steps arduous. We were almost to the market; the constellations teemed above us, like sugar spilled across black velvet, and I drew in a deep breath.

"You never told me about Elle Fielding," he whispered.

Fetching Elle's nightmare already felt like a week ago. "I had to divine the dream. It was . . . unusual."

"How so?" Papa came to a stop and turned to face me.

"The setting was here, in the streets and market. She was being pursued by a knight."

"By night?" He indicated the celestial sky above us.

"No, a *knight*. An armored person of prowess." I paused, remembering the heavy cadence of his feet as he walked, the rust and blood on his steel. The sparks of his sword. "He was a threat, but I couldn't see his face. I couldn't discern what he wanted . . . but it was very sinister."

The silence roared between us. I glanced up to see a flicker of fear in Papa's face.

"What did the armor look like?" he asked sharply. "Was there anything strange about it?"

I tried to describe it, but I had only been afforded a glimpse of his legs.

"And what weapon did he carry?"

"A sword," I replied, frowning. "Have you seen this knight in a dream before?" I asked, which was a foolish question, as I had read all my father's nightmare recordings. Every single one. Unless he had some entries hidden from me. And I inevitably recalled Mazarine's words, spoken earlier that day. *Tell me, Clementine . . . have you read one of my nightmares recorded in your father's book?*

I had never read an entry of Mazarine's, which meant she either drank remedies and kept dreams at bay, like me, or she did dream and my father had broken a sacred law of wardenship by refusing to record her nightmares. I wondered why Papa would do such a thing—willingly omitting a nightmare from the ledger—and yet I couldn't find a good enough answer.

The possibility made me tense, and I stared up at my father, measuring his expression by starlight.

"No, I haven't seen a knight like this before in a dream. Come, daughter. The sons of Amarys are waiting. It's time to send them home." My father's swift dismissal only fueled my sudden reservations.

"You don't like their family?" I asked, remembering the ice in his voice when he had heard the brothers' names.

"Their mother is an old acquaintance of mine." That was all my father would say, and I was too hesitant to pry for a better answer.

Lennox and Phelan Vesper were waiting for us in the center of the market.

They stood like statues as Papa and I approached. They stood like they belonged here, like they had grown roots in Hereswith, and I inwardly despised them for it. Papa and I came to a stop a good distance from them, a safe stretch of grass between us.

"Are you certain you know what you're doing, Mr. Lennox?" my father called to him. "There is still a chance to recant your challenge and suffer no humiliation from it."

Lennox grinned that terrible puppet's smile. "I know what I do, Mr. Madigan. And there will be no humiliation on my part."

His confidence was unnerving, but I thought I saw Phelan roll his eyes, as if annoyed with his brother's theatrics. I watched the quiet brother closely, limned in starlight, seeking a weak point in his spirit.

Phelan looked at my father and said, "We don't want any bad blood between us, Mr. Madigan. Nor do we want there to be any unnecessary injuries tonight."

He is noble of heart, I thought. *Or considers himself to be.* Which almost made me laugh, because there was nothing honorable in arriving to another magician's territory unannounced and seeking to steal it.

"Do you want me to surrender without a fight, then, Mr. Phelan?" Papa countered, his voice edged with ire. "Do you want me to surrender this town and its inhabitants after I've given years of my life protecting it? Is that how wardenship works in the city you hail from?"

Phelan had the decency to appear briefly shamed.

"Of course not, Mr. Madigan," Lennox rushed to say. "And besides, you are here with your daughter, and we are ready to play out the challenge. Whoever defeats the nightmare will win the right to Hereswith."

"Win the right," Papa murmured, and I knew the words galled him, because they certainly irritated me. "Very well, then, Mr. Lennox. When the clock strikes nine, the new moon is announced, and your challenge will begin."

All of us glanced at the market clock, whose face was illuminated by lanternlight. Three minutes remained, and they dragged by like years.

I fought the temptation to pace, to fidget. I made myself stand like stone, just as the two upstarts did, and waited for the clock to strike nine.

Finally, the chime sounded.

And the mountain wind blew through the streets, sweet and dark and full of magic.

Lennox frowned as he glanced about the market, waiting for the nightmare to materialize. Sometimes the dreams were born quickly, as if they were ripe and bursting, eager for the mortal world. Sometimes the dreams arrived gradually, shade by shade, like an artist painting a canvas. Sometimes they were easy to defeat, and Papa and I would be home within the hour with only a few rips in our garments. Sometimes they lasted until dawn, stubborn and vicious and crafty.

As I waited to see whose nightmare greeted me that night, I noticed Lennox and Phelan were rigid, and I knew this victory was ours. Papa was right; we had the advantage. We possessed the knowledge, the experience. I knew every nook and cranny of the streets of Hereswith, every garden, the slant of every roof.

This town was my home, and I would defend it.

I noticed the rain before the men did. Before Papa, even. A drop fell in my hair, then on the back of my hand, the moisture gleaming like a jewel on my skin. I resisted the urge to look up at the sky, because I didn't want to tip off the magicians, but I took hold of Papa's arm and began to guide him away from the market.

"Papa, let's go," I whispered.

Lennox's eyes bugged at the sight of us retreating. I sensed he was tempted to follow us, to mimic everything we did, but Phelan had the same idea as me. He drew Lennox to the protection of one of the market stalls, and they melted into the shadows.

It was wonderful to no longer have to look at them. It was also unsettling, because now I wasn't sure where they were or what they were doing. But I inwardly shook myself alert, giving my focus to the nightmare that was coming to life.

Papa and I stood in the eastern street beneath a hanging shop sign as the rain began to fall thick and hard, drenching us within moments.

"Do you recognize this dream, Clem?" Papa asked me, bending close to my ear so I could hear him over the melody of the rain.

"I'm not sure." But I had an inkling. I looked down to the cobblestoned street, where puddles were beginning to deepen, iridescent.

And I knew it, then.

This was Archie Kipp's dream. A little boy who had almost drowned earlier that summer and now was terrified of water. A child's nightmare, and they were always the hardest ones to champion.

Papa recognized the dream when the puddles became ankle deep within a moment. "We need a boat," he murmured.

I nodded but waited, holding my magic on the tip of my tongue, where it crackled like salt as Papa strove to build us a boat. The water was rising quickly now. It was almost to my knees, and I felt my first true pang of trepidation.

"Papa?" He was taking too long. His magic was weak and dim, beating like a faint pulse. I saw that he was attempting to build something infallible, a small boat of tin and wood, and while I admired his sense of grandness, I knew the flood would rise swiftly. And once it did, the serpents would also arrive, slithering in the water.

"Let me," I said. Papa glanced my way, and I saw how he trembled with exhaustion. The waters were mid-thigh now, and I didn't want to drown tonight.

My father reluctantly nodded and I felt the shift of power flow from him to me. This battle was not ours anymore; it was mine.

I called to the stray pieces of nature around us—stalks of hay, threads of grass, feathers from nests, lichens from roofs, smoke from chimneys. I sensed I needed more, so I reached farther with my magic and gathered the distant sound of an argument leaking from a threshold, the wail of a baby, the song of a mother, the sting from a skinned knee. I wove everything together and I made a small boat, rough-hewn and narrow but sturdy.

It bobbed on the water as Papa lifted me up and set me within its frame. I helped him next, and the boat nearly tipped as he hefted himself up and over with a groan. But we were safe from the flood. I quickly created a paddle from a few floating sticks, propelling us along the streets that had transformed into canals. The water was deep, lapping at second-story windows, and I wondered how much deeper it would become. Would it continue to rise until it reached the mountaintops, until it reached the stars?

"Look for the key, Clem," my father said.

I didn't need his reminder, but I held my retort. Every nightmare had a "key" that could appear in a number of forms and be physically claimed. It was the way to break a dream swiftly. If the dreamer could recognize and claim the key while the nightmare was ensnaring them, then they would wake. It was a similar experience on the new moon. I needed to find the weak point of the dream, locate the key in whatever form it took tonight, and wield it before the Vesper brothers.

"First the flood, then the serpents," I reminded him, because the key to the dream would not appear until all the elements of the nightmare manifested. And so I navigated the boat and wiped rain from my eyes and waited for the snakes to arrive, my body tense as a coil, ready to spring into action.

My boat hit resistance. Frowning, I tried to paddle with deeper strokes, but the boat was hung up on something in the water.

"Can you see what's impeding us?" I asked Papa, since he was sitting at the bow.

He carefully shifted to peer over the edge. "Lily pads."

I sighed. Of course, I had forgotten about that one element of the nightmare. Archie was afraid of drowning, afraid of snakes in the water, and afraid of lily pads.

I quickly began to paddle us backward, and I could see the thick knot of lily pads on the water as we retreated. They seemed innocent, perched on the surface with their green leaves and blossoms, but I knew better than to trust them on the new moon.

I rowed to another street, my eyes constantly searching the water, awaiting the serpents. I imagined I saw something slithering through the depths, but it was difficult to tell for certain. The rain eased, the flood line coming to rest right at the eaves of roofs, and the lily pads were multiplying. I bumped into another nest of them and had to reroute yet again, and my shoulders were beginning to smolder from the effort; my hands were pruned.

I had nearly forgotten about the Vesper brothers until I caught a glimpse of them farther up the street, paddling in their own boat. They rounded a corner, slipping away from sight, and I had a strange urge to follow them.

"Don't lose focus, Clem," Papa said, and I had to swallow another quip.

My attention was drawn to the water beneath me, where a small golden light trembled beneath the surface. I leaned closer, the boat rocking, and realized it was a coin drifting through the water, as if someone had cast a wish into a pool.

"Do you see that?" I cried, and rose with haste, handing the paddle to my father.

"Clem, *wait*—"

But the coin was the key, I thought urgently, and it was about to fade away. I jumped overboard and let the water close over my head as I swam after that tantalizing gleam of gold. It led me through the streets, and I had to surface twice to gulp in fresh air. My father was close behind me, paddling the boat in my wake, and I descended into the water again, chasing the key.

I'm not sure what happened first. The water around me turned bitterly cold and I lost sight of my quarry. Pausing, I treaded in place and felt the corresponding tug in my lungs. I needed air, and I rushed to swim up to the surface. Only I couldn't find it. I was suddenly entangled with lily pads. I couldn't break through them; I couldn't reach the surface. In my panic, I couldn't recall a single convoluted spell for breathing underwater.

I fought and pushed and kicked. The more I resisted, the more I became entangled. My lungs burned; I was overwhelmed, fading in my own skin. Something slid past my leg. One of the serpents. My heart leapt in fear.

I'm about to drown. . . .

I quit trying to breach the surface and grappled for one of the daggers hooked to my belt. *Be calm*, I commanded myself as I methodically hacked at the lilies, hacked at the serpents that were gathering and weaving a net around me with their thin, long bodies.

I was nearing the surface, and I saw the shadow of a boat nearby, waiting for me. *Papa*. I kept my focus on it and broke the surface with a desperate gasp of air. My eyes stung, and I clambered for the boat, hefting myself up into its safety. Sprawled within its hull, I spluttered and coughed. I was trembling, and my head was throbbing, but a sharp sting on my left calf snagged my attention.

I drew up my dress to my knees, exposing a serpent latched to my leg, its fangs buried in my skin. It didn't feel real, even as my eyes smarted from the intense pain, and I merely gaped at it a moment, struggling to remember where I was, what was unfolding around me, my mind foggy from the lack of air.

A blaze of light shot like an arrow, striking the serpent dead. Its writhing body instantly went limp, but its fangs were still caught in my leg, and a hand I didn't recognize carefully unhinged the serpent and tossed it overboard.

My gaze rose.

Phelan Vesper.

I had climbed into *Phelan Vesper's* boat.

For a moment, all I could do was pant and stare at him in numb shock. I coughed again, my lungs burning vividly. I wiped my face and pushed my dress back down, hiding my legs and the blood that was trickling out of the fang marks.

"Are you all right?" he asked.

"I'm fine," I wheezed.

I closed my eyes and leaned back in his boat until I felt steady again. A foolish thing, as I shouldn't trust him. Particularly since I had no idea where his brother was.

I listened to the sound of his paddle dipping into the water as he rowed us away from the lily pads. I could have lain there, limbs melted like wax, for hours, but I forced myself to sit up and take in my surroundings.

I saw Papa farther down the street, the lilies blocking him from reaching me. But our gazes crossed, and he hurried to angle his boat into a side street. I knew what he wanted me to do.

The roofs around us bloomed like mushrooms from the water, and when Phelan rowed us close to one, I leaned toward him. My graceful motion had him instantly wary, and he stopped paddling, his eyes glinting with a dark warning to maintain my distance.

I ignored it, and I dared to touch his face, a fleeting caress that seemed to enchant him into stone.

"Thank you," I breathed. My hand slipped from his cheek and promptly shot a hole in the boat with a beam of magic. He startled as the water began to surge around our ankles.

I leapt to the nearest roof, struggling to find purchase in the thatch. I scrambled up to the apex of the roof and glanced back to see Phelan furiously trying to mend his boat, in vain. It was a moment from being completely submerged, and he glared at me.

"Your gratitude is noted, Miss Madigan," he said, and jumped onto the same roof as me.

I gave him a mock curtsy before I hurried down the other side, where Papa sat waiting for me. I settled into our boat and whispered, "Hurry, Papa."

My father paddled us away, and I glanced over my shoulder to see Phelan standing on the thatched roof, stranded. But I felt the bite of his gaze until we turned onto a different canal and he was finally lost from my sight.

Shuddering, I sat back and took a fortifying breath.

"I told you to *wait*, Clementine," my father growled.

"I know, and I'm sorry," I said, my attention straying to the challenge. "Have you seen Lennox?"

"He's in the water."

I looked over the edge of the boat, where serpents slithered just beneath the surface, and I saw the gleam of the key again. Drifting and taunting me to pursue it. A splash sounded behind me, and I turned to see Lennox cresting the water, slipping back into its domain, effortless as a fish. He swam alarmingly fast; he must have enchanted himself.

I stood in the boat as he passed by us, so swiftly not even the serpents could entangle him.

"Don't forget there's a cost to every charm, Clem," my father said, reading the anguish in my eyes.

"Yes, and we're about to lose this town, Papa." I watched as Lennox rose from the water again, to breathe before diving back beneath the surface. I remembered how it felt to nearly drown, how the water tried to sneak into me and weigh me down, and yet I couldn't bear to face this defeat. To have my home stolen from me by a magician like him.

I inhaled and spoke a long, twisted charm. Wild and spontaneous magic that lurked in my bones. I called upon the last of my reserves and watched the sadness overcome my father's face as gills blossomed in my neck and I struggled to breathe in the air, gasping.

I tumbled back into the water and filled myself with it, my gills flexing in relief. I found my second dagger on my belt and I took it in my hand, swimming and cutting through the serpents. I discovered that if I swam deep, where the cobblestones lurked like a riverbed, the snakes would not bother me, and so this was my path. It was dark and cold and quiet, but I could see the golden shine of the key up ahead. Lennox hovered near the surface, struggling with a patch of lily pads. He had charmed his feet into fins; that was why he was able to swim with such agility.

I neared the key, and my heart lifted as I anticipated ending this challenge. It had at last found its resting place on the street. I swam slow but steady, drawing in water, letting it wash through me, my hair streaming like a fiery pennant. I realized upon closer examination the key was a golden rock the size of my palm, wedged into the cobblestones, and I saw Lennox cut himself loose far above me. He noticed my presence then, and began a furious descent. I quickened my strokes, but my left leg was aching, the serpent's venom affecting how strongly I could kick.

I was reaching for the lambent stone when Lennox's fingers closed about it. He tugged, but the rock held fast, and he frantically worked to uproot it with his dagger. I knew his air was wearing thin—his face was mottled and I wondered if he was about to drown himself, all for pride. I wondered if I should interfere—if I should stab him—and the mere idea drummed an ache in my stomach.

So I waited. Waited for his lack of air to force him back to the surface, for him to abandon the key.

But his dagger found the root of the stone, and he worked it free from the ground. Instantly, the nightmare broke, and the flood began to drain into the hole the rock had left behind in the ground. I felt the water swirl around me, the pressure ease in my ears, my gills flutter in desperation. The serpents turned into silt, the lily pads into pollen.

It was over. I was vanquished.

And through the eddy of draining water, Lennox grinned at me.

7

"You dear, foolish, reckless girl," Imonie said to me, but there were tears in her eyes as she eased my head back beneath the water. I was sitting in the tub, my left leg hanging over the side so she could tend to the serpent bite. But my gills had yet to fade, and I couldn't breathe air. I was confined to the bath, where my gills would allow me a minute or two above the surface before they screamed for water.

There's a cost to every charm.

My father's words haunted me. Perhaps my gills would never fade. Perhaps I would be doomed to live the remainder of my life in a tub or a lake. I sank into the water and breathed it in, suddenly thankful that it muffled the sounds of the world. Sounds of Lennox speaking to Papa just beyond the closed door. Sounds of townspeople ringing the bell, distressed to hear that there was a new warden in Hereswith. Sounds of Imonie simultaneously scolding and praising me as she cried.

I had lost the town. Our home. And the guilt weighed heavily in my chest.

I remained beneath the surface, my heart broken. I felt as if I had been turned inside out of my own body, like I had been split open and I didn't know how to hold myself together. I was uncertain if it was due to the shock I was feeling, to acknowledge I had been defeated by Lennox, or if it was a side effect of my rash enchantment.

I knew a few fundamentals of *metamara* magic, which studied the transformations and adaptations of nature and objects. I knew enough to get me in trouble, and it made me think of my mother. Of what she would say to me if she saw me in this moment, half girl, half water creature.

Imonie's hands were gentle as she drew the poison from my wound with a salve, and when her ministrations were done, she left me alone. I remained in the water for another hour, until I felt the painful shift in my body. My gills closed, forcing me to sit up, to return to the air.

I coughed up the last bit of water. My skin was pruned as I carefully climbed out of the tub and dried off. I pulled the cork and watched the water swirl and drain, swirl and drain until the tub was empty.

I had hesitated. That was why I'd lost. I should have stabbed him. I shouldn't have waited for his air to run out, allowing him the chance to win. There was no one to blame but myself, and I longed to turn back time, to change my actions.

The mirror hanging above the washbasin drew my gaze, and I stood before it, as if I had forgotten my own face.

The gills had left behind scars in my neck. Three thin slashes on each side just beneath my jaw, catching the light like iridescent scales. I gently touched the scars, surprised by their tenderness. They would remind me of my loss, of my foolishness, and yet I didn't feel the urge to hide them.

I stepped into the dining room. Lennox was sitting at the table, papers spread out before him, spectacles perched on his nose. My father sat across from him, bleary eyed and still running a fever, drawing up the contract for the new warden. Phelan stood before the bookshelves, reading the illuminated spines and holding a cup of tea. Imonie was bustling in the kitchen, cooking away her distress. All four of them stopped their tasks and looked at me. I stood on the rug in a slant of morning sunlight, my black dress still wet from my long submersion, my hair a snarled, copper mess around my shoulders.

"Well met, Miss Clementine," Lennox said in a cheerful voice, holding up his glass of mulberry wine. "I must say you were a worthy opponent."

I said nothing, staring at him until his smirk eased and he returned his focus to the papers.

My father's gaze lingered on me the longest—he was noticing my new scars, how they gleamed every time I breathed—and he sighed as he resumed writing the document, his quill scratching over the paper. I walked past Phelan to the kitchen counter, where the teapot was still warm, and poured myself a cup. Imonie set down a pitcher of cream and the honeypot, as she knew my preferences, and I put far too much into my tea, stirring it around and around, my thoughts far away.

"How is your wound?"

I turned, startled to see Phelan was standing close to me. Imonie made a sound of dislike, but the magician didn't notice.

"I would say it's in the same condition as your boat, Mr. Vesper," I replied, and took a loud sip of tea, just to irritate him.

"Then it must be in shambles."

"An adequate word to describe it." I knew he was asking after my leg, but I spoke of the wound in my spirit.

He didn't glance away from me as I expected—it was rude to stare too long at someone in court, where he no doubt had grown up as a countess's son—and I wondered what he saw in me. I dropped my gaze first, unable to hold his uncanny stare.

"And when can we expect you to vacate this cottage, Mr. Madigan?" Lennox was saying.

"We'll be gone tomorrow," my father replied without hesitation.

I set my teacup down on the counter with a hard clunk. *Tomorrow?* The disbelief swelled within me, and I bit the inside of my cheek to hold back the torrent of words I wanted to spew.

"Excellent!" Lennox said. "I do believe this cottage will suit me very well, although there is that rather nice house on the hill. . . ."

"Yes, that's Mazarine Thimble's mansion." Papa's voice cracked with exhaustion. "It's her property and will most likely remain that way."

"Of course." Lennox's gaze drifted to the kitchen, where Imonie was banging pots in her fury. "And the housekeeper? Will she remain behind?"

"No," my father replied swiftly. "Imonie will be going with us.

If you want a cook or a housekeeper, you will have to find one on your own."

Imonie pretended she had not heard as she began to knead dough, but I felt the indignation for her. That this upstart would assume she would stay and work for him.

"And what of the dream tax?" Lennox asked. "How much does the town pay you for your services?"

"They pay us what they can, Mr. Lennox," I said, unable to remain silent a moment longer. "Sometimes with bread, sometimes with coin, sometimes nothing at all if their crop or craft has suffered a bad year."

"Nothing at all!" Incredulous, Lennox looked at my father, as if he was fervently hoping I was jesting. "And you still guard them from their nightmares, despite the fact they cannot even pay you a penny in gratitude?"

"We do," I said.

"Then how do you pay your dream tax to the duke?" Lennox asked, glancing between my father and me. "You *do* pay it, I hope?"

My father nodded. He looked tired, so weary. My heart ached.

"We pay what the duke requires," I said. And I thought of Mazarine and her trickle of coins, which had kept us afloat more times than I could count. "But this is a rural town, Mr. Lennox. This is not the pampered city life you know and are accustomed to. All of us work and pull our weight. Sometimes, a person cannot pay in coin, but we still record their nightmares and we still protect them. Now that you've been informed, you'll have to figure out a way to ensure the duke gets his taxes on time. And if you can't . . . then perhaps your mother can pay them for you."

"Mr. Madigan," Phelan said in a desperate tone, purposefully interrupting Lennox and me, sensing that we were about to strike up another duel. "Please don't feel as if you and Clementine and Imonie must rush away. You're welcome to stay here as long as you need."

"We'll be gone tomorrow," my father reiterated, and he set his glassy-eyed stare on me. "It would be a good idea to begin packing, Clem."

But where are we going to go?

I left my tea on the counter and ascended the stairs. Dwindle was curled up on my bed, purring, and I sat beside her, my hand stroking her calico fur.

Eventually, my damp gown drove me to the wardrobe. I shed the black silk and changed into a simple blue gown. I set to work packing my things, only to realize I had far too many books. I needed to give some of them away, and I began to make piles.

I was halfway through my endeavor when Papa stepped into the chamber, instantly casting a protective charm on the walls, the window, and the door. To keep our voices from being overheard.

"Make sure you pack everything, Clementine," he said. "Leave no trace of yourself behind in this house. No hair ribbon, no letters, no drawings. Not even an old pair of shoes."

I gaped up at my father. "You're worried. . . ."

"I'm not worried," he insisted. But I knew when he lied. His nostrils tended to flare when he spoke falsely. "But nor do I want to give anyone the chance to track where we go, or even summon us, if they were so bold to do so."

I tried to imagine Lennox taking an old ribbon of mine months from now and using it to cast the spell of summoning. It was a dangerous enchantment, one that would draw me into his presence whether I wanted to answer him or not. And I almost laughed at the absurdity until my father's scowl deepened.

"You need to take this seriously, Clem."

"I *am* taking this seriously!" I snapped, and indicated the scars on my neck. "I never wanted to leave this place. Our *home*, Papa!"

He flinched, as if I had struck him. At once, my temper faded.

"It's a great misfortune, and I'm sorry, daughter. I'm sorry I was not strong enough to help you last night."

I glanced away, unable to bear the sorrow in his eyes. My guilt flared again. If I had been craftier, bolder . . . I wouldn't have lost. "Where are we going?"

"I'm still considering our options. The most important thing at the moment is that you pack everything."

"I was planning to give some of my books away to the town girls. Could I still do that?"

His eyes flickered to the piles of books I had made on the floor. I read his mind: books were heavy and cumbersome to move with, even if one enchanted them into tiny charms.

"That would be fine," he replied. "So long as you erase your name on the cover and any notes you may have written in the margins and ensure none of your bookmarks are in the pages."

I nodded and watched him leave. And while I wanted to act

as if I was not rattled by his worry, I was. My hands shook as I went through the books I planned to donate, uttering a charm to vanish my handwriting. Because—*of course*—I was the sort of person who marked every book I owned. And as Papa knew well, I made my own bookmarks. I ended up recovering three of them, lost in the leaves of thick novels. By the end of my scouring, there were eleven volumes that I wanted to give to the Fielding girls.

I gathered the books into my arms and decided I would deliver them now.

The main level of the cottage was quiet. The Vesper brothers were gone, to my immense relief, and my father was in his own bedchamber, packing. Imonie was at the china cabinet, wrapping the porcelain in newspaper, but she didn't stop me when I slipped out the door into the warmth of late morning.

The last thing I desired was to be seen and stopped on the streets. I cast a simple *avertana* charm, one that would make me unnoticeable. And I walked the streets of Hereswith. Everyone was speaking of my father's displacement, because rumors traveled like wildfire here, and everyone had seen the Vesper brothers wandering about the evening before.

Most of the talk was hinged on disbelief and devastation, for my father was sincerely loved in this town. But there were a few conversations I heard, words that were hopeful for the new warden. My father was getting old, anyway. It was good to change magicians every now and then.

I reached the Fieldings' cottage.

With a deep sigh, I loosened my charm so I could be noticed

again, and was approaching the door, preparing to knock, when a sweet voice called my name from above.

"Miss Clem!"

I glanced up at the apple tree that flourished in the front yard. Elle was perched in its branches, harvesting the fruit, and I walked to stand among the roots, gazing up at her.

"Have you come to see my papa?" the girl asked as she began to descend the tree.

"No," I replied. "I've actually come to see you and your sisters."

"Me?" She dropped to the grass and set her basket of apples down. "What for?"

I extended the stack of books to her, watching as her eyes turned alight. "I fear that I'm leaving Hereswith, but I wanted to give these to you and your sisters before I departed. They were some of my favorite books when I was your age."

Her mouth hung agape as she took my books. I didn't realize I had accidentally put one of my art portfolios in the stack until she opened it and leaves of my most recent illustrations began to flutter, threatening to fly away on the wind.

"Oh!" I said, and reached for it. "Sorry. These need to stay with me."

Elle handed me the portfolio and I held it close to my chest as she continued to admire the books.

"Thank you, Miss Clem," she said in a reverent tone. As she hurried inside to share the news with her sisters, Spruce Fielding appeared on the threshold.

"I'm afraid we cannot pay you for the books."

"I don't want payment," I replied. "I give them freely to your daughters."

When Spruce merely stood there, blank with surprise, I bade him good day. I was striding to the gate when he hurried after me.

"Miss Clem! Wait a moment, please."

I tarried, wiping a smudge of charcoal from the cover of the portfolio. "Yes, Mr. Fielding?"

"We're very sorry to hear what happened last night," he said, and removed his cap, wringing it in his hands. "Your father is an excellent warden, someone we trusted. And we're sad to see both of you go."

"Thank you, Mr. Fielding."

"Must you leave? You can continue to reside here," he said. "In fact, we could build you a cottage on my lands, if you like."

This caught me by surprise. It only made my tears surge, and I at last realized why my father and I couldn't stay in Hereswith, why Papa wanted to leave so swiftly. "That's very kind of you, Mr. Fielding. But my father and I feel it's best to leave at once, so Mr. Vesper can begin to settle in and get to know all of you."

Spruce nodded, but he didn't look convinced. "I understand. But if you do change your mind . . . you and your father and Imonie will always have a home here."

The emotion welled in my throat. I smiled at him as I passed through the gate.

It took me a moment to cast my charm again, to go unnoticed as I walked through the heart of Hereswith, back through pockets of gossip and dismay and curiosity. I had just come upon the square when a strange, long scuff on the cobblestones caught my attention. It was a thin mark, as if caused by the tip of something sharp, and it led to a wagon parked not far from me.

I paused, chilled when I recalled Elle's nightmare. The knight had let the point of his sword drag over the stones. He had walked to the wagon where Elle had been hiding. Surely, this scuff mark was just a coincidence.

I crouched down to study it closer, rushing my fingers over the mark on the cobbles. I looked at the wagon, and I began to imagine perhaps the knight had been here last night, walking the streets and hidden beneath the water. But that would mean *two* different nightmares had descended last night—Archie's and Elle's—and that had never occurred. At least, not as far as I knew.

Before I could let that revelation unfold, someone tripped over me.

The impact knocked me down, and my charm of stealth broke as my portfolio went flying. Leaves of my drawings danced on the breeze, and I rushed to gather them before they were carried farther into the market. And through the cascade of parchment, I saw him kneeling on the cobblestones, also hurrying to gather my stray illustrations.

Phelan.

My face warmed when I saw him holding my drawings, these intimate pieces of my heart. He paused to study one, transfixed, and I snatched it from his hands.

He scowled, lips pursed as if he wanted to say something snide until he realized it was me and his expression softened. "Forgive me, Miss Madigan. I didn't see you."

I made no response but folded my now wrinkled papers back into my portfolio. When I continued to walk up the street, he rushed after me.

"May I walk with you?"

"I suppose," I said, and quickened my pace. He noticed and kept perfect stride with me, and all the people of Hereswith seemed to freeze, watching the two of us pass by.

"I know you must think very ill of my brother and me," Phelan began, slightly out of breath as the street took a steep turn. "But I do hope in time that you will come to understand why this happened."

His words infuriated me. I halted and spun. "I think I already understand, Mr. Vesper. You and your brother were raised wanting nothing. Two rich, spoiled brats of the aristocracy. And now that you are grown, you wanted a town to be warden of, so you rolled a die and landed on Hereswith. Quite a challenge, I might add, since it's rather far from your home and resides in the shadow of mountains. But I commend you both for your noble sense of duty and obligation, and while I don't think you will fit in well here, I hope I'm wrong, for the sake of the residents."

The shock in his eyes and the flush of his face were delicious to behold. I smiled as I continued on my way, thinking he would leave me alone. But he was far more stubborn than I anticipated and caught up to me again.

"I'll have you know, Miss Madigan, that I'm not staying in Hereswith."

"Oh, I see! So you assisted your brother in stealing the town and now you are abandoning it?"

"I have responsibilities elsewhere," he said in a near growl. As if I should care.

"Then don't let me keep you from them," I said, my father's cottage coming into view. Phelan relinquished me, coming to an abrupt halt in the street, and I walked the rest of the way home on my own.

But it felt like I was treading an endless nightmare, and it would end if only I could wake.

8

I didn't know where Papa planned to take Imonie and me, and
the uncertainty gave me a stomachache as I waited in the yard,
holding a mewling Dwindle in my arms. The wagon was parked
at our gate, packed to the brim with boxes and crates and burlap
sacks of our possessions. Most of the furniture remained behind
in the cottage, as did the framed artwork and the endless pots of
plants, all of which Papa used a scouring charm over, to ensure no
trace of us remained. I had ensorcelled nearly everything from my
room into one bag, using Mama's shrinking spell.

A crowd had gathered to see us off, most of them dear friends
who had known me for half my life. Lilac Westin brought a bag
of pastries, her eyes rimmed red. The Fieldings were there, the
girls holding my books. And to my great shock, Mazarine. The
disguised troll wore a modest dress of thick brocade and wielded
an umbrella, to shield her skin and hair from the sunshine.

Papa was the last to emerge from our cottage. He carried the book of nightmares, and I watched as he delivered the tome to Lennox Vesper, who waited by a patch of daisies in the yard, Phelan at his side. My father gave him the book and the key to the cottage, and it was officially done and over. Papa was no longer warden of Hereswith, and we were homeless.

I buried my face in Dwindle's fur, to hide the tears that burned my eyes. I felt Imonie's hand on my shoulder, and her attempt to comfort me only made my emotions spin harder. I could feel the weeping in my chest, threatening to rise.

Oh gods, I thought. *Please don't let me cry here. Let me at least get out of sight of the Vespers.*

Despite my resolve, a sound slipped from me. The strangled sound of a girl trying to swallow a sob, and halfway succeeding.

Dwindle let out a disgruntled meow. I was squeezing her too hard, and when I lifted my face, my nose was running. A few tears had escaped, and I hurried to dash them away before anyone but Imonie could notice.

"And where will you be heading, Mr. Madigan?" Lennox was asking. He was a blurry shape at the corner of my eye, but I saw how he cradled the book of nightmares in an awkward stance. The weight of the book had caught him by surprise.

"Wherever the wind blows," Papa said.

He helped me and Imonie settle in the wagon bench before he climbed up himself. His hands trembled as they took the reins and he clucked to the horse, urging the gelding onward.

I wanted to look back at the cottage, at our friends, one last time, but I didn't. Because I feared I would break into hundreds of pieces if I did.

We didn't talk until eventide, each of us lost to our own thoughts until Papa drew the wagon off the road and we chose to camp in a copse of oak trees. Imonie built a fire and made a quick stew of wild onions, potatoes, and some summer sausage, and we gathered around the light and ate, our mood somber.

I had noticed the mountains were growing distant. My father was taking us east, and it made me feel lost. I wrapped a blanket around my shoulders as Dwindle curled up on my lap. And I looked for something I recognized, something to ground me. I found it on the dusky horizon, where the fortress in the clouds was carved into the mountaintop, so distant now I could hardly discern it. But it was a familiar sight and made me feel less adrift. Weary of the silence, I asked, "What do you think is up there? In the fortress?"

Imonie was sitting in the grass, knitting a shawl. "Nightmares. And the lost one."

"The lost one?" I echoed. It had been a long time since she had told me a mountain story, and she knew I was playing innocent in order to draw that tale out of her.

She was quiet for a moment, her focus seemingly on her knitting. But then she began to speak, her voice rich and vibrant.

"Over a hundred years ago, there was a woman who lived in the mountains, alone in a small house in the city of Ulla. In her younger years, she was a faithful lady-in-waiting for the duke's sister, but as she grew older, she preferred solitude, and she listened to the wind that blew in the morning and the evenings. Stories were wrapped within such gusts, and they kept her warm on the darkest of nights. She lacked for nothing and wanted nothing more.

"But a rap sounded on her door one summer midnight, when the moon was full and the wind was quiet and the air was warm. When she answered it, no one was there. No one, until she heard a wail and realized a large basket had been left on her stoop. And in the basket was not one baby but two.

"The woman had never cared for children. They were loud, messy, fragile, demanding. They were wholly dependent on their caregiver, and she did not want to be fastened to such responsibility. But nor could she be heartless and leave the babes on her porch.

"She brought them into her home. Two boys, perhaps only a month old. Ugly and floppy, and she did not know how to hold them. But hold them she did, and their weeping eased. She spoke to them, and they smiled at the sound of her voice. When they grew hungry, she filled a bottle with goat milk and fed them. For months, she sought their parents. For months, she tried to find a new home for them. But in the end, she chose to keep them with her.

"They were identical twins, she swiftly discovered as they grew. It was nigh impossible to tell them apart, and many days she confused them, until she came to learn their personalities. One was intelligent, drawn to books and quiet spaces, and the other was wild, adventurous, a boy who wanted to roam the mountains and drive stakes into rabbits. The quiet one she could raise, but her wild boy . . . the woman did not know how to tame such a heart, if such a heart could be tamed without breaking.

"For all their differences, they both held a vein of craftiness. This she learned when they began to play each other's roles. Her quiet boy would deceive her, acting as his wild brother to take his punishments. And the wild boy would act as his quiet twin, to avoid her wrath when he strayed too far.

"The woman had no choice but to send them both away to school in the city after a decade had passed. Let one become a warrior, she thought, and the other a scholar. And maybe when they grew into men, they would serve the duchy in mighty ways. But even if they did not, she would be proud of them, and she loved them each for their different strengths.

"Grow into men they did. They visited her often in the beginning, after their schooling was complete. Her quiet boy was devoted to his books and knowledge, and her wild one had fallen prey to love, wedding a beautiful girl of the summit. It was good in those days. And then her boys forgot her, distracted by the allures of life. A storm brewed on the horizon. The duke was a cruel ruler, oppressing his people. And it did not matter how much the woman prepared for it. The storm broke and with it the duchy, and her home, her land, was shadowed by the curse.

"She had no choice but to leave. All the people of the mountains . . . they could not stay there. The nights were treacherous, their dreams woven with terror. No one could step foot in the fortress, where the duke had been slain. In the pandemonium of leaving, she could not find her boys. *They are wise and shrewd,* she thought. She made it to the mountain doors, where the summit opens into a valley, and she waited for her boys there.

"Soon, they came. One passed over the threshold freely, into the grass. The other, however, could not. The mountain held him captive, and he could not leave its shadow. When the mountain doors began to close, the woman wept and rushed to her son who was bound to be lost to her, only to be held back by his twin. They watched the mountain doors close and seal, devouring brother and son. Those doors have not been open since, nor will they until the remaining wraiths—the heiress, the lady-in-waiting, the advisor, the guard, the master of coin, and the spymistress—all who once planned the duke's demise, return as one to break the curse."

I was silent, soaking in Imonie's tragic story. When she did not speak again, I realized she was done with her tale, and it left me hollow. I should have asked for a happier story, and I lay down in my bedroll, listening to the wind rake through the grass and the crickets chirp their starlit lullabies.

"Clem." Papa's voice caught my attention, and I turned to see he was holding a remedy vial out for me to take.

I reached for it, the glass cool against my palm, but I hesitated. "Do I still need to drink this now? Since we're no longer wardens?" That had been Papa's reasoning as to why I shouldn't dream at night. It would be difficult indeed to face my own nightmare in the streets of Hereswith. Dreams often revealed one's greatest vulnerability; dreams were doors that led into hearts and minds and souls and secrets.

"Best you do," my father replied, and I watched as he drank one himself before settling in for the night.

Even Imonie took a remedy. I followed suit, uncorking my vial and letting the bittersweet liquid rush over my tongue and coat my throat. A familiar taste, one I had been drinking every night since I could remember.

I lay down in the grass, my eyes growing heavy with exhaustion, and I looked to the mountains, now darker than night against the constellations. And I wondered what sort of things would haunt my sleep, if I ever gave my mind and heart the chance to dream.

Travel was miserably slow.

My father was in no hurry, Dwindle meowed the entire time, and our horse and wagon took a plodding pace as we traveled across the Bardyllis Duchy. But all too soon, the mountains faded away and we were surrounded by crop fields still golden with summer heat, pine forests, and rings of small villages reminiscent to Hereswith. We passed over the Starling River and I noticed the shift.

The dirt roads became cobbled, the forests surrendered to chains of houses, the quiet fragrance of the country gave way to the sounds and smoke and smells of habitation. I could see the haze of the capital in the distance, the sprawling and overwhelming city of Endellion, the seat of the duke's sovereignty, and I suddenly knew exactly where my father was taking us.

I turned to look at him, and his profile was set like granite, his eyes carefully avoiding mine.

He was taking us to my mother.

9

My mother's town house was in the northern quadrant of the city, in sight of the river that flowed through the capital like a silver vein. The last time I had been here to visit her was three years ago, when I was fourteen, and I had longed for Hereswith the entire summer I had spent with her. Longed for the mountains and the meadows and the slower pace of a country town. My mother had sensed the homesickness within me, and I think that was why she failed to invite me the following summer, or the following. We had gradually grown apart when I had chosen to study my father's way of magic instead of hers.

I felt a twinge of apprehension when I approached her door, and I could only imagine how my father was feeling as he waited in the wagon with Imonie, the afternoon beginning to melt into dusk. I rang the bell, cleared my throat, and smoothed the tangles from my hair, to no avail; I looked like a weary, dust-ridden, and windblown vagabond when my mother opened the door.

Her shock was tangible. Her eyes widened when she realized it was me standing at the threshold, and her expression softened.

"Clementine?"

"Hello, Mama," I greeted her with a hesitant smile. I was surprised by how much silver now laced her black hair.

"Where's your father?" she asked, her voice sharp with displeasure. But she gave me no time to reply; she glanced over my shoulder to see Papa sitting like a defeated warrior on the wagon bench. "Ambrose? Ambrose, come inside. You look weary. And Imonie. Come, the two of you."

My father eased down from the wagon, assisting Imonie. They began to gather boxes, which my mother rushed to assist with her magic, charming our possessions to glide themselves in through the front door to the parlor of her town house. After that, Papa insisted on taking the horse to the closest public stable, a block away.

I think he was avoiding the inevitable, which was having to tell my mother we had lost the town and currently had nowhere to go.

And so I did. While he was tending to the horse, I sat in my mother's opulent den that smelled of gardenias and patchouli. Dwindle rubbed up against my legs as I took the cup of tea Mama offered me, and I told her everything. Imonie sat beside me, adding a snort here and there in agreement, particularly when I relayed the arrival of the two magicians.

"The Countess of Amarys's sons?" Mama echoed, and her eyes slid to Imonie's. The two women seemed to hold a private conversation, which irked me.

I paused, uncertain. "You know of them?"

"Doesn't everyone in Endellion," she replied carefully. I couldn't judge her opinion of them, not like I could with Papa. "Her lands lie south of here, but the countess primarily resides in the city, where she has great influence. Her husband, the count, passed away years ago, but since then she has become a close confidant of the duke, in fact."

That only made my indignation flare. Why, then, would Lennox need to uproot my father and me? Why Hereswith, when he could have chosen any town, any village, any slice of the city to be warden of?

"So the sons challenged you and your father," my mother prompted.

I nodded and continued with the doomed tale, and my mother listened, her gaze resting on me and the scars that gleamed at my neck. She was quiet when I was done, and her silence made me feel uncomfortable. As if she was weighing what she wanted to do with us and our predicament.

"Will you let me and Papa and Imonie stay here for a little while? Just until we can find new work in the city," I asked, because I didn't know if she lived alone. If she had a lover or a companion, even though her house felt empty and quiet, full of golden trim that glittered in the shadows.

"Of course, Clementine," she replied, a lilt of offense in her tone, as if I were being absurd to assume otherwise. "It'll be like old times."

It would not be like old times, and we all knew it.

Papa arrived, letting himself in the front door. His footsteps were heavy as he approached, and he stood awkwardly on the threshold of the den, trying not to look at my mother. She rose from her settee, elegant in her lavender gown, her black hair swept back in a loose chignon.

"You haven't aged a day, Ambrose," she said to him.

Papa at last looked at her, unguarded, and I thought I saw regret in his eyes. They had parted ways seven years ago. I remembered how they had reached a point when all they did was bicker and argue. They held different ideologies about magic and the intent behind spells. My mother studied *metamara* and used its whimsy on the stage, captivating audiences as she transformed one thing into another. She believed magic should be fun and entertaining, and my father, with his rigid *avertana* opinions, believed magic should only be used in logical, practical ways. As a means to guard and defend others.

"Same to you, Sigourney," he said. "If Clem and Imonie can reside with you, I'll find lodgings elsewhere."

"Don't be ridiculous," my mother replied. "I live here alone, and this house has far too many empty rooms. Stay here for now."

He nodded but still seemed frozen on the threshold.

I suddenly felt exhausted by the weight of everything—worry as to where we would go, what we would do now, and the sheer amount of homesickness that pinched my lungs every time I drew a deep breath.

That first night in my mother's town house, I lay in bed and relived my new moon battle with Lennox and Phelan, over and over in the dark.

And I finally let myself cry.

Imonie merged into city life with ease, tending to the house and cooking for us. But my father and I were stricken and lost, perusing the classified column of the daily paper for possible work. There were no openings for a dream warden in the city, which seemed unbelievable to me, given how vast Endellion was. So many people, so many nightmares, so many streets. But I swiftly learned that territory was divided into small segments, and there were far too many magicians and not enough positions. A dream warden was a highly contested profession, my mother said when she saw both Papa and I were helplessly searching the ads.

"We could challenge someone this upcoming new moon," I said to him after dinner one night, when he and I sat alone by the fire. "We could win new territory here in the city."

My father studied the dance of the flames. "No, Clem. I won't do what the Vespers did to us."

And I understood why, yet I wanted to regain my position. I needed to be doing something here, for fear I might dissolve into dust.

"Then why don't we return to Hereswith and challenge Lennox? We would still have the advantage, Papa. We know the nightmares." But even as I said it, the words sounded unfeasible, desperate. Dishonorable. I couldn't envision my father lowering himself like that, even if I could—somewhat—see it of myself.

"I think it's time to put away nightmares and dreams and new moons," he said, to my dismay. When he looked at me, I saw that he had fully accepted defeat, that he was done as warden. "We're here now. There are many new avenues to take in the city. Let's put the past behind us and start a new life."

"A life without magic?" I asked, and I could scarcely comprehend it. That he would want to let all his skill and diligence go to waste, until his spells sank into the darkest place of memory, rusted from disuse.

"Perhaps it would be best, Clem."

I buried my opinions, but I was angry. At him, at the Vespers. At myself for losing a challenge I should have easily triumphed.

And the anger smoldered in me like a star.

"Come, you need a walk," Imonie said to me a week later. "I'm heading to the bakery and could use the company."

I hadn't left my mother's house in days, so I set aside my book and laced my boots, following her out the front door.

It was a cloudy, somber day. There was no wind, and the air sat heavy in the streets, stale and warm, even with October's approach. I was still adjusting to the noise, for it seemed like the city never slept, and I tried to find comfort in the bustle of carriages, buggies, and people hurrying on errands, but I only felt more isolated and out of place.

Imonie and I took a side street. We had been walking for nearly half an hour and had already passed two bakeries.

"Are you trying to weary me with a long walk?" I drawled.

"You know I'm picky about bakers," she replied tersely, and it only made me think of Lilac Westin in Hereswith and her renowned cinnamon rolls.

The street spilled us out into a wide thoroughfare. Thin rays of sunlight had pierced the overcast sky by the time Imonie found a bakery to her liking. I had spotted an artist's supply shop across the street, and I planned to meet back up with her after a moment of my own perusing.

A silver bell rang when I entered. At once, I was transported by the shelves of paper, sketchbooks, and canvases, by row after row of paint tins and brushes and bottles of linseed oil. Overwhelmed, I took my time admiring everything until a girl my age with curly brown hair appeared behind the sales counter.

"Can I help you find anything?"

"No, no I'm just browsing," I replied.

"Do you paint?"

"I draw."

"Ah, lovely! You can find those supplies in the next aisle over."

I thanked her and decided I should keep to what I knew best, and that was charcoal and pastels. But perhaps one day I would be brave enough to buy some paint, and a brush or two.

Eventually, I settled on a new sketchbook, and I made my way to the sales counter, where the girl was perched on a stool, reading a poetry book. I was reaching for my coin purse when the doorbell chimed and the girl's attention shifted.

"Lady Raven," she said, sliding off her stool to curtsy. "I have your order ready."

I turned to see a woman of the court, dressed in a dark silk gown. She looked to be my mother's age, with a few wrinkles catching the corners of her eyes, and her blond hair was swept up in a chignon, a net of diamonds holding it in place. Her lips were painted bloodred, and they were pursed, as if she did not smile often.

She approached the counter, her heels clicking on the floor as she rudely cut in front of me. She waited, tapping her fingers as the shopgirl set out a bundle of burlap. Lady Raven proceeded to untie it, her hands hidden beneath two lacy gloves, and she closely examined each item. Every brush tip, every tin of paint.

I glanced at the shopgirl, who had gone pale.

"It's everything you asked for, Lady Raven. Just as you prefer."

The lady finished her examinations and knotted the burlap. "Yes, everything looks acceptable. Thank you, Blythe." Lady Raven turned to depart with her order, and that was when she finally took note of me.

I stood, stark and silent, as her cold gaze swept over me. She studied my wild hair, the features of my face. And then she frowned and said, "You look familiar. Have we met before?"

"No, lady," I said, but my palms had become slick.

"Mm." She lost interest in me and departed the shop.

When I turned to the girl once more, setting my sketchbook on the counter to purchase, Blythe released a tremulous breath.

"I apologize for that. She's one of our loyal customers, and my father told me to always give her precedence when she steps into the shop."

"It's all right," I said. "I'm Clem, by the way."

"Blythe. Will I see you again here soon, Clem?" She handed me the sketchbook as I paid her for it.

"Most likely." I smiled and started to leave, but I smelled a trace of Lady Raven's perfume in the shop, roses and lavender, and it reminded me . . . "By the way, who was she?"

Blythe's eyes widened, as if I should have known. "Why, that was Lady Raven Vesper. The Countess of Amarys."

10

"Perhaps you could take a few art classes," Imonie suggested as she poured me a cup of tea the following morning.

"Where?" I asked, sitting at the table. An art class was enticing, albeit scary to contemplate, as I had never been instructed before.

"The university, perhaps?"

The thought of attending a school full of strangers made my stomach knot. "Maybe."

"Well, you need to find *something* to keep you occupied, Clem. Perhaps taking a class here or there might help you adjust, make some new friends."

I sighed, knowing she was right. Papa had already left for his new employment, working in the mines. A laborious task as far from magic as he could find. And my mother was still asleep, but I felt restless, aching for something. *The mountains,* I thought, *and home.* I longed for my life before the Vespers had stepped within it, and I wearily reached for the honey jar. I was about to melt a spoonful of it in my tea when the newspaper caught my eye.

Papa had been reading it, and there was a smudge of jam on the headline.

I reached across the table to take it and began leafing through the classified column.

> *Wanted*—*a caretaker for an elderly solicitor.*
> *Wanted*—*a tutor in science and literature, for a young noblewoman.*
> *Wanted*—*a dancer for the Disillusioned Tavern.*

I turned the page, my heart heavy with discouragement until I saw the warden notices. Suddenly my hands were trembling, and my eyes raced across the entries.

> *Wanted*—*a warden partner for Lidia M. Lirrey, with the territory of 19 South Elm Street to 25 Reverie West. Experienced magicians only. Contact Ms. Lirrey at the Society as soon as possible.*
> *Wanted*—*a warden partner for Phelan Vesper, with the territory of 1 Auberon Street to 36 Yewborne Street. All magicians are welcome to audition, and interviews will be held from eight o'clock in the morning until noontide at the Luminous Society Museum in Old Village, on Wednesday next. Contact Mr. Vesper for more details.*

I felt heat rise in my face and I read it again, just to be certain it was the right Phelan. The pompous, impolite, selfish, tragically handsome Phelan. The aristocrat who had stolen my home and disgraced me. Bumping into his haughty mother the day before at the art shop had only roused the worst of my feelings. Toward him, toward Lennox. Toward a family that felt as if they could take whatever they desired and suffer no consequences for it.

My anger burned away to cold guilt for losing Hereswith. And then an idea came to mind.

I dropped the newspaper into the plate of eggs and cheese that Imonie had just set on the table. She was already staring at me with a cocked brow.

"I don't like that gleam in your eyes, Clem."

"Imonie," I said, and my mind reeled with possibilities. I could feel my magic wake, like embers being stirred back to life, and I grinned a slow, sharp smile. "Imonie . . . I have an idea. And I need your help."

If she had known what I truly planned to do, Imonie would have never assisted me. But I saw the longing for the mountains in her every time she glanced out the window and viewed nothing but brick walls, chimneys, and wrought-iron gates, and we crafted a plan. She had some estranged family in the city of Marksworth, and she asked my parents for a week's worth of vacation, to go and visit them in the neighboring province.

I made my case to accompany her, and my parents relented after they argued about me leaving the city. Papa said no, my mother said yes, and she thankfully won that spar.

Imonie and I bought a passage on a stagecoach, something that would fly along the roads of Azenor, but instead of taking us north to Marksworth, it took us west to Hereswith. Time was the most vital thread of the plan; I had only a week to get to Hereswith and back before Phelan held interviews for a partner.

"I wish you would tell me what you plan, Clementine," Imonie grunted as the coach jostled us back and forth.

I shifted my satchel of art supplies on my lap. "You'll know soon, Imonie."

"Your plan doesn't have anything to do with that Lennox Vesper, does it?"

"No. He won't even know we are in Hereswith. And we'll be back in Endellion on Tuesday, if everything goes smoothly."

"I'm not going to like this, am I?" She narrowed her eyes.

"I honestly don't know what you'll think, but I ask you to trust me."

She was quiet after that, watching the land pass by in a blur. We reached Hereswith in only three days. I had to pay the driver extra to let us disembark before we reached town, and then Imonie and I carried our satchels and walked through the valley into the forest that crowned Hereswith. Evening was falling, and the air was cool and sweet with the promise of autumn, the mountain wind rushing to greet us among the pines.

Imonie was savoring the fragrance, the gentle sway of the trees, until her nostrils flared and she stopped upright.

"Clementine."

I stopped to look at her in the starlight. She must have smelled it on the wind, the place I was guiding her. "Don't worry, Imonie."

"Whatever you plan to do upon coming here . . . you should change your mind. This is reckless, dangerous. What would your parents think if they knew?"

I didn't know what they would think about my decision, what they would do once they discovered what I had done. The uncertainty churned my stomach, but I had lost too much and come too far to turn around as a coward.

"I'm not changing my mind. I need you to wait here for me. I'll return shortly."

She didn't like that. But she heeded me, settling down on a log with the wind for company, and I continued to weave through the woods.

Soon, the pines grew sparse and I could see the lights of Hereswith, shining like fallen stars. I arrived at the mansion's backyard, a verdant garden meticulously maintained by one of the town boys, and I walked the gravel path to the back door.

My heart was hummingbird swift within me, and a tremor shook my bones as I arrived on the porch, as I lifted my hand.

I had a piercing moment of doubt. But I saw myself and who I wanted to become, and my confidence returned, limning my resolve.

I knocked on Mazarine's door.

She was exactly where I knew she would be—sitting on a plush divan in her library with the curtains drawn, candlesticks burning and dripping wax onto the floor. She was dressed in black velvet with an amethyst hanging at her throat, and she smiled when she saw me enter the chamber.

"Clementine Madigan," she greeted me. "I did not expect to see you again so soon. Although defeat does not suit you."

I wondered if anger had grown a film over my eyes, something I could not blink away, and I suddenly felt a sting of vulnerability. Her comment unsteadied me for a breath.

"I have a question for you, Ms. Thimble," I said, finding my courage once more. "I seek your knowledge."

"Do you? Sit and tell me what knowledge you hunger for."

I sat in my usual chair, the one where I had drawn her human face countless times. I kept my art satchel on my lap, feeling safer with something between us.

"What do you seek, child?" the troll whispered to me in a soft, enticing tone.

I studied her guise boldly. It was so skillfully rendered; she looked every bit of human as I was. Only the mirror had given her away. Only her reflection had betrayed her.

"The magic of disguise you're wearing," I began, and my heart was beating again, so fast it turned my voice into a wisp. "How did you weave it? How did you cast it? Is it *metamara* magic?"

Mazarine's grin widened. "And you desire to know this why?"

"Because I want to cast it on myself."

"Defeat does not suit you, and yet you think deceit would, Clementine?"

Her words provoked me, but my silence only amused her more. She leaned closer to me, her amethyst necklace swinging with her languid movements.

"You want revenge, young one?"

"I want what is mine," I said. "I want to regain what was stolen from me." And I had no doubt that one day I would win back Hereswith and call it home again. But I needed to bring the Vesper family to their knees in order to do so.

"And you believe disguising yourself will enable you to attain such things?"

"Yes."

She sat back, but she was reveling in my answers. "Do you know where I was born? I come from the mountains, from a duchy you can only imagine despite the fact that you lived for so long in its shadow. The magic I wear is not something you have ever encountered here, Clementine. It is old, ancient. I created this enchantment of disguise long before the cruel duke was assassinated."

I had always wondered how old she was. To know she had been alive before the Seren Duchy fell apart informed me that she was well over a hundred years in age, and I shivered. She had lived in an era that was nothing but legends now, and I sought to rectify it. Perhaps trolls had longer life spans than humans. But even as I tried to convince myself . . . something didn't feel quite right, as if time had turned sour in the room. As if Mazarine had stopped the hours from touching her, somehow.

"My magic is very dangerous, and it will require a great cost," she continued. "And I do not know if a human girl is strong enough to bear such a price."

She's trying to frighten me, I thought. *She's testing my mettle. Don't back down, don't be afraid. . . .*

"Then I suppose there is only one way to discover if your words are truth, Mazarine," I said.

"Perhaps. But I also do not give my knowledge and magic away freely," she countered, lacing her long, gnarled fingers together. "And I do not think you have enough gold or bone marrow to satisfy me."

"No, I don't," I agreed, choosing not to dwell on the bone marrow part. "But there *is* something I have that I think you will want."

She waited, watching as I opened my leather satchel. I withdrew a fresh sheet of parchment, a stick of charcoal, and she laughed.

"You have drawn me so many times, Clementine. Why would I want another portrait?"

"I have drawn you in *disguise*, Mazarine of the Mountains. This time, I will draw your true face."

Her humor melted, replaced by longing and the glitter of vanity. I had her, and I concealed my smugness as I continued to hold up the paper, waiting to be marked.

"But then again . . . perhaps you don't want any evidence of your true nature on paper," I said, and began to pack my supplies away.

"Wait, Clementine."

I paused, and she fought a war within herself.

"The portrait of my true face will be enough for payment," she eventually said. "But now the question I must ask is if *you* are willing to pay the cost of my disguise."

"Tell me the cost, then."

She poured a glass of wine. "I will take half of your heart and turn it into stone. It will divide you, and you will turn colder. Because half of who you once were will be no more, you will need to surrender half of something you love to hold the spell. Your art or your magic, most likely, since those are two things that have always been with you, growing alongside you year by year." She took a sip of her wine, but her gaze never left mine. "So what will you choose to give up, Clementine Madigan? Your art or your magic?"

I didn't want to relinquish either one.

For the troll was right: magic and art had been with me always. My two constants, my two greatest achievements. Both light and fire in my imagination, growing year by year alongside me, deepening and flourishing even in the hardest moments of life. And my dream of mastering *deviah* magic, when my magic and my art would coincide as one beneath my prowess, slowly began to die.

"My art," I whispered. "I will give up my art."

Mazarine nodded, but she wasn't surprised. She had known my decision and my weakness, as I had known hers.

"Then let it be done," Mazarine said, and rose from the divan. "Come and draw my portrait, and I will grant you my magic, a disguise of your choosing."

I still had one more burning question to ask her, but I held it on my tongue as I followed her to the mirror. She stood before the glass and I brought out my board and clipped the paper to it, sitting close enough so that I had a clear view of her reflection.

The sight of her was chilling.

Terrifying and magnificent—the elements of a nightmare. I began to draw her true face. I soaked in the wild silver of her hair and the traces of forest that grew within it, the rocky planes of her face, the sharp crookedness of her bloodstained teeth, the shining slant of her horns, the unquenchable pools of her eyes. She was fierce and terrible and yet wholly tame in that moment as I strove to bring her to life on paper.

My hand was aching when I was finished. I stood and unclipped the parchment and set it into her waiting palms. Mazarine's delight was nearly overpowering as she studied herself.

She said nothing, but her eyes were like dew, and she eventually looked at me again. She reached out and brushed my cheek with her cold knuckles.

"Wait here," she said. "I need to fetch a few things for your disguise."

I nodded, my voice hung in my throat, and I watched her depart the room. Thankful for the time alone, I resumed my seat and procured a new sheet of parchment and a fresh stick of charcoal.

I began to draw my final piece of art.

I designed my disguise, how I wanted to appear after Mazarine took half my heart away. An unexceptional face, an ordinary girl who would not garner a second look on the street. A few freckles, because I liked them, and bold brows because I had always wanted that in my own face. But the rest was plain. I traded my wild copper hair for sleek, long tresses the color of summer soil. A medium-brown shade that was rather dull indoors but boasted a hint of gold in the sunlight. No more gill scars in my neck or dimples in my cheeks. My eyes molted their dark brown for a shade of hazel. I gave up two inches of my height. The square cut of my jaw was narrower, and my skin would retain its pale shade.

I finished my sketch long before Mazarine returned. I was exhausted, so I closed my eyes and leaned my head back, resting until I heard the doors groan.

I rose to meet her.

At once, I was overcome by the stench. She was holding a goblet of something foul smelling, a cloudy liquid that made my stomach roil. I didn't want to know what she had cooked and blended to make it.

She seemed unperturbed by the smell, interested by the sketches I had made.

"Ah, your disguise," she said, admiring them. "Although I must say I am surprised."

"Why is that?" I asked, breathing through my mouth.

"I thought you would want to enhance your beauty," she said, arching her brow. "Most of your kind chase after such things. They want an attractive glamour, something to draw the eye and admiration to them. But not you."

"No," I whispered.

I wanted to be unremarkable upon appearance. I wanted to be underestimated, overlooked, on the verge of being forgotten. I wanted a trustworthy face that inspired friendship, a face that could draw out a secret. A face that one would never assume hid something vengeful beneath it.

It was time to speak my burning question. One forged from my greatest fear.

"How long will this magic of disguise last?"

"The longevity of this spell depends on you, mortal girl,"

Mazarine replied. "On how well you guard the stone half of your heart. Be vigilant and your disguise will last unto death. But should the stone within you crack . . . the rest will soon crumble, little by little, until your disguise falls away."

I dwelled on that for a moment. "But you said this enchantment will make me colder. So the chances of me cracking anytime soon are slim."

"It will make you colder. But even the deepest of ice eventually gives way to fire, Clementine."

Her answer satisfied me, and I nodded. I wasn't worried about my disguise failing me anytime soon.

"Although do keep in mind," the troll added, "mirrors are your greatest enemy. They will not lie for you, and your true reflection will always shine brightly upon them."

"Yes, I will be careful in their presence," I whispered.

A quiet moment pulsed between us. Mazarine extended the goblet, waiting for me to accept and drink.

My mouth went dry as I took hold of the cup. She murmured an incantation, one that was unfamiliar to me, a guttural language.

The room was suddenly too warm. My heart was fighting vibrantly in my chest, hammering against my bones. The pain of it breaking was harrowing, and I gasped, falling to my knees.

It felt like I was drowning again.

It felt like I was being cloven by an axe.

I couldn't breathe, and tears were streaming down my cheeks, but through the haze of my anguish, I saw Mazarine clearly. Her face was stark and amused as she held the rim of the goblet to my lips.

"You must take three swallows, Clementine."

I took the first, forced it down like the bittersweet remedies I had drunk all my life.

I took the second, and my heart was an instrument being strummed one final time. The melody trembled through me, a sorrowful ballad that echoed through every bend and corner of me. One that begged me to reconsider.

I took the third swallow, and the pain bloomed unbearable in my chest. I felt heavy, as if I had been filled with molten gold. I was both burning and freezing, and I quivered.

A moan escaped me.

The pain was too great, too bright.

I could not withstand it, and I surrendered to the embrace of darkness.

11

I woke to something tickling my face. It felt like cold dirt was on my skin, on my chest, weighing me down.

Annoyed, I began to lift my hand and brush it away, but my limbs were heavy, prickling with pins and needles.

My eyes fluttered open, but there was a film over them, a transparent material that moved when I breathed. *I should be panicking,* I thought. *I should be alarmed.* But my heart seemed unmoved, beating a steady pulse, and I calmly lifted my hands from the dirt and began to tear away the gossamer that was layered around my face.

I was lying in the forest. Moss, dirt, pine straw, and twigs clung to my half-buried body. I rose from the earth and stood shakily on my feet, brushing my clothes clean.

It took me a moment to remember what had happened. To recognize where I was.

I could see a glimpse of Mazarine's mansion through the pines. My leather art satchel was at my feet. I lifted my hands, studying them.

They trembled, but looked no different.

I noticed my hair. Long, sleek, and brown, flowing down my shoulders. I wrapped a tendril around my fingers, marveling at the sheen of gold that lurked within the threads when the sun touched it.

I rushed my hands over my face, felt the slope of it, the thick brows I had created, the thin lips. Then my neck, where the gill scars were gone.

I laughed, a raspy sound, and I wondered . . . how long had I been lying here? Sleeping, transforming in the shadows of the pines?

I quickly knelt by my satchel and opened the buckles. I sifted through the leaves of paper and found the sketch of my disguise. I would keep it, to remember what I now looked like, since a mirror would be of no help to me. I rolled up the drawing and tucked it into the pocket of my skirt, and then I buried my satchel. The art supplies were worthless to me now.

I walked through the quiet light of the forest, searching for Imonie.

She was where I had left her, although she was pacing, frantic. I stood between two trees and watched her for a moment, her distress so keen that she had not heard my approach. She was muttering a prayer, wringing her apron in her hands.

"I will *kill* that child," she said. "I will kill her whenever she returns to me."

"Imonie," I said, my voice deep and scratchy and yet still my own. I would have to remember to disguise it later, when I saw Phelan again.

Imonie startled and whirled, yanking a slender dagger from her belt. I didn't know she even owned a weapon, and the steel glinted in the light as she glared at me.

"Who are you?" she snarled, and I was briefly taken aback by her tone.

"Imonie," I said, and took a step closer to her. "Imonie, it's me."

She recognized my voice. Her mouth fell open. The knife tumbled from her grip. She suddenly looked grieved, like she wanted to weep.

"Clementine?"

I didn't respond, but I was satisfied. If the woman who had raised me had failed to identify me, then no one would.

The mountain wind rushed through the pines, tangling my hair.

And I smiled.

PART 2

Heart of Stone

12

I stood on the marble steps of the Luminous Society Museum, staring at the elegant colonnade. It was a quarter till noontide, and the sun was high in the cloudless sky above me. I had just returned to Endellion, and I was wearing my black-and-white striped skirt, my white chemise, my velvet bodice. The traditional clothes I once wore on new moon nights, when I had fought beside my father in the streets. It felt right to wear my old armor in this moment, even if the fit was slightly off now and the style was five years out of fashion by city standards.

I ascended the stairs to the heavy wooden doors, knowing I was almost out of time.

I had sent Imonie on to my mother's town house. She was still upset by my disguise, and I made her swear not to say a word to my parents. The confrontation would soon come, but I would think about it later.

The museum greeted me with a wash of cool, musty air. My boots clicked on the floor as I walked to the receptionist, a young magician decked out in a top hat and a brown jacket with a daisy tucked into one of the buttonholes.

"I'm here to be interviewed by Phelan Vesper," I said.

"You just missed him," the receptionist replied, frowning down at the schedule spread before him. "He finished early for the day."

"Did Mr. Vesper find a suitable partner, then?"

"On the contrary. He was woefully unimpressed."

I wasn't surprised to hear this. I remembered the way Phelan had first regarded me in the street of Hereswith, when he had narrowly avoided becoming Mazarine's dinner. He had been underwhelmed by me, or so he had appeared to be. I had spent many hours thinking about how I would snare his attention in this interview, hours I had spent jostled in the stagecoach, suffering Imonie's glares. And I knew his respect for me had not sparked until I had sunk his boat during the new moon challenge.

"Will you call him back?" I asked the receptionist. "The ad said he would be conducting interviews until noontide. And I'm here with minutes to spare. I think he will want to see me."

"Well . . . I suppose I can send word to him. Can you pay for a runner?"

I procured a silver half coin from my purse. The receptionist wrote a hasty message on a slip of parchment and hailed a messenger boy from the streets.

"It might be a while," he said, motioning for me to follow. "You can wait in the gallery." He led me down a corridor into a spacious room with a sad echo.

The gallery was empty save for a table and a chair set in the center of the chamber. The floors were checkered, and the walls were crowded with framed artwork. I stood in awe, craning my neck to study the paintings on the highest row. An unexpected pain shook me. I fell prey to longing for what I had surrendered.

I reached out to trace a gilded frame. My talent was gone, and I felt the aching pit of its absence. I gave myself a moment to experience the pang of regret, to study the beautiful muses of the paintings that surrounded me, whispering their stories in rich oil and sweetened shadows and careful brushstrokes. Paintings of monsters and magicians of old, of creatures and places and landscapes that appeared so vibrant I longed to step within them.

This regret would consume me if I wasn't mindful of its sharp edge. It would chip at the stone within my chest, and so I buried the feeling beneath the ice of my intention and stood in a patch of sunlight, waiting for Phelan to arrive.

It seemed like I waited an hour for him.

At last, I could hear sounds in the corridor, just beyond the gallery. Two sets of boots approached, and one belonged to him. I reached out with my magic, to catch the low conversation in the hallway.

"Who is this person?" Phelan was asking. "Do I know her?"

"I'm not sure, Mr. Vesper," the receptionist stammered. "I've never seen her before. Forgive me, I didn't think to ask for her name."

"But you're certain she's a magician?"

"Yes, sir. She cast no shadow. I *did* make sure to check that."

"Well, I hope she proves me wrong. I fear my expectations are rather low after this morning."

The gallery door opened. I stood like a statue, my breath suspended as Phelan stepped into the chamber.

He was dressed in a black jacket with coattails and a matching top hat, a pheasant feather tucked within its band. His waistcoat was crimson, embroidered with golden flowers, and his boots were spit polished, reaching to his knees. There was no rapier sheathed at his belt this time; the only thing he carried was a book. His dark hair was captured by a ribbon at the nape of his neck.

He took two steps into the chamber and then stopped, his gaze finding me at once.

I felt a bead of perspiration trace down the curve of my back. Why was he looking at me like that? I wondered if he saw through my guise, if he knew it was me. Although how could he? Not even Imonie had recognized me.

"Mr. Vesper?" I asked, pitching my voice deep.

"Yes. Forgive me, I thought . . . I thought you were someone else for a moment." He gave me a disappointed close-lipped smile and walked to the table and chair. The receptionist hurried to place an inkstand on the desk before departing the chamber, and Phelan sat and opened the book, taking a quill within his hand.

"Do you have any experience? Have you ever fought on a new moon before?" he asked, marking a new entry on the page.

"No, I haven't," I lied. "But I've always wanted to be a dream warden."

"Very well," he said, and leaned back in the chair, looking at me again. Dust motes spun in the air between us. "Prove to me that you would be my perfect accompaniment."

I had expected more questions from him. His lack of them was telling—he didn't expect me to last two minutes into this interview. He found me unremarkable, underwhelming, a face that melted into all the others he had beheld that morning.

I turned to hide the emotion that flickered through me. I was fulfilling the very role I wanted, and yet Phelan irritated me so greatly that I wondered how I would be able to work alongside him. How long would it take me to usher his family's downfall?

I would need to enact a stellar performance, and I thought about all the things I had learned from my mother, who flourished on the stage with *metamara* spells. Once, I had thought her tricks simple and harmless, mere whimsies to delight a crowd. She turned handkerchiefs into doves, pennies into fireflies, a sapphire bracelet into falling rain. She made it look effortless, and I stopped before a painting of ravens perched in a persimmon tree.

I suddenly knew what I wanted to do, my *avertana* magic yearning for a spar. I took what I knew best of both threads of magic, and I called the birds to me, coaxed them from the canvas into our realm. They emerged with a thunderous flap of wings, hovering around me like a storm until I whispered Phelan's name and they dove to him.

Phelan's eyes widened. He rose in haste, the chair flipping over behind him, and the ravens swarmed him, clawing at his jacket, his hair, his face. I heard him utter a curse of surprise, and I watched as he winced and outstretched his hand, cutting through wings and turning the ravens into feathers. They drifted to the floor in sad spirals.

I had already moved on to my next painting, one that boasted a knight in plated armor, wielding a great sword. I briefly thought of the menacing knight who had haunted Elle Fielding's dream and summoned this painted one forward. He was tall and slow at first, as if waking from a long sleep, but his footsteps made the floors tremble, and I urged him to Phelan.

The knight did as I wanted. I noticed how Phelan's handsome face drained white, as if he had seen a ghost. His eyes went wide and dark; his hands quivered as he raised them in a defensive stance.

The knight swung his sword and Phelan leapt back, almost a moment too late as my knight cut the table in half. Wood splintered and cracked. The walls shook, the frames rattling in protest. My heart beat cold and swift as I watched Phelan frantically cast a charm that rebounded off the knight's breastplate. The knight grunted and attempted another decapitation, unfazed by Phelan's magic.

Phelan was terrified, uncertain how to fell this knight. And he was no use to me dead or wounded. His fear, though, was intriguing and a touch satisfying.

I curled my fingers and the knight swayed, exposing his neck for a brief moment.

Phelan rushed to meet the weakness, his magic slicing the opponent's neck clean to the bone. Down my knight went, in chunks of armor, like a crumbling pillar of stone.

I wasn't finished yet, though. I stepped to the third painting, one that depicted four wolves running in a snowy landscape. The wolves came to me, docile as pups until I whispered Phelan's name to them. Their coats were thick, each a different shade of gray and glittering with snow, and they stalked to Phelan on silent paws.

He was surrounded, and yet he fought them boldly, even as their claws shredded through his sleeves and pants, and I saw his blood begin to well and drip.

Ease, I told the wolves. I permitted Phelan to vanquish them one by one, his magic radiant, growing in strength and accuracy, as if he at last had learned the steps to my dance. And then it was over. He had slain all four wolves, and they lay as snowdrift at his feet.

Panting and speckled with blood, he looked at me. Between us lay a carnage of magic and charms—black feathers that glistened blue in the light, pieces of armor, an abandoned great sword, icy swaths of snow. Phelan removed his top hat and raked his hand through his hair, and I saw how he bled, how he trembled. He was not badly wounded, his pride and confidence more shaken than anything else.

I gave him a moment, and I called the pieces of the paintings back to me. They returned to their frames, as if they had never seen our realm. Phelan watched as I reversed my charm. When the floor was clean—the poor desk would remain splintered, however—he set his hat back on his head, composed. He studied me closely, a furrow in his brow.

"Who are you?" he asked.

I suddenly was overcome with the urge to leave. How had I thought I could do this? Surely, he sensed it was me beneath the guise.

Before I could stop myself, I strode for the door.

"Please, wait," he breathed. "What is your name?" He reached the door before me, and he laid his blood-speckled hand on the wood. I stared at the brass handle, just out of my reach.

Reluctantly, I met his gaze. The words caught in my throat, and I reminded myself to keep my voice low. "Excuse me, Mr. Vesper. But I think this was a mistake."

"A mistake?" He chuckled and glanced at the disrepair of his clothes. And then he looked at me, how immaculate I was. "I think you are rather brilliant. And you're not here by mistake."

I remained silent, and he shifted his weight, his hand sliding away from the door.

"I offer the position to you. Take the afternoon to ponder it, but if you need help in deciding, join me for dinner tonight at my town house."

"I'll think about it," I said.

"Good," he replied with a smile, as if he already knew I had determined my mind. "I live on Auberon Street, house eleven, in the south quarter of Endellion. About a twenty-minute walk from here. Dinner will be at six." He opened the door for me. "I only ask one thing of you before you go."

I stepped over the threshold into the hallway, but I paused to glance back at him. "And what is that, Mr. Vesper?"

"Your name, please."

"Anna. Anna Neven." I spoke smoothly, as if I had said such a name endless times before. As if that name had always belonged to these bones, this spirit. The stone half of my heart.

"Then I will see you at six, Miss Neven," he said, and I hated how confident he sounded.

"We'll see," I countered.

I didn't slow my pace until I was back in the bustle of the streets and out of sight of the museum. I stopped by a fountain brimming with wishful pennies and sat down on its stone ledge, pressing my palm to my chest, where my heart beat its new, strange rhythm.

My plan was simple. Deceive Phelan. Take advantage of his resources while I positioned myself to uncover dirt on his family, because all noble families had secrets to hide. Set that secret free. Watch the Vespers fall, one by one, into disgrace, including Lennox in Hereswith.

I wasn't sure if I would ever reveal my true self to Phelan after it was all said and done, but one thing I knew for certain: things were going exactly as I hoped.

13

By five fifty-eight that evening, I was walking Auberon Street, rapidly approaching town house eleven. I hadn't gone home that afternoon but wandered the southern quadrant of the city until I worked blisters on my heels, waiting for the sun to set.

I had imagined Phelan's home to be drab and a touch eldritch, with an unpainted door and narrow windows and weeds in the garden. Town house eleven turned out to be unfortunately charming. It was three stories of gray brick with ivy growing up a trellis. The windows shone as if they had just been washed, framed by dark red shutters, and there was a gate off to the sinister side of the house, which led to a back garden.

The shadows were growing hungry on the street, and the lamps were being lit when I made my way to the door and knocked at six sharp.

It opened instantly, like someone had been waiting just behind the indigo-painted wood.

To my shock, it was an older woman. Her thistledown hair curled beneath a lacy cap, and she was dressed in a starched black dress and lace-trimmed apron. "You must be Anna Neven! Welcome, welcome!" She smiled and beckoned me to come inside, as if she had known me all my life. "We're so pleased you are going to be joining us!"

"Ah, yes," I said, and felt a brief flash of annoyance, because Phelan must have assumed that I would accept his partnership and told his housekeeper. But I swallowed the objection and stepped into the brightly lit foyer.

"By the look in your eyes, I don't suppose he told you about me," the woman said with a chuckle, and shut the door behind me. "I'm Mrs. Stirling. I cook and clean for him, and my grandson, Deacon, runs errands."

"How lovely," I said, thinking that Phelan didn't deserve such a cheerful woman to do his chores. Although if I was honest . . . I did have Imonie all my life to wash my clothes and ensure I was fed. So perhaps I shouldn't judge, although I was looking for something—anything—to give me reason to add another mark against Phelan. "And I suppose he didn't tell you that I'm still undecided in my decision of partnership?"

"He told me you were in the midst of deliberation, Miss Neven," said Mrs. Stirling, and her smile deepened, revealing a slight gap between her front teeth. "But after I beheld what you did to his clothes today . . . I do hope you will accept."

I couldn't help but laugh, true and heartfelt, even if there was only half a heart beating within me. "Then I am one step closer in accepting the offer, Mrs. Stirling."

"Good, my dear. He needs a magician such as you beside him."

A creak on the steps caught my attention. Phelan was descending the stairwell, drawn by the sound of my laughter. But he stopped when I looked up at him, and he seemed hung by uncertainty, to see me standing in his foyer. He had changed since our meeting earlier. His clothes were, once again, finely tailored and cut from the latest fashion, and his hair was damp, tamed by a ribbon. I could smell his aftershave from where I stood—a medley of pine and meadow grass, a fragrance that instantly stirred my homesickness—and I had to distract myself with my own raiment. I had chosen to wear the same clothes from before and had ensured they were wrinkled, and that my hair was unbrushed and loose, tangled down my back. I was quite disheveled in comparison to him, but it was deliberate.

I cast a bet as to how long it would take him to begin purchasing new garments for me. It was my intention to steal from his coffer, bit by bit, without him even realizing it. Just as he had stolen my home and livelihood. Just as he had made me pack up everything in a whirlwind with hardly a day to grieve over what I had lost.

"Miss Neven," Phelan said, and continued his descent. "Welcome. I do hope you're hungry. Mrs. Stirling has cooked all afternoon to impress you."

"Then she is in luck," I said, glancing at her. "I don't remember the last meal I ate."

"Oh, dear child! I have plenty for you, then, but I need to return to the kitchen. Phelan? Why don't you give her a tour, and then bring our guest into the dining room."

"Of course, Mrs. Stirling," he said.

We watched as she hurried down the hallway, and then I glanced sidelong at Phelan.

"Is this your house, or hers?"

That coaxed a slight grin from him. "It's mine by law, but it answers to her, I think." He noticed my clothes, wrinkled and gilded in dust, and the long snarls in my hair. I waited for him to say something about it—add another mark against him in my ledger—but he managed to quell his objection and said in a pleasant tone, "Come, Miss Neven. Let me show you around."

I followed him into the drawing room, a wide chamber with wainscoting and striped wallpaper, a plush rug that swallowed footsteps, a marble hearth, and an assortment of furniture. The tang of lemon haunted the air, as if Mrs. Stirling had just polished all the wood.

"This room is for visitors, and most evenings Mrs. Stirling and her grandson, Deacon, and I like to play a round of cards after dessert. You should join us tonight." He indicated the card table that sat between two couches, and I nodded, thinking I should definitely *not* play cards with them. My competitive nature would emerge, and who knew what I might do to win.

Phelan glanced at me, as if he read my thoughts. "I take it you like cards?"

"A little. I don't play very often."

He nodded but seemed unconvinced. I followed him through

the drawing room until I saw the great mirror hanging on the wall, positioned above the game cupboard. I froze, staring at the hungry glass. Why did he need such a large, obtrusive mirror in his drawing room?

Thanks to the thick rug, he didn't hear me come to a frantic halt, and his eyes were set directly ahead, where he was leading me to an open archway. I hurried past the mirror, praying he wouldn't turn. And I caught a glimpse of myself in the glass. A reflection of wild auburn hair and large brown eyes and pressed lips, as if I were holding a song in my chest.

"This leads to the library, where I do most of my work," he said, guiding me through the archway into a back corridor, which wound to a set of double doors with panels of stained glass.

I exhaled, following him into a spacious library. The shelves rose from floor to ceiling, carved from mahogany wood. There was a hearth, swept clean of ashes, and a desk in the center of the room, where a tome sat beside a vase of swan quills and an herbarium. His book of nightmares, I presumed, and I approached it, measuring its thickness, the tattered edge of its pages, the weight it gave to the room.

"How long have you been warden here?" I asked.

"For five months."

"So you have faced multiple new moons in your appointed streets?"

He hesitated, a shadow in his expression. "Not exactly. I've only faced one of the five."

I was intrigued by his response. "Why only one?"

"This most recent new moon I was away due to travel, so I hired an independent magician to cover the streets for me," he explained in a stilted voice. I knew *exactly* where he had been that moon, but I maintained my pleasant facade. "And on my first new moon . . . I was overwhelmed and wounded. It took me a while to recover, and while I was healing, my twin brother fought on my behalf."

Lennox, I assumed, and my lip almost curled in disgust. I was surprised to learn they were twins, because they looked nothing alike. An old story came to mind, the one Imonie had told me of the woman of the mountains and her twin boys. They had been identical, often switching roles to protect each other from punishments. I wondered what it would be like to so seamlessly change places with someone, fooling friends and family alike.

"Your brother must deeply care for you," I said. "I assume the two of you are very close?"

Phelan was quiet, and it prompted me to glance at him. His gaze was distantly set on the shelves of books behind me.

"Our relationship is one built on favors and debts," he replied, still avoiding eye contact with me. "And I swiftly learned that we don't work well together, and I needed a different partner on the new moon nights."

He needed someone to guard his back, which I understood. I had once guarded my father's, and he mine. Strange, that Phelan didn't want it to be his twin brother. Although Lennox was not a likable person.

"What were you wounded by?" I asked, my gaze drifting to his chest. To his perfect posture, which betrayed no visage of weakness, even as I knew my own magic had left lacerations on his skin earlier that day. Nicks and cuts that now hid beneath his garments.

"That I cannot tell you," he replied with a lilt of mirth. "Unless you accept my offer, Miss Neven."

"Touché, Mr. Vesper," I said, and turned my attention away from the intensity of his gaze to the book of nightmares. I considered it foolish that he'd left something so vital and important sitting in plain sight on his desk until I dared to trace its battered cover and was rewarded with a sting.

The shock of it made me wince more than the pain, but I yanked my hand away as blood welled on my fingertips.

"It bites," Phelan belatedly said as he walked to me, pulling a handkerchief from his inner pocket. "Here, I apologize. I should have warned you."

I nearly accepted his handkerchief, my blood welling like a string of red pearls, but I felt a warning in the pit of my stomach. I needed to be careful and give him no piece of me. No strand of hair, no drop of blood, no breath of mine. Nothing that he might use to divine my true nature, should he come to one day suspect I was not who I appeared to be.

I set my fingers in my mouth and licked away my blood, to which he arched his brow, as if secretly repulsed. My blood tasted like warm iron, and I cleared my throat, drawing my fingers from my lips and pressing them against my palm, urging the wounds to clot.

"How long have you lived here, Mr. Vesper?"

"For three years."

"But you have only been warden for five months. How did you come to earn the responsibility?"

"The magician who guarded this territory became a madcap," Phelan replied.

"A madcap?"

"A magician who seeks to find a way into the Seren fortress and break the new moon curse."

Oh, I had come across quite a few of those, milling around Hereswith, seeking information. I remembered how Imonie, Papa, and I had called them "vultures," and how much we had hated them. I remembered how I had thought Phelan and Lennox had been such people the first time I saw them.

"And how many inhabitants do you guard here?" I asked.

"Six streets fall beneath my care. A total of three hundred and five individuals."

An impressive amount for a young magician, I thought.

"And what about you, Miss Neven?" Phelan asked. "Where do you come from? Where do you currently reside?"

"Does it matter?" I countered with a smile. "My life has been rather dull up until this moment. I wouldn't want to bore you with details."

"It matters to me," he said, earnest. "If you and I work together . . . we can't be strangers."

"Of course not," I agreed, but was shifting away from him, my focus attracted to the window of the library, where a vast array of potted plants sat on a table. I recognized all the plants by name, and I brushed the variegated leaves of one. "Do you make your own remedies, Mr. Vesper?"

He had no chance to reply. I was suddenly aware of the glint of two eyes, peering up at me through the tangles of foliage.

"Hello!" a voice chirped, and I startled, my breath hissing through my teeth in alarm.

I watched, astounded, as a boy crept out of the dangling vines, standing before me with a click of his heels. His hair was a mop of tawny curls, his face was freckled, and his clothes were mud stained. He was missing his front tooth as he grinned up at me.

"Deacon," Phelan said with a sigh. "What have I told you about sneaking and eavesdropping?"

The boy glanced at Phelan, his smile fading. "I know, Mr. Vesper. It's rude and I'm sorry, but you told me it was impossible to sneak up on a magician. And I just snuck up on *two* of you!"

"Yes, and that was very dangerous," Phelan remarked. "You took us both by surprise. What if we had responded in another way?"

"Like with magic?"

"Yes. Miss Neven might have turned you into a mouse."

I gave Phelan a flat expression. "Is that the most imagination you have? I wouldn't have turned him into a mouse." And I brought my gaze back to Deacon, softened by his eagerness, his toothless smile. "I would have turned you into a hawk, maybe. A bird who could soar through the clouds. Or a wise fox who knows all the secret ins and outs of the house."

"Or a dragon?!" he cried hopefully.

"Alas, a dragon would not fit in this library. And you might catch all the books on fire," I said.

That made sense to him. He nodded, but his eyes were glazed, as if his mind was whirling with possibilities. "Have you ever turned a human into an animal, Miss Neven?"

"No, I haven't," I responded honestly. "That is very risky magic. It's not that difficult to turn a human into something else if the magician has the imagination and the right spell work, but it's far trickier to return the human back to how they once were. A change is made in the process, and it's easy to err."

"That does sound hard," Deacon mused. "Have you done it, Mr. Vesper?"

Phelan shook his head in a negative response and motioned for the boy to come closer. "Why don't you go and see if your grandmama needs help with dinner. Miss Neven and I will be right behind you."

"All right," Deacon said, but he gave me a smart little bow. "I'm very pleased to make your acquaintance, Miss Neven!"

I smiled, and warmth began to seep in my chest. It emanated a shallow ache, the sort of ache one feels when they have run too far, or when they are about to be reunited with someone they have missed for years.

An ache of stone being shifted, and I couldn't believe it. Not this soon. Not by the kindness I had met here, the welcome and the genuine smiles. Not by the sweet adoration of a little boy and his toothless grin. This would *not* be my undoing, I vowed, and struggled to steady my heart, dwelling on the fact that I'd once had such things until they had been taken from me.

I drew in a deep breath until the ache eased, but Phelan was regarding me intently.

"Are you well, Miss Neven?"

I forced a smile, although I could only wonder what lurked in my gaze when I looked at him. "I think I'm just hungry."

"Then come, let me take you into the dining room."

I trailed him out of the library, down the main corridor—my eyes seeking mirrors of all shapes and sizes. The dining hall was a narrow chamber occupied by a table, velvet-lined chairs, and a marble hearth alight with a fire. Mrs. Stirling was just setting down the last dish.

"Oh good, there you are. Come sit here, Miss Neven." She indicated the chair across from Phelan's.

Wonderful, I thought drolly as I surrendered to the chair. I would unfortunately have to look at him all throughout dinner.

Phelan waited to sit until Mrs. Stirling and Deacon had taken their seats. And then he reached across the table and poured wine into my glass flute.

"Potatoes?" Mrs. Stirling asked, offering the warm bowl to me.

I filled my plate, and the dishes were passed until everyone had taken a spoonful of everything. We fell silent as we began to eat; there was only the sound of cutlery and the crackle of fire.

I relished every bite, eating slowly. The last meal I had taken was dried meat and a plum on the stagecoach hours ago, offerings from Imonie's satchel. Thinking of her made me think of my parents, and my mouth went dry when I anticipated telling them what I had done. What I was doing.

"The food is delicious, Mrs. Stirling," I said, to distract myself from the apprehension. "Thank you."

The older woman smiled and waved off my compliment.

"Do you have any siblings, Miss Neven?" Deacon asked after wiping the edge of his mouth with his sleeve.

I saw the disapproving look Mrs. Stirling sent him before pointing to his napkin.

"No," I answered. Creating siblings, as tempting as that was, would only complicate my story. "Do you, Deacon?"

"I'm the youngest. I have two older sisters."

"That sounds fun. I wish that I had sisters."

"What about your parents?" the boy asked. "Your mama and papa."

"What about them?" I didn't like the idea of lying to a child. But he was certainly full of questions, and I felt my cheeks flush.

"Do they live nearby? Did they teach you magic?"

"I think that is enough questions, Deacon," Mrs. Stirling said. "Remember your manners."

Deacon looked downcast by the chiding, his attention returning to his plate as he pushed his peas around in a circle.

"It's quite all right," I said, reaching for my wine. "I never had the opportunity to know my father. My mother raised me. She was the one to teach me magic."

"I bet she is proud of you, Miss Neven," said Deacon, and I heard the longing in his voice. I had not sensed illumination in him, that unmistakable flame of magic that some of us were born with. But it was apparent that he wanted to become a magician.

"She would be, yes," I replied, and took a long sip of wine.

Deacon's mouth opened, ready to spout more queries, but

Phelan swiftly moved the conversation to other, safer things. I ate my fill, listening more than I spoke, but chiming in when it felt right, and Mrs. Stirling brought out chamomile tea and almond pudding for dessert. I despised almond pudding but swallowed every bite, washing it down with overly sweetened tea.

"Deacon, help me clear the table," Mrs. Stirling said, rising from her chair.

Deacon groaned but then asked, "Can we play Seven Wraiths tonight?"

Seven Wraiths, I thought with alarm. That card game my father had forbidden me to play. The one the Fielding girls loved, even with its enchanted consequences. All I could think of was Elle, terrified of a nightmare she had been given by losing the game. A nightmare that had frightened me as well. I could almost hear the heavy clink of the knight walking through the streets again.

"I think we should," Phelan said, also glancing to me. "Would you like to join us, Miss Neven?"

"I fear I need to return home," I said, standing. "But thank you again for the lovely dinner, Mrs. Stirling."

She smiled and nodded, but I could see the tension in her face. I hadn't shared my decision yet, if I was accepting Phelan's offer or not, and Deacon carefully began to stack the plates. When he came to take mine, he begged, "Please, Miss Neven! *Please* choose us! Mr. Vesper needs you."

"*Deacon!*" Mrs. Stirling called to him through the swinging kitchen door, mortified by his outburst.

I wanted to smile at the boy, to reassure him. But I worried about drumming up that ache in my chest again, and so I merely watched as he retreated into the kitchen with a pile of precariously stacked dishes.

Phelan cleared his throat and rose. "Let me see you out, Miss Neven."

I followed him back into the corridor, where I did find one small mirror hanging in a collage of paintings, gleaming mirth-fully on the wall. But I didn't think it would be likely to give me away so long as I ensured no one trailed me into the hallway.

Phelan opened the front door. The night rushed in, encircling us with the fragrance of sweet cedar smoke from a nearby tavern. We stepped out onto the front porch, and the lantern light trickled over our faces.

"Do you need more time to consider the offer, Miss Neven?"

"No, I've decided. But there is one thing I want to ask you, before I give you my reply," I said.

"And what would that be?" he drawled, gazing intently at me.

I held his stare, even though I felt oddly vulnerable. I didn't know if I liked or disliked the way his attention was so rapt upon me.

"Why did you offer the position to me?" I asked. "You must have had plenty of other promising magicians at the interview today."

"I did. And yet all of them performed for me, as if they were on a stage. Not a single one engaged me as you did," he replied. "I confess, Miss Neven, that there was a moment when I thought your intentions were to kill me. And then I realized how absurd that was, and that you were testing me as I wanted to test you. You challenged me as if you were a nightmare on a new moon, and I knew then that you were the one that I wanted beside me."

His confession took me by surprise. "You must have some terrible nightmares haunt these streets."

Phelan paused. "I do. I've come to learn that they are treacherous on the darkest of nights."

Every street is treacherous, I wanted to say, remembering the gills that had scarred my neck. I resisted the urge to trace where they had once gleamed.

"Then I accept your offer, Mr. Vesper," I said. And before he could respond, I added, "When do we begin?"

"Tomorrow," he answered. "At eight o'clock sharp."

"Excellent. I'll see you here at eight." I took another stair down, only to feel his presence follow me.

"Wait, Miss Neven. Let me walk you home."

I pivoted and held up my hand. "That's not necessary."

Phelan glanced beyond me to the streets, dark patches punctured by the wavering beacons of lamplight. This was a quiet, aristocratic segment of the city, composed of families who were all home for the night. But there were other parts of Endellion that were dangerous to roam alone. I read the lines in his brow. He was worried about this, as well as curious to know where, exactly, I hailed from.

"Then let me call a horse and cab for you," he said.

"No, I truly don't need one," I insisted. "I prefer to walk, especially after that rich dinner." I took another step away from him and he held his ground. "Good night, Mr. Vesper."

I strode over the flagstone path to the gate and slipped out into the street.

I waited until I was three blocks away before I called my own horse and cab. It would have taken me all night to make the walk from the southern quadrant up to the north peak of the city, where my mother's town house resided.

Alone at last, I relaxed in the coach, the cushion smelling of cheap perfume. I leaned my head back and closed my eyes, exhaustion creeping over me. But Phelan's words continued to sound in my mind, like an instrument that would not cease playing.

You challenged me as if you were a nightmare on a new moon.

He had no idea.

14

The front door was unlocked. I let myself in, quietly latching the door behind me. I followed the threads of voices and candlelight into the kitchen, where my parents and Imonie sat at a table, waiting for me to come home.

My mother saw me first.

I stood on the threshold, where the firelight could wash over me, and I waited for her to ask who I was—a stranger in her home. She said nothing but her face went pale. She set her teacup down with a clatter in its saucer and that was when I realized she knew, somehow, that it was me.

"Ambrose," she said, but it was too late. My father was turning in his chair, to see what had transfixed my mother's attention.

He frowned and instantly rose, scaring Dwindle down the hallway.

"Who are you?" he asked, and while he was polite, I saw the

gleam of fear in him. He sensed it, too, and he didn't want to believe it.

"Papa," I said, and he flinched. "It's me."

He took a step back as if I had struck him. Imonie buried her face in her hands and my mother was frozen, watching us with bloodshot eyes.

"What have you done?" he cried, and his devastation was like a dagger in my side. "Clem . . . *what have you done?*"

"You may want to live your life without magic," I said. "But I don't. You may be content to live in the city, working in the mines, but I long to go home to Hereswith. I'm not done fighting for it, Papa."

My father tore his fingers through his hair. He shot a fierce look at my mother and asked, "Did you encourage this, Sigourney?"

"No," my mother said. "Whatever magic she used to transform . . . it was not mine."

Papa paced through the kitchen. "Why? Why have you done this?" he asked, coming to a halt before me. "You were perfect the way you were, Clem."

"This won't last forever."

"How long, then?"

"The disguise will break when I want it to," I answered, hoping my parents believed me. I didn't know for certain how easily this magic would relinquish me. If my spirit was cold, then it might take a long time to chip away the stone in my chest.

"You still haven't answered me," he said. "*Why* have you done this?"

"I want to know why they chose Hereswith, why they chose to challenge us," I whispered. "I want to know their secrets. I want them to feel the same pain as us—to lose something that means the world to them. To feel the sharp edge of their own selfishness."

"Who are you speaking about?" Papa rasped, but he knew.

"I've become Phelan's partner. He's a dream warden in the southern quarter of the city."

"Phelan *Vesper*?"

I nodded.

"He doesn't know it's you, does he?" Papa said, and he chuckled. The sound was familiar; I made the same kind of laughter when I was overwhelmed and furious and afraid. "This is very foolish, Clem. I know what they did to us was agonizing, but you must let it go. This will eat you from within if you don't, daughter."

Let it go.

He might have found peace by doing such, but I couldn't.

"Papa . . ." I reached for his hand, and for an anguished moment I thought he would jerk away from me. But he wove his fingers with mine, fingers that were now smudged and stained from work in the mines. A place he should not be, as if he wanted to forget and hide who he was. "Papa, I know you're worried, but I'm doing this because families like the Vespers need to know they are not invincible. That they cannot just come and steal someone's home for their own amusement."

His eyes flared. He dropped my hand and said, "Go to your room, Clem."

"But, Papa—"

"Please go. I need a moment."

He had never ordered me to my room before like this, and my face flushed as I spun and hurried up the stairs to my chamber. A candelabra was lit, and I sat on the edge of the bed, exhausted. It had been a long day. When my father refused to come see me, I washed my face and brushed the tangles from my hair, and I dressed in a soft chemise.

I climbed into bed and sat against the headboard. Beyond my window, the city still teemed with noises, and I longed for the peace and quiet of the countryside. I stared at the door, waiting, and it must have been sometime past midnight when I finally heard Papa softly rap on the door.

"Come in."

He stepped into the room, haggard and slow, as if his joints ached. I braced myself for the worst until I watched him cast a protective charm around the room, so no one could overhear us. No one, including my mother and Imonie.

Papa stopped at the foot of my bed. He stared at me a moment, like I truly had become a stranger in all ways to him.

"Tell me what spell you have planned to protect yourself," he said. "A spell that will shield you and give you the chance to flee when Phelan discovers it's you, and you've been deceiving him."

"He will never know it's—"

"Clementine."

I swallowed. "I don't have one planned yet."

"Then that is the first order of business. I want you to have it prepared by the end of this week, for me to approve."

"Very well," I said, and my mind reeled with potential spells

I could spin for such an encounter. If I was truly in danger of Phelan harming me.

"Second order of business," Papa continued in a gruff voice. "You will obviously be working with Phelan every day as his partner. How do you plan to move to and from his house and here, without him discovering where you live? If he sees me or Imonie . . . your cover will be blown."

"Yes, and I have a plan," I replied. I knew he wouldn't like it, so I merely smiled, but I realized my dimples were gone, the dimples that he loved, and Papa only scowled at me.

"Explain the plan."

"It may take me a few days, but I'm hoping Phelan will give me a room."

"At *his* house?" Papa demanded.

"Yes."

"I don't like this, Clem. Not one bit."

"I know, but I'm a magician, Papa. You have taught me the best *avertana* has to offer, and I have faced many types of danger, and this . . . this is not something you should be worried about. It's bad luck to harm a guest beneath your roof, remember? And besides, it will give me an opportunity to drain his resources."

"Where is this coming from, Clem? *Draining resources?* This isn't like you."

He didn't know I had given half my heart away, and perhaps I would have felt shame in the past over his disappointment. But not now. I remained quiet, waiting for his acceptance.

He sighed. But when he looked at me again, I saw that I had won this argument, and he reluctantly nodded.

"You will cast a protective charm on your bedroom door every night?"

"Yes," I said, thinking I still had to somehow convince Phelan to even offer me a room.

"And the windows?"

"Yes, the windows as well. Don't worry, Papa."

"I will worry every moment that you're gone," he said, and I felt that terrible ache in my stone heart again. I had to glance away from him and how destitute he appeared. I played with a thread of my quilt until I felt composed.

"Is that all, Papa?"

"No. Once he gives you a room, you're going to tell Phelan that you will have every Monday night off, new moon permitting, and you are going to use your stealth charm to check in with me here. We'll have family dinner together so your mother, Imonie, and I don't worry ourselves to death."

"I can do that," I said.

"And one last thing, Clem." But he hesitated, and I sensed this was the reason why he had charmed the room, so no one could eavesdrop. "You mentioned that you're doing all this because you want to know why the Vesper brothers chose Hereswith. I want to know as well. I don't want you to risk yourself, but if the opportunity presents itself for you to . . . uncover this, I want you to share it with me on Monday nights. And if you come across any information about the countess . . . I would also like to know it, Clem."

"The countess? Why do you want information on her?" I asked, remembering the stilted moment I had met her in the art shop.

She had studied me with cold reserve and said, *You look familiar. Have we met before?*

"She's an old acquaintance," he answered, glancing away. The hair rose on my arms as I wondered what would make a selfish noblewoman interact with a rustic magician like my father. "We were never friends—I was far too lowly for that—but we worked together until we had a falling-out, years ago."

"Do you think she told her sons to take Hereswith, as a way to slight you?"

"I don't know," Papa replied, a bit too quickly for my liking. "Now, do you agree to my terms?"

I nodded.

"Good. Did you drink your remedy tonight?"

"Not yet," I said, but I reached for the small vial, which sat waiting on my bedside table.

"You're a warden again," Papa said. "It would be wise to continue drinking them every night. Particularly since your partner doesn't know who you truly are."

I didn't say that I had been taking them every night since we left Hereswith, as he'd asked me to. And because he seemed to be waiting, I drank the remedy. It went down like a secret, and even after all these years of swallowing them night after night, I still grimaced.

But I knew what Papa implied. It would be disastrous indeed if I strove to be a vengeful eye in Phelan's house, only to let a nightmare, of all things, betray who I was.

15

"Is your book going to bite me again?" I asked, standing in Phelan's library. It was my first day of work with him, our first day of tenuous partnership. It was going as well as could be expected. I had been half an hour late, due to a carriage crash on the lower north quadrant, and I had swiftly come to discover Phelan detested tardiness.

His back was angled to me as he watered the plants on the table, sunlight gilding his dark hair. "No, not today."

"But perhaps tomorrow?"

He glanced at me, noticing the wrinkles on my plaid skirt, my taupe shirt with brass buttons gleaming up the front. My hair was braided, at least, and he returned his gaze to the plants.

"You should begin to read. You have much to catch up on."

I sat at his desk and carefully opened the book of nightmares. I sifted through the most recent of entries, and quickly realized that some of them were written in dark gold ink, while the majority were in black.

"Do you have a reason for using different colored inks?" I asked.

"Yes. The gold entries are the active ones, dreams of people who currently reside here." If a resident happens to move away or dies, I charm their records into black ink, so I keep track of which dreams to study. He pruned a few wilted leaves and then went to work making a remedy. He chopped and scraped an assortment of leaves and petals into a glass flask, where it bubbled over a flame, casting an astringent aroma in the office.

"I suppose it's hard to keep track of everyone who comes and goes within your territory," I said after I had read a few of his entries. "The city is such a fluid place."

"Yes," he agreed. "Some nightmares unfortunately escape my records."

I left him to his task of straining and bottling the remedies, and I read through page after page of golden-hued nightmares. I began to jot down ideas for spells to counter them. The hours crept by. We worked in companionable silence, interrupted only by Mrs. Stirling bringing us a lunch tray of sliced rye bread, cold slabs of roast beef, cheese, and pickles.

Phelan and I sat across from each other at the desk, but I was too focused on eating and reading to attempt a conversation with him.

"Do you have dinner plans, Miss Neven?" he eventually asked.

"No." I kept my eyes on the page.

"Would you like to have dinner with me and two of my friends tonight? We can walk the streets this afternoon, so I can show you the territory boundaries, and then we can go eat with Nura and Olivette."

Nura and Olivette? I reached for my lukewarm tea, suddenly stricken with nerves. He had friends, which meant they would most likely ask me an endless stream of questions.

"I'm not sure. . . ."

"Do you have elsewhere to be tonight?" he asked, and I heard the curiosity in his voice. He wanted to know more of my history and was too polite to directly ask for it again.

I sat back, my fingertips stained gold and black from turning the inky pages.

"I'm not a very social person, Mr. Vesper."

"Neither am I," he quipped. "But I should warn you that if you put Nura and Olivette off tonight, they will insist on meeting you tomorrow night, and the night after that, and the night after that. . . ."

"All right," I said, waving my hand. "If your friends are so persistent, I'll join you."

"Excellent," he said, rising from the desk. "I have a few deliveries to make, but I'll return soon."

I watched him quit the library, the stained-glass doors latching behind him with a quiet click.

I waited a full ten minutes before I began to search through the drawers. I hoped to uncover correspondence—letters between him and Lennox, or perhaps him and his mother—and sifted through reams of blank paper, corked inkwells, bundles of quills, sticks of wax, candle tapers, a bronze stamp, an amethyst cluster, a sack of lemon drops. And then my fingers caught on a sharp edge of parchment. A square calling card. I drew it into the light.

By the seventeenth of November, it read in elegant handwriting. I held the card against a page in the book of nightmares, to compare it with Phelan's handwriting. The script was similar in slant and embellishment, but there were a few differences. I didn't believe Phelan had written this mysterious date down, but perhaps his mother had?

I returned the card to its place in the drawer. But my mind hummed with questions and thoughts. After a while, I decided to return to work. The next new moon was only eight days away, and I still had volumes to cover, new spells to forge in preparation.

I turned a crinkled page in Phelan's recordings, skimming until my attention was hooked by a particular nightmare. Stunned, I leaned closer until I could taste the dust of the pages, and I read Phelan's account:

> *Knox Birch is standing in a great hall of shadows. At first, he does not know where he is, but by the creeping cold on his skin, he feels like he has been here before. When the sunlight begins to flood through the windows, he sees the banners dressing the stone walls—blue banners emblazoned with stars and moons— and he realizes where he stands: the fortress in the clouds. He can feel the great depth of the mountain beneath him, and it is strange how at home he feels in Seren, even though he has*

never stepped foot in the mountain duchy.

Something evil happened here, he thinks.

But his memory wilts the more he attempts to remember why this place is cursed. And soon, he forgets those feelings altogether when the duke's throne catches the sunlight. Knox is alone in the hall, and suddenly, he desires to claim the empty chair. He takes the first step, believing that he will restore whatever has broken by making himself duke. He takes the second step, and then the third. And that is when a shadow emerges, hissing like wind through cracks in the mortar. The shadow fights him, impedes him.

Knox has no choice but to take the rapier that blooms in his hand and cut the shadow down. It lies limp at his feet, and he steps over it, his eyes on the throne. But another shadow interferes, wailing with such intensity that he cannot bear to hear it, and he pierces its heart. The second shadow crumples, and he steps over it, nearly to the dais steps, where the throne waits.

And yet a third shadow rises. It screams and fights him. He cleaves it in two, and it lies at his feet. At last, he thinks. He has defeated the challenges and he alone has earned the throne.

He claims the chair.

As soon as he is seated, the rapier in his hand

vanishes, and the shadows who are crumpled on the floor are exposed for what they truly are: his wife and his two daughters. They lie dead in pools of blood, destroyed by his hand, and Knox lets out a wail that never seems to end.

He wants to claw out his own eyes. He wants to cut out his own heart. If only he had seen them, he cries. If only he had seen their faces, and not their shadows. . . .

The nightmare captured me, and I was shaken, desperate to escape its icy hold. Of all the dream records I had read in Hereswith, no one had dreamt of the fortress in the clouds. And yet I could still taste the brisk air of the mountain castle, feel the cold flagstones beneath my feet as if I had walked Knox Birch's nightmare. I closed my eyes and I saw a glimmer of blue on the walls, and I could hear the distant echoes of lives long lost. I wondered what it had been like before the curse. Why had the seven members of the duke's court killed him? Had one of them desired to take the throne from the Duke of Seren? Was the duke cruel as some of the legends spun him to be?

I couldn't bear to read another word.

And I shut Phelan's book.

Later that afternoon, I walked beside Phelan, learning the winding bends of the streets he guarded. The town houses were well maintained—some were extravagant with their ornate window casements and gates with finials dipped in bronze and lush gardens in the front yard. I wondered about the inhabitants who lived behind each door. The mere notion of trying to learn a horde of new names and faces was overwhelming, and I eventually looked upward, to the reassurance of the sky. It was overcast, threatening rain, and there was a slight chill on the breeze. I imagined Hereswith would have felt her first frost by now, and the leaves would soon change.

"Do you ever dream, Mr. Vesper?" The question slipped from me, soft and genuine.

"Do I ever dream?" he repeated, amused. He walked with his hands in his jacket pockets, and the wind stirred his hair. "You mean if I've experienced my own nightmare, Miss Neven?"

"Yes, I suppose that is the better question."

He was quiet, and when he slowed his strides, I slowed mine, to keep in pace with him.

"I've never dreamt," he replied, meeting my gaze. "But then again . . . I've never given myself the chance to."

I hated how his words resonated within me. I hated how his words could have been my own. I hated how they made me want to ask him more questions.

"You've taken remedies all your life, then? Even before you were a warden?"

He nodded, and a line creased his brow. "I know that must sound strange to you. But my mother, the countess, never wanted my brother and me to dream at night."

I drew in a deep breath. A vain attempt to quench my interest. "And why would she desire that? If I may ask, of course."

"You may ask, Miss Neven," said Phelan. "And I will answer

only if I may ask a question of you, which you must likewise answer."

I grimaced, loathing myself for letting him play me into a corner. "Very well, Mr. Vesper. You can ask *two* questions, and I will choose which one I want to respond to."

"Fair enough," he said, and guided me around a street corner. "My mother didn't want Lennox and me to dream because it meant we would need a warden to record our nightmares down in their book."

"And that's terrible, in her eyes?"

"Not terrible, but a vulnerability. A weakness," Phelan replied. "We would be dependent upon another, who would then know our dreams. And sometimes dreams are ridiculous, but most of the time . . . they reveal our innermost pieces. Our desires, our fears, our ambitions, our plans. Our past, even."

I mulled on that, thinking his mother must be very shrewd. If there were no dream records of their family, then I might have a harder time uncovering their secrets.

"Now," Phelan said, and I could hear the smile in his voice. "You must answer a question of mine."

"Go on," I said, bracing myself.

"Do you have any family in the city, or have you ever dreamt, Miss Neven?"

"I've never dreamt, either, Mr. Vesper."

That surprised him, and he glanced at me. "Really? Why is that?"

"Actually . . . let me take back my words for a moment. I have dreamt. *Once*," I lied, and I was amazed at how smoothly it rolled off the tip of my tongue. "When I was a little girl, I had a night-mare that frightened me so badly I was afraid to leave my room. So my mother began to give me a remedy every night, promising the monster in my dreams could never find me again."

He guided us down yet another street. I admired the old oaks that grew along the sidewalk, their gnarled roots working their way up through the cobblestones. "And does your mother still give you remedies, Miss Neven?"

"No," I whispered. "She passed away last spring."

"I'm sorry," Phelan said, and I was surprised to hear how con-trite he sounded.

We fell silent again until he stopped before a grand town house built of whitewashed brick. I gazed up at its navy shutters and crimson-painted door, its lintel made of carved marble.

"I wanted to show you this house in particular," Phelan said, reaching out to touch a wild tendril of ivy that grew on the iron gate.

"Why is that?" I asked.

"The duke lives here."

I examined the home with an attentive eye. "I thought the duke lived in the Blue Mansion, in the eastern quadrant."

"He does," Phelan replied. "The mansion is his primary resi-dence. But he has other homes located throughout the city. He never sleeps beneath one roof more than a week at a time."

"That's absurd," I laughed until I saw the arch of Phelan's brow.

"It's wise," he amended, glancing back to the town house. "Remember what I told you about my mother, and how she ensured my brother and I never dreamt? The duke has a similar dealing with nightmares. He doesn't want one magician to know all his dreams."

Rain began to fall. I watched as Phelan withdrew a tiny umbrella from his jacket pocket, and with an elegant flick of his wrist, the umbrella grew into its normal size.

"Shall we go to dinner?" he asked, opening the umbrella and holding it between us.

I hated that he stored tiny trinkets in his pockets. But hate could only last so long in the rain.

I stepped beneath the umbrella and we hurried to reach the tavern, elbows bumping in a stiff attempt to keep from touching each other.

The Fabled Tavern was three blocks away, a narrow building wedged between a tailor's shop and a jeweler. It was easy to over-look, built of drab gray stone with an arched entryway choked with wisteria. The corridor ushered us into a courtyard, whose open roof was charmed to catch the rain. Phelan left his umbrella by the coat stand, and I admired my surroundings. There was a reflection pool at the center of the courtyard, and fruit trees grew along winding stone paths. Cushions were spread out on the grass, and couples lounged with cups of tea and wine, listening as min-strels played stringed instruments from a pergola.

This was a watering hole for magicians, I swiftly realized. Good food, tea, wine, conversation, friendship, music, beauty. All the things needed to restore magic of mind, heart, and body.

"Follow me," Phelan said, and led me through the courtyard to an archway that swallowed us into the tavern's indoor seating.

It was a crowded, vibrant place, humming with conversations

and laughter. Tables and chairs were arranged over the blue tiled floors, and booths were carved into the walls. A host of lanterns hung above from the timber beams, bathing the tavern in low, warm light. The air smelled of herbs and sweet wine, and I noticed with alarm that there was a mirror behind the bar. But there were so many people gathered, and the light was romantically dim. I didn't fear my reflection, and I followed Phelan's winding path through the tables to one of the booths.

I saw Nura and Olivette before they saw me.

The girls were sitting side by side, their faces tilted close as they spoke to each other. One had a bob of white-blond hair, a rosy complexion with a sprinkling of freckles across her nose. Her companion had brown curly hair that brushed her shoulders, red-painted lips, and light brown skin. They were both dressed in bright colors, and my anxiety soared when they caught sight of our approach.

"Phelan!" the blonde cried with enthusiasm. "Hurry and introduce us! We've been longing to meet the magician who nearly killed you in the interview!"

"Of course you are," he humored her, but I saw a flush stain his cheeks as he turned to me. "Anna Neven, this is Olivette Wolfe and Nura Sparrow. Olivette and Nura, allow me to introduce you to my partner, Anna Neven."

"A pleasure to meet you, Anna," said Nura. Her voice was deep and smooth compared to Olivette's high pitch. "Come, join us."

I slid onto the bench across from theirs, and Phelan settled beside me.

"I want to know what inspired you to use the paintings in the gallery," Olivette said in a rush. "It was ingenious, but also very risky. How were you able to command someone else's art, Anna? Are you well versed in *metamara*?"

And so it begins, I thought with a twinge of fear. It was the same fear I felt when I saw a mirror, a cold shock that made my spirit coil. And yet I smiled and scrounged up an answer.

"It *was* risky. I won't pretend otherwise. But I've long been an admirer of art, and since I had heard that Phelan was very unimpressed with the other interviews he had held that day . . . I knew I needed to take a dangerous leap in order to catch his attention."

"Hmm." Olivette grinned, glancing from me to Phelan. "She knows you quite well, my friend."

"He's easy to read," I said with a nervous chuckle.

"Am I?" he countered, and I felt him look at me.

"Yes," I said, grateful that the waiter arrived, filling our goblets and setting down a platter of sliced bread, squares of cheese, olives, and an array of colorful jams. "Your eyes betray your thoughts sometimes."

"If that is so," Phelan said to me, his voice low with offense, "then read my eyes now. Tell me what I'm thinking."

I took a sip of wine before I met his stare. His eyes were dark, like new moons, and for all my bluster . . . I had no idea what thoughts haunted him.

"You're thinking that you're hungry, and the noise in this tavern is too loud for your liking," I teased, and lifted my goblet to him.

Phelan begrudgingly clinked his glass against mine, and the tension between us melted as we began to eat.

"Are you an artist yourself, Anna?" Nura asked.

"No," I replied swiftly. "I unfortunately have no such talent, but I love the work of others." And it was time for me to turn the conversation toward them. I smiled and asked, "How do you know Phelan?"

Olivette and Nura exchanged a glance.

"I've known Phelan for years," Olivette eventually replied. "We went to school together."

"And I met Olivette two years ago," Nura said. "When she was looking for a partner. She introduced me to Phelan not long afterward."

Olivette slathered honey butter onto a slice of bread. "Our territory is next to Phelan's, in case he hasn't told you yet. And we have a tradition of eating here at least once a month, before the next new moon."

"A lovely tradition," I said, and I meant it. I longed for this sort of camaraderie.

Our second course of food arrived, distracting us, and slowly, I became more comfortable, but I never let my guard down. If I was honest . . . I enjoyed Nura's and Olivette's company. Perhaps more than I should.

"You'll give us a warning if Phelan decides to go madcap, won't you, Anna?" Olivette asked suddenly.

From the corner of my eye, I watched as Phelan nearly choked on his wine.

"I'm *not* going madcap, Oli," he said tersely, as if they had argued about this before. "I told you. I'm not leaving Bardyllis or my streets for a long time."

Madcap.

Vulture.

I slid my gaze askance to look at him.

"You say that *now*, but you hear the gossip among our kind," Nura said. "The curse of the Seren Duchy has stood for a century, tempting every warden in the realm. An empty throne, a fortress cursed full of nightmares. Which of us wouldn't want to experience it?"

"It sounds dreadful," Phelan said in a flat tone. "And if the curse breaks . . . we'll all be without a job, won't we?"

The new moon curse dictated so much of our lives it was almost impossible for me to imagine living in a realm where nightmares didn't hold such power over us. But Phelan was right; if someone managed to open the mountain doors and ascend to the fortress in the clouds, and then furthermore break the century-old curse, the new moon would become a peaceful night. There would be no need for wardens.

"How can the curse be broken?" I asked. Not even the mountain descendants in Hereswith had truly known themselves, and their stories had been passed down to them from ancestors who had lived through the sundering.

"There are only rumors," Nura said. "But most madcaps believe it will come down to defeating a nightmare in the fortress."

"Phelan, I'm telling you," Olivette warned, pointing a speared olive at him. "If you so much as dare run off to the mountains without telling me and Nura, I'll kill you."

"You have nothing to worry over," he said.

"You talked about it once."

"Yes, once! When we were ten years old, Oli!" Phelan countered. "Do you even know how impossible it would be to reach the mountain summit? The doors are enchanted, and no one has been able to open them."

"It would be an adventure—"

"That would see us all killed," Phelan concluded.

"Anyway, Anna," Olivette said with a sigh. "You'll let us know if he changes his mind?"

"I promise," I said, and to her great delight, I clinked my goblet to hers and Nura's.

When Phelan and I left the tavern, it was half past eight and deeply dark, and while the storm had ceased, the streets were slick with water, shining like obsidian in the lantern light. A chill had crept into the air; it finally felt like October.

"Are you cold, Miss Neven?" Phelan walked in stride beside me. He kept his gaze fixed ahead of us, because the streets were still busy, but I sensed that he missed nothing. Not even a slight shiver of mine.

"I'm fine," I said.

We continued onward in awkward silence, but I was pleased to discover that I was beginning to recognize the crosshatching of streets. We took a turn onto a quiet lane; oak trees stood as sentries along the curb and it smelled like moss and damp leaves and musty stones. We were nearly to his town house.

"May I walk you home?" Phelan asked, just before we reached his gate. He finally looked at me. A thread of dark hair had escaped his customary ribbon. I wondered how he would look with his hair loose, unbound. As if he knew my trail of thoughts, he frowned. I smiled in return.

"No, but thank you, Mr. Vesper." I took a step backward, but my eyes remained on his. "I'll see you tomorrow, then?"

He said nothing, but the rain returned, a cold whisper through the oak boughs.

I was seven full strides away from him when I heard his boots on the cobblestones, chasing after me.

"If you won't let me walk you home, take my jacket, or let me call you a cab," he exclaimed, and I pivoted in surprise. "At least take the umbrella."

He withdrew the small trinket from his pocket and uttered the charm to return it to its natural size. And when he extended the umbrella to me . . . I accepted it, my icy fingers brushing his.

I didn't want it. For all I knew, he had ensorcelled it with awareness, and the umbrella would track me all the way home. But nor could I refuse it, not when the rain turned earnest, drenching my hair and blouse in mere moments. Not when he was staring at me with such intensity, as if he feared I would catch a cold and die on him.

"Thank you," I said, clearing my throat to hide how rusted those words sounded. "That is kind of you. . . ."

"If you think I'm kind, then I've fooled you," he said tersely. Shocked by his admission, I watched the rain drip from his top hat. "I'm no better than all the other nobles at court, and all of us play a game, Miss Neven."

For one heady moment, I feared that he had seen through me. I thought I might have fractured, due to feeling soft at dinner with his friends. I resisted the urge to touch my face, to ensure my disguise was sound.

"I'll see you in the morning," he said in an abrupt tone.

I left him standing in the middle of the street, keen to be gone. I waited until I was two blocks away before I hailed a coach, grateful to be out of the rain. My mind whirled, off-kilter from the strange words Phelan had said to me.

If you think I'm kind, then I've fooled you.

I closed the umbrella and propped it against the bench.

When the coach was three streets away from my mother's home, I disembarked. And just in case my suspicions were true . . . I left Phelan's umbrella in the cab.

16

Word soon came of a nightmare, something I had been anxiously awaiting as the days were beginning to pass and no sinister dreams had emerged. I was in the library, watering Phelan's plants, when he brought the letter to me.

"Do you feel up to collecting a nightmare, Miss Neven?"

I set down the watering can. "Indeed. Am I to go alone, then?"

"It's one of the duke's nightmares," said Phelan, holding up the letter. Its wax seal was like a drop of blood. "Lord Deryn has heard of my new partner, and so this is an invitation to meet you. I would accompany you, but my mother has called me to one of her council meetings on the west side of the city, and I fear it will take me most of the day."

"I can collect the duke's dream on my own," I said. And then I realized that Anna Neven wouldn't know how to divine a nightmare, and I made myself hesitate. "What if his nightmare needs divination? I don't know how to do that yet."

"It won't require divination," Phelan replied, leaving the duke's letter on the tabletop. "His Grace always recalls his dreams with sharp precision. All you need for this visit is the book of nightmares, ink, and a quill. Does that sound acceptable to you, Miss Neven?"

"Yes." I started to gather what I needed. My hands trembled, and I was struck with an unexpected bolt of homesickness. I could almost deceive myself, pretending I was back home in Hereswith, packing what I needed to visit the Fieldings. A day that was only weeks ago, and yet how distant it felt now.

"As I mentioned," Phelan said, breaking my thoughts and handing me a leather satchel to pack my things. I carefully slid the book of nightmares within it. "I'll be gone until dark. But you are more than welcome to remain here and have dinner with Deacon and Mrs. Stirling. In fact, she will probably be offended if you don't."

I smiled. "Then I'll plan to have dinner here." I buckled the satchel and slid its worn strap over my shoulder.

"Very good. I should go now, but perhaps tomorrow I can teach you how to divine a dream?" he asked.

I nodded, and we went our separate ways.

The duke was waiting for me in his drawing room. The chamber was wide and brightly lit. The walls were wainscoted, and thankfully no mirrors were present for me to sidestep around. Spires of golden candelabras were positioned behind couches and chairs. The hearth was cut from blue-veined marble, crackling with a slow-burning fire. Tasseled curtains framed the tall windows, which overlooked the front garden and the street. Busts of heroes sat in corners, and a small olive tree grew in a pot before one of the south-facing windows.

I paused to soak in the grandeur. And I smelled the duke before I saw him; there was a strange scent in the air, like rotting parchment, followed by the sweetness of bergamot.

"You must be Anna Neven," he said.

I startled and spun to face him. My old etiquette training surged, and I dropped a proper curtsy, although the weight of the satchel made me look clumsy.

"It's an honor to meet you, Lord Deryn."

"Enough with formalities," the duke said with a smile. The sunlight gleamed on his perfect teeth. "I am the one who is honored to meet you today. Phelan is destined to become one of the greatest magicians in Endellion, and I am pleased to know that he has found a good match."

Destined to be the greatest, was he?

"Come, join me at the table," Lord Deryn said, ushering me across the room to a round card table. A tea platter was set out for us, with ginger biscuits and small sandwiches.

I sat and carefully arranged the book of nightmares on the table while the duke poured us both a steaming cup of tea. He looked to be my father's age, his hair an ashy shade of brown and trimmed short. The silver in his beard caught the sunlight, as did the trio of emerald rings on his slender fingers. He was dressed in black and gold, and beneath the brief flutter of his jacket, I thought I saw a small dagger sheathed at his side. But perhaps I was mistaken.

"Have you always been a resident of Endellion, Miss Neven?" he asked.

I took the teacup he offered and busied myself with adding cream and sugar. But my palms were perspiring. Lying to Phelan was not difficult, due to our history. Lying to Nura and Olivette was harder because I liked them, as was deceiving little Deacon. But lying to the Duke of Bardyllis's face? I was weaving a dangerous web, one that might catch me. "I have, Your Grace. My mother was a seamstress in the west quarter."

"Oh? Where, exactly?" he asked, settling into his chair across from me. He took note of my garments, which made me stiffen. "I am always on the hunt for a good tailor."

I swallowed a scalding sip of tea. My toes curled in my boots, and I commanded myself to hold it together, to spin the lie. "My mother passed away this past spring, Your Grace. Or else I'm sure she would be honored to work for you. She was of the lower class and was not employed in one shop alone but drifted to wherever she could find work."

"I see," he said, and I thought he was studying me far too intently. "That is unfortunate. And your father? Was he the one to teach you magic?"

"I never knew my father. My mother was a magician and she taught me everything I know."

"You must have been very close to her."

I nodded and dropped my eyes to my tea. To my relief, Lord Deryn ceased asking me any further personal questions, and I prepared to record his dream.

"This nightmare occurred last night, Your Grace?" I asked, opening my ink and scrawling the date, his name, and his address on a fresh page.

"It did," he said, crossing his legs and lacing his fingers together over one knee. "The dream begins in the red room of the mansion. It is spring at midday; the sunlight is pouring in through the windows, and pots of flowers and green vines are flourishing in the chamber, and I realize my brother is standing among the foliage." He paused to give me time to catch all his words on paper.

"Do you dream of your late brother often, Your Grace?" I gently asked, thinking of the duke's older brother, who had died years ago.

"I do," he replied softly, as if the memory still ached. "Returning to the dream . . . he asks me to walk the streets with him, because he is weary of meetings and councils and being trapped indoors. I agree, and suddenly the room melts away and we are walking Verdaner Street toward the open air market. That is when I sense something is wrong. There are too many people, too many noises, too much movement. I tell Charles we should return to the mansion, but he is intent on something ahead of us, something I cannot see. I lose sight of him, but then the crowd opens up. I push my way through to step within the empty space, only to find my brother's neck cut open, and he's lying on the stones, bleeding out."

I wrote every word, the quill's nib biting into the paper. The ink turned gold as I wrote, some crafty charm of Phelan's, and yet I wasn't moved by the duke's dream. I couldn't begin to understand why it rolled off me like rain, as this sort of nightmare used to be the kind that roused my compassion.

Perhaps it was because the duke had dreamt countless nightmares of his brother's death before, recorded in earlier entries. Perhaps it was because I had read so many nightmares as well as encountered them in the streets on new moon nights that I had begun to learn the slant of them.

This nightmare felt fabricated.

I didn't believe Lord Deryn had dreamt it last night.

"I fall to my knees," the duke continued. "I hold him in my arms as he dies. And I watch as his face turns pale as bone, and he tries to say something to me, but I cannot understand his final words."

I finished the recording and gave the ink a moment to dry. I glanced over the sparkling porcelain of the tea, the untouched biscuits and sandwiches, and met the duke's gaze. "I'm sorry, Your Grace. This is a very upsetting dream."

He bowed his head in acknowledgment, and I sensed the deceit as if it were a diamond hanging from his neck, sparkling with each of his unsteady breaths, giving him away.

I closed the book and began to pack, but I waited to rise only after the duke had stood.

"I hope you will be prepared to face the new moon alongside Phelan this upcoming week?" he asked as he guided me to the front door. "You lack experience, do you not, Miss Neven?"

I gritted my teeth but managed a smile. "This is my first new moon, yes, Your Grace. But I have been studying and preparing myself."

Lord Deryn waved his frantic butler away. Alone, we stood in the foyer; I was keenly aware that the duke had positioned himself between me and the door. The cloying fragrance of his cologne washed over me again. Sweet and musty. My head started to ache.

"I am reassured to hear that, Miss Neven. But may I ask you a few questions before you depart?"

"Of course, Your Grace." My fingernails dug into the strap of the satchel, marking the leather with crescents.

"If Phelan is wounded on the new moon . . . would you abandon him in the street to save yourself?"

"I would never abandon my partner."

"Even if it meant your own pain or demise?"

My mouth was parched; I drew in a shaky breath, a medley of bergamot, old wet paper, and my intense desire to leave. "Even so, Your Grace. I'm not one to abandon my duties."

The duke took a step closer to me. I resisted the urge to shift backward, but I had a spell ready. One that would freeze him to the floor if he so much as tried to touch or threaten me.

"Are you aware that Phelan was wounded a few months ago, Miss Neven?"

"Yes."

"Did he tell you what wounded him?"

"No."

"Perhaps you should discover it, then. As you are his partner, he should confide in you."

"You don't know what happened, either?"

"He hails from a very secretive family. But I have no doubt

that you will soon be privy to the truth. Or perhaps encounter it on the new moon. If you learn of anything, Miss Neven, you will inform me, won't you? I pay well for information—riches, jewels, prestige. Position. If you wanted to be warden elsewhere, I could make it happen for you."

"Y-yes, Your Grace," I said, and the words were thick as thistle-down in my mouth. I felt numb as I sorted through the tumble of what he was asking of me, what he was offering me.

Did he know who I was? But how would he? I had never met or spoken to him before, when I was Clementine. And then I realized . . . he thought I was trying to climb the social ladder among wardens. Becoming Phelan's partner was a swift way to do so, in particular for a homely girl with meager beginnings.

At last, the duke unlocked and opened the front door for me.

I curtsied and swiftly departed. I felt his gaze as he watched me walk the stone path and slip beyond the iron gate. But I didn't dare glance behind to meet it.

I sensed he was coercing me, lying to me. A game among nobles.

And I was beginning to think he knew I was lying, too.

17

"You have to stay for Seven Wraiths!" Deacon begged me after dinner.

Night had just stained the windows, and I was anxious, waiting for Phelan to return from his council meeting. Suspicions of the duke and his fabricated dream continued to roam in my thoughts; I wondered if I should say something to Phelan.

"Maybe tomorrow night, Deacon," I said, carrying my plate into the kitchen.

Deacon intercepted me. "Please, Miss Neven!"

"Seven Wraiths sounds like a frightening game," I said in a teasing lilt. But my upbringing inevitably reared; all those times my father had told me how harmful the game was. That I should never play it.

"It isn't too scary," he insisted. "I promise. My grandmama plays, and she doesn't get scared."

"Deacon? Where are those plates?" Mrs. Stirling called from the kitchen.

"Please," the boy pleaded.

"All right, but just *one* round," I said, and let him take my plate. "I still need to get home tonight."

"You should stay the night here, Miss Neven! I saw Mr. Vesper had a room prepared for you!" Deacon chirped before he slipped into the kitchen.

At last, I thought, weary of all the precautions I had to take in order to arrive at my mother's unnoticed. Weary, and yet something else pulsed within me, similar to the feeling I experienced before a new moon unfolded.

I stepped into the drawing room.

Mrs. Stirling had already stoked a fire in the hearth and lit the candelabras. The chamber was a dance of shadows, light, and the flash of golden trim, and I looked at the grand mirror hanging on the wall. As if it had set a hook in me, I walked to stand before it.

My reflection stared back at me. A face I had nearly forgotten. A face that felt like a stranger's now, as if a girl I had never met stood on the other side of the glass, watching me as I watched her.

You're not trying hard enough, said the girl in the mirror, touching a stray thread of copper hair. *You've been passive here, Clem. Do you expect this family's secrets to rise and meet you on their own volition?*

I turned away from the mirror, but my blood was coursing. I sifted through what I had gleaned so far. My father had once worked with the countess, and there was bad blood between them now. The countess was an artist. Her husband had died, years ago. The duke was fabricating nightmares and seemed far too interested in Phelan. Phelan had been wounded by something he was afraid to name and the duke was desperate to know. Lennox wanted Hereswith for reasons I had yet to learn. The seventeenth of November may or may not be a date of importance. But I didn't quite see how this all worked together or how I was going to regain control over my ability to return home.

My thoughts broke when Deacon arrived, wide eyed with delight. He made a beeline to the game cupboard, rustling around its shelves for a deck of cards. Mrs. Stirling joined us, bringing in a tea tray with sugar cream pie, and the three of us gathered around the card table.

I watched as Deacon expertly dealt five cards per player between a spoonful of pie.

"Do you know how to play, Miss Neven?" he asked, crumbs falling from his mouth.

"No, I've never played this game, Deacon. Why don't you explain the rules to me?"

"You know the legend of the mountain duchy, don't you?"

"Yes, of course I do."

"Then you know about the seven members of court who were cursed when the duke was killed?" Deacon queried.

"Yes. . . ."

"You know what they were cursed with, Miss Neven?"

"They cannot die or dream," I said.

"Right," he confirmed with a mischievous smile, as if this were a delightful fate. "So we call them *wraiths*. Anyway, there are seven wraiths in this deck. They're bad—if you draw one, you'll want to find a way to get rid of it by trading with one of us."

"Why don't you explain the game from the beginning, Deacon," Mrs. Stirling suggested.

"Oh, yes," he said, sheepish. "You have five cards in your hand, Miss Neven. Don't let me or my grandmama see them. You want to be able to discard one of your cards here, but it has to match in suit or in number. If you can make a match, you don't have to draw from the deck. If you can't make a match, you have to draw a new card, or you can try to trade a card. The goal is to be the first person to get rid of all your cards, but it's tricky, because you might have one of the wraiths in your hand. And that's the last thing you want at the end of the round. If you lose, you'll have a terrible nightmare when you fall asleep."

I studied the five cards in my hand. Two diamonds, a spade, and two of the wraiths. *Beginner's luck*, I thought with a snort, but then studied the first wraith card closer.

It depicted a middle-aged man dressed in blue robes. Moons and stars were stitched on the edges of his sleeves. His face was melancholy, his head bent, one hand over his heart, the other lifted as if he were in the throes of making a plea. His hair was blond until I tilted the card and the color changed to a fiery red. Or perhaps it was a cascade of blood, which began to drip from the ends of his hair, marring his raiment.

Breathless, I tilted the card again and his hair returned to gold, and the blood marks vanished.

A *deviah* magician had created these cards. A magician highly skilled in art who knew how to layer enchantment within the illustration. Something I once longed to achieve. I felt an ache in my chest and I quickly tamped it down.

The second wraith card surprised me further; it was completely blank, save for the title at the footer: *The Lost One*. But when I angled the card to the light, a scene bloomed on the parchment. Stone walls, blue banners, trestle tables. The grand hall of a castle, with an empty throne on the dais.

I had read about this place before, in Knox Birch's dream. This was the fortress in the clouds, the holding of the Seren Duchy. A chill snaked down my spine as I tilted the card again, watching the scene vanish once more, as if it had never been.

"Miss Neven!" Deacon scolded. "Now I know you're holding not one but *two* of the wraiths! Me and Grandmama won't want to trade with you this round. You have to keep them secret."

"Deacon," Mrs. Stirling warned. "Be nice. This is Miss Neven's first time playing."

I was hardly listening; I studied the first wraith card again. Inscribed at the bottom was the cursed man's title. *The Advisor*. "What are the titles of all the wraiths? It's been a long while since I heard the legend."

"The heiress, the advisor, the master of coin," Deacon began, listing them on his fingers. "The spymistress, the lady-in-waiting, the guard, and the lost one."

"And who is the lost one? I don't see them on the card."

Exasperated that I had now informed him of the exact wraith I was holding, Deacon said, "They are the one who was left behind in the fortress when the duchy fell. As punishment for killing the duke. Everyone else fled before the nightmares arrived."

I wondered if the lost one was just a myth, or if they still lived and breathed, alone in the abandoned fortress on the mountaintop. If they had ever stood on the parapets and looked down into the valley, down to where Hereswith had resided among lush grass and trees. And I remembered Imonie's story, the one she had told me just after we had left home. A legend about the woman with her twin boys and how one of her sons had been lost to the mountain, unable to leave its shadow. Imonie's tale had not stated why one twin was doomed to be trapped, but I supposed that legend complemented the game of Seven Wraiths. If the lost one was the assassin, the curse would not permit him to leave.

"Are you ready to play now, Miss Neven?"

"Yes, I understand the rules," I said. "Let's play."

Mrs. Stirling went first. She set down the three of hearts, to match the three of diamonds that sat faceup on the table, which provoked a groan from Deacon. My turn came next, and I laid down one of my diamonds. Deacon did not have a match for the discard pile and asked to trade a card with Mrs. Stirling.

A few more turns passed around the table, and then my wish was fulfilled: I drew another wraith card from the deck.

The Spymistress. A woman whose age was hard to decipher with her smooth, angular face and long white-blond hair. She was slim and sinewy, dressed in black and dark stained leather, and when I tilted the card, horns bloomed from her head, leaves grew within her tresses. A trail of smoke escaped her mouth.

I froze, gaping at the card. A troll. The spymistress of the fallen mountain court was a troll.

"Miss Neven!" Deacon cried. "You have to guard your face! Now I know you have another wraith card in your hand!"

My attention remained fixed upon the card, how the spymistress changed in my grip according to which angle I looked upon her. Human. Troll.

Mazarine.

I thought of her hoard of secrets, her clever disguise, the old magic she knew. How time seemed to hold no power over her.

Deacon and Mrs. Stirling beat me in that round of Seven Wraiths; I conceded with the advisor, the spymistress, and the lost one still in my hands. But I gained a morsel of knowledge, something that could only come from defeat.

Mazarine had once been the spymistress of the mountain duchy.

She was one of the seven cursed, which meant she could not die, nor could she dream. And if she could not dream, surely my father would have known.

All this time, a wraith from Seren had been living beneath his watch, in our town. And he had never said a word about it.

"Miss Neven? I have a guest room prepared just for you," Mrs. Stirling said to me after four rounds of Seven Wraiths, rounds I had encouraged so I could hold each of the doomed cards. To my own demise and Deacon's victory. "Mr. Vesper asked that I do so, in case you wanted to spend the night here."

I stood in the foyer. It was late—half past ten—and Phelan still had yet to return. I hoped he would stay away longer still.

"I'm not sure, Mrs. Stirling," I said. "I wouldn't want to intrude."

"Oh, my dear! You would not intrude. Mr. Vesper and I both worry about you walking home at night."

I hesitated, but eventually nodded. "I *am* rather weary."

"Come, let me take you to your room," she invited me, and began to ascend the stairwell. "Take care, though. These stairs tend to be slick on odd-numbered days."

The steps were a bit slippery, I noticed with amusement as I followed her to the second floor. The air smelled like roasting wood and evergreen, like meadow grass and the dust of old books.

"I've always loved this room," Mrs. Stirling said with a pleasant sigh as she opened a door, lighting a few candles. "It has a wonderful view of the back garden, and on clear days you can see the sunset."

I followed her into the bedchamber. The room was square, its wallpaper printed with climbing ivy. The bed was a good size, swathed in a canopy, and there was an armoire, a writing desk, and two windows trimmed with dark green velvet drapes.

And an oval mirror, hanging on the wall above the washbasin.

I stopped before I could pass by it, and Mrs. Stirling finished lighting the candles, reflexively spreading a stray wrinkle from the duvet cover.

"There's also some new clothes in the armoire, if you would like to change, Miss Neven," she said.

"Where do you and Deacon sleep?" I asked.

"Oh, we don't live here. I live four doors down and will be here before first light to get the fires started and breakfast cooked."

I hadn't realized that I would live with Phelan alone. I had assumed Mrs. Stirling and Deacon lodged here. This was certainly a detail to keep from my father, and I hoped he would understand that my plan had finally taken root, and not worry when I failed to show up tonight. Tomorrow was Monday, anyway. I would have the evening off to go to my mother's and explain the new arrangement to them.

"And you're certain Mr. Vesper won't mind me staying here . . . with him?" I inquired.

Mrs. Stirling smiled. "Not at all. Unless you feel uncomfortable with the arrangement, Miss Neven. And if that is so, I will sleep here tonight on the main floor."

"No, that won't be necessary," I rushed to say.

"Oh, Miss Neven," she said as if remembering something important, and reached into her apron pocket. "Best you take a remedy tonight, since you lost at Seven Wraiths."

I held out my palm and she dropped one of Phelan's vials in my hand. I proceeded to drink it, surprised by its sweetness. Honey with a hint of spearmint, and far more palatable than my father's recipe.

"Good night, Mrs. Stirling," I said, and waited until she had descended the stairs before I closed my door.

I went to the armoire first, curious to see what sort of garments hung within. There were a handful of colorful dresses, white chemises, embroidered bodices with ribbon laces, silk shirts, and skirts that seemed tailored to my size. Three different cloaks, to keep me warm on my walks. He had spared no expense. Pleased, I reached for one of the chemises. It was luxuriously soft against my skin, and I unbraided my hair and washed my face with lavender water before stepping into the corridor.

I listened to the strange sounds of the town house as Mrs. Stirling and Deacon left for the night, locking the front door. I listened to the walls pop and groan, as if the wood and nails had something to say to me. As if they knew I was here with ill intentions, and they protested my presence.

Quickly, I worked to set an alert charm on the front gate, so I would be warned of Phelan's approach when he returned home. I stepped into his room, where Mrs. Stirling had left a host of candelabras lit.

His bedchamber was modest, composed of earthen colors—greens and browns and grays. A mosaic of a forest graced one of the walls and a wardrobe sat in one corner, a writing desk in another. Stacks of books graced the floor, which I found surprising, since Phelan seemed to love tidiness. The curtains were drawn, and his four-poster bed was spacious, a canopy tasseled to the posts. A mirror hung on his wall above a wash station.

I went to his desk and sat down in a rickety chair, proceeding to open the drawers, minding how things were arranged. It didn't take me long to find the stack of correspondence, bound together with a red ribbon. A stack of letters, all of them addressed to Phelan.

Ravenous, I read the first one. A letter from the duke, and his handwriting was surprisingly crooked on the page, as if he had an unsteady hand.

Your debts have been paid. There is no need to thank me, but let's meet for tea this Friday, to talk about the new moon and how we can better prepare you.

Succinct and tantalizing. I wished there was more. The date read July 12. I folded it back into its envelope and moved on to the next. A bill, a receipt, a reminder about the dream tax, and how much Phelan's streets would owe. I passed through them all, the paper rustling beneath my hands. And then I came upon a small portrait.

The painting was of Lennox Vesper. He was young, perhaps thirteen, and he looked morose, as if the last thing he had wanted was to pose for a picture. The tone and style of art was familiar, like the feeling of crossing paths with someone I had met before, unable to recall their name. It tugged at my memory until I tilted the portrait, to study it closer. And Lennox morphed into Phelan.

I stared at this younger version of him. Still poised with a hint of sadness in his eyes, his dark hair bound by a ribbon. I watched him melt into his brother, and then back again, and I wondered what it would be like to have a twin.

It came to me then. The same artist who had illustrated the Seven Wraiths cards in the drawing room had painted the brothers' portraits. Phelan must know a *deviah* magician of art, and I was suddenly hungry to know for myself who created such wondrous portraits.

I continued to sort through the letters, sensing what little time I had left. A piece of parchment slipped from the stack, floating to the floor. I stared at it for what felt like an entire winter, and an icy finger traced my spine as I leaned down to recover it.

I recognized Phelan's writing. I had been reading it day after day in the book of nightmares, and I had come to know it well.

Stark and simple, the paper read:

Hereswith:
Ambrose Madigan, Warden.
Clementine Madigan, his daughter. Apprentice?
Partner?

I stared at my name.

Trembling, I tucked it away, burying it beneath a sea of wax-sealed envelopes and stray sheets of parchment and the two-faced portrait. I wanted more, though, even as my bones ached, and I was just opening another letter that looked to be from the countess when a chime sounded.

My alerting spell.

Phelan had reached the gate.

I was robbed of breath as I swiftly returned the contents to his desk, just as I had found them. But my hands quivered, and the tang of iron haunted my mouth as I rose, darting across his room, the firelight the only witness to my ransacking.

I shut my bedroom door just as the front door swung open.

I was already dressed for sleep; I climbed beneath my covers, sinking into the plush feather mattress. The light, I remembered a shallow breath later, and whispered a charm. The candles extinguished, one by one, leaving me in the cloying darkness of an unfamiliar room in my rival's house. Slowly, I slid down beneath the coverlet, my hair pooling beneath me on the pillow.

I heard Phelan's heavy footsteps as he ascended the stairs. He paused at the top, as if he sensed me in the guest room. I remembered belatedly that I had promised my father I would cast a ward on my door, on the windows.

Phelan retreated to his bedroom across the hall from mine, shutting the door behind him with a quiet click.

The house fell eerily silent.

My heart would not cease its strange, uneven beat. Was it becoming more stone, or cracking into more flesh? I couldn't tell, but it hurt to breathe deeply. I burned cold with fear and fury, and when I closed my eyes, all I could see was my name, bending to his handwriting in dark, bold ink.

18

"S omeone arrived home late," I said, stepping into the dining
room the following morning. Phelan was there, sitting in
his customary seat. His dark hair was freshly washed and slicked
back, and he sipped tea without making a sound, reading the
morning paper while methodically cutting into a wedge of quiche.
He was dressed formally, as he always seemed to be.

"And someone decided to sleep in my guest room last night,"
he countered with an arched brow, looking up from his paper.

His eyes traced my body. My hair was braided into a crown,
and I was wearing one of the dresses he had had tailored, a simple
yet elegant forest-green dress with flora and fauna embroidered on
the bodice in golden thread. I waited for him to say something,
and when he didn't, I sighed and relented to sit, reaching for the
teapot.

"I won't take advantage of your hospitality again, Mr. Vesper,"

I said, filling my cup. "It was a one-night-only arrangement."

"Were you taking advantage of it, if I offered it to you?" he said, returning his gaze to his paper. But his attention was still preoccupied by me, and I didn't know if that was a good thing or a very bad thing. "You should stay here, Miss Neven. It would be easier for both of us, I think."

"For both of us?" I echoed, cutting a huge slice of quiche.

"Yes. I worry about you, since you refuse to tell me the neighborhood you live in or let me pay for you to take a horse and cab home every evening," he said in a flat tone, as if he didn't care that I kept secrets from him. Which made me think he did, rather deeply. "And there is that other matter."

"What other matter?" I asked. "Are you going to charge me for the wardrobe? You spent far too much on the garments, Mr. Vesper, and I might be indebted to you for years."

"No. The clothes are a gift, Miss Neven. I speak of how you are late for work. Every. Single. Morning."

I took a long sip of tea to hide my smile. I was purposefully late, just to irk him. "I'm afraid I cannot help that, Mr. Vesper. Every morning, there is some sort of carriage crash, and every market I have to pass through is so crowded one can hardly breathe, let alone move at a satisfactory pace."

"You could either leave home earlier, wherever that might be, or reside here."

"Hmm. A difficult choice."

"Should we flip a coin then, Miss Neven?" he said with a hint of sarcasm, snapping the wrinkles from his paper.

That was when the word first bloomed in my thoughts. *Exposé.* I could write an essay on the Vespers, detailing how horrible they were. I could submit it to the paper, anonymously. But I would need more content than just detailing how they had stolen my home. I needed to find the dirt they were hiding beneath their perfect veneer.

"What's the cause for that smile?" Phelan asked, and I realized that one had crept over my face.

I never had the chance to reply. The doorbell rang once, twice, thrice. A harbinger of an impatient guest.

Before Phelan or I could so much as move, the table shuddered between us, and Deacon crawled out from beneath it, leaping to his feet with a flush of guilt.

"I'll get the door, Mr. Vesper!" the boy cried, and bolted down the hall.

Phelan hefted a deep sigh but remained seated, pouring himself another cup of tea.

I was taking my first bite of quiche when I sensed the visitor's presence, like a winter shadow had fallen over the table. And then I saw him from the corner of my eye, standing on the threshold.

"Lennox?" Phelan said with surprise, rising to greet his brother.

I had thought about the moment when I saw Lennox Vesper again. Thought about it so many times that it often made me feel ill. But in my imaginings, the encounter had always happened in Hereswith. Not in Phelan's town house, and not so soon.

It took everything within me—every breath, every thought,

every beat—to refrain from exposing my true self.

But my merciless heart grew hungry.

I took a long sip of tea, my gaze fixed on the upside-down print of Phelan's newspaper, but I watched the brothers from my peripheral vision.

"Lee," Phelan said again, walking to meet his brother on the threshold. "Why have you come? I wasn't expecting you."

"Who is that?" Lennox asked, and I felt the prickling of his stare.

I had no choice but to glance up at him and smile as if I had never seen him before.

"I'm Anna," I said in a pleasant tone. "Anna Neven."

Lennox stared at me for another awkward moment, and then he slid his heavy-lidded gaze to Phelan.

"Anna, this is my twin brother, Lennox," Phelan hurried to say, as if he was embarrassed by Lennox's rudeness. "Lennox, this is Anna Neven, my warden partner."

"A word, Phelan?" Lennox said. "In private." He vanished down the hall, his footsteps sounding in the direction of the library.

Phelan hesitated, glancing at me.

"I'll be fine here," I said.

I listened as Phelan rushed down the corridor, waited until I heard the door shut. I tossed down my napkin and rose, following them all the way to the latched doors of the library. I made sure not to stand before the stained-glass panels, where my silhouette might be noticed by them. Carefully, I coaxed my magic beneath the doors, where I could glean their voices.

"I'm disappointed in you, little brother. You couldn't find a prettier partner?" Lennox asked. "She's so plain. I would grow weary of looking at her every day."

Phelan was silent. When he spoke, his voice was clipped with anger. "Why have you come here, Lee? The new moon is only four days away. You should be in Hereswith."

"Hereswith," Lennox scoffed. "What a joke of a town."

"We have our agreement."

"Yes, yes, I know. I would take the town, you would continue work in the city. I'm tempted to switch our places."

I bit my lip. If the brothers switched places, I would be able to return to Hereswith. I would be home, but my father would not. . . .

"There will be no switching places," Phelan said coldly. "You wanted the town. You now have the town. We don't deviate from the plan."

"The people despise me. All they do is talk about Ambrose Madigan and his daughter with that fruit name."

"Remember your purpose, Lee. You won't have to be there for much longer."

"Yes, I know, *I know*," Lennox barked. "Which is why I'm here, Phelan. There's a problem. Dreams are missing from the book of nightmares."

"As we expected there to be."

"Not exactly." Lennox paced the library. The wooden floors groaned beneath his weight. "The whole purpose of us taking Hereswith was to find the dreamless sleeper. We expected one or two people to have nightmares absent from the record. An obvious and simple path to follow. But there are *nineteen* residents whose dreams are absent, by my reckoning. Nineteen! How am I supposed to find the one out of nineteen by November? That Ambrose Madigan was a wily one, as if he knew one day we would come, seeking the troll. He has protected her well."

My mind reeled.

By November.

My father protecting a dreamless sleeper.

Mazarine.

I remembered how she had asked me on the last new moon, *Tell me, Clementine . . . have you read one of my nightmares recorded in your father's book?* Had she been trying to prepare me for this? Had she foreseen what was coming? I sought to understand Papa's motive in protecting her. Was it simply so she could live in peace, or was someone hunting her? Someone like the Countess of Amarys?

The brothers continued to talk. "Honestly, Lee . . . that's not so difficult. Given that one of those nineteen was the actual warden. You should be able to discern which of the remaining ones are taking remedies every night, and which one is the actual dreamless sleeper, especially since Mr. Madigan has departed."

"Of course, I didn't expect Ambrose Madigan to dream!" Lennox snarled. "He was a warden and we do not risk encountering our own nightmares in the streets. But his daughter, whatever her name was . . ."

"Clementine," said Phelan.

The sound of him speaking my name was like an unexpected kiss on the mouth. I thought of it written on a stray sheet of parchment, tucked away in his desk like a secret, and gritted my teeth.

"Yes, *Clementine*," Lennox said. "She never dreamt, either."

"Which is not unusual, given she was her father's partner."

"She was not his partner but his *apprentice*, Phelan. She should have had a nightmare or two in that book, especially since she had been living there since she was eight years old."

A lull in conversation. My breaths suddenly sounded far too loud, and I feared the brothers had sensed my eavesdropping. I took a silent step back, my stomach in a knot, when I bumped into something. *Someone*, I realized, and turned to see Deacon lurking directly behind me, also eavesdropping.

I swallowed a curse. But now that I realized he was with me . . . well, I might as well linger a few minutes longer. I held my finger to my lips and Deacon grinned, delighted that I was joining him in his crime. We crept closer to the doors.

"Perhaps she drank remedies every night," Phelan said. "Her father was a warden, so perhaps he didn't want to encounter one of her nightmares in the streets on the new moon."

"Yes, I can see your point," Lennox grumbled. "But still . . . something doesn't sit right with me, Phelan. And that brings me to the next debacle: I've lost them."

"Who?"

"The Madigans! I set a charm on their wagon, to track where they went, as Mother desired. Ambrose must have sensed it and rerouted my enchantment. All this time, I believed they had settled in another town, a place called Dunmoor, not far from Hereswith. But they never stepped foot in that village. I've completely lost them, and Mother will have my head for it."

"Can you summon Mr. Madigan?"

"He scoured the house before they departed, so no. There's hardly a bootlace I can use."

Phelan sighed.

I was suddenly very thankful my father took such precautions.

"I'll see if I can locate them from here," Phelan eventually said. "You should return to Hereswith and gather any information about where they went from the residents."

"You're not going to inform Mother, are you?"

"No. *You* will be the one to tell her if we have truly lost them."

"Fine. If that is the way you want to play this . . . I should tell you that *he* was in a Hereswith nightmare, and not too long ago, either."

"What?" Phelan's voice was sharp. *"Who?"*

"You know who I speak of."

"What happened in the nightmare? What did he do?"

"Ah, unfortunately I can't tell you the details, brother. Such are the rules of wardenship, remember? Unless, that is, you want to switch places with me and take this dull little village off my hands."

Silence crackled. I resisted the urge to ease my spell further into the room, for fear of the brothers sensing my intrusion.

And then Phelan said, "Get out."

"Come now, Phelan. You should—"

"Get out of my house."

I urgently motioned for Deacon to follow me into the drawing room, and we rounded the corner just as the library doors burst open.

The mirror, I remembered with a hiss.

I dropped to my knees and crawled on the floor, and Deacon mimicked me, thinking I was trying to be covert. I slithered on hands and knees across the rug until the looming threat of the mirror had passed, and then I bolted upright and settled into one of the high-backed chairs, Deacon close behind me. He collapsed on the divan, and we both reached for a book to hold, pretending to read as Lennox and Phelan emerged into the foyer.

Lennox opened the door but paused to glance at me again, and I saw him shake his head, as if disappointed in his twin. My knuckles drained white as I held my book, the words swimming on the page before me. But then at last he departed, and Phelan slammed the door and leaned against it, as if he were overwhelmed.

I didn't look up at him until he walked into the drawing room and stood directly before my chair.

"Is everything all right?" I asked.

He was pale, and his eyes were distant when he met my gaze. "Yes, perfectly well. Deacon? Will you go and help your grandmama in the kitchen?"

Deacon, who was trying to make himself invisible, groaned in protest but quickly obeyed, leaving Phelan and me alone in the drawing room. "I apologize for my brother, Miss Neven."

"What are you apologizing for?"

"That he is such an ass."

I shut the book and set it aside. "Don't apologize for him, Mr. Vesper. Although I suppose I will have to prove my salt, then, won't I? On the new moon."

"Why would you have to prove yourself?"

"Because I think your brother believes I'm destined to be a bad partner for you." I waited for Phelan to make a remark, but when he remained quiet, I added, "Why didn't you and your brother become partners? Surely the two of you would make a strong team?"

"On the contrary," Phelan was swift to respond. "I don't like working with him. We have fought together a few times before, and I hated every moment of it."

"Oh. I'm sorry to hear that," I said.

Phelan paced the drawing room and eventually returned to the foyer, where he retrieved his top hat and cloak from the rack.

"Are you going somewhere?" I asked, standing.

"Yes, I'm afraid something unexpected has come up and I must attend to it." He knotted the cloak draws at his neck and looked at me. "Will you stay here, Miss Neven? In case a request to record a nightmare comes in the post? With the new moon so close . . . sometimes the dam breaks and the dreams swarm."

I laced my fingers behind my back and nodded.

"Thank you," Phelan said, his voice soft with relief.

I watched him depart, felt the draft of crisp morning float into the house with his leaving.

And I sat back down for a moment, to gather my thoughts. A slight tremble racked my hands, and I stared at the inner curl of my fingers, wondering what I should do.

Because I knew why Phelan had left.

He was searching for my father and me.

19

I fetched a few nightmares, but the remainder of the day proved to be a boring Monday. Phelan was still gone by the time evening arrived, and I took great care with my stealth charm as I traveled to my mother's town house for my first night off.

Imonie's cooking greeted me in the foyer, and I all but groaned as I shed my cloak and followed the smells into the kitchen. My mother was setting the table, and Imonie was stirring a bubbling pot of stew. The warm air smelled of fresh bread and rosemary, and I drew it in deeply.

"Ah, there you are," Mama said, rushing to me as if I had been gone for weeks and not a mere day. She framed my face and studied me closely, and I almost blushed beneath her attentiveness. "I presume Phelan offered you a room?"

"Yes," I said. "My plan has gone off without a hitch."

"Take care, Clem," Imonie said, waving a wooden spoon my way. "Pride always sets a snare."

I sighed at her dourness but nodded, taking my seat just as I heard Papa descending the stairs. He looked weary, and even though he had just taken a bath, his fingernails were still dirty from working in the mines. I tried to imagine what it would be like, laboring from dawn to dusk, hidden from sky and sun. Working by the strained light of a lamp, swinging a pick and forgetting that you had once been a great magician.

It is almost like he is hiding from something, I thought as he sat across the table from me. And while questions swarmed my mind, I held my tongue, waiting.

"Is something wrong, Clem?" he asked. He was grumpy, which meant this conversation might go south if I wasn't careful.

"No. I'm here for my weekly dinner and check-in, remember?" I replied, explaining that I now had a room. He nodded, and while I talked, Papa noticed my nice clothes. He scowled but said nothing about them, to my relief.

Dinner wasn't what I expected. I thought it would feel effortless to return home and be with my family, in a place that felt more familiar than Phelan's town house. But to my shock, the air was tense, and conversation felt unbalanced, as if the four of us didn't know what to speak of.

I waited until dessert and tea before I brought up my news.

"The Vesper brothers were sent to Hereswith to find Mazarine."

Imonie nearly dropped the teapot. My mother froze with a fork in her hand, and Papa merely stared at me, as if he had imagined my announcement.

"Lennox is currently irritated," I continued, "because you have made it difficult for him to find who he seeks, all due to how you withheld more dreams from your ledger than he expected. Nineteen dreamers total, in fact."

My father raised his hand. I sensed my comment had offended him, and he said, "I have broken no laws of wardenship. I have recorded *every* nightmare that was dreamt during the time I was guarding the residents."

"That may be so, Papa. And perhaps you anticipated this happening someday, and you prepared years for it. But I want to know why. Why are you protecting Mazarine?"

"Mazarine Thimble?"

"Don't pretend. I know she's the spymistress of Seren. She's a wraith, and I want to know why you were shielding her."

"I was ordered to."

His quick response shocked me. "By who?"

"That I will not tell you, Clem."

I held his stare, suspicious. I had never doubted him before, and my breath turned shallow.

"Both Lennox and Phelan are hunting us, Papa, with the hope that we will identify the troll. And I think the countess ordered her sons to find Mazarine by November seventeenth," I said. "Does that date ring any bells to you?"

Again, the silence was thick enough to drown in. I glanced from Papa to my mother to Imonie. Why were they acting so strange?

At last, Papa dropped his gaze as he viciously cut into his pie, and said, "I have no idea what that date means. But thank you, Clem, for the news. I hope you're being very careful."

"Yes," I said, but I felt no better for having shared what I had learned. And even though Imonie's chocolate pie was my favorite, it suddenly tasted like ash in my mouth.

Phelan was home when I returned to his place later that night. I followed a trail of light into the library and found him sitting at his desk, his face buried in his hands, jacket thrown over the back of the chair. His cravat was untethered from his neck, his waistcoat unbuttoned down his chest, and he had cast off his boots. His socks were surprisingly mismatched. It was the most undone I had ever seen him.

I stopped just within the threshold, uncertain if he wanted my company until he raised his head and looked at me.

"Long day?" I gently inquired.

"Hmm." He reached for a teapot and poured two cups.

I drew up a chair, keeping the desk between us, and I accepted the cup. I studied him in the candlelight, the lines on his brow, the pallor of his face.

"I know this is none of my business," I began. "But if you tell me what's ailing you . . . perhaps I can be of assistance, Mr. Vesper."

He sighed and leaned back in his chair. "I'm looking for someone."

"Really? Who?"

"A magician."

"He must be an old friend of yours?"

"*She* is not an old friend."

"A former lover, then?"

He nearly choked on his tea. "No, not a lover. A rival would be a better term. She despises me."

"Ah," I said, pleased as I realized he was talking about me. "Why are you seeking this rival, then?"

"She possesses knowledge of something that's very important."

"And you think she would tell you as soon as you found her?" I countered. "Given that the two of you are not friends."

Phelan leveled his eyes at me. For a moment, I feared he had sensed my wicked amusement, savoring this humiliating moment of his, but he exhaled a long breath and said, "You're probably right, Miss Neven. Even if I found her, she wouldn't want to tell me anything."

"You could enchant her to tell you," I nonchalantly suggested, curious to know if he would do such a thing.

"No," he said swiftly. "That sort of magic is illegal and deplorable. But perhaps there is another route I can take."

I was wary as he stood and walked to his bookshelves. He pulled a leather-bound book with an illuminated spine, and turned through its pages until he found a loose square of parchment, tucked safely within the leaves. I watched, horrified, as he set that parchment on the desk. It was one of my charcoal drawings.

I went hot and cold all at once. This little drawing of mine was about to expose me.

How had he stolen it?

And then I remembered. The day we had collided on the street, when I had been studying the knight's sword mark on the cobblestones. My portfolio had fallen open, my drawings scattered in the wind. Phelan had helped me collect them, but I hadn't noticed him pilfering one.

I quelled my trembling and forced a calm mask over my face. I took the drawing in my hand, studying it as if I had never seen it before. My blood felt like molten gold, simmering in my veins. My chest ached as rock scraped against bone, and I determined in that split moment that this was a game I must win. I detached all emotion from my artwork.

"Is she an artist?" I asked, sounding as if I was only vaguely interested.

"Yes."

"She's not that accomplished. Why would you steal her artwork?"

"I . . . *what*?" Phelan frowned at me. "No, I didn't steal it."

"She gave it to you, then?"

"Well, no."

"Then you stole it." I set the drawing on the desk and leaned back in my chair. I drank the tea, hoping it would ease my dread.

"I found it," Phelan said. "A few weeks ago, I bumped into her on the street and some of her art came loose from the folder she was carrying. I helped her recover her pages, but it was not until after we parted ways that I found this one hung up on a bush farther down the road, carried by the wind."

"Why didn't you return it to her, then?"

He was pensive. I was coming to learn that I didn't like it when he was so silent.

"Never mind that." I stood so I could mirror him. "You have a way to find her now. Use this piece of her art to summon her to you."

"Yes, I was thinking to do such," he said, rubbing his chin. His gaze remained on my drawing, transfixed.

I needed him to do it *now*, while I was in the room with him. I couldn't afford to have him summon me when I was away.

Perspiration began to dampen my dress. I prepared for anything to unfold, readying my protective spell in case his summoning broke my disguise and I needed to flee. The enchantment waited on the tip of my tongue like a drop of honey.

I decided I should sit and settled into my chair. "Do it now, while you still have a few days before the new moon comes again. Summoning her will undoubtedly require much of your reserves."

"Have you ever summoned someone before, Miss Neven?"

"No. You?"

"Never. But perhaps you're right," he said. "I should summon her now, while you're here with me."

"And why is that?" I asked. "Do I need to protect you from her?"

He laughed. I realized I had never heard his laugh before. The sound was bewitching, even if it held a hint of scorn. "Yes, you might. She'll probably set a curse upon me when she realizes I've summoned her in such a way."

"Then maybe you should practice on me before you cast."

"Practice for what?"

"The words you will say to this magician when you summon her.

How will you explain yourself? You're about to burn her artwork."

Phelan groaned and paced the library. In and out of the fire-light, the candle flames wavering with his apparent distress. "I don't know what to say to her."

"Well, that *does* present a problem," I said. "You need to have that figured out. What have you done to this magician? Why does she hate you? Is it justified?"

Phelan stopped, his back angled to me. "Yes. I stole her home, her territory. I disgraced her."

I rose and took a step closer to him, my blood singing. "Then you should start by apologizing to her. Genuinely. And then by telling her why you did such a terrible thing to her. And then ask for her forgiveness, preferably on your knees, for burning her drawing. Perhaps she will grant it to you."

He was silent, but he turned and stared at me with a ferocity that made my breath hitch.

He said, "That sounds a bit excessive, don't you think?"

"I suppose it depends on how badly you want to win her over."

"I don't want to 'win her over.'"

"Then what do you want?"

"I want to apologize," he said. "And I want to change what she thinks of me. Then, hopefully, speak candidly with her about the information I need."

"Do you remember what you once said to me, Mr. Vesper?"

He was quiet, regarding me.

So I continued, "You told me that you are not a *kind* person. So why go through all the trouble of apologizing?"

"Have you ever wanted to change someone's opinion of you, Miss Neven?"

"Not really," I replied. "You care very much for what others think of you."

"Don't you?"

"Does it look like I care?" I said, opening my arms.

His eyes searched mine, as if my secrets hid within them. "If you don't, then I wish you would bestow such magic upon me. I would like to not care as much as I do."

I approached him, ignoring how he tensed when I moved to face him, when only a slender space of air remained between us. Rain began to tap on the windowpanes. The night felt heavy and swollen with the storm; the shadows gathered knee deep in the corners of the library.

"If you want to learn," I murmured, "then it begins here." I laid my hand over his heart. "It begins when you acknowledge and respect who you are—scars and mistakes and victories and accomplishments all accounted for." I let my hand slip away, fingertip by fingertip, and watched his deep inhale, as if I had left a scorch mark behind. "Now. Summon her."

I returned to the safety of my chair.

Phelan cleared off his desk. He set my drawing over the center of the wood, along with a silver bowl, a moonstone, a knife, a candlestick. He next selected a spell book, leafing its ancient, crinkled pages open to a spell of summoning.

I watched as he read it, once, twice, as he began to utter the rivers of incantations.

He placed my drawing in the silver bowl and cut his palm with the knife. His blood dripped into the basin three times, marring the parchment, mingling with my art. Next, he held the moonstone over the wavering candle flame, until the stone seemed to come alive, a vein of light pulsing within it. He opened his bloodied palm and the stone gently lowered itself into the bowl, as if gravity had thickened. The moonstone came to rest over his blood and over my drawing. Smoke rose, a dancing blue tendril. The air smelled like cloves, like the wind from the mountains.

It was beginning.

"Clementine," I heard Phelan call. His voice echoed, resounded in my bones. *"Clem, will you answer me? Will you meet with me?"*

He was making no sound with his lips. The conversation was in our spirits—silence in our ears and yet thunder in our minds. His eyes were focused on the smoke as my drawing broke into flames, and my eyes were focused on him, the way the light washed over his face. His lambent eyes as he waited for me to materialize.

I prayed he would not look at me in that anguished moment when I felt the magic tug in my chest. I waged war against the overwhelming urge to rise and answer him.

Sweat beaded my brow, slipped down my back like a taunting fingertip.

"Clem," Phelan called to me again, his voice sharp and beautiful as glass in my mind. Reflecting prisms of color in every direction.

I forced my answer down, down in the tangled vines of my lungs and the wild briars of my being. And yet the tug turned bright and painful. I discreetly braced my feet on the legs of the chair. I held to the armrests, my knuckles strained white.

Hold to the chair, I ordered myself. *Don't move, don't rise, don't utter a sound. Don't answer him.*

The flames rose with crackling intensity, but just as swiftly as they rose did they begin to die. Once my drawing turned into ash, when the spell had nothing more to devour, it would end.

"Clem!"

I closed my eyes, trembling.

If he had only looked at me, he would have known. He would have realized that his magic could not summon me because I was already present.

But his gaze remained on the fire, and I was nothing more than a distant constellation in that moment, gleaming at the edges of his sight. When the flames surrendered into cold smoke, he let out a tremulous breath, slamming his palm on the wood in defeat.

I opened my eyes and looked at him. Phelan was ashen. Sweat dripped off his chin, and his eyes were bloodshot.

"Where is she?" I asked. My voice felt like sand in my throat.

He remembered me, at last. His gaze found mine and he sighed, lowering himself to his chair.

"I don't know. I must have done something wrong."

If there was ever a time for me to reveal myself to him . . . it was now. After this moment passed, things would change between us. I could feel it like the gradual shifting of a season, like autumn giving way to winter snow.

But I was silent, unyielding.

There was too much I knew—he and Lennox wanted to find

Mazarine—and so much I didn't know—what did they plan to do with Mazarine? If I revealed myself to him now . . . I wasn't sure what would happen, and I couldn't take that risk.

I left him in the library, my drawing burned into ashes and my heart beating far too swiftly for my liking.

20

The day of the new moon arrived like any other, save for the fact that I slept in that morning until I was rudely woken by Phelan knocking on my bedroom door.

"Miss Neven?" His voice melted through the wood as he knocked again. "Are you awake?"

I groaned and blearily took note of the daylight that snuck in through a crack in the curtains. It couldn't be later than nine o'clock, and I grumbled as I slipped from the bed, my hair a long, tangled mess down my back.

I opened the door to glower at Phelan, who had claimed I could sleep as late as I desired the night before, in preparation for battle.

To my immense annoyance, he had already showered and dressed. He smelled of soap and spicy aftershave and morning air. He had obviously taken a walk, and had probably already eaten breakfast as well.

"Yes, what is it, Mr. Vesper?" I sighed, and watched as he took note of my dishevelment.

He was speechless for a moment but quickly recovered by remembering what he held in his hands: a rapier.

"Are you sword trained, Miss Neven?"

I stared at the rapier he proudly held and arched my brow. "*This* is why you have woken me from the sleep you promised me last night?"

"I thought you would be up by now," he replied. "There's much to do to prepare for tonight."

"Yes, and I will be useless to you if I'm tired," I snapped, and then remembered myself. "Forgive me, Mr. Vesper. I'm rather grouchy until I've had my tea."

He smiled. A true, brilliant smile that warmed his eyes and made my stomach coil with warning.

"As I've learned, Miss Neven. Here, return to bed. I've brought breakfast to you, as well as your own rapier."

I stepped back and watched, utterly astounded as Phelan leaned the rapier against the door frame and reached for a tray of gleaming breakfast platters, which had been waiting in the corridor, just out of my sight.

"Will you please sit, Miss Neven," he said, taking the first cautious step into my room. "Before I drop this?"

Wordlessly, I returned to bed, and Phelan set the breakfast tray down before me and proceeded to remove the lids, exposing a bountiful breakfast of poached eggs, buttered toast, sliced fruit, diced potatoes with herbs, and a teapot with plenty of cream and honey to suit my appetite.

"Am I to expect this every new moon morning?" I asked as he poured me a cup.

"Perhaps," he teased. "Although the last thing I want is to reward your decadence of late morning sleep."

I rolled my eyes and added a dash of cream to my tea. "Well, then I suppose I shall soak in this grand gesture of yours now, since it may not come again."

"Do as you like, Miss Neven," Phelan said, returning to the threshold, where he had left the sword. "And then once you have eaten and dressed, meet me in the library for a lesson with your new rapier."

"I cannot wait," I said dryly, to which he only smiled again as if exceedingly pleased with himself and shut my door.

I was halfway through breakfast when I remembered the mirror that hung on my wall, and how I had completely forgotten the threat it posed to me. Phelan obviously had not caught sight of my reflection, but it was a sobering reminder of my foolishness. How I had let his thoughtful gesture distract me.

I finished eating and dressed, and I found Phelan in the library, sitting on the edge of his desk, leafing through a book.

He closed it the moment he caught sight of me, and rose with his perfect posture, only a thread of his dark hair defiantly falling across his brow.

I sensed the radiance about him, how his magic teemed in his hands. He was very anxious about this upcoming night, I realized, and I gave myself a moment to imagine what it would be like to fight alongside him instead of against him on a new moon.

The image seemed natural—the two of us on the darkest of nights moving in tandem, and I thought back to our new moon battle in Hereswith, only a month ago—and the ache in my stomach woke again, a flutter of warning.

"You never answered my question from before," he said.

I stopped halfway to him, a square of sunlight on the floor between us. "Oh? And what was that?"

"If you've ever been sword trained."

"No," I lied. My father had taught me how to handle all manners of weapons.

He held out a rapier for me to take. I closed the last of the space between us and took hold of the hilt carefully.

"You prefer to fight with weapons rather than spells on the new moon?" I asked.

"Spells always come first," Phelan replied. "But I've learned it's good to be armed as well."

I secretly agreed, remembering how I had once worn my weapon belt on new moon nights. How a blade had saved my life last time, when I had nearly drowned in a nest of lily pads and snakes.

I listened as Phelan introduced me to the rapier, instructing me on how I should hold it in my hand. When he demonstrated a few stances and thrusts, I mimicked him with ease.

"You have good form," he said with a hint of scrutiny.

"I'm a swift learner," I replied, and then took a daring slash at him.

Phelan was too slow in guarding himself. The tip of my rapier brushed his face and he lurched back with a hiss. I watched a line of blood well on his right cheek before he dropped his weapon and turned away from me.

"Oh, I'm sorry! Here, let me see it . . ." I followed him, setting my rapier down with a clatter.

He continued to evade me, face averted. "It's fine. I'm fine. Don't bother."

I didn't like him running from me. I reached out to snag his sleeve, guiding him to the desk. He surrendered, sitting on the edge of it, his palm pressed to the wound. Blood seeped through his fingers and I had a moment of panic, thinking I had cut open his face until he lowered his hand.

It was only a nick, but it was profusely bleeding.

"It's not as bad as it seems," I said. "Do you have a—"

He reached into his waistcoat pocket, and only when I felt his knuckles brush against my bodice did I realize how close I was to him. But I remained where I was, standing between his legs, and he knew what I wanted. He found his handkerchief, offering it to me with a wry smile.

"Don't smile," I scolded. "You're making the bleeding worse."

He winced as I pressed the handkerchief against the cut. I moved my other hand to the back of his head, my fingers weaving into his hair. He stiffened, as if I had pierced him to the bone. When I met his gaze, I found that his eyes were dark and inscrutable, riveted to my own.

"Is this punishment?" he whispered.

Yes, I wanted to say. Punishment for stealing my home, for burning my artwork. For not being as I expected.

"For what?" I countered, pressing harder on his cheek.

"For waking you too early?"

I tried to hem my laughter, but it escaped in a rush. "No, of course not. This was nothing more than an accident."

But I sensed that he struggled to believe me. And I realized that I hadn't laughed in a very long time as a soft ache bloomed in my chest.

"Who taught you how to handle a blade?" he asked. When his hand slid over mine . . . I was the one to turn rigid. The heat of our skin meeting seemed to burn right through me—a spark of wildfire.

"No one," I said, pulling away from him. "You should keep pressure on it, until the bleeding eases."

To my surprise, he was silent as I strode across the library. But I suppose he didn't like the thought of me running from him either, and his voice chased me just as I reached the doors.

"Where are you going, Miss Neven? Surely you are not conceding this spar to me."

I tarried on the threshold and cast a languid glance his way. "I won this round, Mr. Vesper. And I'm going for a walk."

Autumn hung golden in the air as I wandered. It was October sixteenth, and it felt as if a year had passed since I had lost Hereswith, not a mere month. I explored the streets' winding bends and corners until I felt as if I could walk their paths with my eyes closed and the sun was beginning to set.

I paused on the curb of our territory line, watching as a slight breeze rustled the oaks and people hurried home early, carrying parcels and packages from the market. Soon, this city would feel dead and empty, stricken with terror.

I was lost in such thoughts when I recognized Olivette and Nura walking toward me, hand in hand.

I reflexively turned away from them, wishing I had worn a hat or carried a parasol like some people of the city did, to hide beneath. I was surprised by the regret that suddenly welled within me. Regret that tasted bitter in my mouth, because I longed to befriend them, and yet I couldn't risk such a relationship.

I started to walk away, but Olivette saw me, and it was impossible to act as if I had not heard her bellow.

"Anna? *Anna!*" She frantically waved to catch my attention.

"Hello," I greeted her, and approached them. "So good to see you both again." And then all words fled when I saw what Olivette wore buckled around her waist—a leather weapon belt with two sheathed daggers. The twin to the one my father had gifted to me, years ago.

Nura noticed my stare and said, "It's tradition. Oli likes to walk our streets with her weapons before the new moon rises."

"It's for good luck," Olivette added.

"It's . . . a very nice belt," I stammered. "Where did you get it?"

"My father made it for me," Olivette replied. "If you like it, I can see if he can make one for you."

The sad fact was my own belt was at my mother's, tucked away in one of my trunks. Phelan would unfortunately recognize it; I remembered how he had studied my hips, the way my daggers had shone at the dinner table in Hereswith.

"Oh, no," I said. "But thank you for the offer."

"Would you like to join us?" Nura asked.

"I probably shouldn't. I was walking Phelan's streets, to reacquaint myself before tonight."

"They're your streets now, too," Olivette said. "And where is Phelan?"

"He already had his walk this morning. I would have accompanied him, but I was still sleeping."

"Ah, yes, we only just woke ourselves," Olivette confessed with a disarming smile. "New moons are the *only* morning Nura will let me sleep in so late."

I returned the smile. "Yes, well, I only had until *nine* until Phelan woke me for sword lessons."

"He's very anxious about tonight," Nura said, exchanging a concerned glance with Olivette.

"Is there a reason why he should be?" I asked.

"Did he tell you about his first new moon here? How he was wounded?" said Olivette.

"He briefly mentioned it."

"I think that's why, although he refuses to tell us what, exactly, wounded him so badly."

"And we don't feel it right to press him about it," Nura added. "But it worries us. It's been a year since a warden was killed on the new moon in this part of the city, but it does happen occasionally."

I chewed on my lip a moment, wondering. Phelan had mentioned his near death to me the first night I had shared dinner with him, when he had striven to win me over, but he had not further regaled me with details. It seemed everyone was anxious to know what had happened: Nura, Olivette, the duke. Me.

"Don't worry," I reassured them. "I'll guard his back tonight."

Olivette appeared relieved, but Nura appeared a bit doubtful.

"Good luck tonight, Anna," Olivette said.

"Same to you." I waved farewell to them.

I hurried back to Phelan's town house, the temperature dropping with the sun. A shiver nipped at my bones as I closed the front door behind me. Mrs. Stirling was in the kitchen, preparing dinner. The fragrant aromas embraced me in the corridor, and for a staggering moment, I was back home in Hereswith, and Imonie was cooking and setting the fine porcelain on the table. A place for me and a place for my father.

I laid my palm over the pain in my chest. I was learning how certain things were threats to the stone half of my heart. They were like swinging hammers, eager to form a crack within me, and I was struggling to know how to filter them into my life. Things such as memories of home, Deacon's smile, Nura's and Olivette's friendship. The way I sometimes caught Phelan looking at me.

I forced the memories haunting me into dust, until my homesickness was nothing more than a tiny trace, and I headed to the library. But Phelan wasn't there. I cast an inquisitive net of magic throughout the house, but I failed to sense his presence. He was gone, and I sat at his desk to read through the book of nightmares, only to discover the old tome was absent. *He must have been summoned to fetch a last-minute dream*, I thought, and leaned my head back in the chair, closing my eyes.

Just for a moment, I told myself, and drifted off to sleep.

I woke to the sound of Phelan speaking my name for the second time that day.

"Miss Neven?"

I jerked awake, rubbing a crick in my neck. He stood before me holding the book of nightmares, top hat perched slightly crooked on his head. His face was flushed from cool air, and the cut on his cheek had scabbed at last. Only a thread of sunset filtered through the library window; the rest of the room fell to shadows.

"Dinner is ready," he said, gently setting the book on the desk.

"I'm sorry," I croaked, my voice clogged from sleep.

"For what?"

I indicated the book of nightmares. "For being away. I should have accompanied you to fetch the dream."

"You didn't miss much," he said, removing his hat and tossing it onto the desk. "A recurrent nightmare, and one that is more bizarre than it is frightening."

I continued to rub the stiff muscles of my neck as I followed him into the dining room. Mrs. Stirling had set a feast of steaming platters on the table.

I took my seat first, and then Phelan sat across from me. There were only two places set at the table, for me and for him, and when Mrs. Stirling bustled into the dining room with a pitcher of chilled cider, I asked, "Are you eating with us tonight, Mrs. Stirling?"

"Oh no, my dear," she replied, filling our goblets. "Deacon and I return home early on these nights."

The nightmares wouldn't bloom until the clock struck nine, but I felt the anxious energy in the housekeeper as she set down the pitcher and smoothed the wrinkles from her apron. She was eager to be home with her shutters and doors locked against the night.

"Is there anything else I can provide for you, Mr. Vesper? Deacon and I have tended to all the windows, as well as the back door."

"No, Mrs. Stirling. You have outdone yourself, per usual. Thank you."

She curtsied and gathered Deacon and her cloak. "Good fortune to both of you tonight," she said. "I hope it is an early and effortless night."

"Don't worry, Mrs. Stirling," I said. "I'll take good care of Mr. Vesper."

I felt Phelan's gaze on me, but I resisted meeting it, smiling at Mrs. Stirling and Deacon instead.

"Good, very good," she murmured, scratching her eyebrow. "Don't worry about the plates after you eat. Just leave them on the table. I'll clean them in the morning."

And she was gone, Deacon in her shadow.

I returned to my meal, eating in companionable silence with Phelan.

It took me a moment to rouse my courage, but I finally did. "Are you going to tell me what wounded you moons ago?"

"I've thought many times on this," he said. "How to tell you of that night. But I can't find the words, Miss Neven."

"Oh." I was disappointed with his response, but I hid my feelings and finished my dinner. Silence frosted the table between us.

"I want to prepare you, but I'm uncertain as to *what* we can expect tonight, Miss Neven," Phelan said, breaking the quiet. "I apologize that I can't tell you more. Because of that . . . stay close to me tonight."

Stay close to me.

"I have already promised three of your friends that I will keep you safe tonight, Mr. Vesper," I whispered. "I suppose that means I have no choice but to knit myself to you, to ensure I don't break my own word."

That provoked a small smile from him. The scab on his cheek pulled, as if it wanted to break open again, and I wondered how long that mark would be there, reminding him of me every time he looked at it. He drank the rest of his cider, but he didn't touch his food again. I noticed his face grew wan as the hour progressed, that a sheen of perspiration had formed on his brow. And when he rose and carried his plate into the kitchen, I stood and followed him.

We put away the food in the icebox and washed the dishes, which was sure to evoke Mrs. Stirling's wrath the next day, as we had disregarded her command, but the action of doing something so simple seemed to calm Phelan.

We had another hour to burn.

Phelan built a fire in the drawing room hearth and I made a pot of tea, and we shared it before the crackling dance of the flames. Silent and pensive, waiting for the hands on the clock to tick their path to nine o'clock.

At a quarter till, Phelan rose and left the room.

I braided my hair out of my eyes and checked the buttons on my boots. I retethered the ribbon laces of my bodice, until I felt a pinch when I breathed deeply. I missed my weapon belt and my daggers; seeing Olivette's had stirred up emotions I'd thought I had buried. When Phelan returned to me, he had our two rapiers in hand. I accepted mine and belted it at my waist, a tremor of anticipation coursing through me.

"Shall we?" he asked with an elegant flourish of his hand, as if he were asking me to dance with him.

I was calm until that moment, when my memories crept back over me. The firelight of a cozy cottage, the fragrance of cherry galettes warm from the oven, my father leading me out into a star-dusted night, to the market green of Hereswith. My longing was keen; I wavered for a moment, thinking I might fracture.

I missed those old days. I wanted to return to them until I finally acknowledged that such a thing would be impossible. My life had changed seasons; I could never go back to how things had been. And when I met Phelan's dark gaze, my nostalgia melted away, leaving me standing in a world I had made.

We walked to the foyer with five minutes to spare. I followed Phelan out into the moonless night, as if I had done it a hundred times before.

21

Auberon Street felt cold and dead, like the crooked path of a graveyard. I walked beside Phelan, fog beginning to pool in low places, waiting for the clock to strike nine. I could feel the tension in him when our elbows accidentally brushed; his face looked ghostly pale in the lantern light.

I reached out to touch his arm, and he stopped, as if I had burned him.

"Mr. Vesper," I said, "it's going to be all right. This will be over and done with before we know it."

He sighed and turned to regard me. We had two minutes remaining until the new moon unfolded. The wind was beginning to intensify.

"You must be wondering why I'm so anxious," he stated. "It has to do with the truth that I don't deserve to be here."

I frowned up at him, thinking now was not a good time for

such dramatic statements. "Why not?"

He reached into his jacket for his pocket watch. "Because I wasn't born with illumination. I wasn't born with the magical flame, like my twin brother was. Everything I've accomplished I've had to learn. It took me many grueling years of lessons."

I almost laughed at his ridiculous statement, but thought better of it, as that was something Clem would do. Anna, on the other hand, would be impressed.

"Then that only solidifies your place and accomplishment, Mr. Vesper," I said. "You've earned the right to be warden here."

His watch chirped, and I knew the time had come. He slipped the golden orb back into his pocket and looked at me, whispering, "We can talk more about this afterward."

I wondered if he had even heard my compliment. He turned away from me, so that our backs were aligned.

We watched the street, my gaze fixed on the southern end while his scanned the north.

It was the sort of quiet that makes you fearful to breathe too loudly. The fog continued to gather, and my feet were cold in my boots as I strained to see through the mist.

Was this the element of a nightmare? I racked my mind, trying to recall if I had read any entries in Phelan's book that were made of fog.

"Look to your right, Miss Neven," Phelan said, and while his voice was calm, I knew the nightmare had begun.

I looked to see the row of town houses, shuttered and bolted with only stray beams of firelight slipping through the cracks.

And then I saw it, a heraldic banner unrolling from the roof, covering the house's face with a proud bolt of blue. Silver moons were stitched upon it, and diamonds winked like stars in the fabric.

"That's the mountain duchy's banner," I breathed, my memory surging.

"So it is," Phelan agreed, and we watched as more banners and tapestries unrolled from the roofs of houses around us, flapping slightly in the breeze.

The cobbles beneath me hummed, and I glanced down to watch them become large, smooth flagstones in shades of copper and gray, freshly swept. The air smelled of fresh sun and sweet red wine.

I knew where this dream had taken us. Phelan and I were standing in the fortress in the clouds, in the hall of the mountain castle.

"A dream of the Seren Duchy," I said.

"Did you ever read Knox Birch's most recent nightmare in my book, Miss Neven?" Phelan asked.

"Yes," I whispered, and I remembered it with a shudder. Mr. Birch had dreamt of the Seren throne and had unknowingly cut down his wife and two daughters in his hunger to claim it. "Do you see the duke's chair?" I asked, unwilling to take my eyes from the southern end of the street.

"Yes," he said. "It's ahead of me."

"Then Mr. Birch will be coming from my direction."

"Do you want to trade places?"

"No," I said, but I drew my rapier. "I'll tell you when I see him approaching."

I had yet to meet Knox Birch in the flesh—I had only read the account of his dreams—but I knew he lived one street over. I waited for him to appear, my palms slick with sweat.

At last, a man emerged from the darkness, striding through swaths of fog. He reminded me of my father, middle-aged and tall, with hair the color of a faded penny. His eyes gleamed gold, as if he was haunted, and yet his face was cold and merciless, like nothing could break him from his ambitions.

"He's coming," I said.

Phelan turned, and I felt a swell of cold air wash over me as he put some distance between us.

"He cuts down three shadows," he reminded me. "I suspect you and I are two of them."

I thought the same, but I had no time to agree with him as a woman with a pale, sorrowful face and long hair materialized from the shadows. Knox's wife, I realized, and she boldly intercepted him, pleading, "Please, Knox . . . please don't do this. Choose us, *choose us.*"

A rapier bloomed in his hand. He cut her down quickly, his blade piercing her core. She fell with a sickening thud, crumpled as a rag doll on the flagstones, her blood spreading beneath her like a crimson cloak. I knew he saw only a sinister shadow. He didn't see her until the end, when he got what he thought he wanted: a place in the duke's chair.

I was the next barricade in his path.

I drew in a deep breath and cast a spell net over him, one that would slow his movements. I sought the key of the dream—the crux to break the nightmare—and thrust my rapier at him, aiming at his heart. He blocked it, his movements like honey warming over fire, returning to their previous swiftness. We continued to circle each other, lunging and parrying, until the cross guards of our blades met; I was in the throes of uttering another spontaneous charm to freeze him to the stones, but the force coming from him slung me back and away. My hand tingled from the jar of clashing steel and I bit my tongue, my charm dissolving. I stumbled but Phelan caught me, ushering me behind him while I regained my balance.

I watched as he engaged Knox in a fraught spar, eager to rejoin the fight.

A new spell was rising within me like a song. I took a step forward and winced when I felt a sudden blaze of pain. My belly stung with the movement, and I glanced down to see the bottom half of my bodice hung open, its ribbon laces sliced into dangling shreds. I laid my hand over the torn fabric and felt something warm and sticky. My blood, I realized with a pang of shock, staring at its red stain on my palm. Knox's rapier must have grazed me, but the cut wasn't deep, to my immense relief. Although a few inches deeper and he might have given me a mortal blow.

I returned my focus to Phelan, sparks blazing along his rapier as he continued to fight. Knox wasn't slowing or wearying; he was like a storm, gathering strength, pushing us closer and closer to the dais and the throne. And when he nearly cut Phelan in half, I cast another charm to slow him down. As soon as Knox felt my enchantment hinder him, his face snapped toward me, furious. I met his gaze as steadily as I could, even as it intimidated me. Within his eyes, gold shone like two coins catching the light.

"His eyes," I said to Phelan, my voice ragged. The gold in his eyes had become a film, preventing him from seeing through the veil of his greed. "The dream's weakness *is his eyes*."

Phelan heard. He had to lurch back to avoid being skewered by Knox's blade, but the momentum swung around in his favor. He aimed and thrust the point of his rapier into Knox's left eye, and the gold that covered his pupil burst and ran down his face like ichor.

Knox went still and then gasped—his moment of realization—before falling to the ground in the puddle of his wife's blood.

Phelan withdrew his blade, watching the nightmare reach its harrowing end.

I stood a few paces behind him, staring at the blue banners on the town houses, the moon and stars and the promise of mountains, waiting for them to melt away, for the nightmare had been championed. But the banners remained as stubborn fixtures, and the flagstones and the duke's chair refused to fade. The elements of the nightmare were firm and solid in the street.

Something wasn't right.

Phelan was breathing heavily behind me. When I glanced over my shoulder, I saw he was still staring at Knox and his wife, their bodies refusing to vanish on the stones, and I had a sickening thought that perhaps it had all been real, that Phelan and I had in some way been fooled.

Had there been more to the dream, and Knox Birch had failed to divulge it to Phelan?

"Mr. Vesper . . ."

My voice died with the wind. The world around us became silent and still, as if we were trapped in a painting of a forgotten place, and then I heard it—the clink of armored feet approaching. A heavy, methodical gait that made the flagstones tremble beneath me. Silvered footsteps I had once heard before in a dream that didn't belong to me, but a dream I had divined.

"My gods," I whispered. It felt like a bone was wedged in my throat as I waited for the knight of Elle Fielding's dream to appear, his footsteps growing louder, louder, the dream rippling around me like it was under duress.

I forgot where I stood, where I was. I forgot about Phelan at my back, my entire being focused on this inevitable meeting.

And then the knight appeared, the fog swirling around him.

I had only seen his legs and feet in Elle's dream, when she had been crouched beneath the wagon. Now I beheld his entire self, fully covered in steel-plated armor that was splashed with blood. He was tall and broad as he walked with purpose, striding toward us. But it was not the blood or the long sword that he unsheathed at his side that coaxed my horror. It was the helm he wore, a helmet forged with tapers at its brow. Seven sharp points crowned him. I couldn't see his eyes, but I felt his piercing gaze.

Terror held me until I felt a warm hand take hold of my arm, drawing me back.

"Get behind me, Miss Neven," Phelan said.

As soon as I felt his presence, his magic's illumination overlapped with mine and bolstered my courage. I inhaled a deep breath, flexing my hand.

We walked backward in unison, to give ourselves more time to hammer a plan together. The knight followed with his steady pace; he seemed fixed on that gait. He couldn't run, but neither could he slow. We were faster but he was persistent, and I was uncertain about his weakness.

"Who is this?" I whispered to Phelan as we continued to walk backward, our eyes trained on the knight.

"I don't know. But he's the one who wounded me, months ago."

"You fought him?"

"Yes. Weapons are useless against him, as are any offensive spells."

I didn't quite believe Phelan, and I cast a disarming spell on the knight. My magic hissed into smoke when it met his breastplate, and he continued following us, undeterred. I tried again, desperate, to no avail.

"Save your magic, Miss Neven," Phelan said dryly.

"He must have a weakness." I studied the knight's armor. "He can't be wholly invincible."

Phelan was quiet, but then he said, "There are two of us and one of him. I will slip behind while you engage him."

I nodded and threw a blast of light at the knight's feet, to cover Phelan's movements. But it was futile; the knight sensed Phelan's presence and turned with him, swinging his sword. Phelan ducked and rolled, barely missing the edge of the blade, and I surged forward, anger smoldering within me. I roused that fire and funneled it, and my magic streamed toward the knight, striking him in the spine and limning his armor as if he had been electrified by lightning. He hesitated, and I took that moment to study the plates of steel and chain mail, searching for a golden scale or link that I could puncture and usher his demise. There was nothing, and he pivoted so swiftly he took me by surprise.

I lurched back in response and saw his sword arcing for me. Everything suddenly slowed. My motions, my breath, my heart. A warning prickled at the nape of my neck, and this horrible encounter felt strangely peaceful. This moment before death. This moment before the knight beheaded me.

I felt a hand on my ankle, a warm hand that pulsed with both life and terror. It yanked me so hard that I went down on the flagstones with a jar, my rapier tumbling from my hand. The knight's sword whistled harmlessly above me.

Phelan, I thought, dazed from hitting the ground. His magic clung to my ankle and he pulled me quickly to his side, over the stones.

I scrambled to my feet, swallowing the tang of iron, and I wiped the blood from my lip and watched as Phelan resorted to his rapier. The knight's blade broke Phelan's like it was made of glass.

Phelan stumbled back, but his opponent followed. I roused my magic just as the tip of the sword caught the front of Phelan's waistcoat. I heard the fabric rip, heard his grunt of pain, and he was hurled up and away as if he had been struck by a giant's hand.

I kept my eyes on the knight, despite the nagging temptation to look at Phelan. I heard him hit the flagstones behind me, and I coaxed the light of my hands to flood the knight's helm. His focus shifted to me, and I suddenly became aware that I was too close to him. I was within his striking range, and I had no choice but to flee to where Phelan was sprawled in the center of the street, his blood blooming like a rose across his torn waistcoat.

"Phelan," I breathed. "*Phelan*, can you stand?"

We only had moments before the knight reached us. His heavy tread began to sound again, and I reached down to haul Phelan up to his feet.

His eyes were glazed, but he responded as I supported his weight, his arm draped over my shoulders.

"To the house, Miss Neven," he said, his voice wispy as if he was about to faint. "If you please."

I wildly searched for his house, my bearings lost in the fray. I knew it must be nearby—we hadn't strayed far from it when the nightmare manifested. And then I saw house eleven, with its gray brick and climbing ivy, three doors away, and my relief nearly crushed me as I began to haul him to the front gate, the knight hounding us.

Don't look behind you, I ordered myself, even though I wanted to see how close the knight was to catching us. *Don't look down*, even though I wanted to see how much blood Phelan was losing.

My eyes on the door, Phelan limping at my side, the knight hounding us. This new moon was unraveling around me.

I dragged us through the gate, up the path and porch steps, the lantern light flickering as if beckoning us to hurry, hurry, *hurry* . . .

"The key," Phelan moaned. Of course, he had locked the front door when we had departed, and I frantically searched his pockets. He was steadily bleeding, and it coated my hand as my fingers darted from pocket to pocket.

The front gate creaked behind us; the knight was in the yard. Cold air washed over my back, like winter had arrived early. The ivy on the trellis withered; frost spangled the shutters. At last, I found the iron key, tucked within the inner pocket of Phelan's jacket, and I struggled to unlock the door, my hands numb, trembling.

"Miss Neven," Phelan whispered into my hair. *"Anna . . ."*

He was begging me to rush, because the knight was only steps away from cutting us both down.

I kicked the door open and heaved Phelan inside. Every fiber within me burned from exertion; I had to let Phelan go. He slid to the hardwood floor, groaning, and I turned to see the knight ascending the porch stairs, four steps away from us. From *me* as I stood on the threshold, watching his approach. An unspoken challenge glimmered like an enchantment between us, waiting to be inhaled and spoken.

Who are you? I wanted to ask, but my voice was a splinter in my throat.

"Anna," Phelan panted. "Anna, lock the door."

My ears roared. The floor seemed to tilt as the knight stared at me, as I stared at him. I thought I saw the sheen of his eyes in the slits of his helm. The sheen of something alive and angry and ravenous. The knight lifted his sword in one hand, but with the other he reached for me.

"ANNA."

Phelan's desperation dashed my suspended thoughts. I didn't know when I would have this chance again, when I would encounter this knight and his mysteries face-to-face. And that uncertainty was a thorn in my pride.

We couldn't beat him; we had lost this battle.

I slammed the door shut.

22

I closed my eyes, sweat dripping down my temples, and I pressed my ear to the door. The knight hadn't moved. He stood at the threshold, unable to pass over it since the door was locked.

I struggled with my desire to remain in safety and my hunger to oppose the knight again.

Someone wheezed behind me.

I turned to behold Phelan, lying on the foyer floor. He was watching me, his face blanched and furrowed with pain. His hand was pressed over his abdomen, where his blood was pooling.

A slender, cold part of me was satisfied to see him brought low, wounded, and humbled.

But then I knelt at his side and I took hold of his hand, drawing his bloodied fingers away, and those jaded feelings in me were eclipsed by worry.

"Can you help me up the stairs?" he rasped. "To my bedroom?"

I nodded and pulled him up to his feet. With me supporting his weight, we laboriously ascended the stairs with the assistance of my magic.

A lone candle burned in his bedroom. The fire in his hearth had died into embers, and I walked Phelan to his bed and eased him down on the mattress. I swiftly roused the fire back to a crackling dance and lit a few more candelabras, so I could examine him in better light.

I inevitably glanced at the mirror that hung over his wash station. If he sat up in bed, the glass would catch his reflection. And I would have to walk past it to leave the room. I felt trapped and annoyed, and struggled with my temptation to shatter the mirror.

A moan slipped from Phelan.

It drew my attention, to where he was lying in bed, his back slightly arched as he struggled to unbutton his waistcoat with one hand. I needed to leave now while he was preoccupied, to harvest an herb from the library and make a potent tonic that would render him unconscious. Then I would tend to his wound and my own, which I had all but forgotten about in the cascade of adrenaline.

I started for the door.

"Where are you going?"

I halted on the rug, just before the mirror, and met his gaze. "To the library, to make you an herbal tonic."

"I don't want an herbal tonic. I need you to stitch me up."

"Then you're going to want something for the pain. Lie back down. I'll return in a moment."

Phelan stared at me. "I don't trust you."

"What?" His words caught me by surprise.

"Come here, Anna."

I had no choice. He was watching me like a hawk, as if he could see through me, and I took a wide berth to his bedside, staying just out of reach of him and his mirror on the opposing wall.

"Why don't you trust me?" I asked, my voice low and far rougher than I intended.

"Because you want to slip away," he said. "You want to open the door and face the knight again without me."

I let out a huff of breath. "Fine. I was tempted to, yes."

"I forbid it."

"You *forbid* it?" I echoed with a hint of laughter. "And how do you propose to do that, lying in bed, wounded like a fair nobleman in war?"

"All right," he said. "I can't forbid you, but I ask that you stay here and help me. The knight will no doubt challenge us another new moon, but in this moment . . . I need you."

I need you.

His candor softened the hard edges that hid within me.

"Lie back down," I whispered, and he obeyed. I waited until his head rested on his pillow before I moved to stand at his bedside. Gently, I undressed him. I slid his arms from his jacket. I unbuttoned his tattered waistcoat, unknotted his cravat, and eased him out of his shirt. Once his chest was naked, I surveyed the damage.

His wound wasn't deep, but it was long, cutting across his stomach. I saw another scar, one that ran from his heart down to his hip, as if he had once been sliced open, and I couldn't help myself. I traced it with my fingertips.

"Did he do this?" I asked. "The knight?"

"Yes," he whispered, and his blood continued to trickle out. I took his rumpled shirt and pressed against the wound, and Phelan winced.

"How do you want me to stitch this?" I asked.

"In my wardrobe," he said, his voice hoarse with pain. "In the bottom drawer. You'll find my medicine box."

I hurried to fetch it, and Phelan remained still, staring up at the ceiling as I opened the wooden box. There was a pack of needles, dark thread, rolls of linen, a few small jars of healing salve, and antiseptic.

I cleaned the wound first before threading my needle, planting stitches along his skin. I had done this once before, with a cut on my father's arm, and while this wasn't a new experience, it was one that still made my heart quicken, to see Phelan's wound close beneath my fingers. To watch a different sort of magic spill from my hands.

"I've noticed something about you," he said just as I was finishing.

He was quiet until I looked at him. I was pleased to see some color had returned to his face.

"Your name," he said. "*Anna Neven.* You can spell both of your names forward as you can backward."

I cut the thread and wiped the lingering traces of blood from my fingers. "My mother was fond of palindrome names."

"Hmm."

I spread healing salve over my handiwork, and the fragrant smell of herbs began to drift in the air between us. I watched the steady rise and fall of Phelan's chest as he breathed.

"It's not your real name, is it?" he said.

I smiled as if he was ridiculous, finishing with my ministrations. "Of course it is. Why would you doubt me, Phelan?"

"Because you have told me so little about yourself."

"That doesn't make me a liar."

"No, but it gives me moments of doubt, Anna. And I . . . I don't want to doubt who you are."

I didn't know what to say. I couldn't afford to have him doubt or suspect me, and I did the only thing I could think of, the only thing that felt natural. I traced the hard cut lines of his stomach, the contours of his bare skin. I traced his scar.

"You doubt me in this moment, Phelan?"

He made a low sound that seemed forged from both pleasure and irritation and grabbed my hand with his, to halt my caress. "You wanted to leave me here, floundering on my bed!"

"I wanted to fetch you a tonic to dull your pain, you fool!" I leaned down closer to him, so that our mouths were a breath apart. My braid had come partly unwound in the battle, and my hair fell around us. "Now, I'm going to the library to harvest some herbs, and make you a tonic that will help you sleep. You will stay here and trust my word and not move, and when I return, you may ask me anything you want and I'll answer you."

He was silent, but he continued to hold my hand, pressed

against his heart. I could feel the frantic beat, pounding against my palm. A rhythm that made me realize things had started to shift between us.

I didn't hate him as I had before. How could I after this harrowing night had bound us together, in fear and courage and wounds?

And while his face had been difficult to read in the past . . . I saw the lines in his brow fade the longer he regarded me, our breaths mingling. I saw the shock of hope, tender and fragile and surprising as a flower breaking winter ground, rise within him.

I was beginning to think he liked me—Anna, not Clem—more than he let on.

When I stood, he released me. I took my time putting his medicine box away and gathering his clothes off the blood-speckled rug, because he was intently watching me, and I needed him to close his eyes before I passed the mirror.

At last, his eyes drifted shut, and I hurried by the mirror and out the chamber, down the stairs to the library. It was dark and solemn as a tomb, the air thick with the musty fragrance of books and the loam of plants, and I took a moment to drop my guard. To gasp in relief and lower myself to my knees. To lie prostrate on the floor and sift through the events of that night—in the streets and in his bedroom.

But all too soon, I made myself rise and light a candle.

Every muscle in my body felt sore and tense, and I kneaded a knot in my shoulder as I approached the plant table. I gathered what I needed, a recipe that was similar to making a remedy but without the fuss of draining plant pulp. I added a hearty dose of fiddle's spark, an herb that brought on swift, deep slumber. There was no chance of Phelan drinking this and not succumbing to sleep within a few moments.

I carried the tonic back up the stairs, pausing in the middle of the staircase to glance behind me at the front door, to the bronze handle that winked in the dim light. I wondered if the knight still stood on the threshold, waiting for me to answer the challenge he posed, but I forced myself to continue my ascent.

Phelan was just as I'd left him, his eyes closed until he heard me step into the room.

I hastened past the mirror and set the cup of tonic on his bedside table. I realized I couldn't linger beside him, not with the glaring reflection of my secret, and I awkwardly stepped away, far from his and the mirror's reach.

"Thank you," Phelan said, but I detected a hint of mockery in his tone as he struggled to sit upright on his own.

I pretended to be distracted by the piles of books he had on the floor, kneeling to study their titles, to touch their worn covers.

"What did you put in this, Anna?" he asked after a moment, stifling a cough.

I glanced up to see his lips pursed in disgust. "It'll aid your healing and sleep. Drink all of it, Phelan."

I listened to him struggle to swallow my tonic, and I angled my face away, so he wouldn't catch my smile. I eventually felt the sting in my skin, and I knew that I could not ignore my own wound any longer.

Gingerly, I stood and turned to speak to Phelan, surprised to see his eyes were closed, his head slightly inclined back against the wooden headboard.

Well, then. My tonic had accomplished its purpose.

I walked to his wardrobe to retrieve the medicine box again. A stool sat in the shadows beside the furniture, and I drew it into the candlelight and took a seat upon it, my back to Phelan. I slowly unlaced the last of my bodice's ribbons and let it fall to the ground with a whisper. Next, I eased my chemise off my shoulders, down to my waist, so I could examine my wound.

A shallow scratch arced above my belly button, already forming a scab.

I reached for the antiseptic and was cleaning it when Phelan spoke.

"Are you wounded, Anna?"

I paused, a hitch in my breath. Here I was sitting half-naked in his room, when my tonic should have dragged him into dreamless sleep. I glanced over my shoulder to look at him still propped up in bed, his eyes heavy lidded but regarding me with attentiveness.

"No, just a scratch." I returned my focus to the cut, but I felt his gaze linger on me and the bare curve of my back. I was comfortable in my skin, and I didn't mind his attention, not as I probably would have if this had happened a month ago, or even a week ago.

I drew my chemise up to my shoulders and knotted its drawstring tight. The bodice was ruined, so I left it in the pile with his bloodied clothes.

"Ask your one question, Mr. Vesper," I said. "Unless you want to wait until tomorrow, when you have a clear head and will remember my answer."

"I have a clear head," he said, but his words were slurred as he fought the cloying effects of the tonic. "Come, sit here, Anna." He patted the bed beside him, and I merely stared at it, the mirror still a threat.

"Lie down, and perhaps I will."

He heeded me, easing his head to his pillow, his boots close to dangling off the bed.

I approached the other side and sank into the feather mattress beside him, a few generous hand widths between us.

"Ask your question, Phelan."

His eyes were closed but he smiled. "I want to know your real name."

"Mm, very well, although I think that's a sorry thing to waste your one question on."

That prompted him to crack open his eyes and look up at me. "Which means I have asked a very good question, because you don't want to answer it."

He was beginning to read me rather well, which stirred my apprehension. I resolved to be more careful around him. And I hadn't thought of myself as performing a role, but I should have, from the moment we'd had our interview.

"Anna Bailey is my true name," I said. "I chose *Neven* for myself after my mother died, to hide me from a few of her old acquaintances who might give me trouble. She had some old debts that she never paid before she passed away. That's why I haven't told you much about me."

"You could tell me who she owes a debt to, and I will pay it."

I frowned. "No, Phelan. I don't want you paying my mother's debts."

Go to sleep, I thought with desperation, and listened as his breaths pulled deep, his eyes closing more and more with each stubborn blink. I delayed a minute more, just to be certain he was asleep this time, before I began to edge my way off the bed.

"Don't leave, Anna," he whispered. "Stay here with me."

I wondered if he truly wanted my company, or if he was worried about me slipping away into the night without him. But I lingered.

Eventually, though, I couldn't deny my weariness. I found a dreamless remedy in Phelan's side table and drank it, surrendering to the soft embrace of the bed. And I fell asleep at his side.

23

"Miss Neven? *Miss Neven!*"

I woke to the shock and horror of Mrs. Stirling. She stood at the foot of the bed, her face blanched as she stared at me. Why did she look so upset? I wondered, groggily wiping the drool from my lips.

And then I realized this bed was unfamiliar, and Phelan was sleeping close beside me, his chest exposed and scarred and sewn up, his fingers entwined with mine. . . .

The memory of the new moon flooded through me and knocked away the last gossamer of sleep.

"Mrs. Stirling. Don't worry, he's all right," I started to say, but my voice died when I saw another figure step forward. One that sparkled with diamonds and moved with terrible grace. I recognized her. We had crossed paths in the art shop last month. The countess. Phelan's mother. Her blue eyes studied me with icy reserve, and I suddenly felt as if I were naked.

"Miss Neven, this is the Countess of Amarys," Mrs. Stirling rushed to introduce us, but she couldn't smooth away the tension in the air. "Lady Raven Vesper."

"It is an honor to make your acquaintance, Miss Neven," the countess said with a smile, which only made her eyes burn colder. I noticed she cast no shadow on the floor. "My son spoke very highly of you when I saw him last week."

My mind went blank as I held her stare. I was acutely aware of the bloodstains on my chemise, the wrinkles in the gauzy fabric, the snarls in my hair. I knew I appeared like I had just risen from the gutter, and I swallowed, uncertain how to save this first impression of myself.

Phelan, of course, blithely continued to sleep, and I regretted giving him such a strong tonic.

"My lady," I said, and slipped hastily from Phelan's bed, as if the coverlet had caught fire. "Your son fought valiantly last night but was wounded. I felt it best to stay beside him until morning."

"And I thank you for your diligence, Miss Neven," said Lady Raven. "I can handle it from here, and I would appreciate if you kept my son's wound a secret."

I dropped a crooked curtsy, feeling as if every one of my bones had come out of socket. Mrs. Stirling hesitated before granting me a gentle nod, but I departed as swiftly as I could, retreating to the safety of my bedchamber.

I sat in the shadows until my cheeks had cooled, and I opened my curtains and my shutters, basking in the morning light. I washed my face and shattered the mirror that hung on the wall because I was weary of seeing myself. I watched the cracks in the glass spread into a glittering web, until Clem was broken into an array of pieces, and yet I still didn't feel satisfied.

I needed to get out of this house, and I swiftly dressed and brushed the tangles from my hair, quietly descending the stairs.

I emerged onto the front porch, standing in the very place the knight had stood only hours ago. I shivered in the sun, longing for home. To rest in a place where I didn't have to pretend. And I cast my stealth charm and began to walk north.

Imonie was shocked to see me at the door. She had the town house to herself, and was in the middle of scrubbing the hallway when I arrived.

"What happened?" she asked, tossing down her bristle brush to greet me.

"Why does everyone assume something terrible has happened every time they see me?" I asked, exasperated.

Imonie pursed her lips, but I noticed how her eyes flickered over me, from head to foot. As if ensuring I was hale. "Well, it *was* the new moon last night. I take it you were victorious?"

I only sighed.

Her eyes narrowed. "I think this conversation calls for tea. And a hot breakfast. Come here, Clem."

I followed her into the kitchen, thankful that she didn't ask questions while she cooked, but that she listened as I rambled on about the night. I wanted to tell her of the knight but refrained, and perhaps it was only because Phelan had seemed so intent on keeping it a secret. I was on my second cup of tea when I confessed, "I saw the countess this morning. I just so happened to be sleeping in Phelan's bed when she arrived."

Imonie's face paled. "And why were you in Phelan's bed?"

"Nothing happened. He was wounded and he asked me to stay with him."

Imonie eased into the chair across from mine. She wrapped her fingers around her teacup, her eyes glazed in fear. I had never seen such a thing in her—she kept her emotions as guarded as she did her past.

"I want you to stay away from her," she said.

"Who? Lady Raven?"

Imonie nodded. "She's dangerous, Clem. She will stop at nothing to get what she wants."

"How do you know that?" I asked, breakfast suddenly like lead in my stomach.

"Have you ever heard about the Count of Amarys?"

"Her husband? No."

"That's because he's dead," Imonie said. "Been dead for almost sixteen years now. There was much speculation at the time he died. One day he was fine, the next? He fell sick. He died three days later, bloated and choking on his own blood. The countess was a young mother to two boys, and it all seemed rather tragic until rumors began to fly that the Duke of Bardyllis was the boys' true father, and not the count. And that perhaps the countess had poisoned her husband to get rid of him."

I gnawed on my lip, processing Imonie's story. This would be perfect for my exposé on the Vespers. "Do you think she killed her husband?"

Imonie wiped a wrinkle from the tablecloth. "Yes, I do. She poisoned him."

"But why?" I asked. "Why would she kill him? She hasn't gotten with the duke since then."

"Perhaps the count had come to know too much about her. Perhaps she wanted to raise her boys on her own. Perhaps she had simply tired of him. Perhaps he was in her way." Imonie shrugged. "No one knows, so that's why I'm telling you to give her a wide berth."

That did nothing to reassure me. Not when I recalled how Lady Raven's gaze had been icy, beholding me in her son's bed.

"Papa said she's an old acquaintance of his," I said.

Imonie snorted. "Yes, and why do you think he's now working in the mines and has given up magic and wants nothing more than to evade the Vesper boys?"

I wasn't sure, so I remained quiet.

Imonie began to gather the plates, carrying them to the wash bin. I thought the silence would continue to hang between us, but then she looked at me and said, "He doesn't want the countess to find him."

I was relieved to see the countess's carriage was gone when I returned to Auberon Street. The minute I stepped into the foyer, Mrs. Stirling met me with a sigh of relief and a tray of tea and biscuits.

"There you are, Miss Neven. Gave us all a fright, wondering where you had gone!"

"I'm sorry," I said, flushing when I realized I had been absent most of the day. I'd honestly thought no one would care. "I went for a walk."

I was worried that Mrs. Stirling would have that reserved gleam in her eye, the same from that morning, when she found me in Phelan's bed. But she only nodded and extended the tea tray to me.

"Do you mind carrying that up to Mr. Vesper?"

I accepted it and carefully ascended the stairs.

Phelan was sitting upright in bed, loose papers spread before him. He was intently reading, his hair damp from a bath. He was wearing clean clothes, my stitches hidden beneath his shirt. It almost felt like I had merely imagined the events of last night. As if it had all been a dream.

"Did Deacon find her yet?" Phelan asked, presuming I was Mrs. Stirling.

"He didn't need to," I replied, drawing his attention.

I stood on the threshold holding his tea tray, and for a moment, he and I stared at each other. Words seemed to be lost between us.

"I thought . . . ," he began, but his voice faded.

"That I had run away?" I finished with a teasing cadence.

He hesitated—where, indeed, did he think I had gone?—but withheld whatever he wanted to say or ask me.

"Come in, Anna." He dropped his gaze to the papers before him.

That afforded me the chance to slip past the mirror, and I set his tea tray down on his bedside table, mindful of the new jars of herbs that now sat by his glass of water.

"I see the doctor has been here," I remarked, watching as Phelan gathered his papers into a heap.

"Yes. And my mother."

"I know. I met her this morning."

Phelan's eyes darted back to mine. "Did you? She failed to mention that to me."

"No, I don't think she would have," I said, wandering to the window. The curtains were tasseled back, the shutters were open, and I stood in a stream of sunlight, watching the street below. "I was in bed beside you when I met her."

"Oh."

I couldn't resist glancing back at him, how he flushed and hurried to pour his cup of tea, thankful for the distraction.

"Do you remember anything from last night?" I asked.

Phelan took a sip, but his gaze found mine again. "I remember everything."

I had to break our stare first. My skin warmed when I thought about how I had touched him last night, how he had seen my bare back, how he had asked me to stay with him.

"I need to tell you something, Anna."

I braced myself. Surely, his mother had convinced him to dismiss me, and I waited for it to come, for Phelan to let me go. He set his teacup in its saucer. He was drawing this out, to no doubt make me nervous.

"What is it, Phelan?" I asked, impatient.

"I'm going away," he said.

I gaped at him, unable to hide my shock. "To where?"

"I can't tell you. But I'll return in a week or so, and I need you to remain here. To record the nightmares that may emerge and to give the portion of dream tax to the duke's collector, who will be arriving any day now to claim it. I also need you to discreetly pass on a payment to a friend. You will note that there is a purse with a red ribbon in the safe, where I store the money. When they stop by to 'borrow a book,' I need you to ensure they receive that money."

I was quiet so long that he frowned, concerned.

"Anna?"

"Yes, I will do these things for you," I said, inwardly shaking myself. "When do you leave?"

"Tomorrow."

"This must be a trip of great importance, since you should be at home, recovering in bed."

He refused to answer, returning his attention to his stack of papers. I sensed that his mother had given him this order.

And then the realization hit me like a strike to my body, and I turned to the window quickly, before Phelan could see the emotion ripple across my face.

I knew where he was going.

Hereswith.

24

Three days after Phelan departed, Lord Deryn called.

I found him waiting in the library, standing before Phelan's bookcase, intently studying the volumes on one of the shelves. He pivoted when he heard me enter, a well-practiced smile on his face.

I smelled the bergamot of his cologne. A sickly sweetness, mingling with that odd scent of molded parchment. And I knew he was here for me, not the tax.

"Miss Neven. It is good to see you again."

"Your Grace," I said with a curtsy.

"Forgive me for calling so unexpectedly, but I wanted to speak to you. Please, sit."

I obediently lowered myself into the chair, but my dread kindled. A few spells rose to mind, in case I needed to cast them on a whim.

"I wanted to inquire about this last new moon," he began, taking Phelan's seat behind the desk. "Was it my nightmare that materialized?"

"No, Your Grace."

He waited for me to elaborate, and when I didn't, the duke raked his fingers through his beard.

"I know you cannot tell me which dream manifested," he said. "Forgive me for asking. But I need to know how Phelan was wounded."

"How do you know he was wounded, Your Grace?"

"I have ears and eyes everywhere, Miss Neven. Nothing happens in this province that I do not know about."

His words were unsettling, but I was determined that he would never know how much he rattled me. I sighed as if relieved and leaned closer to him, my elbows impolitely resting on the desk.

"I'm happy you already know of it, Your Grace. Did the countess inform you?"

"No, she did not." There was no emotion in his face, in his voice when he spoke of her. The monotone only made me more suspicious of their relationship.

"I confess that I have been worried about him, especially since his mother sent him away. He should be resting in bed."

The duke didn't rise to my bait. He made a noise of contemplation and then said, "What wounded him? An element of the nightmare, or something beyond it?"

I was quiet, wondering if he was accusing me of being a poor partner.

"Choose your answer carefully, Miss Neven," the duke warned in a voice like honey. At last, the threat I was anticipating. "I want the truth, even if that gives me no choice but to remove Phelan from this post. Or you, for that matter."

He doesn't want Phelan in danger, I realized, and then saw this as my chance to have Phelan's aspirations and accomplishments shattered. I could tell the duke Phelan was weak, vulnerable. But even if my desire had originally been to see Phelan lose his home and sense of purpose . . . I was now tied to him, and I didn't want to relinquish what I had gained just yet. I reveled in being a warden again.

"Phelan and I vanquished the nightmare," I said. "But then something else emerged. Something unexpected and malevolent. It wasn't recorded in his ledger."

"What was this unexpected thing, Miss Neven?"

I hesitated.

The duke sensed it and softened. "You will not betray him by telling me."

Oh, but I certainly felt like I would be. Phelan hadn't told two of his closest friends. He couldn't even describe it to me, his partner. It was almost like Phelan had been ordered not to speak of it.

"I think you should ask Phelan when he returns, Your Grace."

Lord Deryn smiled and leaned back in the chair, but his gaze never left mine. "I am going to tell you something, Miss Neven. Something not many people know, and yet I am going to trust you with this secret."

I sat frozen, hating how eager I was to hear what morsel the duke had to offer me.

"Phelan was not born with illumination," he began. "He was not accepted into the Luminous School until I waived his entry. In fact, he failed every single entrance exam, but I saw the potential in him. I gave him a place in the school, I funded his education, and I ensured he received this portion of territory when he was ready to become warden. I have had a hand in shaping him into the magician that he is despite the fact that I have no light in my bones, and it would be a shame to see my investment lost before its time."

I listened, and his words began to spark thoughts I had never entertained before. The duke had been married years ago, but his wife had died not long after their vows. He was a widower, childless. Heirless. And if the duke had played such a quiet but steady hand in Phelan's upbringing—if he thought of Phelan as an *investment*—then the duke had greater plans for him. Whether Phelan knew it or not remained to be seen.

"You plan to name him as your heir," I whispered.

The duke was silent, studying me with sharp intensity, as if he had underestimated me before now. "Yes, Miss Neven. You must not breathe a word of it to him or any other, you understand?"

"I understand, Your Grace."

"And I want to know what is threatening him on the new moon nights."

I could see no other way to avoid it.

I told the duke about the knight.

He listened with a scowl. "This sounds like someone who can control and influence nightmares."

"I've never heard of such a thing," I said, transfixed by the imagining. "How is the knight able to do this?"

"Something, or some*one*, is providing him with a door to enter the dreams on the new moon."

"Who would have such power? A magician?"

Lord Deryn was pensive for a moment. "I do not know, but you will not be able to vanquish him in the dream realm. You will have to locate him in the waking world and defeat him here."

"Not a small feat," I said, but I was surprised by how eager I was for this challenge. I wanted to uncover the knight's secrets. His purpose. His source of power. Even if that entailed me working with someone like the duke.

"Indeed, it is not," Lord Deryn agreed. "But if you can find a way to remove his helm in the nightmare . . . you would see his face. And if you see his face and describe it to me, I would be able to locate him in the province."

The duke was not making a suggestion; he was giving me an order. I thought about the places I knew the knight had appeared: Months ago, on Phelan's first new moon as a warden. Hereswith, the night before Phelan had arrived. And then again on one of Phelan's streets, this October new moon. This didn't feel random to me; it felt like the knight was after Phelan, and it chilled me.

"If the knight arrives on this upcoming new moon, then I will find a way to do that, Your Grace."

"And you will come to me at once with the description, Miss Neven."

I nodded, although my mind was whirling, remembering how the knight had almost beheaded me and sliced Phelan open.

"You have a concern, Miss Neven?"

I met the duke's gaze. "Yes. The knight is a formidable opponent, immune to magic and blades. I don't know how Phelan and I will manage to remove his helm without suffering damage to ourselves."

Lord Deryn steepled his fingers together and pressed them to his lips. "If magic and weapons are useless against the knight's armor, that must mean the armor was forged by a *deviah* magician."

That hadn't crossed my mind. But now that it had, other pieces began to fall into place. Wild speculations. I wondered if the card game of Seven Wraiths somehow influenced the ability of the knight's armor. If both of them were tied to nightmares, and both of them made by *deviah* magicians . . . perhaps they were linked, somehow.

"There is a smith not far from here," Lord Deryn continued. "He is one of the best in the province. A *deviah* who can layer enchantment into steel. I will have him forge something that will help you both."

"If it's armor, it will be more of a hindrance than a help, Your Grace. It will only slow us down, and we must be swift."

"It is not armor, Miss Neven," the duke said, rising from the chair. "I will put the order in, but the smith will most likely want to meet with you about measurements."

"Very well, Your Grace. And what shall I tell Phelan about where this gift arrived from?"

"Tell him it is from me." He fell silent, pensive. But his gaze remained on me. "Phelan speaks of you often, Miss Neven." And I didn't know why he would say such a thing until the duke shocked me further by adding, "Would you want to be a duchess?"

"No."

"A reflexive answer, Miss Neven. As if you have contemplated it before."

The truth was I had *never* thought about it, but the duke was making me anxious. What I did know was the last thing I wanted was to be a pawn in a noble's game.

"If I ever became a duchess," I said, "it would be by my own choice and merit, and not by marriage."

"Ah, you could become the Duchess of Seren, then. That throne is open to anyone who could ascend the mountain and break the new moon curse."

"Which I hear is not nearly as simple as it sounds," I said. "The mountain doors won't open unless all the wraiths are together. And who knows where the seven of them are hiding these days, if that legend is even true."

"How do you know this?" he asked sharply.

I bit the inside of my cheek, the pain my punishment for speaking so freely. "Just a rumor, Your Grace. My mother used to tell me a few mountain stories when I was a girl."

The duke's calculating silence continued to roar.

I felt the urge to state, "I'm not a madcap, if that's what you truly want to know."

"I think we all are madcaps, in one way or another. And a warden like you already has all the training one would need to defeat whatever nightmares lurk in that old mountain fortress," the duke countered, arching his brow. "But as you said, Miss Neven. The wraiths are but a myth. Faces in a card game meant to frighten young children. Now, then. I have taken more than enough of your time today."

I rose, thoughts muddled by all he had said to me, and began to follow him to the library doors until I remembered the dream tax. "Your Grace, the tax . . ."

He paused and gave me a smile, one that crinkled the corners of his eyes. I wasn't fooled by the gentleness of his demeanor. I saw the glint of greed within him. "My collector will arrive later today, Miss Neven. The money never passes through my hands, not until it has been marked and accounted for."

I curtsied and waited until Mrs. Stirling had seen the duke out, and the house fell quiet once more. But I could smell a trace of the duke's cologne again, and I opened a window to let the potent fragrance escape. The library seemed to soften in relief that the duke was gone, and I approached the hidden safe in the wall.

I whispered the spell into the dust motes and watched the safe's door appear in the wall with a mercurial gleam. The door conceded to yawn open beneath my hand, recognizing me, and I stared at the bundles of coins that rested within its belly.

A small portion of this money was mine, for Phelan and I took a percentage and split it between ourselves. *My first proper paycheck*, I thought before locating the bundles Phelan had set aside for the tax collector.

Four bags, each the size of a cantaloupe, swollen with coins. I studied them, one by one, and felt their weight in my palm.

So much money, I thought with a disbelieving heart. *So much money.*

Two days after the duke's visit, I received a request from the smith to come to his shop. It was a tricky place to find, and I walked past it twice before I finally found the shop door, which was so unremarkable that it nearly blended into the brick wall.

The doorbell rang when I entered. The shop was composed of a small chamber, smelling of leather and iron and cleaning oil. Swords of all kinds were displayed on one wall, as well as axes and daggers. A few suits of armor caught my attention. I paused before a steel-plated set that reminded me of the one the knight wore, only far less sinister. Indeed, I felt as if I had stepped back in time. All these weapons and armor . . . not many people possessed such things anymore. They were figments of the past. And the air was dusted with nostalgia, with the memory of fading things.

"May I help you?"

I turned to see a middle-aged man with thinning brown hair and sharp eyes, a pair of wire spectacles perched on his hawk nose. He wore a leather apron, and his hands were covered in grime.

"I'm Anna Neven," I said.

"Ah, yes. I need to take your measurements." He hurried behind his desk and found a spool of measuring tape.

I had told the duke that armor would slow Phelan and me down considerably. And I wanted to protest until the smith measured my height and my left arm, studying my shoulder and the way I stood.

"You're not making armor?" I asked.

"No. A shield."

A shield would *be helpful*, I thought. Although I remembered how the knight's sword had shattered Phelan's rapier like it had been composed of glass. It could just as easily sunder a buckler, but I held my doubt.

"How long have you been practicing *deviah*?" I asked.

The smith glanced at me, a suspicious arch in his brow. "Long enough, I suppose."

"Were you a warden before?"

"No. But I am familiar with *avertana*."

"Do you often create enchanted armor?"

He gave me an exasperated expression. "Do you often come into shops and ask a hundred questions?"

I blushed. "I'm sorry. I just find your vein of work quite fascinating."

That mollified his gruffness. *Slightly.* "Creating enchanted armor is extremely difficult, even for the most experienced magicians. It would take years to achieve one suit. Now, then, Miss Neven. I'll deliver the shields to Mr. Vesper's town house when they are ready." He wrote down a few notes, which I took as his way of dismissing me.

I began to leave the shop when something caught my eye. A leather weapon belt, hanging overhead. It was the twin to the one I had possessed, the one my father had purchased for me when I began to fight at his side on the streets of Hereswith. The twin to the one Olivette had worn the other day.

My breath caught.

The resemblance was uncanny, undeniable. Papa must have bought it from this shop.

"Another question, Miss Neven?" the smith asked, noticing my rapt attention.

I wondered if this smith was Olivette's father, remembering how she had told me that her father had made the weapon belt for her. And I opened my mouth to ask more about the belt, to tell him I knew Olivette, but something gave me pause. A warning, as if I had felt a draft. "No. Good day to you, sir."

That afternoon, I began writing my exposé at Phelan's desk. I used his ink and quill, and a blank journal I had purchased, and started listing the things I wanted to include:

—The countess buys art supplies (for herself?) and is a magician. Potential <u>deviah</u>?
—The countess poisoned her late husband, the count, because . . . ? (She was bored of him/she had a liaison with the duke/he had uncovered a secret of hers she wanted to keep buried.)

—*Lennox and Phelan may or may not be the duke's children.*
—*Phelan failed his entrance exams, holds no illumination, and would have never become a magician if it wasn't for the duke's influence.*

"Miss Neven?" Mrs. Stirling opened the library door. It startled me so badly my quill shot across the page, and I hastened to close my journal. "I'm sorry to interrupt, but a visitor has come to borrow one of Mr. Vesper's books."

"Yes, give me one moment and then send them in, Mrs. Stirling."

She nodded and left. I hurried to charm my journal so no one but me could read it before opening the enchanted safe, retrieving the purse with the red ribbon. It was swollen with coins, and I wondered what Phelan had set this sum aside for.

A creak sounded on the threshold.

I spun to greet the visitor, only to stiffen in shock. Words froze on my tongue as I stared at the girl from the art shop. Blythe.

She gave me a tentative smile, tucking a stray curl behind her ear. "I'm so sorry to interrupt you, but I'm here to borrow one of Mr. Vesper's books. He said you could help me."

I swallowed my shock, as well as the hope that she would remember me. I was in disguise, and I had nearly forgotten it.

"Y-yes, of course." I walked to her and extended the coin purse.

Her delight was tangible. She beamed at the purse, cupping it with both hands. "Oh, this is so much more than I thought it would be! Please thank Mr. Vesper for me!"

And what am I thanking him for? I wanted to ask. "Of course."

"Thank you," Blythe whispered again, sliding the purse into her leather satchel. "My brother is a warden of a few streets that have fallen on hard times and cannot pay the duke's tax. So Mr. Vesper's donation is much appreciated."

"Phelan will be pleased to hear of it," I said, struggling to hide my surprise. This side of Phelan was new to me. And I didn't like how it made me doubt my prior assumptions of him.

"I also have a message, for you to give to Mr. Vesper," Blythe said. "A few weeks ago, he asked me if I had seen someone named Clementine in the art shop. I told him there had been a pretty girl named Clem with red hair, and he wanted me to inform him if I ever saw her step foot in the shop again."

"And has she?" I asked, clearing my throat.

Blythe shook her head. "No. But the strange thing is his mother, Lady Raven, *also* asked about the girl. She wanted me to follow Clem home the next time she visited the shop. I thought Mr. Vesper would be interested to know his mother is also looking for her. I hope Clem is not in any sort of trouble."

"On the contrary," I said with a slight grimace. "Perhaps they want to commission her."

"Perhaps. Well, good day to you . . ."

"Anna. Anna Neven."

"Anna," Blythe said.

I remained standing in the library long after she departed. The shadows grew long, gnarled roots around me.

The Vespers knew I was in the city. And I thought of the spell I had planned, in case Phelan discovered who I was. The spell my father had insisted I have prepared.

At the time I created it, I had believed that I would never have to cast it.

Now? I was no longer sure.

25

Phelan returned after a week and a half's absence, and he brought the first frost of autumn to the city. I reunited with him in the library that evening, where he stood before his shelves, frantically leafing through a book. And when that failed to entice him, he set it down and reached for another, his fingers swiping through the pages.

"You were away longer than you said you would be," I greeted him, closing the library doors behind me.

Phelan turned. His hair was tousled, his clothes uncharacteristically wrinkled from the journey. "Yes, forgive me, Anna. I hope things were uneventful here?"

"Quite," I said, joining him before the shelves. "The dream tax has been passed on to the collector. And I gave the red ribbon purse to your contact. She was very thankful for the amount."

"Good. Did she have any other messages for me?"

"She hasn't seen your old rival Cordelia—"

"Clementine," Phelan corrected me.

"Yes, whatever her name is, in the art shop."

He sighed and carelessly dropped a book on his desk. "Just the news I wanted to hear."

"What else have you done to try and locate her?"

"I've contacted a few art shops and checked her Luminous Society files," he said. "There's not much there to glean, as both of her parents are highly private people and paid to have their records guarded. But it seems her mother is proficient in *metamara* and performed stagecraft, so I've begun to check with theaters in the area."

My pulse skipped. I had never thought about him tracing my mother to me, because she went by her stage name, and had been doing so for nearly a decade, since she split with my father. Despite that, I was tempted to dismiss myself and send an urgent message to my parents, but I quenched the impulsivity and chose to take another route.

I lingered in the library, watching him draw book after book from his vast shelves.

"What are you looking for? Aside from Clementine, that is."

"A certain volume," he said. "I can't remember its title, but it has an essay on trolls that I need."

"Trolls?" I echoed, thinking of Mazarine. "Why is that? Did you encounter one?"

"Perhaps." Phelan sounded distant, resuming his search.

I watched. There were moments when Phelan looked at me or when our skin brushed and I felt something electric pass between us. I told myself it was merely from two enemies being in close quarters, until I realized that I had—unfortunately—come to miss him during the time he was away. But more than those unsettling feelings . . . I needed to distract him from Mazarine, from hunting me and my parents.

"This house is far too quiet at night without you," I said.

That brought him back to me. He met my gaze, and I wondered what he saw in my eyes, because Phelan smiled.

I took a step back, and it was like we were bound by an invisible tether, because he suddenly forgot about the mess of books around him and took a step forward.

"Leaving so soon, Anna?"

"Well, you're knee deep in books," I said, waving my hand. "We can talk more tomorrow."

"Talk more about what?" he asked. "The fact that you missed me?"

I suddenly couldn't tell if he was humoring me or deadly serious. "I never said that I missed you. I said that it was *quiet* here."

He took another step closer. "Then let me be the first to confess. I missed you."

"I have no doubt."

"I should have taken you with me."

I tried to imagine that scenario—going to Hereswith with him. Staying in my old house with him and his brother. Walking streets I knew like the lines on my palm, and pretending it all meant nothing to me.

"You should have." My voice was husky, full of longings he would never understand.

"And I'm weary of trolls and dusty journeys and missing Clementines and having to deal with my brother's snark," he said, and the space between us closed a little more.

I had to tilt my chin to look up at him. "And what can I do about that?"

"Distract me."

He shouldn't challenge me with such a thing. I could give him all sorts of distractions, and I raised my hand and grasped the ribbon that held his hair at the nape of his neck. Slowly, I pulled it loose, and I listened to his breaths quicken as his dark hair spilled around his shoulders. Not once did he look away from me as my hands deftly unfastened the top two buttons of his waistcoat. My fingertips traced the faint scar my rapier had left on his cheekbone.

I stepped back to regard him. "Yes, you look much better as a rogue."

Surely, that comment would offend him. But he laughed, and the sound was golden, incandescent. I longed to hear it again, as soon as it melted away.

"Come, the distraction is not over yet," I said, inviting him to follow me from the library. "Go set a pot of tea to boil, and then meet me in the drawing room."

"What for?"

"That would spoil the fun, now, wouldn't it?"

He only arched his brow, but a smile lingered on his mouth. And I hated how I suddenly wanted to taste it.

Phelan took the corridor to the kitchen; I stepped into the drawing room and found the cards. I stoked the fire in the hearth and lit a few candles by magic, and then I sat in a high-backed chair and waited for him to arrive with the tea. He must have used magic as well to prepare it, because he arrived sooner than I anticipated. The mirth that had been in his eyes just moments ago waned when he saw Seven Wraiths laid out on the table.

"Honest to gods, Anna . . . I'm tired of this game," he said, setting the tray down. "It's all Deacon wants to play, night after night, and—"

"As I know," I replied. "But I have something important to say to you, and I think it will help if we are holding the cards."

He only sighed and poured us each a cup of tea, settling into the chair across from mine. I had a strange feeling that he would do just about anything I asked of him, and it made my hands tremble. He watched as I dealt, and the silence was thick as we studied our cards.

I wanted to gather as many of the wraiths as possible and was delighted when I drew the heiress, a young woman with long dark hair and sorrowful blue eyes, a white dress accentuating her lovely figure. A golden belt was cinched at her waist, where a small dagger was sheathed in a bejeweled scabbard. When I tilted the card in the light, tears of blood streamed down the heiress's cheeks, marring the ivory sheen of her gown. It was a disturbing sight, one that made me forget where I was until Phelan nudged my foot beneath the table.

"It's your turn, Anna."

"Will you trade with me?" I asked.

To my surprise, he did. I gave him the eight of clubs, and he gave me another wraith. The guard. He was decked in armor, his face obscured by a helm. But when I tilted the card, flames began to lick up his body, melting the steel into quicksilver, and I could see his face, screaming in pain. . . .

"You are *terrible* at this game," Phelan drawled.

I ignored him and asked, "Do you know who illustrated these cards?" I had an inkling that his mother had painted them. I had seen her buying supplies in the art shop—a place I now wished I had never step foot in. She cast no shadow. And there was that uncanny portrait of the twin brothers, tucked away in Phelan's desk.

"Yes, I do."

"Who is it?"

He shifted in his chair. I sensed his discomfort, and his voice was wary when he said, "What's this really about, Anna?"

I laid down my cards, faceup, so Phelan could see them. The two wraiths caught the firelight, gleaming as if they breathed, as if they lived, trapped on the paper.

"I think the enchantment surrounding these cards is giving the knight a way into dreams that are not his own," I began.

Phelan frowned, contemplating. "Go on."

I couldn't tell him that my conclusion had not only come from the duke, but also from Elle Fielding in Hereswith, who had lost a round of Seven Wraiths and suffered a nightmare for it. A dark dream where the knight had trod. The cards and the armor, both made from different *deviah* magicians, were somehow linked together by nightmares. I just did not know *how* yet, and I hoped

Phelan would give me insight.

"We know that whoever loses this game will have a nightmare as punishment," I continued, tracing my fingertip over the burning guard, the weeping heiress. Both who had betrayed their duke a century ago. "I think the nightmares spawned by this game are providing doorways, or portals, for the knight, who is wearing enchanted armor, to physically pass into them."

Phelan, frowning in contemplation, set down his cards to mirror mine, and I saw that he had been holding the spymistress. Mazarine. Her horns flared and then vanished, and I swallowed the questions I wanted to voice, questions that would betray all the things I shouldn't know.

"My mother painted these cards," he confessed at last.

"I noted that she is a magician when I met her in your bedroom," I said carefully. "I didn't realize she is also an artist."

His gaze flickered to mine. "Not many people know of her skill. She hardly speaks of her *deviah* magic to me."

"Have you ever asked her why she paints these cards?"

"No."

"Does she know that the knight has wounded you twice, now?"

"Yes, of course she knows." He was becoming agitated with my questions.

I swept the cards off the table and shuffled them. Phelan watched me with hooded eyes as I dealt us a new hand.

"Your mother is making these enchanted cards, unaware that she is also giving someone the chance to wreak havoc on the new moon," I said. "You and I need to discover who the knight is, and what they want. Perhaps they are simply seeking a challenge, but perhaps they have a bone to pick with your mother. Hence why they have attacked you twice now, Phelan." And why the knight appeared in Hereswith, the day before the brothers had arrived. As if the knight had known they were coming.

Phelan looked pale in the firelight. "You think the knight will come on the November new moon if one of us loses at cards and dreams tonight?"

"Yes," I said. I didn't tell him that I believed the knight had specifically targeted him, and that it was vital we discover who this vengeful person was before they killed him.

"Then whichever of us loses must also choose to forgo a remedy, in order to dream tonight, Anna."

"Yes," I said again, softer. I bit my lip. I couldn't afford to be the one to lose and dream. I needed it to be him.

He stared at me for a long, uncomfortable moment. I didn't look away from him; I held his eyes as he held mine. Even as he seemed to steal my breath.

"Very well." He picked up his cards, as did I. And my hopes were dashed when I saw that I held three different wraiths. The advisor, the lost one, and the lady-in-waiting. If I was going to win, I would need Phelan to trade cards with me three times.

He refused to trade at all.

I lost with the three wraiths in my hands, and when I surrendered them, faceup on the table, Phelan fell quiet.

"Another round," he murmured, and worked to shuffle and deal.

I didn't want to acknowledge what he was doing, or why. But

he purposefully lost the second round.

Defeated, Phelan rose with a weary groan and drained the last of his lukewarm tea. "Take a remedy tonight, Anna. I'll be the one to dream. Surely, the knight will be *delighted* to use my nightmare as a doorway this upcoming new moon."

To my shock, I stood and said, "No. Let us both dream tonight."

Perhaps it was because of the late hour, somewhere long past midnight when reality begins to blur into recklessness. Or perhaps it was because we were both exhausted. Or because I liked him more than I wanted to, and the thought of him suffering through the night so I wouldn't have to vexed me. Or perhaps it was merely because I had never allowed myself to dream at night, and I longed to experience it.

"All right," he agreed.

Together, we banked the fire and extinguished the candles, ascending the stairs to the second floor. There was an awkward pause before his door; Phelan stalled for a moment, holding a candlestick. The solitary flame carved shadows on his face; pinpricks of light shone in his eyes. I knew he wanted to say something else to me, and so I also tarried on my threshold.

"I'll leave my door open tonight," he finally said, darting a glance at me. "If you need me, call and I'll come to you."

I nodded and slipped into my chamber, shutting the door behind me. But I stood there for what felt like years, stiff with apprehension. And I decided to open my door and leave it that way, just as Phelan had left his, and I prepared for bed.

I lay down in the dark, drawing the coverlet up to my chin. If

I dreamt of my old life—of a girl with auburn hair and charcoal-streaked fingers, walking the streets of Hereswith—I would break all laws of wardenship and fabricate a nightmare to record in Phelan's book. And if this nightmare happened to spawn on the new moon . . . then I would be exposed and I would flee, as Papa had prepared me to do.

I drifted into sleep before I felt wholly prepared for it.

When I woke hours later, the sheets were crumpled around me, the night pitched dark and cold. The hour before sunrise. It was not a nightmare that had startled me awake. It was the emptiness. The howling quiet. A terrible sense of unease crept over me.

I hadn't dreamt at all.

I sat forward in bed with a gasp.

I was chilled to the bone; I trembled, full of aches I had never felt before. It was as if I had slept in a snowdrift on midwinter, and I struggled to rise. My fingers and toes were like ice.

My sleep was dreamless, although it shouldn't have been. My mind was hollow, but I told myself it was nothing to worry over. Nothing to worry over as I left my room and crossed the hallway, to where Phelan's door sat open with invitation.

I took two steps into his chamber and then halted, as if I was truly losing my mind. I shouldn't be here. I shouldn't seek him out for comfort.

"Anna?"

He was awake, as if he had been waiting for me. I listened as he shifted in bed, sitting forward. "Anna, are you all right?"

"Yes," I replied, and the lie sat in my mouth like glass.

Something that would tear me up as soon as I swallowed it. And I said, "No. No, I'm not."

"Do you want to join me? There's room for both of us."

I already knew there was room in his bed. I had slept at his side once, and it had been one of the best nights of sleep I had experienced since leaving Hereswith.

I couldn't see in the dark, but I surrendered and felt my way to his bed. I listened as he moved the blankets, as he fluffed a pillow, as he made space for me.

I eased into the warmth of his bed. The sheets were like silk, steeped with pine, meadow grass, rain, and spices. The smell of his skin and his soap. And the ice I had felt upon waking dreamless began to melt. The bed was generous enough that we could both lie side by side without a chance of touching, and I relaxed, sinking into the feather mattress. But I could sense him, how slim the distance was between our bodies. If I reached my hand out to the gentle darkness, my fingertips would brush his shoulder. His hair. The line of his jaw.

I felt safe lying beside him. As the tingling left my limbs, I asked myself why I didn't dream. A voice echoed in my memory, as if in reply. *Tell me, Clementine . . . have you read one of my nightmares recorded in your father's book?*

Mazarine's words, haunting me weeks after she spoke them. And then it was like she was speaking to me, because I heard her whisper, *"Have you read one of your* own *nightmares in your father's book?"*

"Anna?"

"Mm?"

I was thankful he spoke, breaking me from my reveries. I listened to him breathe, wondering if he was about to tell me what nightmare he had dreamt. If I would need to write it down for him. And when the silence deepened like a canyon between us, I thought he had drifted asleep until he spoke again, and his confession echoed through me. . . .

"I dreamt of nothing."

26

"It must have been the cards," I said later that morning, watching Phelan pace the library. "Perhaps the enchantment has worn away in them, from being passed through so many hands."

"No," he said. "Those cards will never lose their enchantment. Not while the curse still lives on the mountain."

"Do you think the curse will ever end?"

"I don't know, Anna."

I fell silent. I hadn't told him that I was also dreamless. As far as he knew, I had suffered a nightmare while he had suffered nothing. And if I was honest, there was a piece of me that wanted to tell him the truth. To confess and watch the furrow in his brow ease. But I feared it would make me too vulnerable.

"How does your mother create the cards?" I asked. *How does she enchant her illustrations with nightmares* was what I truly wanted to know.

Phelan stopped pacing. His back was angled to me; his attention was fixed on the frost-laced window. One would never think he had experienced a bad night; he was impeccably dressed, and his raven-dark hair was held by his customary ribbon. But his eyes were bloodshot and distant. Even when he looked at me, I sensed he was far away.

"I'm not sure. I know very little of *deviah* magic." He sighed. The sound could have come from my own lips, as if our worry was the same. "I need to go tend to a few things. You can have the rest of the day off, Anna."

He left in a rush, grabbing his top hat and coat from the rack on his way out.

For a moment, I didn't know what to do with myself and this unexpected day of freedom. And then I smelled the aroma of Mrs. Stirling's cooking drift down the hall, browned butter and golden crust and strawberry preserves, and I knew exactly where I wanted to go.

I went to see Imonie.

She had the town house to herself again. Mama was at the theater, Papa at the mines. I sat on a kitchen stool with Dwindle purring on my lap—even in a different shape, my cat knew me. Bright October sunlight flowed in from the windows as I watched Imonie bake. It almost felt like the Vespers had never happened to us and we were back in Hereswith.

Almost.

"It looks like they've been feeding you well," she said as she kneaded dough on the counter.

"The food is good," I replied. "But I do miss your galettes."

She tried to hide how much my comment pleased her; only a hint of blush warmed her cheeks. "If I had known you were coming, I would have a whole tray ready for you."

I smiled, but I said nothing else for a while, the words suddenly feeling too heavy to speak. I would have been content to simply sit silently in Imonie's presence until she looked at me with her keen eyes.

"What's troubling you, Clementine?"

It was a relief to have someone I trusted, someone who knew me in all my shades, ask me a direct question.

"What does it feel like when you dream, Imonie? Do you dream every single night if you don't take a remedy?"

"It's been a long while since I dreamt," she replied, returning her gaze to her dough. But her attention remained fixated on me. "Once, when I was younger, I dreamt vividly every single night. The good dreams were like sustenance, feeding me all throughout the following day. And the bad ones? Well, I think you know what nightmares are like, Clementine."

I mulled over her reply, and then asked, "Is it common to wake up and forget what you dreamt the night before?"

That brought her eyes back to mine. Sharp and probing. "Why do you ask, child?"

"I'm merely curious."

"Then yes. Sometimes."

The stiffness in my shoulders eased. I stroked Dwindle's calico fur and thought perhaps that had been the case for me last night. But the longer I tried to convince myself, the weaker it felt. Because both Phelan and I should have been battered by nightmares. And nightmares were not the type of dream to be forgotten come sunrise.

"There's something I want to tell you, Clem," Imonie said, wiping her hands on her apron. "The other week, when you came for Monday night dinner. You asked if November seventeenth held any significance."

"And does it?" I prompted, my interest catching.

"It doesn't in Bardyllis, but once, long ago, that date meant something in Seren. It was a night of feasting, when the people of the mountains lit fires and ate their favorite foods and danced beneath the stars. It was the last feast of autumn, because the snow comes early in the mountains."

"Why didn't you mention this to me when I first asked?"

Imonie glanced away. "You know speaking of the mountains grieves me, Clem."

She was about to say something else, but the front door creaked open, and we both turned, surprised to see my father appear on the kitchen threshold.

"Papa!" I greeted him.

He stopped upright and gaped at me a moment, and I noticed that he had washed the grime of the mines away, and that his hair was brushed, and he was wearing fine clothes.

He wasn't pleased to see me.

"Why are you here, daughter?" he asked in a brusque tone. "Shouldn't you be with Phelan?"

I slowly rose from my stool, setting Dwindle on the floor. "And shouldn't you be at the mines?"

Papa glanced beyond me, to look at Imonie, but by the time I spun around, their silent conversation had ended.

"Forgive me, Clem," my father said gently. "You're taking a risk by coming here in broad daylight. I didn't expect it."

"I haven't forgotten my stealth charms."

"Come, sit with me in the drawing room."

I moved to follow him until I smelled something odd. It was faint at first, and I told myself it must be coming from the kitchen. But when I stepped into the drawing room and could still taste the bergamot and parchment in the air, I halted, watching my father sit in a leather chair.

"You've been with the duke," I stated.

Papa gazed up at me, his face frozen. His lips hardly moved as he asked, "What makes you think that?"

"You smell like his cologne."

"Don't be ridiculous, Clem."

"Don't *lie* to me!" I cried. The emotion welled, sudden and fierce. It took me off guard, and I drew in a deep breath to calm myself. "What does he want with you?"

My father continued to stare at me; his face was like a stranger's, cold and suspicious. I couldn't read him, and fear sparked within me.

"Sit down, Clementine."

"Was he the one who ordered you to protect Mazarine?" I asked. "Does he hold something over you, Papa?"

"Yes, and that's all I can say to you of the matter." I hadn't expected my father to reply. So when he did, it nearly made me keel over. He rose and approached me, cradling my face in his palms. I could smell the bergamot on his skin, as if he had shaken the duke's hand.

"Did you make a bargain with him, Papa?" I asked in a hoarse voice. *Please*, I thought. *Please tell me no. . . .*

My father only studied me, as if he was desperate to find a semblance of his daughter in my disguise. "You've met the duke, Clem?"

He was turning the conversation on me. I tried to step away but he held me steady. "When?" he asked, and I heard a thread of worry within his voice. "What did you meet with him about?"

"Papa . . ."

"Answer me."

"To record a dream of his. Weeks ago."

"Is that all?"

"Yes." But I had hesitated, and Papa had heard it. He knew I was lying.

"Clem," he whispered. "What else happened?"

I had always trusted my father. And I saw how naive that was of me. To never question him, to always tell him everything.

"That was all," I said, and I felt the stone of my heart settle. As if it would never crack and relinquish me. "But perhaps you should tell me why *you* met with the duke."

"I don't want you to worry over this, Clem," he said. "All is well. What I want you to do is continue playing your role as Phelan's partner safely and shrewdly. Do you understand?"

I nodded, even as his hands continued to cradle my face, firm within his grip.

"Good," he whispered, and his fingers fell away. "Now, then. Do you have any news about the countess?"

I did. I knew that she was a *deviah*, and she had been creating enchanted cards for Seven Wraiths. I knew that she was trying to keep Phelan's new moon nemesis an absolute secret, for reasons I could only marvel at. I had an inkling she had once had an affair with the duke, and Phelan and Lennox were the offspring of that liaison.

But if my father would not be forthright with me, then why should I be with him?

"No news, Papa. But Phelan is searching the theaters, seeking Mama."

"I'll let her know," he said. "You should return to your post before you are missed."

I let him walk me to the door, Imonie slipping a few cheese pastries into my hand. My father and I paused in the foyer, and I knew he wouldn't open the front door until I had cast my stealth charm. But I delayed; I was still hungry for answers.

"What would happen if I ceased taking remedies at night?"

Papa frowned. "That would be a foolish thing to do, Clem."

"But what would happen if I *did*?" I insisted. "Would I dream, Papa?"

He was silent, but his stare held mine for a long moment. "You would dream, daughter. And there is no telling how terrible those dreams would be."

I cast my stealth charm. He opened the door for me, and I slipped out of the town house without another word. I walked a few blocks before I came to a stop near the river, and I stood on the mossy bank for a while, acknowledging the truth like a bruise on my skin.

My father was deceiving me.

I didn't drink a remedy that night.

I lay in bed with the door open, like it had been the night before. As Phelan's was, on the other side of the hall. As if some channel had been forged by our dreamless slumber, and if I dared to rise, its current would guide me to him.

I stared up into the darkness, afraid to fall asleep, afraid to discover what awaited me on the other side. Afraid of the answers that I sought.

I slept beneath the shadows of a canopy, beneath the watch of the stars. I woke to the fragile light of the sun. And I was cold again, as if I were in an empty cavern, or lost on a winter sea.

There was nothing for me to experience in sleep, despite what my father had sworn.

Again, I hadn't dreamt.

27

The shields arrived.

I had honestly forgotten all about them, and Phelan and I stood side by side in the library, staring at the two shields laid out on the desk. The larger one was for him, made of dark, glistening wood and silver studs. Its companion was smaller, crafted from a red wood with golden accents. The one the smith had made for me.

They were beautiful, and when I traced the edge of mine, I felt a chill in my hand. I tasted mist and rust and salt in my mouth. Enchantment that was forged deep into the essence of wood and steel.

"Why did these arrive?" Phelan asked tersely. He had been in a foul mood since the day before, and I could only assume it was due to his dreamless sleep. "I didn't order them."

I cast a careful glance at him. "The duke had them commissioned for us."

"Please tell me you didn't, Anna."

"That I didn't *what*, Phelan?"

"Tell the duke about the knight."

I was silent. Phelan groaned and dragged his hands down his face. "He knows too much and all but owns me. I don't want to be any more indebted to him than I already am!"

I remembered what the duke had said about Phelan. *His investment.* I dared to wonder if Phelan was his son, but I would never breathe that assumption aloud. At least, not yet.

"You don't like the duke?" I asked.

"I won't say that I *dislike* him," Phelan replied. "But he is everywhere I turn. Watching me, advising me. Ordering me." He paused, and a light of realization flickered through him. "He came here while I was away, didn't he? Did he force the truth about the knight from you, Anna?"

"No, but he was concerned about your well-being."

Phelan groaned again and walked to the window, to gaze beyond the glass. "Well, then. I suppose we have no choice. The shields it is."

"The shields are to protect us while one of us removes the knight's helm," I said, and Phelan turned to stare at me. "We need to identify whoever it is."

"Removing the helm will be impossible."

I sighed at his pessimism and lifted my shield. It was heavy, but not to the point where I would be unable to wield it. I slid it onto my arm and met Phelan's stare. "I think you and I can do it."

"He might not even appear this upcoming new moon."

"Why? We've been playing Seven Wraiths every night. We've all but rolled out a welcome rug in our dreams, inviting him to the streets on the new moon."

"But I still haven't dreamt."

I glanced at him. "Were you able to speak to your mother about it?"

Phelan never answered, as we were interrupted by Mrs. Stirling, who brought in a pot of slippery elm tea and a pile of letters that had just arrived in the post.

Phelan and I sat at the desk, drank tea, and sorted through the correspondence. Most were nightmare requests, and I made a list of names we needed to visit.

"This one is for you," Phelan said, handing a thick envelope to me.

I accepted it with reservation. Who would write to me? And then I saw the golden wax seal, and I slowly opened it, slipping out an exquisite invitation.

Lady Raven Vesper was inviting me to a dinner party, following the next new moon. November seventeenth.

I stared at that date until it swam on the paper. Imonie's words flooded back to me: *It was a night of feasting, when the people of the mountains lit fires and ate their favorite foods and danced beneath the stars.* Did the countess know this? Was this all some coincidence of dates? I didn't think that it was, and I must have been staring at the invite too long, because Phelan asked, "Would you like to attend it with me, Anna? As my date?"

My heart quickened at his offer. I hated that it did; I hated that

I wanted to go with him. I winced, swallowing the pain and the desire, and dropped the invitation on the table.

"I'm fairly certain your mother loathes me," I replied.

"She doesn't loathe you."

"I have nothing to wear."

"I'm afraid that excuse won't do, Anna. I'll provide you with something."

"Of course you will."

"Is that a yes, then?"

Yes. "No."

Phelan leaned across the desk and said, "I know you dislike this sort of thing. As do I, but my mother has given me an order, so I cannot escape it. And I told her I would not attend without you."

That caught my attention. "She *orders* you to attend dinner parties?"

"Not often. But this time, yes." And he smiled, as if that would help change my mind.

It was not the charm of his smile, but the enticing thought of seeing the countess again, in her mansion. I would have access to her private residence—a *deviah* magician with a multitude of secrets—and I knew this opportunity would not come again. It was the perfect chance to glean more information for the exposé I planned to write about the Vespers.

"Very well," I conceded. "I will go as your date, but only if I am the one to remove the knight's helm on the new moon."

His smile melted into a scowl. I waited for him to protest, but instead he extended his hand across the desk and said, "I agree to your terms."

I hesitated only a beat before I reached out and let my hand slide into his.

We shook on it.

The moon waxed.

Phelan and I gathered nightmares. We walked the streets in the evening with our shields on our arms, growing accustomed to their weight. We planned strategy, we planned a dance with the knight, we planned for the unexpected and the expected.

The moon waned.

I no longer drank remedies at night. I never dreamt, and I refused to dwell on what that might mean. I blamed it on the tattered state of the cards; I told myself the magic of the game was weak and worn. I never asked Phelan about his nights, but I knew he wasn't dreaming, either. I knew the long, dreamless nights were wearing him down with worry, because I felt it too. How it made one crave warmth, to feel something other than numbing emptiness.

Sometimes, I found myself concerned for him, and how distant he was. Something had changed within him; he seemed guarded and preoccupied. I occasionally wished that I had been honest with him about my own sleep. For despite how close I felt to him now, my lack of vulnerability had built a wall between us.

Two nights before the November new moon, he came home late from visiting his mother. I was already in bed, but I heard the front door slam, followed by a crash that shook the walls.

My pulse leapt in my throat as I grabbed a robe and flew down the stairs.

I found Phelan in the throes of dismantling the library. I stood, stunned, as he viciously swiped his books off the shelves. Volume after volume was hurled to the ground, until the floor was nearly covered in exposed pages and scuffed covers. He took to his desk next, completely unaware of me. There was a whirlwind of fluttering papers and quills and shattering glass, ink spilling like dark blood.

"Phelan," I said, but my voice was nothing more than a rough whisper.

He went to the window, where his potted plants were arranged. He took each one in his hands and hurled them against the wall. Vines and flowers went limp in clumps of soil. I dared to step closer to him.

"Phelan."

He froze, at last hearing me. When he turned, I saw that his eyes were red rimmed, and his cheeks were flushed, from anger or from weeping, I didn't know. But I had never seen him like this.

He released a sharp breath when he met my gaze.

I wanted to ask him what had happened. But I couldn't find the words. They lodged in my throat as I stepped over his ruin.

"Anna," he said. His voice was hoarse; he no longer sounded furious, only sad. "Anna . . . you should leave."

I halted. "Leave?"

He set down the pot he had been about to toss. "Yes. Get far away from me, my family."

My fingers curled into fists as I wondered if he had discovered my true identity. He hadn't mentioned Clementine Madigan since the day I'd conveyed Blythe's message, but I sensed he was still searching for me.

"You would tell me to leave two days before the new moon?" I asked, incredulous. "Why?"

Phelan turned away, surveying the damage he had wrought. "I can't tell you why. But I want to give you the opportunity to leave while you still can."

I stared at him, stunned, as he began to pick up books and set them back on the shelves.

The volume of nightmares was sprawled in the middle of the floor; I retrieved it, smoothing the pages that had bent. Phelan paused, watching as I walked the tome to his desk and set it down.

"Remember that night you told me that you weren't *kind*?" I asked. "Well, in case you failed to notice, neither am I."

"Anna," he began, desperate. "You sh—"

"No, listen to me! I have invested too much time, sweat, and blood in you and your streets for you to dismiss me over some family matter you refuse to divulge. I'm not going anywhere, Phelan Vesper."

I left him to clean the library on his own, but I sat in bed by candlelight, too anxious and angry at him to sleep. I reached for my journal and reread my exposé, eventually turning the page to write what Phelan had said to me earlier: *Get far away from me, my family.* I stared at those words, and I wondered what had inspired them. I needed to know—his mother must have done something awful—and I shut the journal.

My door was open, as it had been every night, and yet I was

still surprised to see him appear, standing on my threshold long past midnight. He had never come to me in the dark as I sometimes did to him, to lie close enough to feel his heat but far enough that we never touched.

We stared at each other for a long, fragile moment. A moment when I wondered if he was about to ask if he could sleep in my bed, and I felt terrible warmth course through me.

"You're right," he said. "I'm sorry."

"For what?" I would never be above making him grovel.

"That you had to see my fit, downstairs. That I told you to leave." He paused, but his eyes shone like gemstones in the firelight. "I need you. And if you had departed as I first wanted, I would have soon come after you."

I shivered, but I refused to dwell on how his words made me feel, like I was sugar melting in tea. I needed to know what his mother had done to upset him. "You can talk to me, Phelan."

He was quiet. His gaze dropped for the briefest of moments, down to my throat and the loose neckline of my chemise. "I know. Good night, Anna."

He left, striding to his bedroom across the hall. I thought it was probably for the best and slid into the safety of my cold sheets.

28

The November new moon arrived, at last. Phelan and I walked the cold, darkened streets with shields on our arms, waiting for the dream to arrive.

The trees were succumbing to bareness, limbs creaking in the wind and leaves gathering on the cobblestones, damp and golden and fragrant beneath my boots. I could see my breath, a steady plume of smoke, and I felt the chill of the air bite my cheeks.

It began to drizzle.

The streetlamps cast hazy circles of light and I shivered as moisture gathered in my hair, beaded on my raiment. A dankness settled into my bones. My shield sat snug on my arm, but the uneven weight of it was agitating my shoulders.

Phelan said nothing as he stood at my side, but he frequently checked his pocket watch. We hadn't discussed the library dismantling again, or what had driven him to do it. In fact, he had kept me at a polite distance, and I hated to admit that his reserve bothered me.

I could barely see his face in the darkness, but when he looked at me, his eyes were bright, almost feverish.

"This weather is granting us a disadvantage," he said.

"As long as we stay close together, we should be fine," I replied. But I couldn't deny that he was right about the disadvantage: the streets were slick from the drizzle and patches of leaves. We continued to wait as the rain began to fall steadily, soaking through our clothes.

"If something goes amiss," Phelan began to say, "I want you to retreat to the house and lock the door."

"I'm not retreating and leaving you."

He never responded, because the nightmare manifested in the streets with a sudden and fierce gust. It blew us both off our feet. We sprawled on the wet cobblestones, breathless and wide eyed and clumsy with our shields.

"What was that?" I asked, scrambling to my feet, my gaze peeling the darkness.

We both heard a clatter behind us. The sound of something climbing up a trellis, rattling the shutters of a nearby house.

I turned. It looked like a man upon first glance, but then I saw that he was some manner of demon, with pale, scaly skin, sinewy wings, and long talons in place of nails. His eyes were lambent and he hissed when the shutter remained locked against him. He flew to the next window, seeking to unlock it. I was alarmed, to see a figment of a nightmare so intent on breaking into a house.

"Is this a child's nightmare?" I asked Phelan, because I failed to recognize it.

"Yes. The demon comes and takes the child through the window," he replied.

We would have to climb after it on the trellis, which would be difficult with our shields. Phelan shed his buckler in the street and I followed suit. Together, we approached the town house.

"Is there anything else that happens?" I asked.

He waded through a bush to reach the base of the trellis, taking hold of the lattice. He glanced at me and said, "No. Just the demon and the kidnapping."

The demon finally noticed us.

He hissed from his perch on a second-story window ledge before flying to the next house.

"We'll have to be more discreet." Phelan headed to the path that wound to the backyard.

But the demon had his eye on us now, watching with a taunting glare.

"Wait, Phelan," I said. "We need to set a trap for it, or else we'll be chasing it from town house to town house until dawn."

Phelan paused. "What sort of trap?"

I was already taking a step back, returning to the street, my eyes on his house.

"Anna?" He hurried after me.

"I'm going to sit in my room with the window open and the shutters unlatched," I said, breathless. "You need to be in the backyard, prepared in case the demon manages to drag me out the window."

I waited for him to protest. To my surprise, he didn't. I slipped in the front door and locked it behind me, and Phelan went to the garden in the back, where he could see my bedroom window.

I hurried to light a candle in my chamber. I opened the window and unlatched the shutters, and I drew a chair up center to it and sat.

The rain continued to fall, a quiet melody. I was frozen to the bone, waiting to hear the demon's claws rap on my shutters.

It didn't take long.

The demon burst into my room with needles of rain. He expected to find me in bed, so I had a moment of surprise to cast my magical net. He screeched and flung himself against the wall, attempting to cut through the binds I had draped over him. They held, and I watched for a moment, until the demon had tired himself. I sought the golden key, thinking it should be somewhere on the demon's body. A place to stab him.

There was no golden weakness.

But from the corner of my eye, there was an alluring gleam.

I turned to my open window, the casement slick with rain. There was a hint of gold at the edges, and I suddenly understood, although it seemed very reckless.

I didn't give myself another moment to doubt. I called my magical net back to me, felt the corresponding recoil like a whip striking my hand. But I gritted my teeth through the shock of pain and leapt for the demon as he made to flee through the window.

He hissed as we glided into the night, as if I was suddenly a great hindrance to him, and I thought about being a child dreaming this nightmare. I thought about how the entire crux of this dream was that the child was terrified to let the demon carry them out the window. And yet how it was the key to ending it, to awaken.

The demon dissolved into smoke beneath me.

I was flying, falling, tumbling. I aimed for the closest roof and eased myself down with a slowing spell, but it was still a rough landing. I hit the shingles, knocked a few loose as I slipped, scrambling for purchase. I cursed the rain and my temerity, thinking of all those lessons when my father had instructed me to be cautious.

Those lessons felt as if they belonged to another life, another girl.

I hung from the gutter and eased my way to the corner of the house, where I could drop down to a trellis. Halfway in my descent, the lattice groaning like it wanted to break, I heard Phelan on the ground beneath me.

"Are you all right, Anna?"

I paused to glance down at him. The rain sat on his face like tears. His dark hair swept across his brow in a terribly endearing manner.

"I'm fine. The demon is gone." And the lattice responded by finally cracking beneath me. I was suddenly spilled into the darkness below, into Phelan's frantic arms.

The impact sent us sprawling into a bracken patch. My hands delved into the damp soil above his shoulders, my legs straddled his waist, and I felt every point of contact between us. The heaves of his breaths beneath me. How his warmth chased away the cold nip of the night.

I attempted to slip off him, stiff and awkward in my drenched clothes. He grasped my waist, tightening his hold on my hips as if he wanted me to remain. Or perhaps to simply cease moving.

One of his hands rose to carefully tuck a thread of tangled hair behind my ear. So he could behold my face in dim light. And when his thumb traced my lips, as if he had imagined kissing them . . . a gasp escaped me. I felt a hint of pleasure and pain, both lurking deep in my chest. I winced as if a needle was prodding my heart.

"Anna?" he whispered, uncertain.

I instantly shrank away, realizing this was foolish. To allow myself to be so close to him and enjoy it. His fingertips grazed my jaw as I retreated. I refused to acknowledge the confusion and chaos of my feelings then, but I knew I would have to later, like a sunburn appearing on my skin.

"We should go," I said, successfully sliding off him this time. "Another battle awaits us."

That sobered him. Maybe the knight would come, and maybe he wouldn't. But lying in a garden entwined with Phelan Vesper was a bad idea, either way.

We returned to our original post, the streets empty and lamplit, gleaming with rain. I fixed my shield upon my arm, preparing for the second leg of the night. My adrenaline was beginning to ebb. I felt sore and weary, and my drenched clothes were chafing my skin.

It's almost impossible to judge time on a new moon night. I don't know how long Phelan and I stood there, our breath like clouds, our skin pebbled from the cold, our shields waiting on our arms.

But it felt like hours until the silence was broken by an unexpected sound. Someone was singing in the distance, a slurred chorus that echoed off the town houses.

Phelan and I both whirled to look behind us. In a ring of lamplight, I saw a man stumble. I could see he had a bottle of wine in his hand, and he continued to sing, defiant and foolish and utterly unaware of himself.

"Gods above," Phelan said, exasperated.

"I take it he's not part of the nightmare," I said, but I felt a jolt of worry. It was always dangerous for residents to wander the streets on the new moon, even after a nightmare had broken. I had heard horrible stories of how magicians had inadvertently slain innocent mortals who had been in the streets, because the wardens believed they were part of the nightmare. Of course, this typically only happened to magicians who were unprepared, those who did not study and memorize their nightmare ledger.

"It's Allan Hugh," Phelan groaned. "And no, he's not part of the nightmare. He's very real."

"You should do something," I whispered, thinking it would be disastrous to have a drunk Allan wandering the streets if the knight appeared. "Can you take him home?"

But even *that* was a risk—to make Allan's wife have no choice but to unlock her door on this capricious night.

Phelan sighed. "Yes, he lives one street over. I'll take him there now. Will you—"

"I'll wait here for you," I said.

Phelan must have heard the resolve in me. I was not about to trail him and this drunk individual. He nodded and began to run up the street, splashing through puddles, calling for Allan's attention.

I watched until they had vanished into the darkness. I soaked in the silence again; I closed my eyes and leaned my head back, face upturned to the sky.

And that's when I felt it. A tremble in the cobblestones beneath me.

A shift in the wind around me.

The rain eased, as if nature was retreating, hiding.

I opened my eyes and watched the knight appear.

He was unchanged. He walked his same steady, heavy-footed pace. His armor was still bloodstained. His helm still inspired a blaze of terror in me. He drew his sword and the tip of it rang on the stones alongside him, a warning for me to run from him.

I walked to meet him, shield ready on my arm.

I'm faster, I reminded myself. *Stay out of his reach and if you stumble, remember the shield.*

He took his first swing at me. I danced out of the sword's path. I would wear him out, and I taunted him again, stepping close to provoke him, darting away from his reach. He swung, I evaded. I believed I could continue doing this until dawn, and I had every intention to until the knight feigned a move and I misread him. He turned and caught me by surprise, but my reflexes saved me.

I swung my shield around to block. His sword lodged within the wood and I expected my buckler to crack in two, but it held firm, suddenly illuminated as its enchantment stirred. I was drenched in golden light, and the knight bent to it, to me. I stumbled backward, and his sword came with me, embedded in my shield. I was amazed at the sight of him disarmed.

He seemed stunned as well.

And I claimed that moment of surprise, just as I had done with the demon. I swung my shield and the hilt of his sword at his chest, and the blow rocked him from his feet. He went down with a grunt on his back.

"Anna!" Phelan shouted from a distance, and I knew he was running to me. But I didn't spare him a glance.

I let my shield slide from my tingling arm and stood over the knight, my foot on his chest. He was dazed. Frozen on the cobblestones. I knelt and removed his helm.

The streetlight spilled over his face. A face I knew alarmingly well.

It was my father.

29

I couldn't breathe; I couldn't move. I hovered above the knight and stared at his face—familiar and yet hauntingly strange in the darkness of the new moon. A face that was beloved to me. And yet there was no recognition within him as he stared up at me. His eyes were unforgiving and sharp as flint; his auburn hair was lank in the rain. His mouth was pressed in a hard line, and vengeance burned within him like stars.

I recognized him, and yet part of me denied it.

My father appeared younger with the shadows playing over his features. Startled, I realized I had seen him like this before. On the night when the Vesper brothers had arrived to Hereswith and Papa had been sick. He had asked me to glamour him to look hale, and as I cast the spell, I had caught a glimpse of his younger self.

Before I could demand why he appeared this way, what he was doing, how he had walked into this nightmare, my father reached out and took hold of my throat. His grip was fierce, unrelenting. I gasped and clawed at his hand, but my fingers were useless against his armor.

He is going to kill me.

The thoughts burst in my mind as the world tilted. I struggled; I viciously fought him, and it only made my blood thrum faster. I could hear Phelan shout my name again, his boots echoing on the street as he ran for me. My sight was dimming, my lungs burning. And yet I held my father's vicious gaze, unwavering, and rasped, "Papa . . . *Papa!*"

My father grew still.

He stared at me, his eyes widening like he had woken from a dream. Before I could rouse another strangled word in my throat, he released me, hurling me up and away from him as if I were weightless. My hair streaked across my face as I glided through the rain, as I hit the cobblestones with a painful jar.

Phelan reached me a moment later.

His arms came about my body, drawing me up and holding me firm against him. At first I thought I didn't need his strength until I realized that my feet were numb.

"Anna? Anna!" Phelan turned me toward him.

I gasped a broken, terrible sound. My neck throbbed as I leaned into him. My voice emerged, weak and brittle. "Where is he?"

Phelan glanced beyond me to where the knight had been just moments ago.

"He's gone, Anna."

I didn't believe him. I looked to where I had seen my father, gleaming in bloodstained armor. Where my father had almost strangled me.

It was as Phelan said. The knight had vanished, retreated. But his sword remained lodged in my shield, and my shield lay on the cobblestones. A testament to what had happened.

I felt my awareness fading and I bit my lip until the pain sharpened me.

Stay awake, stay awake . . .

Phelan's breath was labored as he led me to his house and ascended the porch stairs. He bore me inside and kicked the door closed. The sound reverberated through my body and I could see the concern in his expression, a wrinkle of fear on his brow.

He carried me upstairs, past my bedroom, into the lavatory. He spoke and the candles ignited, washing us in rosy light. Gently, he set me down on the tile floor, propped up against the cabinets. I knew there was a mirror, directly above me, and it hovered like a blade about to fall.

If I wasn't so drained, I would have shattered it.

Phelan knelt and drew my hair away from my neck, studying the column of my throat. I imagined bruises would soon bloom.

"I'm fine," I said, and I wanted to send him away but couldn't find the strength. His fingertips traced my neck up to my jaw, to the arch of my cheek. A soft caress that made me ache. He held my face in his hands, and I closed my eyes, surprised by the surge of trust I felt for him. I breathed deeply until I had calmed myself. Slowly, I could feel my limbs again. Slowly, my fear faded, and a bitter coldness replaced it. The ice seeped into my chest.

I opened my eyes.

Phelan was watching me intently. Whatever shone in my gaze made his hands fall away.

"I'm going to draw you a warm bath," he said, reaching for the handles. Water began to flow from the faucet, and he cast a heating spell over it. The chamber became warm, steamy. Lavender intoxicated the air.

I could have fallen asleep, propped up against those cabinets, lulled by the sound of running water.

But I continued to see my father's hauntingly young face, feel his hand on my neck, choking me.

"Did you see the knight's face?" I asked.

Phelan was still on his knees, tending to the tub. A jar of bath crystals was in his hand, and he poured them into the water. "No, I didn't. But you did, Anna?"

"Yes," I whispered, and Phelan waited until the tub was full before turning off the faucets. He returned to me, on his knees.

"Did you recognize the knight?" he tentatively asked. "You seemed to hesitate when the helm was removed."

"I've never seen him before," I lied, and Phelan nodded. But I thought I saw his eyes shutter, his jaw flex.

"Do you need me to help you into the tub?"

I almost laughed until I realized how shaky I was. I tried to unlace my bodice, but my hands were trembling. "If you could help me undress . . . I can do the rest."

He did so with great care, unbuttoning my boots first. He slipped them off my feet one by one. He unlaced my bodice and drew my skirt down, and I could hear him breathing, deep and steady, like his heart was pounding. Soon I was sitting in my damp chemise and my knee-high stockings, and he hesitated before he reached beneath the hem of my undergarment to find the top edge of my right sock. I felt his fingertips trace my skin as he slowly pulled the wool down my leg, leaving goose bumps in his wake.

I closed my eyes as he reached for the second one, and I was wondering if I should let him completely undress me when he paused, my stocking pooled around my ankle.

I looked at him, brow arched. He was frozen, staring at something on my left calf. Two scars made by fangs, on a night not unlike this one. When I had nearly drowned and had pulled myself into Phelan's boat. They were scars I thought he would never see, and so I had left them when Mazarine transformed me.

He met my gaze. I couldn't read the thoughts that lurked within him—if he suspected I was not who I appeared to be—but nor did I have the energy to reassure or lie to him.

"I can handle it from here," I whispered, and waited for him to slip away, the door latching behind him. I drew myself up with help of the cabinets, kicking off my left stocking. I let my chemise fall away and I stepped into the bath, sinking into the warm water with a tremor.

Alone, at last, I indulged the softer side of myself. I covered my mouth and wept.

I don't know how long my mind whirled before a wave of misgivings crashed on me. I embraced the pain and finally relived my father's betrayal, seeking to make sense of it. How long had he been hiding enchanted armor, and why was he stepping into nightmares? What power was he channeling to do it? Why had he not recognized me? Why had he appeared to look twenty years younger?

I wiped away my tears, my neck aching from his brutal hand. And then I studied my own palms, my fingers, the length of my brown hair. All of them lies, a facade that I had made for myself.

"Oh my gods," I whispered, watching my hands quiver. My father must also be wearing a disguise. He was two-faced, as I was. How old was he, truly? Why would he need to hide his face? His age?

I would have to go to him and insist he answer my questions. Questions that threatened to burn through me, questions that I wanted to hone into swords and pierce him with.

He had lied to me. He was a hypocrite. *He had nearly strangled me.*

I laid my fingers over my neck; I felt the stone half of my heart grow colder than the ice on the mountains.

I would have to take him by surprise at the mines that evening, when he left his shift. And while I felt too restless for it, I slept most of the day. Late afternoon sunlight crept through my curtains when I woke, and I saw that Mrs. Stirling had left a tray of food by the bed. It must have been hours ago, because the tea and soup were cold.

I rose and dressed, avoiding my reflection in the shattered

mirror. My neck was sore; I imagined the bruises were beginning to show on my skin as I silently crept down the stairs.

I paused in the foyer, listening. I reached out with my magic, mindful to go gently, or else I might gain their attention.

Mrs. Stirling was in the kitchen. She stood at the counter making dumplings. Flour was on her apron, on her face. She sang beneath her breath. Farther down the corridor, I sensed Phelan in the library. The doors were open, and he sat with the book of nightmares cracked before him. He was so still he could have been hewn from stone as he stared at the page. His worry hung in the air like a thundercloud. And then beyond the back door, in the garden, was Deacon. He was supposed to be gathering herbs for dinner but he was preoccupied with whittling a stick into an arrow.

I called my magic back to me and slipped away from the town house, careful to make no sound.

I hurried down the street, fighting the sensation I was being followed. It eventually overcame me so greatly that I did pause and wait in the alley between two shops, to see if anyone was trailing me. Phelan, most likely. But I never saw him, and I imagined I was simply being paranoid, after discovering that my father was not who I believed him to be.

I called a horse and cab and traveled to the northwest point of the city.

I lingered in a shadow by the mine yard, waiting for dark, when my father's shift would be over.

It seemed like I waited an eternity before the miners began to file out of the earth, their faces streaked with grime. My father was at the end of the line, his head bowed, his boots dragging. I intercepted him, grasping hold of his shirt and tugging.

"What—?" He let out a startled sound until he realized it was me. He followed me to an alley, and his concern nearly smothered me.

"Has he discovered you? Do we need to flee?"

I gaped at my father. He acted as if nothing had happened the night before. As if he had not tried to strangle me.

"Clem," he urged, impatient.

"Who are you?" I countered coldly.

He blinked, taken aback. I could just discern his face—the face of a forty-seven-year-old man who I had implicitly trusted—as a nearby lamp limned us with faint light.

"What?"

"You heard me," I snapped.

"I have no idea what you mean, Clem."

"It's Anna. And you do know, Ambrose." I drew my hair away from my neck, so he could see the bruises.

The shock and fury on his face were electrifying. My father reached for me but I evaded him, my stomach knotting. I was going to be sick. I was shaking, fuming. My anger was so keen it felt like I might break apart.

"Did he do this?" he demanded, his voice trembling.

"No, Phelan did not do this to me. *You* did. Last night."

"Last night?" he whispered, bewildered, and then he realized it had been the new moon. "Wait a minute, Clem. *Wait!*"

But I had already taken a step away from him. When he moved to follow, I held up my hand and he halted.

"Where did you get the armor? What spells are you casting to step into the dreams? Why did you wound Phelan twice? Why are you disguising your face?"

He stared at me as if I had lost my mind. I felt trapped in an upside-down world with him, one where nothing made sense, and all I could hear was my own uneven pulse, beating like a drum in my ears.

"I have no idea what you speak of, Clem!"

My eyes burned with angry tears. "I know you're wearing a glamour. One that makes you look far older than you are. And I want you to stay away from me, in both worlds. The waking as well as the new moon realm. Stay away from Mama and Imonie. Do not come near me or Phelan again, or I will have the duke eviscerate you. Do you hear me?"

"Daughter, please," he said, stepping nearer to me. "Explain to me what happened. Did you see me in a dream?"

For a moment, I almost believed him, that he had no recollection of last night. But I wouldn't be deceived by him and his act.

"Don't come any closer to me!" I warned. "Did you not hear me? I don't *trust* you. You are vile and deceptive and I want no part of you."

I turned and began to stride away.

"Clem! *Clem!*" he shouted, which only fueled my anger as he recklessly exposed my cover.

I gathered my stealth charm about me, slipping from his reach and his sight. And yet I couldn't resist. I glanced over my shoulder to see my father on his knees in the street, dazed as if I had just given him a mortal wound.

30

It was late when I returned to the town house. Mrs. Stirling and Deacon had departed for the night, and I found Phelan sitting in the drawing room before the fire, a glass of wine in hand.

"Miss Neven," he greeted me as I joined him in the room. I should have known then that something was wrong, but my mind was trapped in a daze. "Are you all right? We were worried about you."

I sank into the chair across from his. "I'm fine. I went for a walk. I apologize for missing dinner." I met his gaze, shocked when I saw that his dark hair was unbound, brushing his collarbones. Why was he regarding me in such a way, as if he were memorizing me?

"Is there something on your mind?" he asked.

"No." It was strange how his eyes, slowly taking me in, made me ache to be known. To not have to hide and pretend and feel this rock in my chest.

"You know you can confide in me, Anna."

Let it crack, I dared myself. *Let yourself fall and come undone and be who you want.*

"I know."

The enticement lasted for a minute before I regained control of myself, glancing away from his intensity. I watched the safety of the fire. And I realized I was just like my father, cut from the same cloth. Deception and secrets and vengeance and lies ran thick in our blood.

"Can I tempt you with a round of Seven Wraiths?" Phelan asked quietly.

"I'm sick of Seven Wraiths," I replied, pinching the bridge of my nose when I inevitably envisioned my father in that blood-stained armor.

"Then grab another game. I think it'll take your mind off whatever is troubling you," he said. "At least for tonight, while you are here with me."

I sighed but conceded to look at him once more. His gaze was on my neck. On my bruises, I realized, and I watched as his knuckles drained white.

"Very well," I said, and rose.

I was glad to turn away from him, walking to where the cupboard sat against the wall, just beneath the mirror. I crouched to avoid its taunting gleam, opening the cabinet and sifting through the other board games until I found one that seemed promising. I stood without a second thought.

I hadn't heard him move.

I hadn't sensed his presence, not until it was too late.

Phelan stood behind me. I met his stare in the mirror, and his shock sent a pang through me.

He beheld me as I truly was, the girl he had first met and championed. Neither of us moved or spoke. It felt as if ice had fettered my ankles, sprouted in my chest, making it difficult to think through the frost that gleamed between us.

And then he broke it with his voice—the ice and the uncertainty and my entire facade.

"Clem."

The sound was beautiful and terrible, piercing me like an arrow. I felt a crack in my chest. It wasn't deep; it was only a hairline break, the stone faithfully holding to my heart, even as the pain swarmed. I pressed a fist to my breast, clenching my teeth until I thought they would chip.

Hold yourself together. Don't crumble like this.

I did the first thing that came to mind. I hurled a spell at him, even though he hadn't moved or threatened me. No, all he seemed capable of doing was staring at my reflection, stricken.

Vines rose up from the rug. Thorns and leaves and indigo blossoms. They wove together in a whispering rush, and my intentions were to trap him, to form a cage about him. It would give me the time I needed to flee, but when I thought about running . . . I had nowhere to go. For that had been my father's plan all along, and it was now worthless in my eyes. And when I saw the pain and betrayal in Phelan's face . . . I could not entrap him. I reined my spell back a fraction, so that my vines would form a wall between us. A barrier.

He studied it for a moment. My impulsive defense.

I watched through the gaps in the vines and leaves as he slipped a dagger from the inner pocket of his jacket. He began to cut through my enchantment, hack by hack, and it gave way to him. Flowers sundered beneath his blade, their petals cascading to the floor. The vines snapped and recoiled; the leaves hissed into steam as he dashed through them. My spell held valiantly, giving me the time I needed to run.

Run, I thought, and yet I couldn't move.

My desire ran dark and deep. I wanted to face him again, wholly known. I wanted to answer his challenge.

I wanted to clash with him.

And so I waited and watched him work through my enchantment. My thorns dragged over his face, leaving bright scratches behind. They clawed at his hair, at his clothes, and when he finally emerged on my side of the wall, he looked the most disheveled I had ever seen him. He looked untamed, half wild.

He stared at me, panting, blue petals and silver leaves in his hair. He tossed his dagger aside.

Slowly, we circled each other, our gazes holding as if we were both prey, both predator.

Say something! I wanted to shout at him. His silence was overbearing, crushing. I couldn't read his thoughts.

And then he smiled, but it was scathing. Sharp and unfamiliar.

The sight of it sent a thrill through me.

I hurled another spell at him, an arc of light. He was ready for it, taking it in his palm, dissolving it into shadows. For all my disguise, he knew me well, and that was maddening. I struck him again, again, but he caught my spells effortlessly, as if he knew exactly what to expect from me. He turned my fire into smoke, my wind into dust, my light into shadows. He accepted everything I gave him and yet he didn't retaliate. He refused to counter my moves, and I didn't know if he was waiting for me to tire myself or if he simply didn't want to risk hurting me.

This would never end. The two of us circling, me striking, him absorbing.

I turned away from him, frustrated that he wouldn't spar with me, and he caught me around the waist. I tripped over my own vine, snaking across the floor, and down we went. We tangled, our limbs entwining and our hands catching and our breaths mingling.

I saw it in his eyes, at last. The shock of my deception was wearing thin, and the realization kicked in like a second heartbeat. I watched his eyes darken when he remembered my interview, how I had attacked him. When he remembered all the lies I had spouted to him. When I had told him to get on his knees and apologize. When he had tried to summon me and thought he had failed.

"I should have known it was you," he whispered, his mouth dangerously close to mine.

His skin flushed with anger, indignation. I was satisfied to see it, to know my vengeance had run its course. That I had hurt him as he had once hurt me.

We rolled on the floor, caught up with each other, unable to separate ourselves as if a spell had bound us, and I finally emerged on top. I straddled his waist, held him beneath me, and before I knew it, I called his abandoned dagger. The weapon came willingly into my hand; I set its glittering edge to his throat and he went still, his gaze fixed on mine.

And I thought . . . *Is this who I am becoming?*

I didn't recognize myself in this tenuous moment.

"Clem," Phelan said. *"Clem . . ."* He dared to take a gentle hold of my wrist.

I recoiled from him. I tossed his dirk away; it landed with a plink in the rug. I slid off him and stood, trembling.

He sat forward and rose with fluid grace, putting a safe distance between us.

I felt him stare at me, a heated moment I was reluctant to acknowledge. But soon the draw to meet his eyes was irresistible. I glanced up and held his gaze, unrepentant.

I knew I had wounded him, deeply. He lowered his guard; he looked devastated.

"I hope you enjoyed every moment you played me a fool," he said.

"Phelan," I whispered, but my voice turned to ash in my mouth.

"I hope you achieved whatever it was you wanted. I hope all your lies were worth it." He took a step back; I felt the space between us like a chasm had formed in the floor.

I felt completely hollow.

"Bravo, Miss Madigan." Phelan held out his arms to grant me a mock bow. He spoke a charm beneath his breath. I had never heard it before, and I tensed until I realized it was not directed at me but at him. I watched him fade away.

He was gone.

Alone, I sank to the floor, to the remains of my vines and thorns and withering magic.

31

He didn't come home.

I sat in the library at his desk, watching patches of sun travel across the floor. I waited for him, words gathering in my chest, building like water behind a dam. Words I wanted, *needed*, to say to him. An explanation. An apology, even. Maybe. But Phelan never returned.

My disguise still held firm as my own skin. When I drew a deep breath and held it in my chest, I could feel the small crack within me. I wondered how much longer I had until the stone half of my heart shattered. If I could suffer a few more blows before the spell relinquished me.

Mrs. Stirling found me at noon, concern creasing her brow. "Miss Neven? May I ask what happened in the drawing room?"

I had cleaned it the best I could, but my vines had left a few fissures in the wall and the mirror. "A slight altercation, Mrs. Stirling."

Her eyes widened. "I hope no one was harmed?"

"No, all is well." The lies still flowed smoothly from my mouth. Gods above, I sounded just like my father.

She nodded but didn't seem convinced. "A package has arrived for you."

At first I thought it must be from Phelan. Something ominous, something to make me pay for all my deceit. But Deacon carried in a narrow clothes box and set it carefully on the desk before me.

"What is this?" I asked, wary.

"Your dress, Miss Neven," Mrs. Stirling said. "For the countess's dinner tonight."

Oh. That was tonight. It was the seventeenth of November, and I had hardly known it.

I rubbed my brow, keenly distressed. But I tempered my feelings before Mrs. Stirling or Deacon could detect them, and I smiled. "Thank you. Have you heard from Phelan this morning? He left early, before I woke."

"Yes, Miss Neven. He wrote and said he would be away for a few weeks."

"Oh?" A few *weeks*? I paled at the thought, wondering where he had gone.

"Did he . . . did he not tell you?" Mrs. Stirling asked kindly. She finally inferred that the "slight altercation" had been between us and that I was completely in the dark.

"He didn't. But no matter. I'll tend to things here while he's away." I granted her and Deacon a smile, but it was weak, and they saw through it.

"Oh, and you received a letter." Mrs. Stirling reached into her apron pocket to extend an envelope to me.

I accepted it, immediately recognizing the duke's crest.

"Let us know if you need anything, Miss Neven," the housekeeper said as she herded her grandson from the library.

I scowled as I opened the duke's letter. I was not surprised by his message, succinctly written:

Miss Neven,
I surmise that the new moon was a success.
Please send me a detailed description of
the man in question, as soon as possible.
Lord Ivor Deryn
Duke of Bardyllis

I held the duke's letter over a candle flame and watched it burn. I was not ready to expose my father. And yet I didn't know what I was waiting for, either.

I stared at the clothes box, but refrained from opening it. I quickly gathered my cloak and departed, heading to the town house that Olivette and Nura shared a few streets over.

They were sitting in the dining room still wrapped in their robes, eating a late brunch. I was suddenly overcome with strife, wondering if Phelan had revealed my deceit to them. . . .

"Anna!" Olivette greeted me warmly. "Come join us! There's plenty."

Her vibrant response was a relief. But Nura sensed my distress, even as I sought to hide it. She set down her teacup and bluntly said, "What's wrong?"

I hesitated on the threshold. "I was wondering if you two had seen Phelan today. Perhaps he dropped by this morning?"

"Phelan?" Olivette echoed, glancing to Nura. "No, he hasn't."

"And he hasn't sent a letter in the post to you?"

"No," Nura said, rising. "Did something happen?"

"Yes," I breathed. "We got in an argument."

"During the new moon?"

"No, afterward. He left and I haven't seen him and I don't know where to find him." What was *wrong* with me? I sounded desperate. If I didn't know better, one would think I had feelings for him, and I cleared my throat, embarrassed.

You are afraid he will expose you, I told myself. And there was a kernel of truth in that statement. He now held something over me, and I was uncertain what to expect from him. If he would use it against me. If I should go ahead and reveal myself before he did.

Nura reached out to gently take my arm. "Here. Sit and eat. Things always feel worse on an empty stomach."

I sat. My shoulders were sore; my knees ached. I drank a cup of tea and relented to eat a few bites of egg and steak, Olivette watching me with obvious concern.

"Do you want to tell us what you quarreled about?" she whispered.

I set down my fork. "I . . . no. It was foolish, though. And he is quite angry at me."

"That is so hard to imagine," Olivette said. "I don't think I've ever seen Phelan angry! He's so mild, so even-tempered."

Until he met me, I thought.

"It's natural in our line of work, Anna," said Nura. "Partners will inevitably butt heads. You shouldn't beat yourself up over it. I'm sure Phelan is taking the time he needs to sort through whatever has come between you. But you'll see him tonight, to smooth things over with him."

I frowned. "Tonight?"

"At his mother's dinner. He wouldn't miss that."

"He wouldn't?"

Olivette smiled. "Of course not! His mother gives him an order and he follows it, every time."

"Oli," Nura warned. "You shouldn't speak of the countess like that."

"What?" Olivette shrugged. "It's the truth."

I stood, suddenly overwhelmed by nerves. "I probably shouldn't go tonight."

What if he planned to expose me at the dinner? But the more I imagined it . . . would Phelan do something like that to me?

"What? Yes, you should come, Anna," Olivette insisted. "You can ride with us tonight!"

I was silent, contemplating all my options. To go, to stay. To run, to confront. Nura stood beside me. Gently, she drew the hair away from my neck and saw my bruises.

"Is this Phelan's doing?" she asked in a low, sharp voice. One that made me shiver.

"No, it wasn't him," I replied. "An unfortunate result of the new moon."

Olivette gasped, also seeing the bruises from across the table.

"Anna! Oh my gods, what happened?"

"It's nothing," I said, taking a step away from them. "I'm perfectly fine." And it was a good reminder for me to glamour the bruises until they healed. "I think I will ride with you tonight to the dinner, if you don't mind."

"Of course," Nura said. "We'll come pick you up at half past five."

I left before they could press me for further answers, retreating to Phelan's town house.

I rested most of the afternoon, but soon my uneasiness swelled, and I prepared for the countess's dinner.

The dress Phelan had tailored for me looked to have been spun from gold. It rushed off my shoulders and softly held my curves, tiny jewels sewn along the hem and the neckline. I had never worn something so beautiful. It felt like sunlight on my skin, warm and soft. Alluring.

I glamoured my bruises and then touched a few lank strands of my hair. I decided to braid it into a crown, weaving within the plaits a golden ribbon that I found in my wardrobe.

The sun set. The stars were beginning to smolder in the sky when Olivette and Nura arrived. I sat on the bench across from them, rocking with the sway of the cab, and listened to them talk. A low, pleasant stream of conversation, one that I failed to join, because my thoughts were distant, roaming.

"My father will be so delighted to finally meet you tonight, Anna," Olivette said.

I blinked, returning to the cab. "Your father will be at dinner tonight?"

"Yes."

"How many people will be here, do you think?" I asked non-chalantly, but my dread rose. Something was going to happen tonight, and it wasn't going to be pleasant.

"I'm not sure," Olivette said, glancing at Nura. "This is the first time we've been invited to one of the countess's dinners. They are selective affairs, though. Many of the upper class hope to win an invitation."

That did nothing to ease my sense of foreboding.

All too soon, the carriage arrived at the countess's mansion.

It was a grand estate, out of reach from the street by a long, private driveway. The house was built of creamy stone and a gray shingled roof, three storied with large mullioned windows, creeping ivy and multiple chimneys. The front doors were on the second story, and two curved staircases blossomed from the court-yard up to the entrance. Through the dusky light, I could see a long stretch of shallow water to our left—a reflection pool—and the hedges of a garden.

I followed Nura and Olivette out of the coach and up the stairs.

A butler took our cloaks and led us deeper into the mansion, to a spacious ballroom, where the floors were blue-veined marble, the ceilings arched and coffered. Hanging chandeliers burgeoned with silver wrought leaves and candles.

Music haunted the air, and servants milled about with flutes of sparkling champagne. I expected to see a crowded room, a night full of people I could lose myself among. But it was a small, inti-mate party.

Nura and Olivette drifted toward the musicians, but I remained standing, soaking in the grandeur of the room. And I couldn't help myself; I looked for Phelan among the black jackets and top hats.

He was nowhere to be seen, and I buried my disappointment just as the countess caught sight of me.

"Miss Neven," she said, and I sank into a deep curtsy. "I am honored you have accepted my invitation."

"Thank you, lady. The honor is mine."

"Come, take a turn around the room with me," she invited. "We are still waiting on a few more guests to arrive, but let me introduce you to an old friend of mine in the meantime."

I fell into a stilted stride beside her and soon realized she was taking me directly to the duke, who was standing beside a man I recognized—the smith who had created the shields for me and Phelan.

"This is Lord Deryn, the Duke of Bardyllis," the countess said. "And this is Aaron Wolfe, the most renowned smith in the province, as well as Olivette's father."

"Miss Neven," the duke greeted me with a languid smile. "A pleasure, as always."

"Your Grace." I curtsied, and then looked at Olivette's father. "Mr. Wolfe."

"I shall leave the three of you," the countess said suddenly, as if it had been her task all along to deposit me at the duke's feet. And perhaps it had been, I thought irritably as I watched her stride across the room.

"Were the shields a success, Miss Neven?" Mr. Wolfe asked.

His face and voice were so carefully guarded that I couldn't tell if he was surprised to see me here tonight.

"Yes, Mr. Wolfe. Thank you."

The smith nodded, and there was an awkward lull until he glanced at the duke and said, "I should go say hello to my daughter."

I wanted to beg him to stay, to not leave me alone with the duke, but I held my tongue. When Lord Deryn stepped closer to me, I flinched.

"I trust you received my letter today," the duke said in a low voice, offering me his arm.

I hesitated, but only for a breath. I rested my hand in the crook of his elbow and permitted him to slowly walk me around the edges of the room.

"Yes, Your Grace. I apologize that I have not had time to write a response."

"You saw the knight's face?"

"I did."

"Can you describe him to me?"

I envisioned my father's face. The words rose to illustrate him, but I couldn't speak them. Even with his betrayal, I couldn't find the desire to expose him. "No, Your Grace. I fear it was a dark night. It would be impossible for me to describe it in detail to you."

"Then we are in luck," the duke said, coming to a stop.

I glanced up at him, but his gaze was elsewhere, cutting across the room.

"Did the knight perhaps look like that man?" he asked,

indicating a new dinner guest.

I turned to see who he spoke of, and the hair rose on my arms.

My father stood just within the ballroom, speaking to the countess. Clean, his beard trimmed, his hair slicked back. He was not a miner but the magician I had always known him to be. He wore a top hat and white waistcoat and black jacket with a rose in his lapel. On his arm was my mother, dressed in a bloodred gown overlaid with a net of black stones. And trailing them was none other than Imonie, wearing a blue dress with lace sleeves, her steel-blond hair swept up in a loose bun.

I froze, but my mind flooded with anger, shock, a multitude of questions.

What were they doing here?

My silence was answer enough for the duke.

"Good, Miss Neven," he said, amused. "I am glad Mr. Madigan could whet your memory. Now, if you will excuse me."

My hand slipped from his elbow as he rejoined the countess. I continued to stand, stranded. My father sensed my stare, his eyes rising to meet mine.

He appeared just as surprised to see me, his mouth going slack. If not for my mother guiding him away, distracting him with a flute of champagne, I'm sure my father and I would have fought in the countess's ballroom, ruining my guise for good.

Even Imonie paused, setting a tense gaze on me. I almost went to her; she had always been my refuge, a safe place for me to call home. And yet tonight she was like a stranger.

Ignore them, I told myself. *You have never seen them before. . . .*

The ice thickened in my chest. I was cold, calm, poised. A girl with a stone trapped in her ribs. And then I felt his stare.

My eyes scanned the ballroom until I found Phelan nearby, standing in one of the archways, draped in shadow, watching me. I wondered how long he had been leaning against the frame, observing my precarious walk around the room. But the moment our gazes met, the glittering, firelit world faded around us. There were only shadows and a path that connected him to me, a path that felt treacherous to walk in the sense that it might undo me.

His face was smooth of expression, his eyes inscrutable. I wanted to know what he thought of me, when he had started to suspect I wasn't who I claimed to be. And I didn't know if he planned to expose me, or if he would ever forgive me. I told myself not to care, but a small fracture was within me now, and my regrets began to trickle through it.

Even the deepest of ice eventually gives way to fire, Mazarine had once told me.

I turned away from Phelan, unable to look upon him a moment longer.

I found my way back to Nura and Olivette, who were in high spirits.

"Oh, there's Phelan," Nura said, looking beyond me.

"Why isn't he joining us?" Olivette wondered, waving him over. "Have you spoken to him yet, Anna?"

"No."

Nura exchanged a swift glance with me before saying, "I'll go speak with him."

She left me and Olivette, and I tried to focus on conversing with her, but my worries tugged, and I watched Phelan speak to Nura across the room. He was saying something solemn to her. She frowned, listening. And then she glanced back to where Olivette and I were standing, and I thought for certain he had just exposed me.

"Shall we go speak with your father?" I asked Olivette with a hint of desperation, lacing my arm with hers. But no sooner did we begin to approach Mr. Wolfe did my parents begin to speak to the smith, and I came to a halt.

"What's the matter?" Olivette asked.

"Do you know those people? The ones speaking to your father?"

She studied my parents. Papa looked up at me, held my gaze for a beat too long.

"The woman is Sigourney Britelle, one of the most esteemed performance magicians in the province. Have you ever been to one of her shows, Anna?"

"No, I have not."

"Phelan should take you to one soon, then," Olivette said. "As for the man . . . I've never seen him before, but he seems familiar with her." She paused and then added with a hint of anger, "And he keeps looking at you. Do you want me to say something to him?"

"No, but thank you, Olivette." I narrowed my eyes at Papa. He finally ceased glancing at me with that worried gleam.

Sweat began to bead my skin and I reached for a flute of champagne, a tremor in my hand.

I watched Imonie next from the corner of my eye, and when the countess walked a loose circle around her . . . my dread turned into a leaden thing, weighing me down. Their conversation didn't look friendly; I openly observed as the countess finally ceased her predatory walk about Imonie, and their lips moved but I couldn't read them from where I stood.

Why would someone as haughty as **Lady Raven** invite my parents, Imonie, me? Why would she invite someone like Olivette's father, who worked with his hands and kept to the shadows? Why would she invite Nura and Olivette? I couldn't make sense of this dinner party and the odd mixture of guests, and it only heightened the sense that something was wrong.

Nura returned to us. I struggled to focus on her, waiting to feel her scathing glare, for her to expose me for the fraud I was. It never came; she was too preoccupied with Olivette. She wove their fingers together—brown and white—and whispered, "Come here, Oli. We need to speak."

I watched them retreat to a quiet corner of the ballroom. I felt bare, alienated. I drained my champagne and decided I would leave. This night held nothing promising or good for me, and I didn't care if I offended the countess.

I turned and nearly stepped into Phelan.

"Going somewhere, Miss Neven?" he said, cordial but cold. The cadence he would give to a stranger.

"Yes. I'm going home. Wherever that might be." But I didn't step away. I stood facing him, so close I could smell the spice of his aftershave. "Will you let me pass, Mr. Vesper? I know I'm the last person you want to see tonight."

"You read minds now?"

"Yes. For three gold coins."

"You seem to have already emptied my pockets," he said. "Or else I would pay."

"Go ahead, then, Mr. Vesper."

He arched his brow. "Go ahead with what?"

"Expose me. Reveal who I am. That's why you told your mother to invite my parents and Imonie here tonight, no? Take your vengeance on me and let's call a truce. We can part ways and you never have to see my deceptive face again."

He smiled, but it wasn't gentle. It was a wince, as if something within him ached, and he leaned closer to me. "I know you believe this night is about you, Miss Neven. Let me assure you: it's not. And you can leave now if you want. I won't stop you. But you will come to regret your impulsive departure when the sun rises."

"You speak in riddles," I said, breathless with anger. "Why are my parents here?"

"You will discover that soon enough," he replied. "If you choose to remain."

It was a challenge. One he knew I couldn't resist.

The dinner bell rang.

I followed the stream of guests into the dining hall, surprised when Phelan chose to sit beside me. The table was long and narrow, sparkling with fine china and glasses and silver candelabras. Once everyone had taken a seat, I noticed that two chairs were empty.

"Two more guests will be arriving later," said the countess, as if she had heard my thoughts. She was the last to sit at the head of the table, the duke to her left, Imonie on her right, and only once she had taken her seat did the servants file into the dining hall bearing the first course.

It was a thick green soup I had never seen before. It was also chilled, and I didn't know what I thought about it when I forced a spoonful into my mouth.

Nura and Olivette also seemed disgusted with the green mystery. They were sitting to my left, and I watched from the corner of my eye as they took only a few polite sips. My father, who had somehow managed to sit directly across from me, drank the entire thing, savoring it.

Conversation flowed quietly. I didn't even try to engage with Phelan. He, too, was often silent, speaking minimally when the duke attempted to draw him into a discussion about dreams.

The second course arrived. Another strange dish I had never tasted before, but it looked to be roasted poultry on a bed of sautéed greens and buttery porridge, with pickled beets on the side. I didn't know how to properly eat it, so I watched my father, who once again acted as if this dish was one of his favorites. Were these recipes from Seren? I was too shy to ask, but it was the only explanation I could come up with, especially when I recalled how Imonie told me the significance of November seventeenth to the mountain duchy.

Course after course was served. All of them were bizarre and unfamiliar, and I struggled through this seemingly endless dinner, thankful that no one took much note of me. I was beginning to believe that Phelan had fooled me into staying when the dessert was delivered, a lemon pudding with berries and cream, and Phelan leaned close to me, to whisper into my ear as one does to a lover.

I didn't move as his lips brushed my cheek.

"Something is about to happen tonight," he said. "You must not expose who you are. Hold your act."

And then he leaned away from me, as if he hadn't spoken such dire words, dipping his spoon into the pudding.

My father was watching us, though. I lifted my eyes to his, and the tension eased in his face. As if he also knew what was about to unfold and he was waiting for it. . . .

The doors opened with a bang, startling half of the table.

The candlelight flickered as Phelan's brother, Lennox, entered the room. He looked windswept, his clothes wrinkled, his cravat knotted crookedly as if he had arrived here in great haste. He wasn't alone. Mazarine accompanied him. Mazarine in her human disguise.

My breath left in a rush. My body tensed until I felt Phelan's hand on my knee, beneath the table.

Hold your act.

The countess smiled and rose. "At last, you have arrived, my son. And I see you have brought our guest of honor."

"Indeed, Mother," Lennox said with a triumphant smirk. "Ms. *Mazarine* Thimble of Hereswith."

I couldn't take my eyes from her. There was a trickle of blood flowing from her lip, and her silver hair was snarled. It was almost impossible to believe that she had been bound and brought roughly into the city. Mazarine, a bloodthirsty, dangerous creature of the mountains. But in this moment, she had been tamed. Her hands were fastened behind her back.

"Perhaps you would like to sit and join us, Mazarine," the countess said. "Or perhaps you would like us to call you by your true name."

Mazarine smiled. It was frightening, even with her human face. "I will not sit and eat at your table, even if you tried to serve the best of Seren foods. Call me by my name, heiress."

Lady Raven stared at the troll. The only evidence of her displeasure was the tightening of her jaw. "Welcome, Brin of Stonefall. It has been a long time since last we met. Ambrose Madigan has shielded you well the past decade, but alas, all good things must come to an end."

Mazarine spat on the table.

Lennox took a fistful of her hair and yanked her head back, and I felt compelled to rise until Phelan tightened his hold on my knee.

Even my father gave me a sharp glance. One that ordered me not to interfere or respond.

I watched, but my mind was reeling.

"You have us all together, Lady Raven," Mazarine—*Brin*—said with a malicious gleam in her eyes. "Why delay? Prove your point."

The countess lifted her hand in response. An emerald ring gleamed on her finger.

Five servants, who had been standing against the wall, stepped forward. They no longer held platters; they held daggers. And they moved in unison, approaching the table.

Mazarine was stabbed first. A servant plunged the blade into her chest, where it met her bone with a *crack*. The troll laughed as dark blood ran down her dress, as it seeped into the silver tangles of her hair.

Next, Aaron Wolfe. Olivette's father. He didn't fight or protest as a dagger split his heart. He seemed to welcome the mortal blow, and Olivette lunged to her feet, overturning her chair, screaming and screaming and screaming. Her father didn't even look at her. He closed his eyes, sorrowful, peaceful. As if he were already dead.

The blood dripped from his chair, pooling on the rug.

My heart pounded in my ears.

An uneven rhythm.

I trembled.

Phelan's hand remained warm on my knee, holding me steady, holding my guise in place. I drew in slow, deep breaths, but the air was full of copper, the metallic taste of blood.

The duke was next. He didn't fight it either but surrendered to the blade. It pierced his broad chest and he only sighed, complaining how the countess had just ruined his best waistcoat.

When a dagger found Imonie's heart, I nearly rose from the table, to lunge across it to reach her. *No, no, no*, my thoughts rang, until she looked at me and gave the slightest shake of her head. I had seen that look before plenty of times; she was scolding me, even as her blood marred her blue dress.

Stay there, Clem. I read her thoughts. *Be patient, be shrewd.* And then my father.

The last servant approached Papa's chair. A noise of distress slipped from me when I saw the flash of the blade. The dagger sank deep into my father's heart with a wet thump, down to the silver hilt. His blood rushed forward, fast and bright like a rose had bloomed over his breast. It sprayed over the white tablecloth, speckling the china and the candelabras in crimson. I watched its cascade, numb with shock, waiting to feel my face crack like an eggshell. Because I sensed it rising; somewhere deep within me, Clem was screaming in my bones. Furious to escape. Witnessing Imonie's and my father's murder was going to shatter my disguise.

This is the end of me. My lips parted, full of ragged breaths, as if I had run for hours.

But my father remained upright. Soon his blood slowed and then ceased altogether, leaving only a red stain on his waistcoat. He sat in his chair and breathed with a pierced heart. My mother remained at his side, eyes closed and her face pale, but even she was not surprised. She wasn't protesting or reacting to the violence that was unfolding around the table.

I couldn't fathom it. I prepared myself to see Papa slump in the chair. To gasp his last breath. But the dagger held no power over him.

My father cannot die.

Olivette continued to weep, but Nura held her in her arms. Nura had known this was coming, I realized. That was what Phelan had whispered to her earlier that night, and Nura stared at him now, both furious and fearful. But Phelan's focus remained on his mother, who stood at the head of the table, calmly watching the demise of her dinner guests.

I waited for Mazarine the troll, Mr. Wolfe the smith, Lord Deryn the duke, Imonie, and my father the magician to drop dead. But they continued to breathe, sitting in their blood-soaked raiment. Waiting. Their gazes strayed to the countess.

Mazarine laughed, and the sound broke the brittle tension in the room. "You have proven who we are, Lady Raven," the troll said. "Now prove yourself to us."

The countess didn't hesitate. She took the last dagger from the servant who waited beside her chair and she plunged the blade deep into her side.

I felt Phelan flinch, but he said nothing. Beneath the table, I reached for his hand. Our fingers intertwined.

The heiress, I thought, studying the countess. And then I dwelled on her companions—the wraiths who I had held as cards in my hands. Her companions, who she had commemorated by painting them, over and over, lending her magic and her sorrow to a card game. They had been mere illustrations to me in those moments when I had been playing a game, and I had never dared to believe that I would one day sit at a table with them, beholding their accursed state of being. I had never contemplated that I was the daughter of one of them.

The advisor, I thought, staring at my father. *He was the mountain advisor.*

And Imonie? I wasn't sure what her title was among the wraiths, but all my life, I'd believed what she had told me—that her ancestry was rooted in the mountains, but she had been born in Bardyllis. Never had I imagined she had been part of the court that had sundered Seren. That she had been there when it fell apart.

My childhood, my entire life, had been built upon lies.

"Welcome, old friends," the countess said. "It has taken me years to find some of you, thanks to Brin of Stonefall's magic of disguises. But here we are, reunited after so much time apart."

"What do you want with us, Lady Raven?" the duke asked, yanking the dagger from his chest. "I was quite happy in Bardyllis. So were you."

"Happiness never lasts for our kind," the countess said before glancing at my father. "Ambrose's twin brother, Emrys, has withstood the curse for a hundred years on the mountain. We left him behind a century ago, the lost one of our alliance. He has carried the curse and walked the fortress in the clouds as penance for slaying my brother, the Duke of Seren, but now Emrys has found his way out.

"He walks dreams on the new moon, taunting us to come home. Twice he has wounded my son, and by the vengeance of his blade, I no longer had a choice but to gather you all to answer his challenge." She held up her chalice of wine, as if preparing for a toast. "We scattered like chaff when the curse began. We went our own ways and sought to live our own quiet lives. I lost track of you, as you did with me. But the time has come, my old friends. It is time we returned home. It is time we remembered ourselves and dreamt again. That we no longer wake from cold, dreamless slumber. That we live and feel as mortals do. That we die when the time comes. For we have dwelled hidden and forgotten in this province for far too long."

She paused, and I was suddenly hanging on to her every word. I felt them resound in my soul, in the dreamless depths of my being. "It is time for us to return to the mountain. It is time for us to end the curse."

PART 3

Mountain of Dreams

32

I stood in the foothills of the Seren Mountains, on the edge of Bardyllis province, savoring the cold bite of the wind as the sun set. It had taken our party a full week to travel from the city to the border, but now we were here, full of anxious thoughts and a heavy sense of foreboding.

We would approach the mountain doors the next day. Part of me hoped the doors would refuse us entrance, but Imonie had once told me that they would open if all the wraiths approached together.

I studied the fortress in the clouds, carved into the summit.

I had been traveling with the Vespers' party, everyone believing me to be Anna Neven. Save for Phelan and my parents and Imonie, all four of whom I hadn't properly spoken to since the countess's bloody dinner. I had an act to perform, and I ignored my family. But at night, when I was alone and embraced by darkness, my anger burned so bright it felt like a fever was ravaging me. Lie after lie, my parents and Imonie had fed me, allowing me to grow up beneath deceit.

I didn't want to even look at them.

But I knew I needed to eventually speak with Imonie and my father, whose twin brother I had mistaken as him. I needed more information about this mysterious uncle who had almost strangled me on the new moon, and I deigned to ask the countess more about Emrys during our journey.

"He's Ambrose's identical twin, and the mastermind behind the assassination," Lady Raven had said to me. "He slayed my brother and the mountain made him pay for it, holding him captive while the remainder of us left. If he wasn't so coldhearted, or better yet, if he hadn't tried to kill my own son, I would feel pity for him."

"Who made him the armor?" I had asked next. To say I was nervous to meet Emrys once we ascended was an understatement. He had only released his hold on my neck when I had called him "Papa," and I surmised it was because he realized I was his niece. Which meant he knew who I was, and I couldn't afford to be exposed as Clementine Madigan yet.

"Why, Aaron Wolfe made the armor," the countess had replied, as if I were daft to not realize it.

We had been traveling in a coach together. Phelan and Lennox were in another, as Phelan was still avoiding me as much as I was avoiding my own family.

"How old were you when the curse happened, Lady Raven?"

"That's impolite to ask, Anna," the countess had replied stiffly, but it only confirmed my suspicions that she was wearing an aging glamour, just like my father. To look older than she was, even though she had lived well over a century. In fact, most of the wraiths had become magicians—the countess, my father, Mr. Wolfe. Imonie never had, but then again, Imonie wasn't wearing an aging charm to fool unsuspecting people. I was almost certain of it.

I had then dared to press my luck and asked her, "Who is that other woman in our party? I think her name is Imonie."

"Ah, yes, *Imonie*," the countess said with a hint of malice. "I once called her by another name, long ago. She was my lady-in-waiting before the curse. She used to dream with me about how we could make Seren a better place if my brother was off the throne. And gods, I remember . . . I remember the day she told me twin boys had been left on her door stoop. She did not know what to do with them, and I told her to take them to the orphanage and wash her hands of them. Someone else would eventually want them. But no. She kept them and I knew they would grow up and break her heart, as children are prone to do."

One of those twin boys had turned out to be my father. And I had not pointed out that the countess herself had borne twin boys, and that life sometimes had a twisted sense of humor.

"Regardless," Lady Raven had continued, clearing her throat as if the memories still haunted her. "Imonie hid from me a long time after the curse, when we wandered the province and tried to make new lives. I recommend that you stay clear of her. She's as slippery as an eel."

That conversation had happened days ago, but I was still mulling over it.

I sighed and turned away from the mountains and my recollections. Our party was setting up camp, and I walked to where the Vespers' servants were rushing to erect the tents. I had a tent of my own, as did Lennox and Phelan, although the countess ensured to set her tent between ours. As if she had anything to worry about. Phelan had hardly looked at me this past week, speaking to me only at a polite minimum. Most of the time, I didn't care. But then there were other moments, usually at night when I watched the moon begin to wax, when I felt the sting of his dismissal.

I longed for the way it had once been between us.

I had tried to speak to him. One evening, I found him standing alone a few yards from camp, and I had joined him.

"I know why you came home angry that night."

He had glanced at me, and I waited, hoping he would talk. That we could settle this rift between us. Of course I didn't truly know why he had stormed home and destroyed the library that evening weeks ago, but I could imagine that was the day his mother had told him who she was, who *he* was—the son of a wraith—and that she was gathering up her erstwhile companions with the intention to return to the mountain.

"Perhaps," he had said before walking away. "But I don't want to talk about it with you, Anna."

His words still stung when I recalled them, but I also couldn't fault him for being angry at me. I swallowed that memory and watched the first star break the dusk as I returned to the camp.

Tents were pitched in a ring with a fire in the center. Olivette and Nura were currently struggling with their tent, until Nura gave up and enchanted it to rise. My parents and Imonie were already camped as well, Imonie beginning to cook dinner over the flames. And then there was the tent for Mazarine, who everyone gave a respectful berth, and the duke's.

I drifted to a log beside Nura as she began to chop carrots for a stew. I helped by peeling a mealy potato, and I waited until Olivette, who was tending the fire, rose to fetch more sticks.

"Have you figured out who is who?" I whispered to Nura.

She knew I spoke of the mountain court—the seven wraiths—and was quiet for a breath, but her eyes darted around the bustle of the camp. Some of the wraiths were obvious; others, I was still trying to identify.

"I believe so," she began in a low tone. "Mazarine is the spymistress, obviously. The countess is the heiress. I think the woman called Imonie once served the countess as her lady-in-waiting." She paused to dump her carrot rounds into a cast-iron pot. "I think Olivette's father is the advisor."

I held my tongue. I believed that was *my* father's former position, but I was still uncertain.

"And what about the duke?" I whispered.

"The master of coin," Nura said without hesitation, and I nodded.

"But what I'm wondering," I began, lowering my voice a shade more as one of the Vespers' servants tossed a split log on the fire, "is how the master of coin was able to worm his way into being

Duke of Bardyllis. If he can't age, and wasn't born into the Deryn family, then how did he manage it . . . ?"

"It's a mystery," Nura agreed, "and I think there is some old magic at play here. The duke is obviously disguised, as Mazarine is. Maybe she fashioned a glamour for him to appear just like the real duke, so the master of coin could seamlessly take his place without anyone realizing there had been a swap."

It alarmed me to think the master of coin had been wearing a full-blown guise, just as I had been. That he had been masquerading as a well-known, beloved person—Lord Deryn. But this would explain why the duke had ordered my father to guard Mazarine, over a decade ago. Because if something happened to the troll, then the duke's disguise would surely crumble.

I discreetly glanced up from my peeling to catch sight of him on the other side of the camp, speaking to Phelan.

"His Grace certainly pays a great deal of attention to Phelan," Nura said sharply.

"I've noticed that as well."

She glanced at me. "You and Phelan are still at odds?"

"He refuses to speak with me."

"Well," Nura said, scraping her second batch of sliced carrots into the pot. "Sometimes conflict can't be resolved with words alone. Sometimes it requires settlement of a different sort." And she gave me a shrewd smile.

A burst of laughter escaped me.

"Ah," she whispered. "You have drawn his eyes now."

"Is he hurling daggers my way?"

"On the contrary. He looks immensely jealous of me, as if he longs to be the one who made you laugh."

I smacked her arm, which made her chuckle.

"Don't tease me, Nura."

"If you doubt me, then look for yourself, Anna."

I did, unable to resist. As soon as my gaze touched his, Phelan languidly glanced away, back to the duke, as if I didn't exist.

"Oh yes," Nura said, also noticing. "You have certainly gotten under his skin. Whatever did you do, my friend?"

I focused on my potato peeling, thinking if she knew the truth . . . she would despise me. "Perhaps I enchanted him, and the spell has broken."

Olivette returned with an armload of branches and dropped them before us, and I didn't realize she had been crying until Nura leapt to her feet.

"Oli? Oli, what is it?"

Olivette glanced at her father, who sat on a nearby rock. Mr. Wolfe froze, stricken. He made to rise and approach until Olivette turned away.

"I'm not going with him," she announced, dashing tears from her cheeks. "He's lied to me my entire life. Why should I believe anything he says now? Why should I risk myself by returning to some cursed mountain fortress?"

"Come, let's chat." Nura took a gentle hold of Olivette's hand, guiding her away from the camp.

I hesitated until I saw the sheen in Mr. Wolfe's eyes, and I stood, following Nura and Olivette. I could relate to Olivette more than anyone else in this camp. Her words could be my own, as if she and I were reflections of each other. And I wanted to say, *I understand how you feel. My childhood has also been built upon lies.*

I considered confessing to them—these two girls who had become my friends. What if I opened my mouth and told them everything? That I was a girl named Clem who had lost her home and wanted Phelan to pay for it. Would they still trust me afterward? Would they hold my secret?

Don't be a fool, I told myself.

I quietly approached Olivette and Nura.

"Shh, Oli. It'll be all right," Nura was saying, drawing Olivette into an embrace. "We don't have to ascend if you don't want to."

I wondered if seeing the mountain had churned up these feelings in Olivette. To realize how close we were to returning to a place that our parents' sins had cursed a century ago. The sight of it had done so to me. I felt as if my blood was singing. It was nearly impossible to sleep at night.

"This isn't *my* curse," Olivette said vehemently. "It's *theirs*. They're dragging me into it, and you, Nura, and even you, Anna! And everyone is still holding so many secrets, and no one knows who to trust or what awaits us when we reach our destination. I . . . I can't do this anymore!"

She buried her face in Nura's neck and sobbed.

My gaze drifted to the meadows that lay south. Hereswith was not far from here, perhaps half a day's travel. I was so close to home and yet it felt as if all along, I'd belonged here at the footstool of the mountains.

I knew why the wraiths wanted me and Phelan and Lennox and Nura and Olivette to accompany them. The legend claimed that nightmares roamed the fortress in the clouds. It was the heart of the new moon curse, and all of us were trained to fight such dangers. But it didn't make the uncertainty any easier to bear.

Olivette finally wept the last of her tears, Nura stroking her hair.

"I know much has changed lately, Oli," she said. "But your father is a good person. Perhaps he wanted to tell you who he was, but he didn't know how."

Olivette was silent, but she was listening.

"And he's doing the right thing," Nura continued, framing Olivette's tear-streaked face in her hands. "He's partly responsible for this curse, and he's now returning to hopefully see its end. And if we are successful . . . then the Seren Duchy can be restored."

"And who will take the throne?"

Nura paused, but she glanced at me with an unspoken request.

"Who would you want to see on the throne, Olivette?" I asked.

Olivette was quiet for a beat, wiping her nose on her sleeve. "I don't know, but not me. I don't want it. What about you, Nura?"

"I don't want it, either. Not without you." Nura tightened her embrace. "But don't you remember how you once wanted to be a madcap, Oli?"

"Gods, don't remind me."

"You thought it would be a grand adventure to see the fortress in the clouds. So did I, after I met you."

Olivette's gaze drifted to the summit. "And now I realize how foolish I was to want that. We could all die tomorrow, up there in that dank fortress. It took me this long to realize how much I love Endellion. And those music classes we thought about taking? I don't want to die before learning how to play the flute, Nura."

"We aren't going to die, Oli," Nura whispered with a smile. "After this is over, you're going to learn how to play the flute, and I'll learn how to play the violin."

I decided to give them a few moments alone and walked to the fire, the stars gathering overhead as the dusk deepened. Soon, Olivette and Nura returned, and I remained on the Wolfes' side of camp with them, even though I made sure I ate the food the Vespers' servants had prepared.

No one talked much that night. Not even the duke, who had strangely seemed the most affable out of our traveling party.

We continued to sneak glances at the mountains, at the fortress. It was dark; there was no visage of life in the stone, and yet all of us knew my uncle resided there, walking those corridors, waiting for us to return.

The lost one.

I wondered if he would challenge and kill us on sight.

"Lady Raven," the duke finally drawled. "Since you are the one who has so generously collected us all and dragged us across the province to the mountain . . . what is the plan for tomorrow? How are we to prevail?"

Lady Raven took her time in responding, holding her goblet up for a servant to refill with wine. "We'll approach the mountain doors tomorrow morning. They'll open, because all of us are present. And then we'll ascend and speak to Emrys."

"What if he doesn't want to speak?" Mr. Wolfe asked. "He nearly killed your son, Raven. *Twice.*"

"I know what he did, Aaron," she snapped. "He attacked Phelan to prompt me to act. That is all."

"Good thing we have plenty of wardens," Mazarine said wryly from where she sat in a shadow, crunching on chicken bones. "The nightmares will no doubt run rampant."

"We are prepared," the countess insisted. "All of us are here and ready. There is nothing to worry about."

"But someone is missing from our party," Mr. Wolfe said. His statement made me glance around the fire ring. Everyone was accounted for.

"Who do you speak of?" Nura asked.

The smith glanced at my father. "Where's your daughter, Ambrose?"

Everyone froze either to gape at my father with surprise or regard him with suspicion. I played the act, looking at him with an arched brow.

Papa calmly ate the last spoonful of his stew and set his bowl aside. Imonie, who was visibly anxious at the turn of conversation, took his bowl and began to wash it. My mother sat on a rock nearby, her long dark hair boasting a blue sheen in the firelight, her face sorrowful.

"Yes, where is Clementine?" the countess asked. "I've heard so much about her. Should she not be here with us? Both of my sons are. Aaron's daughter is here. Where is yours?"

"I don't know where my daughter is," Papa said. "After our town was lost to us . . . she was angry with me and ran away. I haven't been able to locate her."

"You don't have any tricks up your sleeve, do you, Ambrose?" the countess queried with a laugh. "Although perhaps I should also ask the same of you, Ms. Britelle? Since you are a seasoned stagecraft performer."

My mother narrowed her eyes. "What are you implying, lady?"

"That you have schemed for Clementine to arrive at the mountain fortress after we have ascended and taken all the risk and danger."

Mazarine snorted and cracked open a new chicken bone. Thankfully no one paid her any heed but me.

I told myself to inhale, exhale. To not draw any attention. But my body was wound tight and I think Nura sensed it, sitting beside me.

"Clementine has no idea who I truly am," Papa answered. "I have withheld my past from her. And when she does discover it . . . the last thing she'll want is to be anywhere near me."

His words dampened the mood of camp. My father stared into the flames, as if his only daughter was truly lost. But through the fire and the dancing shadows and the starlight, I felt someone watching me.

I lifted my gaze to meet Phelan's.

This time, he did not look away.

33

I couldn't ascend the mountain the following morning without speaking to my father in private. The questions were devouring me. And I remembered the things I had once said to him, when my heart had been wrung by betrayal.

You are vile and deceptive and I want no part of you.

I retired to my tent and waited for the camp to fall quiet. I cloaked myself with stealth and slipped into the night, cautiously approaching my parents' tent.

I hesitated a beat. I was anxious to enter unannounced, because I was uncertain about the status of their relationship. I had been surprised that my mother chose to accompany my father on this journey, given their past.

But perhaps love was not something easily forgotten, even when it had burned down to ashes.

I was beginning to understand why their marriage had unraveled all those years ago. My father was deathless, dreamless, cursed. A magician of the mountains. And my mother wasn't. She was of Bardyllis; she would age and die. She could dream.

And yet she had guarded his secret.

As Phelan was guarding mine.

I slipped into their tent without stirring the canvas.

They had not gone to bed yet, to my vast relief. But they sat close to each other, a few candles burning around them, casting monstrous shadows on the tent walls. My father startled when he saw me materialize.

"Clem," he rasped, and I held my finger to my lips, silently rebuking him.

"Anna," my mother said. "We were just speaking of you."

I drew a deep breath, burying the resentment and bitterness that bloomed within me. I told myself that I would handle this conversation as Anna would, as an outsider with little emotions attached, and whispered, "I don't have long, but we need to talk, Ambrose."

He nodded, glancing at my mother. She rose, brushing the wrinkles from her dress, and said, "I'll keep watch."

She departed, touching my shoulder on her way out, and I took her place on the ground, facing my father.

He cast a quick spell; I sensed his magic drifting around us like feathers. Enclosing us in the tent, so our voices couldn't be overheard.

"What can I expect when we stand in the mountain fortress tomorrow?" I asked.

"I don't know, but I imagine my brother will greet us." He paused, his gaze drifting to my neck. He was remembering the bruises that had been there, inspired by Emrys's hand, and he said, "I'm deeply sorry that he hurt you on the new moon."

"I thought he was you."

My father smiled, but it gleamed with pain. "You would have known who he was if I had told you the truth from the beginning."

"Yes, the truth would have been nice," I said, my skin flushing. "You and your brother are the twin boys in Imonie's story." I remembered that tragic tale of hers. At the time, I hadn't realized she was sharing a glimpse into her own past. "You and your brother . . . she raised you, didn't she?"

"She did."

I studied my father's face in the candlelight—lean and handsome and yet creased with sorrow. I wondered if he had been Imonie's quiet boy. The lover of books and knowledge. Or if he had been her wild boy. Reckless and untamed and full of challenge.

"How old are you, Papa?"

He chuckled. "Well, I was twenty-five when the curse fell. But I've been alive for nearly one hundred and twenty-seven years now."

"Can I see your true face?"

He hesitated but nodded. I watched as his glamour melted away, and I saw him as he was, frozen in time as a young man. And even though I was prepared for the sight, it was still strange to behold.

"It's one of Mama's spells, isn't it?"

"Yes," he answered, and the glamour returned. "Without it, I was unable to stay in one place too long, for fear of people becoming suspicious of my agelessness."

"Why did you choose to become warden of Hereswith?" I asked. "Did you want to be as close to your brother as you could? Even as the curse kept you apart?"

He was quiet for a moment, but his brow furrowed. "Yes and no. I do miss my brother. Some days, it is nearly unbearable. But I was also given an order to protect Mazarine."

"The duke's order?"

"Indeed."

"He's wearing one of Mazarine's guises."

"He is. As you know well yourself."

"And he must have killed the real duke quietly," I surmised. "And then had Mazarine enchant him, so he could replace Lord Deryn without anyone knowing there had been a swap."

My father was silent, but I saw how my spoken revelation softened his eyes.

"How did you get dragged into this, Papa?"

"The duke found me by chance years ago, even though I had tried to melt into Endellion society. My marriage to your mother was on the rocks by then, so when he offered me Hereswith with a few terms attached, I took it."

We both heard a sound beyond the tent. A nightingale's call.

I knew it must be a warning from my mother, and yet there was still so much more I wanted to ask my father.

"The countess thinks we are scheming," I rushed to say. "She's concerned about me arriving. Why?"

"Because for the era of the curse to fully come to an end, a new duke or duchess must claim the mountains and reinstate a court," Papa said. "The Countess of Amarys no doubt thinks I am going to try and position you as sovereign. I believe she has similar plans when it comes to one of her two sons."

I held his stare, wondering what my father saw within me. If he saw light or darkness. If he saw truth or deceit. If he would make a case for me to rule or if he thought me too reckless, too ambitious.

And I . . . I didn't know what I wanted. These thoughts were new to me; they swarmed like a hive, and I didn't want to entertain them for too long, for fear they would overcome me.

Another bird call.

I stood but lingered, because I had one more question.

"Papa . . . why can't I dream at night?"

"Because of me, Clem," he said, rising to his feet. "Because of the curse in my blood. It runs through you, daughter."

Did that mean the mountains owned a part of me? That I had a place among the clouds? Would I dream again, once the curse was broken? Where did I truly belong?

I felt divided, yearning for Hereswith and my old life. But that had been a life built upon a facade. And so I acknowledged the other half of me, which secretly longed for something new and dangerous.

Papa must have read my slant of thoughts. He continued in a low voice, "You inherited the curse, but something else as well. You also have a claim."

"A claim?"

"To sit upon the throne."

"Is this what you want for me, then?"

"Mere weeks ago, I wanted you to lead a normal life," he said. "One where you could draw, paint, become a *deviah* magician if you wanted. I sensed the countess was hunting us when her sons arrived in Hereswith, and I fought it as long as I could. I tried to keep us from being discovered by her, so our lives could move forward here. But everything has changed now. We've been drawn into this century-old conflict, and you are the only one I would see end it."

I stared at him. "How can I trust you now? After all the lies you have raised me beneath? In what world would I believe what you are telling me? In what world would I follow you up the mountain?"

My questions wounded him. Agonized, he reached for my hand. I sidestepped his touch, a knot in my throat. There was a warning in my chest, a painful scrape of stone against tendons.

"Listen to me, daughter. When we ascend the mountain tomorrow, alliances will be formed. Not all of us are promised to survive. If you want to throw your lot in with the Vespers, then by all means, you are grown and your own person. But if you want to take the throne, you have my support, as well as the duke's."

"The duke's?" I remembered how my father had met with Lord Deryn one afternoon not so long ago. How his hand had smelled of bergamot. A cologne the duke must wear to hide his true scent—that rotting smell of parchment.

"For years I protected Mazarine for him," my father said. "And now the time has finally come for me to call in a favor; he will support your claim to Seren, should you desire it."

Another bird call, this time more insistent. I didn't want him to see how his words had affected me and I asked, "Was the Duke of Seren good or cruel?"

Papa had never told me mountain legends when I was a girl. Imonie had occasionally, and her myths had depicted the duke as an oppressor. But I wanted to hear what my father thought.

"He was cruel, Clem. A man bent by selfishness. But that doesn't absolve me for what I did. What I planned as a member of his court. And it's all the more reason why I refuse to see someone unworthy take the throne again."

I nodded and slipped from the tent. I tried to put myself in his place, in Imonie's place. What would I do if I was in the court of a cruel person? Was it right to kill them? I kept to the shadows, tossing off my stealth charm halfway to my tent.

I entered through the canvas door. I heard the clink of beads, the rustle of fabric, and I startled to see the countess standing there.

"Lady," I said, rigid with shock. I felt a spasm of fear that she had uncovered my journal with my exposé, which was sitting just behind her, tucked away in my satchel. What would she do to me if she read it?

"Where were you?" she asked.

"Visiting the privy."

"For ten minutes?"

"I had to walk a good way to find a private place," I said. "Your servants mill around the camp like ants."

She was pensive for a moment, as if weighing my voice for a lie.

"May I help you with something?" I asked.

"You and my son have quarreled," she stated tersely. "What about?"

"I think you should ask him, lady."

"I have, and he will not tell me." She pulled her fur cloak tighter about her, but her eyes never left mine. "Whatever has come between you . . . you need to settle it before we arrive at the fortress tomorrow morning."

I sighed. "What is this truly about, Lady Raven?"

"Phelan cares for you, Anna," she said, and I couldn't help it: my mouth fell open, drawing a snicker from her. "Do not act so surprised. Any fool could see it."

"Any fool could see he can hardly bear to look at me."

"That may be, but I know my son very well. And when he does allow himself to look at you, there is an ocean in his eyes," the countess said. "I will not see you usher his downfall."

"His downfall? Lady Raven . . . I am his *partner*." A partner who had once schemed of gathering all his family's dirt and publishing it in the paper. A partner who had once drawn his blood with a rapier and reveled in his groveling.

She wasn't wrong to doubt me.

"Partners have turned on each other before," she countered. "I want you to swear allegiance to my family. Your vow will come into great importance when we stand in the fortress hall tomorrow, when the curse realizes we have all returned to the place of our betrayal."

The last thing I wanted was to swear my allegiance to the Vespers.

My father's words rang in my thoughts; I had his support, as well as the duke's, although I was reluctant to believe it just yet. I could most likely also garner Mazarine's support. But I didn't know if I desired any of it. I hoped I would have a better sense of what to do and what I wanted when I reached the summit.

In the meantime, I held an advantage, and I wasn't afraid to play it.

"I will swear my allegiance to you, Lady Vesper," I said. "I will fight on your behalf until the curse is broken and the mountain duchy is restored."

"Good, Anna. Come, kneel before me and give me your vow."

I did as she wanted.

I knelt among the blankets and furs of my makeshift bed and held out my right hand. She unsheathed a small dagger from her belt and bestowed a quick, shallow slice to my palm. The wound stung as I spoke my vow to her.

"I, Anna Neven of Endellion, pledge myself and my magic to your service, Lady Raven Vesper, Countess of Amarys. I will serve you and your family from this moment until the curse breaks on the mountain and the Seren Duchy is restored. Should I break my word, you have the power to bring me harm by whatever way you see fit, according to my betrayal."

She nodded, pleased with my words.

I rose and she wrapped the wound on my hand with a strip of cloth torn from one of the blankets.

"The first thing I ask of you is to make amends with Phelan," she said. "You once guarded his back on the new moon nights in Endellion. I would ask it of you again."

"You believe someone in our circle would harm him?" I asked.

She nodded, and I could sense she was warring with her words. To tell me or to withhold what she thought. When she continued to hesitate, I said, "The duke, perhaps?"

"The duke and I do not often see eye to eye, but he would not hurt my son," she replied. "I do not trust Ambrose Madigan."

"The magician? Is there a reason, lady?"

"His loyalties are questionable," the countess replied. "He was once very close to his twin brother. They were inseparable before the curse. I would not be surprised if he chose to defend his brother instead of restoring the duchy."

"I'll keep that in mind, lady, as well as watch over Phelan," I said, and I hated how her statement about my father planted a seed of doubt in my mind. "Although your son tends to hold grudges. I don't know if he will ever forgive me."

"Oh, I have no doubt that he will," she said.

I watched her walk to the tent entrance, the night wind stirring the canvas as she departed.

I stood for a moment longer, contemplating all the paths before me.

Anna Neven might have given her vow to the Vespers. But Clem Madigan's allegiance remained to be seen.

34

We rose early with the sun and prepared to ascend, leaving our tents pitched, as if we would soon return for them. The Vespers' and the duke's servants would remain behind, tending to the camp. I didn't carry much: a satchel stuffed to the brim with several changes of clothes, green apples, a wedge of cheese, the journal with my exposé notes, an inkwell and quill. My father had snuck a dagger to me, and it was hidden in its leather sleeve, tucked away in my boot.

I walked with the Vespers' party through the long, frosted grass, my father, mother, and Imonie leading the way. We were silent, pensive. All too soon we reached the mountain entrance.

Two great wooden doors sat before us, thrice the height of a woman, arched and latticed with iron. I thought about how long it had been since the passage or the lift inside had been used.

"And how are we to open these doors?" Lennox asked with a huff.

"The doors will open on their own, since all six of us are together again. Emrys, the seventh, is already here, of course," Mazarine said from the back of the line. "Approach the doors, Ambrose."

My father closed the distance between us and the entrance, and just as the troll predicted, the doors creaked open on their own, streams of dirt cascading from the stone lintel above. The mountain seemed to rumble, as if recognizing the broken court that stood at its feet. The twin doors came to a rest, gaping open like a mouth, eager to swallow us. The passage was dark; I could smell damp stone and rich earth and rotting wood.

"Brin," the countess said crisply, pivoting on her heel to regard the troll. "Why don't you lead the way?"

Mazarine snorted, but moved to the head of the line, passing my father with a polite nod.

"Do you need fire?" he asked, but she didn't answer.

She stepped into the darkness of the passage and vanished, and we waited, uncertain.

"Should we follow her?" Nura whispered from behind me.

No sooner did she speak the words than fire bloomed in the passage. Torches bracketed on both walls ignited one by one.

We followed Mazarine's path. I could feel the heaviness in the air—cold, quiet, sentient air. The floor beneath our boots was swept clean, set with stone. The walls on either side were recessed and carved with moons and suns and people. Relics of the duchy that had once dwelled here.

This place felt like a tomb.

The passage opened up into a vast, cavernous chamber. From the faint reach of the firelight, I could see wagons full of cobwebs and crate upon crate, stacked in clusters. A storeroom of sorts, or once a place of trade, and it felt vast, endless. I stayed nearby the Vespers, but my eyes roamed my surroundings with its high ceilings that melted into darkness and the stone pillars that stood like trees. I kept waiting to come across skeletons, thinking it must have been pandemonium when the curse unfolded here.

"Ah, here is the lift." The countess's voice broke the heavy silence.

Mazarine had already located it. The troll stood beside a sleek platform of wood, its railings made of iron; she studied its pulley and gears. Lanterns burned at the four corners of the lift, granting light to see. "It is still functional."

My father joined Mazarine's side, examining the lift's operation. "Yes, it looks just as we left it, all those years ago. It hasn't aged a day."

"Enchanted," Olivette whispered in awe.

"Cursed," Nura added.

Mazarine glanced up from the lift to study us, her eyes catching the firelight like those of a cat. "Ambrose was brave enough to lead us to the doors. I took it upon myself to lead us into the passage. Now it is your turn, Lady Raven of Amarys, to be the first to take the lift."

I watched a shadow dart across the countess's face as she frowned, but then she seemed to have a change of heart and smiled.

"Of course, Mazarine. My family and I will be the first to

return to the fortress. It is only fair. Come, Lennox and Phelan. And you too, Anna."

I followed them onto the lift. I remained near the railing, but my palms were slick with perspiration as I imagined being toted upward, into the darkness and unknown, on this piece of shaky wood.

The duke stepped forward to unexpectedly join us. "I will ascend with you, Lady Raven," he announced gallantly.

"How kind of you, Your Grace," the countess replied, but I heard the twist in her words. She didn't want the duke to accompany us.

"Are we ready?" Mazarine drawled.

The countess nodded.

The troll shifted a lever and the lift began to groan and shake. The chains tightened and rotated through a great wheel, and up we went.

I held on to the railing and looked down at my parents and Imonie.

They were staring at me, worry and fear drawn in their faces. I was being carried away from them, out of sight, and I felt a twinge of anxiousness.

I glanced away from them first, casting my eyes up to the darkness and the unknown.

It was a slow but steady rise.

We began to pass by different stone landings, silent and shadowed, but the lift did not stop. We continued to inch upward, the chains ticking like a heartbeat, and I knew we were in the fortress, surpassing the lower floors. No one spoke, but I sensed the duke watching me. I ignored him, and kept my eyes on the wall of stone, waiting for us to reach our destination. The darkness was gradually fading around us, as if we were ascending from night into day.

The lift jerked to a halt and I stumbled backward into Phelan. He grasped hold of my arm, steadying me, and he didn't let go until the countess took the first step off the lift, onto the highest landing of the fortress.

Sunshine streamed in through skylights in the ceiling. The floors were set with stone, smooth and polished and accented with small blue jewels. The landing opened up into a wide chamber that broke off into four different corridors.

We stood in the sunshine and drifting dust motes, staring at each of the passages, and behind us I could hear the lift beginning to lower with a loud clang.

"Mazarine has inadvertently given us an advantage," said the countess. "We should explore before the others arrive. See if we can locate Emrys." She glanced at me. "Anna, you will go with Phelan. His Grace and Lennox will come with me."

"Should I not accompany Anna and Phelan," the duke dared to say, "since you and I are familiar with these passages, and they are not?"

Lady Raven's annoyance was nearly palpable. But she nodded at the duke and said, "Very well."

She and Lennox took the western corridor, while Phelan and I followed the duke into the eastern one.

Lord Deryn and Phelan both had rapiers sheathed at their belts, and their hands strayed to the hilts as we walked deeper into the silent fortress. I didn't sense danger, only sorrow and cobwebs of memories. Vibrant tapestries dressed the walls, pleading to be admired after so many years missing a beholder.

I paused before one, captivated by its quaint beauty. It depicted a view from the mountain fortress, overlooking a lush valley. The longer I stared upon the tapestry, the more I felt as if I could step into this scene and find myself in a sun-drenched meadow, cradled by the mountains. . . .

I began to reach out, my fingers touching the finely woven threads.

"Miss Neven," the duke said, breaking my reverie.

I glanced to where he and Phelan waited a few paces away, both of them regarding me.

"Please stay close to us," he said. "I do not know where Emrys is, and I do not wish to risk losing you to him."

The duke led us to the fortress hall, a place Phelan and I had both walked on the new moon, in Knox Birch's nightmare. The scene the countess had painted on the card of the lost one.

It felt strange to stand in a place I had seen dimly before as a bewitched reflection.

But I recognized it. The blue banners of heraldry on the walls, the arched windows, the multiple hearths, the tables and benches. The dais. But the duke's throne was missing, and I exchanged a discreet glance with Phelan.

"We shall sit here and wait," the duke said, drawing out a bench at the nearest table.

"What are we waiting for, Your Grace?" Phelan asked.

"For the others to arrive. I do not know why your mother thinks wandering around is an advantage, Phelan."

I struggled to understand her reasoning as well, and I conceded to sit at the table, eager for my parents and Imonie and the Wolfes to arrive. Phelan remained standing, too restless to sit. He paced the hall, the click of his boots echoing off the walls.

I waited until Phelan was out of earshot before I addressed the duke.

"What is it like, Your Grace? To return home after so many years away?"

He glanced at me from across the table. I couldn't help but wonder what his true face looked like. "It is bittersweet, Miss Neven. My thoughts and heart are full of memories."

I thought about the conversation I'd had with my father the night before. The duke had given my father Hereswith, but with orders. And I didn't know what the duke wanted, but it seemed he was the countess's opposition. I didn't trust the countess either, although I did Phelan.

I trusted him because he was protecting me by keeping my true identity a secret, for unknown reasons.

Although sometimes I imagined that I knew why, when Phelan looked at me.

"What was your position in the mountain court?" I asked, and the duke gave me a toothless smile.

"You have not uncovered that yet, Miss Neven?"

"I have my suspicions."

"Which are . . . ?"

"You were once the master of coin."

He studied me closer. "Not the guard, or the advisor?"

"No." And I remembered how many coins Phelan's territory had paid to satisfy his dream tax.

Does he truly want to break this curse? I wondered, because once the curse ended, so did the new moon nightmares. There would be no need for wardens and the dream tax. Perhaps the duke had lied to my father about supporting my claim.

Phelan eventually grew weary of pacing and joined us at the table, sitting a few hand lengths away from me. That ended my conversation with the duke, and we waited for the others to arrive.

Mr. Wolfe, Olivette, and Nura finally appeared in the hall, and not long after them my parents, Imonie, and Mazarine arrived.

"Where is the countess?" Imonie asked with a concerned frown.

"And Lennox?" Nura added, noticing that he was also missing.

"They are exploring the fortress," I replied, and I saw the suspicion in my father's face.

"We should not progress without them," said Mr. Wolfe, rushing his hands through his wispy hair. "We need to make plans as one."

And so we waited.

I was beginning to wonder if Emrys had slain them both in some shadowy corridor when the countess and Lennox appeared, no longer toting their bags.

"Ah, good," Lady Raven said, taking note of everyone. "We are all gathered here."

"Where were you?" my father snapped.

She cast him a surprised glance. "I was reacquainting myself with my old home, Ambrose. My former quarters are exactly as I left them."

Papa opened his mouth to say something else, but a loud bang stole our attention. We glanced to the dais, where a hidden door had been opened and shut without our notice. There stood Emrys, watching us with jaded eyes.

He wasn't wearing his enchanted armor, as I'd half expected him to. He was dressed in blue robes stitched with silver moons, with a dark shirt and trousers beneath. His auburn hair fell across his brow, just like Papa's, and his mouth was set in a firm line, also like my father's. I stared at him, amazed by the resemblance. If my father dropped his aging glamour, it would be difficult to tell them apart from a distance.

"Emrys," Papa greeted him, slowly approaching the dais.

"Hello, brother," Emrys said, gazing down at him. "It has been a long while. And yet look at you. Wearing an old face like a man with something to hide."

My father's shoulders drew back, tense. This reunion felt fraught, icy. I swallowed and hoped I could evade Emrys's attention.

"I see you have brought your companions," Emrys continued, regarding the rest of us. We remained close together around one of the tables. No one spoke; we hardly dared to breathe.

Emrys's gaze found Imonie and lingered on her. His mother. Imonie, who stood quiet and still, as if she had anticipated this moment for years and now that it had come . . . she didn't know what to do, what to say to him.

She remained silent, and I ached for her. I wanted to wrap my arms around Imonie and bury my face in her dress, to breathe her in as I had done as a child. Oh, how she had loved me, the granddaughter she could not claim in word because of her and my father's secrets, but she had claimed me in love. And that love had given me a warm, safe childhood, despite the pain of my parents' separation. That love had clothed me and fed me and raised me, protected me.

I hadn't fully appreciated her until this moment.

Emrys opened his mouth, and I expected he would greet her. But different words spilled out, and his eyes coldly passed over her to Phelan, to the Wolfes. To the duke. "At long last, the traitorous court is reunited. I hope your lives in Bardyllis have been idyllic, a dream. Was it you, Ambrose, who gathered and rallied our alliance to return?"

"It was me," the countess answered, and boldly took a step toward him. "I found those who wanted to be forgotten. Your brother, for one. As well as the spymistress and the master of coin. The three of them would have continued on for another hundred years if you had not found a way to haunt the new moon. And so it is I who answered your summoning, Emrys. I have brought us back to end this curse."

"Raven," said Emrys, his eyes shifting to her. "You have not changed either. Do not lie and claim that you returned to ease my suffering."

The countess acted like he had struck her. Her face went pale; her eyes glittered like she craved to stab him.

"You are perhaps looking for the throne," Emrys continued, motioning to the empty dais. "The chair your brother once graced as duke, before you plotted to kill him, Raven."

"*We* plotted to kill him, old friend."

Emrys only smiled, but there was no kindness within it. I wondered if walking this fortress, abandoned and alone for an entire century, turned a heart into stone, deeper than Mazarine's old magic. "The throne does not appear until nightfall," he continued. "When it appears, your dreams will manifest. Be ready, for they will be eager to cut you to the quick."

"Dreams?" my father echoed.

"You have not dreamt since you left," Emrys said. "That has changed now. You stand in the mountain where the crime was committed, where the curse hooked your souls. Your dreams, then, will now return when you sleep. And there are no remedies here to keep them at bay. Nor will these corridors and this hall be safe when the sun sets. If you do not wish to encounter the nightmares, remain in your room with the door bolted. But if you want to end the curse, one of you must break the dream and claim the throne."

His words wove together all the stray pieces of my wonder, questions, and dread. We would dream, and our dreams would roam this place at night, just like they did on the new moon.

What would my mind spin and create, now that it could?

"Oh, and one final warning," Emrys said, raising his hand. "Your deathless state is no more in these halls. You can bleed and feel your life ebb; you can feel the mortal sting of a blade. It would be a shame, indeed, to watch a number of you fall before the curse breaks."

A hush settled over the group. The wraiths looked shocked to learn this. I snuck a worried glance at my family.

"Go now and rest," Emrys said. "What little daylight you have remaining should be used to prepare for tonight. Bread, meat, and water will appear in your room by magic every evening an hour before sundown. I am sure I will see some of you in the hall when darkness falls."

I waited for the duke to rise first before I stood, hoping to remain hidden in the group. My father and the countess returned to us, and I had to remind myself to follow her instead of Papa.

Emrys's gaze found me just before I left the hall.

With a chill, I realized he knew exactly who I was.

35

I chose a bedchamber across the corridor from Phelan's, near the countess's grand suite. The room was small but clean with a trio of windows, a bed with a feather mattress, a wardrobe in one corner, and a fireplace where enchanted flames burned. I unpacked my bag, eating one of my apples while I hung my clothes in the wardrobe. Who had once dwelled in this room? I wondered as I eventually sat on the edge of the bed. Blankets were folded at the foot of it, and a wolf pelt was draped over the middle.

I tried to judge the time of day by the slant of light on the floor and surmised it to be around one in the afternoon. And then I waged a war with myself: to fall asleep so I could last the night, or to resist, for fear of dreaming.

I eventually decided I would at least lie down. I stared at the ceiling for a while until my eyes felt heavy.

The bed was soft beneath me, the fur warm across my legs.

I drifted to sleep before I knew it.

I am in Endellion.

I walk the streets I guard with Phelan, and I don't know what I look like—who I appear to be—until I pass by a gilded mirror in a storefront. I'm Anna in the reflection, and it surprises me. I lay my hand over my breast, covering my heart. The stone within me holds, emitting a heavy permanence. It has grown into my flesh; it cannot be removed, nor will it ever crack and crumble.

I suddenly feel lost, within myself and in the streets.

I turn, struggling to breathe, until I see Aaron Wolfe's shop. I step inside and walk among the swords and axes and armor. I approach the leather weapon belt but it is something else that captures my attention. A slender dagger with a jeweled hilt. As I reach for it, Mr. Wolfe appears. Olivette's father.

"How much for the dagger?" I ask him.

"The price is the secret you hold," he replies.

And I know if I take this dagger within my hand, it will cut me, and Anna will bleed away.

Mr. Wolfe disappears, and I am left with the decision, to bleed or not.

I choose not to, and it's not because I am afraid of the pain but because I hear the pounding of an anvil in the distance. I follow the sound through a back door, down a dark tunnel that makes me shiver, into a workroom.

Mr. Wolfe is nowhere to be seen, but something claims the center of the chamber.

I approach it cautiously, a warning ringing in my mind. It's a full suit of armor, standing upright, waiting for someone to step *within it. As I draw closer . . . I recognize it. This is Emrys's armor, the one he wears on the new moon, trespassing into nightmares.*

Fresh blood drips from it. I watch it spill down the breastplate, pooling on the floor. I hear something move behind me and I whirl to find Mr. Wolfe standing in a doorway, framed by light, staring at me with shadows in his eyes.

"Whose blood is this?" I ask.

He doesn't answer, but an axe gleams in his hands.

"Whose blood is this?" I ask again, louder.

He takes a step closer to me, the floor creaking beneath him.

I startled awake.

It was twilight, and my clothes were drenched with sweat. I had no idea where I was. Not until I sat forward and studied the sparse chamber that held me.

Trembling, I slipped from the bed and warmed myself at the fire, although the dream's chill lingered in my mind. Why on earth had I dreamt such a thing? Olivette's father, of all people. I quickly ate a few bites of bread and meat that had appeared on my table as Emrys foretold, washing it down with water.

I donned my boots and then sat on the edge of the bed, waiting for night to arrive. That's when I noticed a folded slip of parchment sitting on the floor, as if it had been snuck beneath my door.

I rose and picked it up, suspicious until I recognized Imonie's handwriting.

Be patient, be shrewd.

I smiled, remembering how she said this to me every new moon. But the warmth of the memory faded when I realized what she was saying to me.

Don't get yourself killed, Clem.

I took the dagger my father had given me into my hand, pacing the room, anticipating what was to come.

The night deepened.

Ready, I approached my door, but my fingers paused on the iron handle. What if it was my dream that materialized in the hall? I shouldn't have let myself sleep this first day. I had already failed on the *shrewd* part of Imonie's message.

I stepped into the corridor with such thoughts nipping at my mind, catching a glimpse of Phelan up ahead, striding through the candlelight toward the hall.

I wasn't surprised to discover he was venturing out to encounter the night's offering, but I did wonder how many of us would. Six of us were wardens, but that didn't mean all of us would roam the fortress, seeking out what could be our own nightmare.

I followed him through the winding passages, past door after door, tapestry after tapestry.

When I reached the entrance of the hall, though, I hung back, concealed in a shadow. I had a clear vantage point of the hall and could see Nura and Olivette limned in firelight as they paced, waiting for the dream to appear. I sensed Phelan was nearby, but I could no longer see him.

I tarried in the shadow, the stone wall rough and cold against my back.

"I'm not surprised to find you here," Phelan said, his voice emerging from the darkness on my right.

"I could say the same about you."

We stood in awkward silence together, close enough to sense the other but far enough away to have no chance of touching.

"Did you sleep this afternoon?" he asked.

Did you dream was what he meant.

"Yes," I replied. "Did you?"

He was quiet for a beat, and then said in a husky voice, "Yes. I did as well."

Another round of silence. I watched as Nura and Olivette grew weary of pacing the hall, choosing to sit on the edge of a table. They hadn't slept; I could see the exhaustion in their faces.

"Is your brother coming to fight tonight?" I asked.

"I don't know."

You should, I thought, biting the inside of my lip. I didn't desire to see Lennox take this duchy and restore it back to life. But I had no doubt he would believe himself to be the best candidate.

I was opening my mouth to say something snide when I felt a rush of air. Phelan was in the shadow with me, and our arms brushed as he whispered, *"Anna."*

He had never said my faux name like that, with urgent awe. And I swiftly learned why, when I saw the dream that manifested in the hall.

I was walking the streets of Endellion.

I stopped before a mirror in a storefront, to look upon my reflection.

This was my dream.

Heat spread through me like a fever. Mortification and dread unfurled in my thoughts, and for a moment I could only stand and helplessly gape as I watched my nightmare overtake the hall. I started to rush forward, only to be stopped by Phelan.

"Wait," he hissed into my hair.

I froze until I remembered that Olivette's father appeared in the dream as a sinister force. And Olivette was in the hall, watching everything with wide eyes.

I pulled away and Phelan let me go.

I entered the hall; I stepped into my dream.

It was like treading a river, one that deepened with each step. The currents tugged me toward myself, this terrifying flesh-and-blood copy of Anna. What would she do if I caught her attention, if our eyes met? What would *I* do?

I was relieved that I had not taken that bejeweled dagger, that I had not exposed my true self. Nothing about this dream gave me away as Clem, although it did mention my secret and it raised suspicions about Olivette's father.

We had nearly reached the end of the dream. The armor shone and dripped blood.

"Father?" Olivette cried, staring at Mr. Wolfe holding the axe.

I knew she was caught up in this dream just as I was, struggling to tell what was real and what was fantasy. She saw her father and thought it was truly him, arriving to assist in fighting the nightmare.

"Olivette!" I called to her, hurrying to close the gap between us. My friends didn't know this dream like I did. I was the only one who held the advantage.

The sound of my voice drew dream Anna's and Mr. Wolfe's attention. The moment they looked at me, I was overwhelmed. I sank to my knees, dazed as if I had been struck across the face.

Nura was the one of us who responded.

She cast a defensive spell as Mr. Wolfe approached with the axe. Her magic arced with blue light, finding its mark in his chest. The smith stumbled back but did not fall. It roused his anger and he moved faster.

"Wait, Nura," Olivette shouted. "It could be him!"

"This isn't your father, Oli," Nura said, hurling another charm to slow him down.

I could feel my pulse in my ears as I rose.

Olivette was shouting and Nura's magic was teeming in the air, scorching Mr. Wolfe's clothes, burning his skin. But he continued to press us, swinging his axe.

Nura blocked it with a charm and attempted to wrench the axe from his grip. Her magic rebounded and tossed her back a few yards. She landed lithely on her feet several tables away, and I saw the tension in her face as Olivette attempted to speak to Mr. Wolfe's phantom.

"Father, lower the axe," she said.

He swung.

Olivette gasped and lurched backward, scrounging up a magical shield, but the edge of the blade sliced her raised forearm. Nura launched herself over the tables, teeth bared as she struck

Mr. Wolfe again with more force. He stumbled, granting her enough time to ease Olivette up and away safely out of his range.

Phelan appeared. He engaged with the smith so Nura could continue retreating with Olivette, who was weeping, her forearm leaving a trail of blood on the flagstones.

We were all so distracted by Mr. Wolfe's attack that we forgot about Anna.

I glanced to where the shade of myself continued to stand by the bloody armor. I saw the gleam of gold at Anna's breast, the jewel she wore about her neck.

I was the key to ending this dream. My stone heart was the weakness, the break. It had to be broken, and as soon as I realized this, Anna began to retreat from the hall.

I pursued her.

I didn't realize Phelan was chasing after me until I was about to slip out the side door Anna had vanished through. I felt his magic encircle me, slowing me down.

"Wait," he panted, reaching my side. His magic loosened, and I spun to look up at him. "Let me come with you. Let me guard your back."

I entertained the temptation, because the more I realized I would have to give my phantom a mortal wound, the stronger my reservations grew. But when I looked at Phelan . . . I knew he would struggle in wounding this reflection of me as well.

"Help Nura and Olivette to their chamber and lock the door," I said. "Quickly, before Mr. Wolfe reaches them. I will meet you there after I bring this to an end."

My words struck a chord between us.

We glanced at the dais, where the duke's throne had appeared, illumined by a stream of moonlight. Emrys stood beside the regal chair, an observer as the night unfolded. His face was like marble, unreadable, but he was watching Phelan and me, watching Nura, Olivette, and Mr. Wolfe. Watching and waiting to see if this dream would break.

I slipped from the hall; Phelan didn't follow me this time.

The corridors were cold and dark, punctured by the flickering light of sconces. I followed the trail Anna left for me, sounds of her boots on the stone floors, a flicker of movement as she rounded corner after corner. She was leading me deeper into the fortress, down to the very heart of the mountain. In my dream, I had felt lost. And that sensation welled within me once more.

I must have chased her for an hour, through every vein of the fortress.

I walked through the dark kitchen, through dusty storerooms, through the armory, where swords and crossbows and shields hung on the wall, glinting in the dim light. Through a library with endless shelves of musty books. Through rooms and suites long abandoned.

I stopped in the main corridor, thinking she was about to bring me back into the hall. I stood ragged, bewildered. Surrender was softening me until she appeared at the end of the passage, waiting for me to follow.

I no longer ran. I walked, which gave me the chance to draw my dagger from my boot. I slid the steel free from its leather sheath and held it in my hand, following Anna into a spacious suite.

I knew at once this was the Duke of Seren's chambers.

The moon was setting, but the last of its silver light streamed in through the open balcony doors. The wind sighed, stirring the curtains. Anna came to a halt, a strange mark on the floor between us. It was wide and dark. Old blood that had dried long ago.

"This is where it happened," she said to me, meeting my gaze. "Where the Duke of Seren was murdered. Where the curse was cast. His sister always believed she was the true heir, not him. And when she hatched a plan to be rid of her brother, six other court members readily joined her, never dreaming of what their ruthlessness would inspire."

The golden jewel gleamed at her chest. I let out a long breath, the dagger slick in my hand.

"Why have you brought me here?" I asked.

"Because you need to see it," she replied. "You need to stand on the same ground where the crime was committed."

"Did my uncle kill the duke?"

She chose not to answer. I could hardly discern her face—the face I had drawn for myself months ago.

"They say the duke was a cruel man," I said.

"Does that excuse the court of the murder they plotted? Lady Raven may have first spoken the idea aloud, but it lived in the other six hearts."

I was quiet.

"Go on," she taunted me when my hesitation continued. "Strike me and bring about the end."

"You act as if you're not a part of me," I said. My hands shook, much to my dismay.

She smiled. "Of course I'm a part of you."

Knox Birch's nightmare suddenly came to mind. He had wanted to claim the throne of Seren, and he had cut down his wife and daughters to do it. He had sliced through his own heart and had not even realized it until afterward, when the blood stained the ground, when he had obtained his desire at an unthinkable cost.

But there is no other way, I thought. The dream had to be vanquished so the throne could be claimed and the curse broken. I wondered if the greed shone in my eyes like a film as I prepared to pierce Anna's heart. I wondered if one had to become a monster in order to end the curse.

I took a step closer. One moment, it was just her and me. The next, a rough hand yanked me backward. I collided with someone's broad chest, the point of a dagger prodding my side, just beneath my ribs. A little more pressure, and it would pierce me.

I froze when Lennox hissed into my hair, "Did you think I was going to let you be the victor here, Anna? Do you truly believe you are the one destined to break the curse? You, a girl from the gutter who never deserved to be warden with the likes of my brother. You shouldn't even be here."

I didn't reply. But I thought on the past, when he had defeated me for Hereswith. When he had stolen my home, all because I had hesitated.

I stared at phantom Anna, whose eyes slid to Lennox as he held me roughly against him. Behind her, the balcony doors sat open, eerily as if they had been left that way a century ago. The sun was just beginning to rise, the mountains incandescent with gold.

And I dared to spin and turn, risking the dagger he held at my side. It cut through my dress; I felt the blade bite my side, but I forgot the pain as I cast a repelling spell at him with deadly accuracy.

Lennox was blown off his feet, hurled up and away to the other side of the room. He slammed into the wall and for one wild moment, I thought I had killed him. I only felt a tiny bit of remorse.

He slid to the floor with a grimace, his eyes shining with fury as he charged again. I dodged the spell he spouted at me; I effortlessly danced around the green fire he created, and we met in a clash that robbed our balance.

On the cold, bloodstained floor, I struggled to slow him down. Because he was crawling to reach Anna, and it was a race to break the nightmare before the sun did. The light was creeping ever closer through the window and doors, and I bared my teeth and dragged Lennox by the ankle back to me. Among the scrambling, I thought I saw the glistening of bones, lurking beneath the duke's bed. As if a skeleton had been swept beneath it.

Lennox was dazed, but he fought me until I disarmed him. I flung his dagger away and held my blade at his throat.

"Anna . . . ," he whispered, suddenly trembling. "Anna, think of Phelan. He will come to hate you if you wound me."

"*Wound* you?" I taunted.

"You mean to kill me?"

I stared at him, but from the corner of my eye, I watched as the sunlight inched closer to where Anna stood. She was becoming transparent, about to melt away.

"Do you know I swore allegiance to your mother?" I asked, pressing my dagger deeper into his neck, just to see him squirm beneath me. He let out a yelp when a bead of blood welled. "You *fool*! I'm fighting on your family's behalf, but if you get in my way again . . . I won't hesitate to cut you down."

"All right, all right," he panted, lifting his hands. "Get off me, will you?"

Around us, the room became illuminated. Dust and cobwebs and the patina of memories. The shadows gave way to light.

Anna sighed. She turned into a wisp of smoke, victorious. The nightmare had slipped through my fingers.

And the curse remained to be broken.

36

I couldn't stop shivering.

I fetched a fur-lined cloak from my bedroom and laced it tightly at my collar before I knocked on Olivette's door. Exhaustion was heavy as a millstone on my shoulders; I waited for someone to answer. I could hear murmurs within the chamber, and then the lock was unbolted and Nura cracked the door.

"Anna?" she asked, glancing beyond me.

"It's me," I reassured her, and she welcomed me inside.

Olivette was sitting upright in bed. Phelan stood before one of the windows, framed by sunrise, and Mr. Wolfe was tending to the fire.

All of them looked at me when I entered. I stopped, feeling my vulnerability like a burn. I could hardly look Mr. Wolfe in the eye.

"How are you, Olivette?" I asked, my voice hoarse.

She held up a bandaged forearm. "I'll be fine, Anna. It wasn't bad."

"It only required twenty-five stitches," Nura said pointedly.

"And thank gods you could sew it up without a hitch," Olivette replied, just as sharply. I sensed the two of them had quarreled, but it was centered on the fact that Nura had nearly witnessed her partner's dismemberment.

"Is it safe to assume you did not break the dream, Anna?" asked Mr. Wolfe.

"Unfortunately. I failed." I felt Phelan's stare from across the chamber, but I didn't lift my eyes to him.

"You didn't fail, Anna!" Olivette cried.

Ah, sweet Olivette, who only saw the good in people. I smiled at her, but it sat on my face like a wince.

"Is there anything I can do for you?" I asked, eager to wash away the stain of my dream.

"Can you brew a pot of tea from thin air?" Olivette asked, and I laughed.

"How I wish." The meat, bread, and water once a day was fine, I supposed, but I couldn't deny that I craved a good stout tea.

"That's what I want the moment I leave this mountain," Olivette stated with a sigh. "A pot of tea with cream and honey. And some blueberry scones."

I caught the worried expression that crossed Nura's face as she gazed at Olivette. We might be on the mountain for a while.

"Miss Neven?" Mr. Wolfe gently drew my attention. "May I speak to you in private for a moment?"

I nodded, but my throat was narrow as I followed Olivette's father into the corridor.

"Nura and Phelan told me the details of the dream," he began with a stammer. "I feel like I must apologize, Miss Neven."

I stopped walking so I could face him. "No, Mr. Wolfe. Please, don't apologize. The dream was mine. You are not at fault."

He sighed, struggling to believe me. I imagined it was horrifying to see your daughter dragged into a room, crying and bleeding from a wound your phantom had given her.

"That may be, Miss Neven," Mr. Wolfe said. "But there was truth within it."

I wondered if he was hinting at my secret—the price for that bejeweled dagger. And then I recalled the armor.

"You forged the armor that Emrys used to walk the new moon," I said.

He nodded. "I made it long ago. But the inspiration for it has always been betrayal. I began my service to the duchy as a guard, but my mind was given to other things, mainly the spells of *metamara*. Transforming one thing into another. My father was a smith, and as I held no other skill but to protect and guard, I began to learn how to craft armor and weapons. I soon joined Raven's inner circle, only because her brother the duke wanted me to create more and more weapons that I felt were dangerous and wrong. And Raven was the only one who was powerful enough to protect me from her brother's bloody whims.

"She asked me to make enchanted armor. The seven of us who desired to see the duke gone had formed an alliance, and we were to draw stones, to see who would give him the killing blow. Whoever was selected would wear the armor, as a way to protect their identity and themselves from any magic the duke might cast in defense. So I began to forge it, and I thought all would be well with the plan, but none of us realized how slow the armor would make us. And to kill the duke . . . one would have to be swift.

"I completed the armor, but we never used it. I left it in a storage closet in the castle armory, locked away. I forgot all about it when things fell apart, when I fled to Bardyllis."

I was silent, thinking on his words. I envisioned the duke's chamber, the bloodstain on the floor. The bones beneath the bed. And I wanted to know who had been the one to kill the duke.

"Who drew the stone?" I asked.

Mr. Wolfe glanced away from me, as if he could not bear to look me in the eye. "What do you mean?"

"Who drew the stone to assassinate the duke?"

"Emrys did."

I retreated to my chambers. The sun streamed in through the arched windows, and the floor was bitterly cold beneath my feet as I removed my boots.

My mind whirled, thinking of stones and armor and what the wraiths must have been like before the curse had fallen.

I had just pulled the ribbon loose from my braid when a knock sounded on my door.

"Come in," I said.

The door opened. Phelan stood on the threshold, hesitant until I motioned for him to step inside. He did, shutting the door behind him. His boots were scuffed from the nightmare, his trousers ripped at the knee. His cravat and jacket were abandoned. His shirt hung slightly open at the neck draws, and I remembered the scars on his chest.

"We need to talk," he said.

I waited for him to speak and began to unwind my braid with my fingers, my hair coming loose in rich waves. He watched me, transfixed, until I asked, "What did you need to talk to me about?"

"This is Mazarine's magic, isn't it?"

I knew he spoke of my disguise, and I looked away from him, bracing myself for this conversation. One that had been brewing between us for well over a week now. I sealed the door and windows with a quick spell to hold our conversation private. "Yes."

"Can you tell me why?"

"Why I donned a disguise and became your partner?" I walked to the small round table by my hearth, where a pitcher of water sat. I poured myself a glass but didn't offer one to him. "I was angry. You and your brother arrived without warning and challenged my father and me for my home. You won it, fairly, and yet I couldn't let it go. The way you both disgraced us. How we were now homeless."

He sighed and dragged his hand through his hair. "Why did you come after me? What did you intend to do, Clem?"

I made myself take a long swallow of water, but I was trembling, torn between my desires. To be shrewd and continue withholding things, or to let the truth unfold. I set down the glass and drew my cloak tighter around me, as if it could protect me from the discomfort of both choices.

"Did you plan to kill me?" he asked.

"Honestly, Phelan! Do I look *that* merciless to you?"

He stared at me. "I don't know what I see in you."

"I wanted to disgrace you, as you had done to me," I confessed, walking to him. "I wanted to hurt you and your family, to make you feel the things that you had inspired in me. I wanted you to be devastated. And I wanted to win my home back."

He stiffened, as if my words had cut him. But he held my gaze, insistent. "Did you ever plan to reveal to me who you were? Or were you going to up and leave me without word, without a trace?"

"I wanted to tell you. Eventually."

"To bask in your victory, I suppose."

"Yes." I sounded callous, and I watched Phelan flinch.

"So Anna was all an act?" he asked.

"In some ways," I replied carefully. "But in others, no. I was and still am exactly who I was before. Even in the moments when I was with you as Anna . . . I was Clem."

"Did your father put you up to this?"

"No. It was all my doing. My decision."

"And do you feel the same as you did at the beginning?" he asked. "Do you want to see me devastated? Disgraced? Do you want to hurt me, Clem?"

How should I respond? I was suddenly terrified to be vulnerable in his presence, uncertain where such a path might guide us.

"No, Phelan. You were not who I thought you to be at the beginning," I said, my cadence clipped with frustration. "You turned out to be different. And I wanted to despise you. I wanted to throw more kindling on my hate and yet you gave me nothing to burn, because you are simply too good. Even now, you are too *good*."

I shoved his chest for emphasis. He didn't budge, but his hands rose to capture mine.

"How so?" he said. "I told you I wasn't kind."

"You gave me a room when you thought I had nowhere to go. You clothed me and spared no expense. You listened to me when I began spouting wild claims about Seven Wraiths and the knight. And even after you realized who I was . . . you protected me," I said. "You should expose me now. I don't know why you are holding my secret like it is one of your own."

"And yet perhaps I will expose you," he said. "In time."

I froze, my hands still caught in his. "Are you threatening me now?"

"If my dreams are a threat, then yes." He fell silent, as if he wanted me to find the explanation in his eyes. I couldn't see it and pressed him for more.

"What are you speaking of?"

"I dreamt of you yesterday, Clem."

My divided heart all but stopped.

"I dreamt of you," he whispered again.

"A nightmare, I presume?" I countered, unable to help myself.

He smiled. "That I won't say. Although you may see it whether I want you to or not." He paused, his mirth fading. "Do you understand what I'm saying to you?"

I stepped back, suddenly overwhelmed. My hands slipped from his and I walked about my chamber, in and out of the light. His dream might be the one to materialize tonight. Apprehension took hold of me like a claw.

"How did you see me in your dream?" I asked.

"In both ways," he answered. "I saw you as Clem. And I saw you as Anna."

"That won't necessarily expose me," I said, breathless from the shock of his confession. But when I met his eyes from across the room . . . I realized that it would. Whatever his dream held, it was going to reveal my secret.

"I'm sorry, Clem," he murmured, and he did sound contrite, as if he could control what his mind created in sleep.

I almost laughed. "We have never dreamt, you and me. All our lives, we have been void of dreams until now. And at last, we dream, and your first is tainted by a treacherous girl who you must despise."

"I would not trade such a dream," he was swift to say. "Not for me, not for the world. Not even to break this curse. But for your sake in this strange game we find ourselves trapped within . . . I would."

"Well," I said, glancing out the window. "Thank you for the warning. Although perhaps you'll dream of something else this afternoon."

"Perhaps." But he didn't sound confident. And I was swiftly learning that our dreams were intent on unmasking us and our plans. Our secrets, our past. What we hoped for.

What we desired.

An awkward lull beat between us. My face felt hot when I pressed my hands to my cheeks, and I wondered if I was getting ill.

"I should go," Phelan said. "Let you get some rest."

I turned and watched him leave, the door latching quietly behind him. I was still staring at it two breaths later when the door unexpectedly swung open again, Phelan's gaze finding me instantly.

"I wanted it to be you," he said, his voice deep, rough-hewn. "When I returned to the museum for that final interview . . . gods, how I wanted it to be you."

And he had gotten his desire, only not how he had envisioned it.

I took the first step to him, and it broke the storm that had been building between us. He met me in the center of the room, and I had enough sense to flick my fingers and charm the door shut before we collided.

His hands grasped my waist, drawing me to him. I took hold of his collar, my mouth hungry to taste his. Our lips met, cautiously at first as we explored each other. My fingers drifted into his hair as I drank his sighs, his breaths. His hands moved to the curve of my neck; his fingertips traced the dip of my collarbones. I arched into him as he pressed me against the wall.

Vaguely, I heard an inner voice remind me that I was held together by stone and ice. Vaguely, I remembered my disguise, and I told myself that I had not come all this way as Anna only to break now into Clem.

My heart sang a vibrant ache; the pain branched through me, a sharp warning that stole my breath.

"Phelan," I gasped, my fingers tightening in his hair.

He drew away. Cold air washed over me.

I opened my eyes to meet his gaze, afraid that he would see me come undone. But he was looking at my side, where he had pushed aside the drape of my cloak to touch me. His hands fell away; his right palm was smeared with blood.

"You're bleeding," he whispered frantically. "You didn't tell me you were wounded."

I had forgotten about the swipe his brother had taken at me, hours ago. And everything seemed to crash over me at once: my exhaustion, my worry, my desire.

"Come here." Phelan guided me to the bed, easing me down to sit on the edge of the mattress. "Let me tend to you."

"Do you mean to undress me again?" I asked wryly.

He wasn't amused by my humor. "You might need stitches, Clem."

I winced, feeling the wound with each breath. "And what are you going to stitch me with?"

"I brought my supplies."

"Then perhaps you should fetch them."

He stroked a tangle of hair from my brow. His thumb grazed my cheek to find my mouth, tracing my parted lips before he brushed them with his own. A soft, fleeting kiss. Heat flared through me as I watched him depart.

Alone, I inhaled the solitude and pressed a fist to my chest, aching. It took me a moment to regain my composure, and I rushed my fingertips over my face, measuring my disguise. It was still intact, holding fast. But I sensed the frays along my edges. It wouldn't be much longer now.

I stripped and examined my wound, arcing just over my hip bone. It wasn't deep, but it was steadily bleeding again, most likely reopened when Phelan had pressed me against the wall.

A knock on my door. "Anna?"

It was him. His voice made everything leap within me, breathless.

"Anna?"

I swallowed and reached for a clean chemise. It was wrinkled from being shoved in my satchel, but it was soft against my skin as I unlocked the door.

Phelan stepped inside, carrying his medicine kit.

"I can stitch myself," I said, reaching for it.

He withheld the box, glaring at me. "Are you serious?"

"As the grave. Hand it to me, please."

"You're pushing me away from you. Why?"

I hesitated, even as I longed to tell him everything.

"No more lies, Clem," Phelan whispered. "We have both held our secrets long enough. Tell me what is troubling you. Tell me how I can help you."

It was strange how those words of his struck deeper than his kiss. I wavered, leading him back to the bed. I lay down and let him stitch my wound, because I knew that I needed him to do it. And this was a good opportunity to get the answers I still needed from him, as he wouldn't be able to up and run if I asked something he didn't want to answer.

I stared up at the ceiling while he stitched my side. "How long have you known of your mother's plans?"

He exhaled, as if he had been waiting for it. "I sensed she was up to something when she gave me and Lennox orders to take Hereswith and study the book of nightmares for a dreamless sleeper. We suspected she was looking for a particular wraith, but I didn't realize her full intentions yet. When she finally told me that she herself was a wraith, and that she had located nearly all of her kind and planned to return to the mountain and break the new moon curse . . . I was furious. That was the night you saw me tear apart the library. It made me question everything . . . who she was, who I was. What was to come for all of us."

I bit my lip against the sting in my side. "When did you realize who I was?"

"When I saw those scars on your leg," he replied, cutting the thread. "That entire day, I kept telling myself it was ridiculous, that there was no way you could have fooled me for so long. But I started to examine every single one of our interactions, and I realized I should have seen it, right from the very beginning when you viciously attacked me at the interview."

I struggled to hide a smug smile. "I wasn't *vicious*."

Phelan was silent so long it prompted me to look at him. As soon as I did, he leaned so close that our lips almost touched. "You were indeed *vicious*," he breathed, but pulled away before I could kiss him. "That's why I wanted you. And then after the new moon, you snuck from the house. I followed you, all the way to the mines. I saw you speak to Ambrose and I knew without a doubt it was you."

He wiped my stitches with antiseptic, the air between us full of static. And then I whispered, "Why didn't you reveal me to your mother?"

Phelan glanced away, repacking the medicine kit. "I thought about it, at first. I was so angry at you for deceiving me. But I couldn't do it. Every time I approached her about it . . . I couldn't speak the words."

I felt like he was withholding something else. Why wouldn't he meet my eyes when he answered?

I chose to be vulnerable in that moment, hoping it would encourage him to be the same, and sat forward, my stitches pinching my side. I took his hand and I laid it over my chest, where my heart was beating. Phelan's eyes widened at first, uncertain of my intentions until I said, "My heart is only mine by half."

He continued to kneel before me, pensive, his eyes studying me as his hand continued to rest against my breast. As he felt the uneven song beneath my skin. "And where is the other half, Clem?"

I told him the truth, about Mazarine's tonic, and what I had to surrender. I told him half of my heart was stone and my disguise as Anna was dependent on its survival.

"That night when you caught my reflection in the mirror," I said. "When you said my name . . . the stone within me suffered a crack. And I don't regret that it did, because I had forgotten how vital it is to be known for who you are, and not for who you pretend to be. I had forgotten how good it is to be seen, even with flaws and scars. I *wanted* you to see me. But I can't risk it now. Not until the end comes. You are making it more difficult for me because I've grown fond of you, in the most impossible of ways."

There was a long beat of silence. I was suddenly eager to know his thoughts, but I was too proud to beg for them.

I waited, full of blazing tension, watching him.

"Then I will guard you until the end, even if that means I must do it from a distance," he said. His fingers traced down my arm to twine with my own, lifting my hand to his lips. To kiss the hollow of my palm, as if sealing me with a vow. "Rest now, Clem."

He relinquished me and stood. I sensed he was anxious about the things I had shared with him, but he hid his emotions well.

"Do you need anything before I go?" he asked, halfway to the door.

I studied him, wondering how this had happened to us. I yearned to say one word to him. *Stay.*

But I shook my head, surrendering to the cold bed.

"No."

He left.

I soaked in the silence of the mountains, drawing my fingers through my tangled hair. Phelan had become my greatest alliance while also becoming my greatest threat. And a few strands of auburn now shone among the golden brown of my hair.

37

Imonie had slipped another message beneath my door.

I found it as soon as I woke from my afternoon sleep, still heavy from dreams of Hereswith.

This time, she wrote: *The master of coin?*

I stood and puzzled over it and why she had sent it to me. I contemplated going to her; she and I still needed to talk. But I knew it was too dangerous for me to be in any way associated with her, especially since I had cast my lot with the countess. And I winced whenever I imagined asking Imonie why she'd lied to me all those years. I honestly knew what her answer would be: to protect my father and the life he had built in Bardyllis.

To protect *me*, until the right time came to tell me the truth.

I burned her message, as I had with the one the day before. I couldn't risk having them lying around my room, and as I watched the parchment curl into ash, I realized what she was trying to tell me.

She wanted me to take the throne. And she must be doubting the duke's—*the master of coin's*—agreement with my father to support my claim.

I threw on my charm of stealth and walked the corridors, my eyes keen to find the duke. I eventually located him in the fortress's garden, meandering among tangles of shrubs. I stood behind the courtyard doors and watched him through the glass windowpanes. He paused to gaze at the astounding view that rolled beyond the garden walls—an overlook of the mountain city of Ulla, built in tiers with houses of stone. Abandoned and empty now, with nature overtaking it.

I needed to speak with him, but I couldn't do it in the open, where the countess might see.

I hastened to the duke's chambers. His door was locked, but I picked it easily enough with a charm. I settled in a chair where I had clear vantage of the door, my stealth still cloaking me, and waited.

A quarter of an hour later, the door opened.

The duke entered the chamber, wholly unaware of my presence. If he had been more attentive, he might have noticed the odd wrinkle against the wall panel. A break in the pattern. But as my luck had it, he was too preoccupied.

I gave him a moment to cross the floor. He came to a stop before the mirror, and he gazed at himself. From where I was positioned, I could only catch half of his true face in the reflection.

He was old. Much older than his disguise. His hair was long and silver, his face pale and crinkled as parchment. There was a scar on his brow, and a beard covered his face, gleaming like frost.

He sighed.

I understood a fraction of that feeling, and I watched as he turned to his refreshment table, as he poured a glass of water.

The cup was halfway to his lips when my voice broke the silence.

"The water is poisoned, Your Grace."

The duke startled.

He dropped the glass and I watched it shatter, the harmless water spilling across the floor. I released my charm as he turned, finding me instantly sitting in the chair against the wall.

"Miss Neven," he said, and he somehow managed to sound pleased to see me. Although he was an exquisite pretender. "You have taken me by surprise."

"Forgive me, Your Grace. I thought it best that I give you warning."

"And who seeks to poison me?" he asked, glancing down at the puddle.

"I will tell you, but only if you honestly answer two of my questions first."

He laughed, a deep robust sound. "Very well, Miss Neven. Come, why don't you take a seat next to me, and we can share what little bread and meat I have remaining, unless it is poisoned as well?"

I rose and joined him at the table, but I declined the meal.

"Your food is safe, but I'm not hungry."

He nodded but seemed to hesitate before breaking the brown loaf. "Ask your first question, Miss Neven."

I waited until he had taken a bite. "Do you want the new moon curse to end?"

"Of course I do," he answered, but he spoke too swiftly. "The nightmares have haunted us long enough in Bardyllis. My people are weary of them. They are a great inconvenience every month."

"Even if the dream tax fills your coffers?"

He narrowed his eyes at me but took another bite of bread. "That tax not only serves the betterment of the land, but pays magicians like you, Miss Neven. Do you want to do such dangerous work for free?"

"Wardens deserve to be paid," I said. "But the tax on dreams is excessive and unnecessary."

"I suppose that means you are in favor of breaking this curse, Miss Neven," he stated. "At the cost of losing your profession and income."

"I'm in favor of breaking it," I replied.

I had never imagined I would find myself in the throes of ending the new moon curse, and the duke was right—to see it broken would change my way of life. But I wanted the mountain duchy to be restored. I wanted the realm to be healed. I wanted my father and Imonie to feel less like wraiths and more like humans again.

I wanted to do something beyond fighting nightmares, moon after moon, trapped in a vengeful cycle.

"Then that settles your first question," he said. "Ask your second."

"Who do you support when it comes to new sovereignty?"

"Ah, we have at last reached the meat of the matter," the duke said, and as if to make a point, speared the roast with his fork. "This is not easily answered, Miss Neven. There are many factors at play."

"Such as?"

He chewed, and I knew he was giving himself time to form his answer. "I think the members of the original court have been given our chance and we squandered it, didn't we? I am in favor of one of the children ruling."

"Lennox, Phelan, or Olivette?"

"There is another one."

"Who?"

"Ambrose's daughter." The duke cut another slice of meat. "Clementine Madigan."

"A strange name," I mused.

The duke only arched his brow and ate his roast.

"Well," I said. "Where is this girl?"

"You heard Ambrose the other night at the camp. She's missing."

"Then she is not a candidate for the duchy," I replied simply. "So we shall set her aside. Who, out of the three present, would you support?"

"*You* could also take the throne, Miss Neven. We talked about this before. One doesn't need a claim to rule Seren, although it does help garner approval and protection."

And that was when it hit me: what I wanted, and what I didn't. I stared at the duke and said, "I don't want to rule."

"Very well." He sighed and set down his fork. "You know of my investment."

"You speak of Phelan." Who was a human, not a sum of money. But I held that comment between my teeth.

"Phelan is for Bardyllis. I only need his signature on the papers to officially deem him as my heir."

"Are he and Lennox your sons?"

The duke didn't seem shocked by my blatant query. He only smiled and said, "You are not the first to wonder that. But no. They are not."

"You must have some agreement with the countess, then," I said, and watched how his expression shifted. It was only a minute change, but enough to inform me that I had struck a nerve. "And that agreement must have been forged long ago, because it seems as if the two of you don't see eye to eye now."

"The countess has always been ambitious," he answered. "I've known her her whole life. She only makes decisions that serve her interest in the end. Phelan as duke is one of them, because she thinks he is her weaker son. She thinks she can manipulate him and rule through him. And you see . . . she has always wanted to rule. She never got over the insult that her brother was deemed more fit to be duke, and not her. Ever since then, she craved power."

"Then who do you think she wants to see rule the mountains?" I dared to ask. "She was the one who was so keen on seeing this curse overturned."

"My dear girl," the duke said, and reached for my hand. "*She* wants to rule the mountains. She always has. A century has not changed that ambition of hers."

I slipped my hand away from his hold. "But the nightmare must be broken before she can claim the throne."

"And her two sons are wardens, aren't they?" he said. "She will have Phelan and Lennox break the dream and she will claim the right to rule."

I was quiet for a moment. And then I said, "Do you want to see her reign?"

"I have already told you that I think our court has had its moment."

"Then would you support Olivette Wolfe? Or Nura Sparrow?"

He chuckled. "Olivette has made it quite clear she wants nothing to do with the mountains. She is Bardyllis, through and through. As for her partner . . . I fear I do not know much about her to say if I would support her claim or not."

He wasn't wrong. I sensed Olivette was uncomfortable here. She longed to return to Endellion. I sensed Nura did, too. And it didn't feel right to put such weight and responsibility on them now, not when Olivette was still reeling from her father's secrets and had been wounded by a nightmare. Not when both girls had outright said *I don't want it.*

"You dislike Lennox?" the duke asked.

I did my best to keep my face neutral. "He's not who I envision for the mountains."

"But Phelan is."

"Yes."

The duke sighed. "As I said, Miss Neven, he is—"

"For Bardyllis," I finished the phrase. "And Bardyllis is a well-established province. Anyone could be polished and trained to be sovereign over it, to inherit the land from you. But that is not so when it comes to Seren. Its people have been scattered for a hundred years. Its fortress has been abandoned. Its court broken and cursed." I paused, hoping my words were finding their mark with the duke. *The master of coin.* "I don't know how long you've been disguised, Lord Deryn. I don't even know your true name, and I won't ask for it. But I want you to consider releasing Phelan from Bardyllis and supporting his claim for Seren. You say he is your heir, and yet your blood is of the mountains, not of the meadows and the coast. This fortress was your first home, Your Grace. Remember where you have come from."

He was pensive, listening. I wondered how easy he would be to sway, if he would remain faithful to the bargain he had agreed to with my father, or if he would shift course. I knew my wisest action was to let him simmer on what I had said.

I rose from the table.

"Take the remainder of the day to mull it over," I said. "But if you do decide to join me in supporting Phelan's claim, come to the hall at sunset and raise your glass to me."

"I shall consider it, Miss Neven," he said with a nod. "Now, then. Who sent you to poison me?"

I began to walk to the door, but I turned to regard him one final time. I caught a glimpse of his true reflection in the mirror.

An old, shrewd man was he.

But two could play that game.

"The countess, of course," I said, and departed without another word.

38

Eventide fell.

I began to prepare for the night. I washed my face and braided my hair, hiding the auburn strands. I donned a plaid skirt, a fresh chemise, and a black bodice to lace over it. The clothes I felt most comfortable in. I drew my stockings up to my knees and put on my boots, my dagger tucked in its hiding place, and then ate the meal that appeared on my table. Pumpernickel bread and a roasted hen and water still cold from a mountain stream.

I was one of the first to reach the hall that night.

The Vesper brothers were present, leaning against one of the trestle tables. I made a point to avoid looking at Lennox, but my gaze drifted to Phelan. He was already looking at me; I took three deep breaths before I broke our stare, walking the length of the hall.

Every minute that passed heightened my worry. The potential

manifestation of Phelan's dreams was the root of it, but there was also the possibility of my parents' dreams, or Imonie's, or even Mazarine's to expose me. I didn't know if they dreamt of me or not, and it made me anxious.

As soon as I thought about Papa, he appeared in the hall, dressed in his best and prepared to fight. I shared one fleeting glance with him, and then we both ignored each other.

Nura and Olivette did not arrive, and I presumed they were resting that night, safe in their bedchamber.

I watched the last of the light fade through the windows and was surprised to see the duke enter the hall, just as I'd requested. He held a glass of water, and he meandered over to Phelan and Lennox, speaking a few words with them.

Perhaps he had only come here to taunt me. But then the duke met my gaze from across the hall and lifted his glass to me.

I acknowledged him with a bow of my head, just before he departed.

Alliances were not carved in stone, it seemed.

Phelan noticed our exchange, but only because I was never far from his attention. And I couldn't help but notice his every detail in return. The garments that fit him perfectly: fawn-brown trousers and knee-high boots, a waistcoat embroidered with the phases of the moon, a cravat, a black tailed jacket, and a rapier sheathed at his belt. His dark hair was loose, just as I preferred.

The countess entered the hall next, to my shock. She wore an ink-black dress with a fur draped diagonally across her body, cinched tightly at her waist with a belt of gold. A dagger was sheathed at her hip. I wondered why she was there—she was a magician, but not a warden—and I made my way over to Phelan's side after Lennox had vacated their table.

"Your mother is planning to fight tonight?" I asked.

"She plans to watch," Phelan replied. "But your—" He caught himself, clearing his throat. "Mr. Madigan is joining us, I see."

"Yes," I said, keeping my voice low. "I hear he was once a great warden."

"I believe he still is," Phelan said gently.

"Phelan," I whispered, and I wanted to ask if he would claim the chair should the dream break tonight. He was the hope of the mountains, because Olivette and Nura didn't desire it, and Lennox was crooked in heart, and I was full of contradictions and lies. But I lost my courage; the words wilted within me.

He waited, but his mother approached us, and the moment was lost.

"Ah, I am glad to see you here tonight, Anna," the countess said.

"Yes, Lady Raven," I replied. "I'm ready to fight beside Phelan, per usual."

She smiled, but the warmth failed to reach her eyes. "May I have a word with you, my son? Over here with your brother?"

Phelan released a soft sigh, one that I knew expressed his reluctance, but he accompanied his mother back across the hall to where Lennox stood.

I took note of the three of them, plotting in a shadowy corner. My father, who walked the aisle alone. And then there was me, caught between the two, full of hope and doubt and plans of my own.

The night arrived at last. The shadows in the hall sweetened until the multiple hearths ignited with enchanted flame, casting streams of light across the floor.

It took a while for the throne to materialize on the dais. But once it appeared, Emrys arrived to stand beside it like a magistrate at court, and the nightmare was not long to follow.

I watched the hall shift, molting its tables and benches and heraldic banners. The floors rippled into white marble with threads of blue; the timber beams in the ceiling sank to become arched and coffered. Chandeliers bloomed, glittering with silver leaves and candles.

I recognized this place. It was the ballroom at the countess's mansion in Endellion.

I glanced across the way to look at Lady Raven. Her face was stark, her eyes wide with dread.

This was one of her dreams.

I hung back at its edge and watched.

The phantom countess stood in the center of the ballroom, and beside her was a man, tall and trim with thick dark hair. He reminded me of Phelan, and I knew this was her brother, the Duke of Seren. The magician who had cursed this court and the new moon, whose bones now gleamed beneath his bed.

The phantom countess startled to see him. "What are you doing here, Isidore?"

"You are not pleased to see me, sister? Not even in dreams?"

She was quiet, but I saw how she traced her belt, seeking the hilt of her dagger.

Isidore noticed and smiled, fearless of her. "You cannot kill me in this realm."

"I was not seeking to."

"Then what is this blood on your hands?" he asked.

The countess glanced down to see she had smeared blood on her dress. She held up her hands, and they trembled as blood dripped from her fingers and gathered on the floor, inch deep.

"Shall we see all the people you have killed, and those you hope to end?" drawled Isidore, and with a sweep of his hand, more people appeared in the ballroom.

There were ten victims in total, counting the Duke of Seren, and I didn't recognize any of them, but the air grew tense when they looked at the countess, the woman who had set their deaths in motion. I saw a flash of red hair, long and loose and wild, as a girl walked across the ballroom through the blood.

I felt a stitch in my side when I saw her face.

It was me.

Clem.

And I didn't know why I was in the countess's dream. Not until I stood beside the Duke of Seren and the truth sank into me like a blade.

The countess planned to kill me.

I glanced around the nightmare, seeking Phelan. I couldn't locate him among the fantastical gleam of our surroundings, but I longed more than anything to behold his face in that moment. To see if he had known of his mother's plans.

Whatever else the dream had in store was altered, because Lennox stepped forward to walk among the victims, his rapier drawn and his hand up, ready to cast. He should have been more patient, I thought with gritted teeth. Now he had interrupted the nightmare, and it would run its own reactive course. I would never know how the countess's dream truly ended, if she succeeded in killing me.

But perhaps it didn't matter. Lennox was focused on Clem; he wove his way through the victims to reach her, and I realized that she wore the golden jewel around her neck, just as Anna had the night before. The weakness was me and my stone heart, and I swallowed a curse, irritated that the dreams here seemed fixated on exposing my secret.

Phelan appeared, trailing his brother. "What are you doing, Lee?"

Lennox paused to glance over his shoulder. "She is the key to breaking this dream. Don't you see it?"

Phelan gazed at Clem. His eyes were dark and filled with longing, and I wondered what thoughts ravaged him as he looked at my phantom.

Clem was silent and pale, rooted to the bloody floor like a statue. The sight of her stillness made me nervous, and I took a step deeper into the dream.

"This is not her, you know," Lennox taunted, sensing his brother's attachment, and prepared to pierce Clem's chest with the tip of his rapier.

"Wait, Lee!" Phelan struggled through the crowd, who began to turn on him. The peaceful guise of the ballroom shattered, and Phelan had no choice but to divert his attention to defend himself.

My father stepped forward, entering the fray. I watched him strike down one of the countess's victims with a beam of light. He cut the Duke of Seren in half, unrepentant, and Isidore gasped, melting into smoke.

The countess must have been waiting for her brother to be conquered, for she interfered at last, her face flushed from the mortification of watching her dream on display. She ignored the phantom of herself and the teeming violence, and withdrew the dagger from her belt.

"Kill her," she ordered Lennox, nodding at Clem.

My eyes drifted back to Clem, and my body coiled with energy, preparing to impede the countess should the dream break. I watched this phantom of myself, who continued to stand, docile and gentle, and I wondered if I would go down quietly, if I would do nothing while Lennox attacked me.

Lennox drew back his sword, preparing to strike Clem.

And she waited until he had begun his forward thrust, the rapier glinting in the light. She moved her hand in a terribly familiar way, a movement I had performed many times, and her magic caught the blade before it could pierce her breast. The rapier submitted to her, bending back on itself to sting its wielder, and Lennox went wide-eyed in shock, emitting a scream as his own blade punctured his shoulder.

How pleased I was in that moment.

I stood in the shadows and watched with satisfaction as Clem flicked her fingers and hurled Lennox back. He landed on the floor with a groan, his rapier still lodged in his shoulder, and he mewled in pain, blood soaking his clothes.

The countess turned bug-eyed, glancing between her son and Clem.

"Phelan!" she cried, shrill. "Come and finish this."

Phelan's clothes were shredded. There was blood splattered across his waistcoat and hands, although I didn't believe it was his. His hair was tousled, dark threads of it framing his face. He stopped fighting, and I could tell he was weary by his shoulders, how they curved inward. His old wounds must be hurting him.

"Come here," the countess said, sharper, and he obeyed.

Phelan walked to her in a heavy gait. My father continued to fight the remaining phantoms in the dream, but his attention was now split, divided between what he battled and the sight of Phelan approaching his daughter.

"Go on," Lady Raven prompted. "This is yours to vanquish."

Phelan stared at Clem, his breaths ragged. He held up his rapier, pointing to her heart, to that promise of gold. The nightmare's fault line.

He froze in that stance, but his arm quivered.

Gradually, he lowered his sword and said, "I cannot do this."

"Yes, you can," his mother encouraged him. "This is just a phantom. Whatever power this girl holds over you . . . now is the time to break free, Phelan."

He took a step nearer to Clem, unable to look away from her.

From me, I thought, and a warning rang deep in my bones.

I moved silently, drawing closer. Blood soaked the hem of my skirt. It rippled in my wake, and yet no one noticed my approach. No one but my father, who had finished slaying the rest of the dream's phantoms and was sore for breath.

I wasn't sure what to expect from Clem, if she would treat Phelan with the same regard as she had Lennox. My stomach clenched when Phelan gently reached out to her.

I saw the shift in her expression, the cold glitter in her eyes. There was no love, no forgiveness, no mercy within her. Vengeance had devoured those parts of her, scraped her clean, and she was hollow, so endlessly hollow. I felt an echo of that emptiness as Clem prepared to strike Phelan down, her magic gathering.

He stiffened and inhaled a sharp breath, his realization coming a moment too late.

I lunged forward and cast a shield. My magic came between them, absorbing the brunt of force that had been directed at Phelan. The shock of my interference rocked all three of us, and we stumbled back a few paces, our surroundings rumbling in response. A crack formed in the floor, and the blood began to drain through it, filling the ballroom with a perpetual trickling sound.

I regained my balance and stood a few paces away, my hand aching. I watched as Clem likewise straightened her willowy frame. Auburn hair tangled across her face like a net. I remembered that feeling; I could nearly sense it over my own face. Her eyes met mine over the fissure and blood and shadows and firelight, and she smiled, as if she had been waiting all along for me to appear.

"Anna!" the countess cried in relief. "Thank gods, dear one. Finish what my sons cannot. Break this dream, Anna, and I will extravagantly reward you."

I hardly paid her any attention. I was focused on Clem. I stepped over the crack in the floor, into her striking range. We circled each other, prey and predator, girl and phantom. I was both, and yet I felt like neither. My emotions were snarled, cold and hot feelings entwined together, radiating a pleasant numbness in my chest.

How was I to defeat her? I knew her arsenal of spells. As she knew mine.

Clem at last came to a halt.

I mirrored her motions.

Over the slender slope of her shoulder, I saw the dais behind her. The throne, gleaming like it was carved from bones, and Emrys standing beside it, watching me with wicked amusement. And then the countess walked into that view, waiting on the dais stairs. She was positioning herself, I realized. As soon as I broke this dream, she would claim the sovereignty of the mountains.

And more than anything . . . I didn't want to bend the knee to her. I didn't want to see her sit on that throne.

I held Clem's stare, and I knew she saw the cascade of my thoughts. My desire for her to take victory over the dream.

She nodded and lifted her hand toward Lady Raven. Down went the countess, with a shriek and a tumble. She lay prostrate on the stairs, frozen. Had my phantom just killed her?

There was no time for me to wonder. Clem pivoted and shot a spell at Lennox next, even though he was still writhing along the floor, wounded. He went limp as a rag doll, limbs splayed out.

Phelan, I thought, and panicked. I took a step toward him, the phantom's spell grazing my ear. The enchantment hit him square in the chest, and I watched, wide-eyed, as a trail of blood began to flow from his nose. He sank to his knees, his gaze fastened to me. I was the last thing he saw as he surrendered to the floor.

And then my father, who was swift, but not swift enough when the nightmare was his daughter. He could have struck Clem down; he could have broken the dream. But he hesitated, and she took advantage of that moment. Down he went, like a folding house of cards.

I stared, stricken, at his unconscious form. Blood also trickled from his nose.

I tried to convince myself this was just a dream; they weren't dead. But a wave of devastation broke over me, and pain sparked from my chest up to my neck. As if I had been branded. Hissing, I touched my throat. My fingertips traced sleek marks, embedded in my skin.

"The throne is yours for the taking," said Clem. "I will concede, but only to you."

I stared at her. Before I knew it, I struck her down with a spell, aiming for her heart. She melted into smoke, into oblivion, and I realized on shaking legs that I had just vanquished the nightmare.

My eyes drifted to the dais. To the throne, where Emrys continued to wait. He held out his hand, inviting me to take the chair.

I took a step closer to it. Suddenly, it was all I could see, all I desired. I walked through blood, stepped over the countess's body, and I was rising, rising to take it. All the things I could do, all the things I could change.

My ambition was broken by Emrys, whose gaze flickered beyond me, as if someone else had entered the hall. I paused on the steps; a warning crept over my skin. Someone was following me.

I spun to see who it was but was met by the blur of a shield, swinging to knock me off my feet. Pain bloomed across my skull, burst behind my eyes.

And down I went. Deep into the darkness.

It was peaceful; the darkness held me like a vise. But when the light started to creep in, I was met by a sea of strange sensations.

Cold fingers tracing my face. Cold fingers on my neck, covering my throat.

A ring of voices, calling a name that sparked nothing within me. *Anna? Anna!*

A pant of breath, breaking through the watery commotion, saying, "No, let me take her. She's mine."

Arms carrying me, up into the clouds. Down into the depths of the mountain. A soft fur and bed and the crackle of fire. The smell of pine and meadow grass.

"Clem."

It was Phelan, trying to rouse me.

My head felt split open. My chest wept with pain.

"Get the dagger out," I whispered to him, but I couldn't open my eyes or show him where I hurt.

"Clem."

I drifted away from him and his hands, down into a place where not even dreams could reach.

39

When I woke, my memories were scrambled.

It was afternoon again, but the light was icy and tinged in blue, as if a storm brewed beyond the windows. I was lying on a bed of furs, Phelan close beside me. I watched his chest rise and fall as he dozed. Slowly, I put the pieces together, and I remembered what had led me here, shut away in his room with a splitting headache.

The moment I moved, he woke.

"Easy, Clem."

"I want to sit forward," I croaked, and he eased me up. The world spun, and I fought a wave of nausea, settling against the wooden headboard. "How long have I been asleep?"

"For several hours." Phelan moved off the bed to stir the fire in the hearth and pour me a cup of water. He brought it to me, and I took long, greedy drafts. "It's about noon now, although the snow is making it difficult to tell time."

I glanced out the window, struck by the haunting beauty of the snow as it fell. I watched its dance for a moment longer, until I raised my hand to feel the back of my head. There was a tender lump, hidden in my snarled hair.

"Who hurt you, Clem?" Phelan asked.

"It wasn't the nightmare," I replied. "Someone struck me."

I didn't tell him that I had been ascending to take the throne. Or that I had stepped over his mother's prone form to do it.

I remembered the blur of wood and steel, just before impact. I hadn't been struck by a spell, but by a shield. Something of the physical world. Had it been the duke? Or had it been someone like Mr. Wolfe?

My suspicions stirred. Whoever had rendered me unconscious didn't want the curse to end; if they had, they would have taken the throne, instead of leaving it empty until the sun rose and the chair vanished along with Emrys, waiting for evening to reappear.

Phelan was quiet. His silence drew my eyes to him, and he studied me with a frown.

"What's wrong?"

"You're changing, Clem."

"How do you mean?" My heart gave a nervous twitch, as if he sensed the shadows gathering within me. But he only sat on the edge of the bed and caressed my hair.

"There's more auburn in your hair now. And your neck . . ." His fingers traced my throat. "The gill scars have returned."

I swallowed and touched the sleek scars. "I saw my phantom strike you and my father down, and I thought you both were dead."

Phelan's hand drifted from me. "Not dead, but in a painful sleep. I don't think I care to encounter your dream form again anytime soon."

He was teasing me, but my face felt too stiff for a smile.

"Did you know that your mother wants to kill me, Phelan?"

"No, Clem. I swear that I didn't know she wanted to see you dead. And even if I had known, if she had told me the full extent of her plans, I would have *never* revealed you to her."

My thoughts hung on his words. *Revealed you to her.*

I looked at him, saw the crushed hope and anguish within his eyes. "But you told me to *hold my act.* You have held my secret as your own, playing this charade alongside me. So you must have come to realize that she planned me harm, or else it wouldn't have mattered if I was Anna."

He briefly covered his mouth with his hand as if deep in thought, but when he met my gaze once more, I saw that I had spoken truth.

"Clem . . ."

"Tell me the truth, Phelan," I said. "I'm sick of people lying to me. And if you can't be honest . . . you and I are done being partners."

He drew a sharp breath. "Then let there be no more lies between us, Clem. I knew she wanted to keep tabs on you and your father after you left Hereswith. She told me to find you. I didn't know why and I didn't question her. But I should have. I didn't know she wanted to harm you, not until she told me the entirety of her plans."

"When you came home and trashed the library."

"You'll never let me forget it, will you?" he countered with a slight smile. But the mirth faded as he continued, "I couldn't bear to see anything happen to you. Yes, I told you to hold the act, and I've been carrying it alongside you, because I don't care for my mother's plans."

His voice held a tremor, one that made me think his heart was beating in his throat. He slid off the bed and sank to his knees.

"You told me to get on my knees before you and apologize," he said. "This is me saying I'm sorry, for all that I have done to you, for all the heartache I have caused, for giving you no choice but to resort to the wildest of plans to ease the pain I wrought. I don't deserve your forgiveness, but this one thing I seek, so that I may remain near you."

I must have stared at him for a long, excruciating moment, because he whispered my name. I shifted across the mattress, sitting on the edge of the bed before him, my feet touching the floor. I still was afraid to speak—even his name might break me—and I took his face in my hands.

Phelan's arms came around me. "Tell me what you want me to do," he said. "Tell me to leave, and I will."

My fingers slid into his hair. "Stay," I whispered.

He kissed the shine of scars on my neck. His fingers traced the curve of my back as he kissed my collarbones, down to where my heart pounded a stilted dance of flesh trying to break away from stone, and stone determined to hold fast.

Whatever came tonight, I hoped it ushered the end. For I didn't know how much longer I could withstand this veneer.

"Why does your mother want to kill me?" I asked, to dampen the embers flaring between us.

Phelan leaned back so he could look up at me. His hands drifted to my hips, a warm, possessive touch. "You're a threat to her."

"In what way?"

"You're Ambrose Madigan's daughter. Emrys Madigan's niece. The blood of the mountains runs through you." He paused, but his dark eyes measured mine. "You're a strong contender for the sovereign claim of Seren."

I snorted. "And so are you and Lennox. And so is Olivette."

"My mother doesn't see Olivette as a threat."

"Are you certain, Phelan? Perhaps you should still warn Nura."

He pressed his lips together but nodded. "Yes, you're right. I should warn them both. But Mr. Wolfe is devoted to my mother. She gave him favor and protection in the era before the curse and I don't see him turning against her now. I have no doubt he will support my mother's claim to sovereignty."

"And do you?" I countered. "Do you support your mother's claim?"

"No."

This is the moment, I thought. The moment I told him what I hoped for. Who I wanted to see bring life back to these mountains.

There was a knock on the door.

Phelan stiffened. He eased my hair forward, so that it flowed over my shoulders, concealing the auburn strands as well as the scars in my neck. Reluctantly, he went to answer the door.

It was the countess. She stood on the threshold, holding a platter of roasted hen.

"What is it, Mother?" he asked, sounding just as surprised as I felt.

Lady Raven glanced at me, her eyes as cold as the snow drifting beyond the window. "I hope you have recovered from last night, Anna."

"You're interrupting her rest, Mother."

"She has been resting for hours, and in case you forgot, Phelan . . . *all* of us suffered a hard night," Lady Raven stated. "I would like to speak to Anna alone."

"I don't think—"

"It's all right, Phelan," I said.

He didn't want to leave me alone with his mother. I read the lines in his brow, the set of his jaw. I noticed how his hands clenched and released as he strode past the countess, out into the shadows of the corridor.

As I felt the draft of his leaving, I wondered if she had discovered my deceit. If she knew who I was beneath my guise.

Perhaps the countess had come to kill me.

Lady Raven kicked the door shut. She crossed the chamber to set the platter of hen down on the table.

"You shouldn't have troubled yourself, lady," I said.

"Oh, this is not for you," she replied. "It is for the troll."

I blinked. "The one called Mazarine?"

"Yes. Brin of Stonefall."

I hadn't seen Mazarine since the day we'd arrived. She had kept to herself in her chambers. I often forgot about her presence.

"The duke tried to poison me early this morning," the countess said, brusque.

"He did?"

"Yes. And so the time has come for me to finally rid myself of him."

"Are you certain it was the duke?"

"He is no duke," she all but snarled. "He is a master of coin, and his greed knows no bounds. It took me nearly eighty years to locate him after the curse. That was the extent of his desire to never be found."

"How were you able to find him, lady?"

"My sons," she replied, glancing at me. "The duke, who was close friends with my late husband, treated my boys as his own when they were born. When his wife died and he remained child-less, he began to lavish great gifts upon us. Particularly Phelan, who needed intensive schooling to amount to anything."

I held my tongue, although I burned to give a retort. I thought of Phelan's self-deprecation on the first new moon we had fought together. How he believed himself unworthy of his title and magic, even though he had striven twice as hard as me to earn the illumination.

"Three years ago," she continued, oblivious to my ire, "the duke approached me about naming Phelan as his heir, the future Duke of Bardyllis. And I do not know why, but it roused my suspicions.

It took me another two years to fully understand that this was not Lord Deryn but my old companion from the mountain, and that he must also know where Brin of Stonefall was hiding herself, for as the spymistress of Seren she once wielded the ancient and hazardous magic of guises."

Hold your act. I heard Phelan's voice in my memory. *Hold your act. . . .*

But how close the countess was to uncovering me. I felt as if I walked on glass.

"So you desire to kill the duke for vengeance, because he evaded and deceived you for so long?" I asked.

"I desire to kill him because he is going to oppose the curse breaking," she said. "He does not want to see the Seren court reinstated. He does not want to see the new moon nightmares come to an end. It is too lucrative for him, this business of taxing dreams."

Her words sank into me slowly, like a long knife, and for a moment I wavered, overcome with doubt. The duke said he would support me as well as Phelan. And yet the countess believed he would oppose anyone claiming the sovereignty.

I felt her gaze, an icy assessment of my demeanor, and I rallied, focusing on her.

"So you want to bribe Mazarine with a chicken?"

The countess smiled, as if I were some adorable, dense creature. "No, child. The hen is poisoned. And once Mazarine falls, her magic crumbles. The master of coin will lose his guise as duke, and then he will have nothing. No title, no prowess, no fortune. He will have no choice but to support my plans to end this curse."

"Oh," I said. "A brilliant move, Countess."

"Indeed. Now, deliver the chicken to Mazarine. But do not rush away. Delay and talk to her, to ensure she begins to eat it. Trolls are vain creatures, and they like stories and shrewd company. You will do fine, Anna." Lady Raven was obviously scared of Mazarine. And she was sending me in her stead.

"I'm not in danger from this troll, am I, lady?"

The countess opened the door and looked at me. Another one of her pitying expressions. "No, my dear. So long as you give her the hen." She took a step over the threshold but then paused.

I braced myself, my hand eager to find my dagger, hidden in my boot.

"Oh, and Anna?" she added, just before she departed. "Last night, you hesitated, and the nightmare got the best of you. See that you don't let it happen again."

40

Ten minutes later, I knocked on Mazarine's door with a headache and a chicken. She had chosen a room in the northern wing of the fortress, where the colder, darker chambers sat with minimal sunshine and an interior view of the mountains.

"Who knocks?" she growled through the iron-latticed wood.

"It's Anna Neven," I replied, balancing the platter of hen.

I heard her footsteps as she approached the door. The multiple locks turning. And then I stood face-to-face with her, and a frightening smile lit her face. Her yellow teeth flashed like amber.

"Anna," she crooned. "It has been a while. Do come in."

I entered, struck at once by the abundance of candlelight and the heavy scent of moss and damp stone that filled her chamber. Her windows were open, and snow was swirling into the room. The temperature was frigid.

"Careful," she warned. "The floor is slick in some places. And mortal bones are quick to fracture."

I took heed of her warning and set the platter down on the table, which was scattered with chicken bones, all split and sucked dry. I felt her presence trailing me like a shadow.

"And what is this?" she asked.

"A gift from the countess," I replied.

"Ah, my old beloved enemy," said the troll, bending her head close to the hen. She sniffed it, her nose scrunching in distaste.

"It's poisoned," I said.

"Any fool could smell it and come to that conclusion," Mazarine said, straightening. "Why does she poison me?"

"She wants to use you to strike at the duke, who I suppose I should begin calling the master of coin."

"Ah, I see. Her ambition never ceases to amaze me." She studied me closer, one eye smaller than the other. "And you are involved with the heiress?"

"For now."

"You have surprised and delighted me, mortal girl."

"How so?"

"You have used your guise to the greatest advantage. You find yourself in a dangerous game to secure a new sovereign, and yet you move effortlessly. Tell me, does your stone heart still hold true, unmovable as this mountain?"

"I've guarded it well," I carefully replied, but I could still taste Phelan's lips on mine. I still saw him on his knees before me, captivated. I still heard the way he said my name.

"Time will tell, won't it?" Mazarine said, as if she sensed the cracks in me.

"May I ask you a question?"

"Perhaps."

I took that as a yes. I held her beady gaze and asked, "Can I trust the duke? The master of coin?"

"Hmm." She drummed her fingers on the table, her long nails clicking on the wood. "Can you trust him, you ask. He often says one thing and does another in secret. Who do you think spread rumors of how great the cruel duke was a century ago? And yet who bribed the guard at the duke's door the night of the assassination? The master of coin. But who promised the master of coin an endless cave of jewels and gold once she reigned? The heiress, who you call countess."

Her answer did nothing to bolster my reassurance. The duke might be playing me, or he could be genuine, eager to see the countess's ultimate plans dashed.

"Does that answer your query, mortal girl?"

"Yes."

"But there is another question in your eyes. Speak it, Clementine of Hereswith. I will answer with truth."

It was so cold in this room I could see my breath, and the snow was swirling, gathering in my hair. And yet I had never felt more alive than at that moment.

"Will you support Phelan if he takes the throne?"

She must have been expecting this question, because she answered it smoothly. "I support *you*."

"But I'm not a worthy contender."

"You are a daughter of the mountain, even beneath the veil of my magic." Mazarine began to walk a circle around me. "You have crept into my stone of a heart and softened me, to my immense dismay and utter astonishment. I would support your claim without fail, but if you forgo it yourself, I would support your choice of sovereign."

She rendered me speechless.

And it pleased her. She came to a halt before me, studying my face. "I always knew you would help guide us home."

"What do you mean?" I asked.

"I used to watch the world spin from my third-story windows in Hereswith," Mazarine began. "Time does not feel the same to me as it does to you; minutes are long and empty, and seasons feel endless. Yet I was patient. I was waiting. Waiting for someone to come along to set things in motion. The moment I saw that red hair of yours—you were eight, skipping along the street beside your father—I knew that you would be that change. Ambrose would never want it, of course. I could smell his fear every new moon; he wanted you to lead a normal, safe life despite the bruise our curse had left on your soul. But fathers often underestimate their daughters, don't they?"

Her words roused emotion in me. *How ironic*, I thought, *if I crack and crumble right here and now, at her feet.* The one who had disguised me.

She must have sensed it. She took hold of my chin, her fingers frigid against the flush of my cheeks. Her long nails bit into my skin, reminding me to be careful. To bury my feelings. "Take care tonight, Clementine. The end draws nigh and many of us are not as we seem."

"Do you know who struck me last night?"

"I was not watching the hall," she replied, releasing me. "But the smith is wholly devoted to the heiress, in case you did not know."

And she picked up the countess's platter of hen and tossed it out the open window.

I walked the fortress corridors after my meeting with Mazarine, finding my way into the Duke of Seren's abandoned chambers. The suite that Anna in the dream had guided me to.

It was a different experience to see this chamber in the daylight. The walls were wainscoted with painted oak panels. A massive tapestry dressed one wall, and the marble hearth held a heap of ashes. There were four large windows curtained with red damask and a set of balcony doors that remained wide open, ushering in wisps of snow. The bed was large and sunken in the middle, framed by a grand headboard carved with mountains and moons, and there was a reading chair in one corner, flanked by bookshelves.

I stopped before the bloodstain on the floor.

I imagined Emrys drawing his blade over the duke's throat, and the duke fighting, clawing for life. It had been a nightmare, a new moon. A bewitching, soul-changing hour.

A mountain wind sighed through the balcony doors. It touched a wardrobe in the corner, whose carven doors were slightly ajar. Something silver flashed within, and I stepped around the blood and snow to behold the heart of the wardrobe.

The knight's armor hung within.

I stared at it a moment, remembering it from Elle Fielding's dream, from the nights I had fought beside Phelan.

I reached out to trace its steel. A chill raced up my arm.

"Even now, you are not afraid."

The voice took me by surprise. I spun to see Emrys standing a few paces away from me, the stain of blood between us, holding gravity like a hole in the floor.

I took a frantic step away from the wardrobe, but I felt trapped. The balcony was at my back, but my uncle was impeding my path to the corridor.

"Forgive me," I said in a calm voice. "I shouldn't have wandered here."

"I seek no apologies," he replied. Even his voice was like my father's—deep and gentle. A rumble of thunder. "You are free to explore this place, niece."

I tensed.

Emrys seemed to know the cause of it, because he glanced over his shoulder to look at the open doorway and then said, "Rest assured. No one comes near this suite but me. And now you, I suppose. We can speak freely here."

I struggled to believe him. Someone could be lingering just outside the door, eavesdropping. Someone like the countess or Lennox . . .

But I drew in a deep breath and calmed the flutter of my pulse.

"Do you take delight in harming magicians on the new moon?"

He grimaced. "Ah, I was waiting for you to bring that up. My sincerest apologies, Clementine. I did not know it was you."

"It doesn't matter if you knew it was me or not."

"Oh, but it does," Emrys countered. "You are my brother's only child. I would long for death if I had inadvertently killed you."

I didn't know what to say in response. I glanced around the room, looking at anything but him. My terrible, murderous uncle.

"Imonie told me a story about you."

"Did she?" He sounded amused. "Which one, Clementine?"

"I prefer Clem."

"Very well. *Clem.*"

I met his gaze, for he had not taken his eyes from me, as if measuring the depth of my guise. "She told me how you were abandoned on her doorstep one summer night. How she disliked babies but she came to love you both. One of you was quiet and intellectual, the other wild and reckless."

"I take it you have discovered which one your father is?"

"Yes, I believe that I know," I said, but I didn't share my thoughts with him. "Have you spoken to your mother yet?"

"No. Why should I?" he countered. "Imonie fled with all the others and left me to my fate."

"A fate you carved for yourself. In this very room."

"That may be, but they say a mother's love is unconditional."

I fell silent, unwilling to argue with him. But my gaze wandered back to the suit of armor. The bloodstains marring the steel.

"You wounded Phelan twice on the new moon," I said. "Why him? Why not Lennox?"

"Wounded, yes, but I did not kill him," Emrys replied. "Nor would I have. I knew Phelan was important to his mother as well as the master of coin. To strike him would be to strike them both, which was quite effective in getting the court to return home, because here you all are."

I was quiet again, pensive.

"Clem," he said. "Clem, do you have no compassion for me? I have carried the curse that the entire court deserved to bear, living alone in this place with nightmares, unable to die, unable to leave. I carried it so the others could lead normal lives despite our collective treachery, and so they did for an entire century. Do you fault me for growing lonely here? For wanting to see the end?"

"I don't begrudge your loneliness, uncle," I said. "But nor do I have compassion for you."

I began to walk around the bloodstain, my posture stiff, as if I expected him to interfere with my departure. He didn't move, not until I was almost to the door, and he turned on his heel.

"Wait, Clem. There is one more thing I would ask you."

I paused.

"I understand that you are close to Lady Raven," Emrys began in a careful tone. "Does the heiress plan to harm your father?"

"If she did, I think he would have appeared in her dream last night," I said.

"As you appeared?"

I nodded. "She dislikes him, but she has set her attention on others in this fortress. Besides, I don't think you truly care about what happens to my father."

Emrys went rigid. "What makes you say that?"

"Have you even spoken to him since he returned?" I asked. "Do you still judge him, resent him for being the one who escaped your fate? So close, you and he once were. So close that Imonie couldn't even tell the two of you apart when you were boys. She said you would take each other's punishments. That is how deep Ambrose's love for you was. And I don't presume to know what it's like to share a face with another. But whatever it is you're holding against my father . . . you should see it settled, before night falls. Because I think he misses you, more than he will ever confess. That's why he became the warden of Hereswith—to be close to the mountain. To be close to *you*."

I had shocked my uncle into silence. But he laid his hand over his heart and said, "As you say, then." He granted me another bow, but I was gone before he could lift his head.

I returned to my bedroom and saw another note had been slipped beneath my door.

The paper unfolded like wings; I stared at the familiar slant of Imonie's handwriting until the words seemed to melt away.

Do not trust your eyes alone.

41

Night arrived with a whisper of snow. It seemed like the fortress had carried Mazarine's words from earlier that day, delivering them down the winding corridors and slipping them under doors like notes. *The end draws nigh.* Because all of us appeared in the hall that night, dressed in our finest and armed for the unknown.

Mr. Wolfe was present with Nura and Olivette, who was much recovered, although her arm was still bandaged. Mazarine sat at one of the tables loudly crunching her chicken bones, much to the countess's chagrin. The countess sat at a table on the opposite side of the hall, close to the dais, of course. Lennox was at her side, pale faced and sullen, the wound in his shoulder bound in swaths of linen. His arm was in a sling. A rapier sat on the table between them, in addition to a crossbow. Phelan was pacing, lost in his thoughts. The duke stood in one corner draped in shadows, as if he was keenly uncomfortable witnessing a nightmare manifest. I caught a glimmer behind him, and realized it was a weapon of some sort, which he must have pilfered from the fortress armory. And then my parents and Imonie. Mama and Imonie took a seat before one of the hearths, but my father remained standing, his gaze expectantly fixed on the dais. Waiting for the throne and his brother to appear.

It seemed to take forever, but I suppose when you are waiting for something to happen, the minutes feel as long and heavy as years.

I stood between shadows and firelight, looking beyond the windows, where the snow froze like lace.

A bittersweet thought crossed my mind.

This might be the last waking nightmare I faced.

As soon as I came to terms with that truth, time flowed swift and true once more, and the throne materialized, limned in firelight. It quietly beckoned to us all to *come, come and claim me* until a door opened in the wall behind it, and Emrys stepped onto the dais, coming to a rest beside the chair.

This dream arrived gently. I smelled it first—sweet mountain wind, summer grass, cherry galettes still warm from the oven.

A mountain cottage unfurled around us, the walls made of stacked stone, lichens dangling from the thatched roof. The windows were open, inviting rivers of sunshine into the small, simple chamber. There was a kitchen nook with pots and herbs hanging from the rafters, and a worn table that held bowls of abandoned porridge. A few tattered pieces of furniture sat around a hearth.

Books were stacked on a mantel, as was a vase of wildflowers.

I heard the sounds of children playing. Fighting, more like it. One boy laughed, the other began to sob.

And there was Imonie. She appeared in the kitchen of the house, and she was younger, but that scowl still marked her face. She cursed and set down a steaming pan of galettes, following the sound of distress to the back door.

"Boys? *Boys*, inside, now!"

Two auburn-haired boys spilled into the house. They were identical save for the objects they held. One wielded a wooden sword. The other one, the boy who was loudly wailing, held up a book with ripped pages.

"He tore the pages out of it, Mam!"

Imonie's nostrils flared as she looked at the twin with the sword. Her wild one. Emrys.

"Is this true?" she asked him.

"Yes," Emrys replied, solemn.

"Apologize to your brother, then."

Emrys huffed, but he looked at Ambrose and said, "I'm sorry for tearing pages from your book."

The apology did nothing to ease the sting in Ambrose's heart. He retreated to the divan by the hearth and lay facedown on it, weeping into the cushion until he fell asleep.

"You must be gentler, son," Imonie said to Emrys. "What do I tell you every night before bed?"

"To think before I act," Emrys grumbled.

"Give me the sword, then. You will not get to play with it for a week, as punishment," Imonie said, and held out her hand.

Emrys surrendered his wooden sword to her with a sigh.

The scene melted away, instantly replaced with another. The twins were older. They were young men, now—the age my father and Emrys were frozen at—and I struggled to identify who was who as they walked a corridor of the fortress.

"The time is now," one of them whispered. The shadows danced across his face but his eyes were luminous, as if he burned from within.

"Are you certain?"

"Yes."

"When?"

"Raven deems the new moon will be appropriate."

"But what does Lora think? What of your wife?"

"She supports me. She supports this plan."

Silence fell between the brothers. With a pang, I realized that I couldn't identify whose dream this was. If it belonged to my father or to Emrys.

"I will not move forward with these plans, not without you, brother."

A long sigh. "Fine. I will join you, then. I seem destined to keep you out of trouble."

The dream shifted again, pulling us along its currents.

We were in the Duke of Seren's bedchamber. Isidore stood near the foot of his bed, reading a letter by firelight. The night was dark, bitterly cold. Emrys was present, dressed in the blue robes of an advisor. He withdrew a dagger silently, but its blade flashed a warning.

My uncle sliced Isidore's neck.

The duke gasped his name, a name that rose like a hiss of smoke, the sound of a curse sparking—*"Emrys"*—before he sank to his knees, his blood pooling on the floor. Hunched but still breathing, Isidore held out his hand and called to the moon, to nightmares. He cursed his court and died facedown in his blood.

Emrys ran the halls, his heart beating in his throat. A woman with long brown hair and a scar on her face was waiting for him in the courtyard. The stars bled in the sky as she embraced him, and her voice trembled when she said, "We have to go. We cannot stay here." She took the dagger he had slain the duke with and threw it over the balcony. It clattered among the rocky slopes.

The dream took us to the mountain passage, to the opening in the foothills. Two wide doors that I had passed through days ago.

The court was fleeing. I saw them all—the master of coin, the heiress. Mr. Wolfe. Mazarine. My father holding the hand of the woman named Lora. His wife, I realized, and my alarm began to swell.

The only member of the court who could not pass from the mountain was Emrys.

Emrys in his blue robes.

"Come, brother." Ambrose beckoned him, frowning. He stood in the grass and the sun, but his twin remained in the shadows of the passage.

"I cannot, Ambrose," Emrys said. "The mountain holds me captive."

Ambrose passed over the threshold and took his brother's hand, struggling to draw him out, into the light. A sound of pain rose from Emrys. Steam began to rise from his garments, as if he was catching fire.

"Go," he cried, shoving Ambrose into the grass. "Go and forge new lives. I will hold the curse."

The doors closed.

Both Imonie and Ambrose stood in the foothills for a long while, staring at the wooden doors that had sealed. The place where they had been separated from Emrys.

Lora eventually drew my father away, but she had grown old. Her hair was gray, her body withered. She was old but my father was not, and he wept over her grave when she died. It was Imonie who pulled him up and led him to Endellion.

"Death follows me, Mam," my father said to her. "Nothing good comes from my hands."

"Then you must determine to make something new with your hands, son," Imonie replied.

He heeded her, and magic bloomed in his palms.

Imonie turned away and my mother appeared, young and bright and alive, her beauty like a flame that my father couldn't look away from.

Sigourney tore the fabric from her skirt and wrapped something small within it. A baby, and she extended it to Ambrose.

"Your daughter," she said, and my father took me in his arms for the first time.

The world grew quiet as he gazed at me. Quiet until a tiny flash of gold caught the light. A golden scale just above my small, fresh heart.

If I had thought it was difficult to pierce Anna's and Clem's hearts to break a dream, then it was impossible to imagine driving a dagger into my infant form.

I stood and trembled at the edges of the dream—my father's dream.

I stared at him, how he held me, how he smiled at me.

The wonder faded when my real father stepped forward. He approached his phantom, and when he held out his hands, dream Ambrose surrendered me into his arms.

I also moved forward.

My father paid me no heed, gazing down at the baby in his arms. With polished confidence, he withdrew his dagger. Both light and darkness danced on the blade as he lifted it, and my breath hung in my throat when a scream split the air.

My mother rushed to him, horrified. I didn't know if it was actually my mother or her phantom. The realms bled together, and I was lost between what was real and what was imagined.

My father didn't spare my mother a glance. He drove his dagger into the baby's chest, swift and deep, and the baby let out a wail as the dream broke at last. The infant turned into smoke, slipping through my father's arms. And the strange world that had been layering around us melted away.

I closed my eyes until the colors had passed, until the only sound I could hear was my breath, whistling through my teeth.

The hall was silent, and I opened my eyes to behold my father.

He stared at me. He still held the dagger in his hand, and I wanted to ask if he had harbored any doubt before he had plunged that blade into my heart. If it had been difficult for him, even if he had kept his senses straight.

I was both relieved and angry. I was grateful the nightmare had broken, and yet I wanted to shout at him, *How could you?*

But his eyes were jaded and cold. A stranger's gaze. And the longer I studied him . . . I realized he was not my father. It was Emrys, wearing my father's clothes and aging spell, pretending to be him.

Do not trust your eyes alone, Imonie had warned me.

I swallowed the knot in my throat and looked at the dais, where my father stood beside the throne, stripped of his glamour and dressed as Emrys. My father in those blue robes. His cheeks shone with tears.

The truth was slow to overtake me. But I felt its sting, and I acknowledged that my father was not who I believed him to be.

He knew the taste of blood.

"Daughter."

I glanced back at Emrys, shocked he was speaking to me, continuing with this charade.

I heard something buzz by my ear, felt it whoosh and nearly graze my cheek. And I watched as an arrow sank into Emrys's chest.

It happened so quickly. I didn't believe my own eyes, not until Emrys's blood began to drip down his chest and he gasped. It was a sound to summon the spirit of death. A mortal blow. He slowly sank to his knees and I rushed to catch him, easing him to the floor.

"Where is my brother?" he rasped, clutching my hand. The aging glamour faded, leaving behind a young yet ancient face, marred in pain.

"I'm here," my father replied. He knelt on the other side of Emrys, drawing his brother into his arms. "I was supposed to shield you this time, Em. You fooled me."

You fooled me.

I dwelled on my conversation with Emrys from earlier that day. He had asked if my father was in danger. I had said no, but Emrys had seen through the countess. He must have convinced his brother to swap roles to keep him safe.

I looked up to see Lady Raven standing nearby with the crossbow in her hands. Her shock seemed to radiate from witnessing someone in the deathless court die. She trembled as Phelan yanked the weapon away from her.

"I could not let your life end like this," Emrys whispered to Papa. A pallor was creeping over his skin. I watched his blood continue to flow down his chest and drip onto the floor. "You have so much . . . to live for, Ambrose." He looked at me, and there was tenderness in his eyes.

I felt Imonie's presence draw near, and when she spoke, her voice was soft, agonized.

"Let me hold him."

I shifted away and let her take my place on the floor. My father eased Emrys into her arms and she held him close to her heart.

"Mam," Emrys whispered.

"Let me hold you one last time, my quiet boy," Imonie said with a smile, stroking the hair from his brow. "My scholar of dreams."

I remembered Imonie's story, her words like an echo returning to me after months. *Her quiet boy would deceive her, acting as his wild brother to take his punishments. And the wild boy would act as his quiet twin, to avoid her wrath when he strayed too far.*

I had assumed wrong.

I had thought my father was Imonie's quiet boy. But all this time . . . it had been Emrys. The boy who had loved books and school and peaceful spaces, who had wept when my father tore the pages in his book. Who had let my father wear his robes to deceive and kill the duke. Who had taken the fall for my father's crime.

Emrys closed his eyes.

Imonie continued to hold him. And he breathed his last in her arms.

42

A wail rose from my father. His brother's blood stained the floor and Papa buried his face in his palms and wept.

It was the sound of a heart breaking.

The waves of his grief cut through me. I stared at Papa, at his bloodied hands. He was Imonie's wild boy. The assassin. A reckless coward.

And I was his daughter.

The betrayer's blood ran through my veins like quicksilver.

I rose, my feet throbbing with pins and needles. I drew a deep breath to steady myself, my gaze roaming the hall. My mother rushed to Papa's side. Mr. Wolfe remained at a respectful distance, but his eyes were wide with shock. Nura and Olivette walked toward me, but I had no time to go to them, to try and sort the tangle of my emotions.

Someone was rushing to the dais, their boots clicking over the stone floor.

I knew it was the countess before I turned to look in that direction. She was ascending the stairs, furtively glancing over her shoulder to see if any of us were following her. Because of that action, she didn't see Mazarine emerge from the shadows behind the chair, a crossbow in her hands. The troll shot at the countess before I could yell an order for her to hold her fire. The arrow sank into Lady Raven's thigh, violently halting her progression, and she emitted a scream that made the hair lift on my arms.

The countess collapsed on the stairs.

Lennox stood and watched like he was hewn from stone, but Phelan rushed to assist her, gently easing the countess up and carrying her to the table.

"You'll be fine, Mother," he said as he briefly examined her wound.

The countess whimpered and then promptly fainted from the pain.

Mazarine continued to linger by the throne, guarding it with her crossbow. The hall fell painfully quiet, and then the troll looked at me. She arched her brow and said, "Clem?"

She'd blown my cover. The one who had cast her magic upon me now unapologetically exposed me. And yet . . . I found that I didn't care.

I was relieved.

"Clem?" Nura echoed.

I glanced at my friends. Olivette's brow wrinkled with confusion, but Nura was furious. The pieces had just come together for her, and I watched the betrayal brighten her eyes.

I walked to the dais stairs, expecting someone to protest my approach. For all they knew, I was about to claim the sovereignty for myself. But the silence held and simmered, and I paused on the steps and looked at Phelan.

"Phelan," I called to him. I watched his face slacken in surprise. "Phelan, will you join me on the dais?"

He slowly left his mother's side, as if he understood my intentions and was resisting. But he ascended as I knew he would, and he stood before me, casting a wary glance at Mazarine.

"What is this about, Clem?" he whispered, but his voice carried. Everyone could hear us.

"I want you to claim the sovereignty of Seren," I said. "Will you sit on the throne and reinstate a new court? Will you restore the mountain duchy and bring her people home?"

He stared at me for a long moment. And then he said, "Why not you?"

I swallowed scathing laughter, but I glanced at my father, who continued to sit on the floor. He had ceased weeping and now watched the events unfolding on the dais with rapt attention.

I returned my gaze to Phelan and whispered, "I'm unworthy."

Phelan shook his head. "I've never heard something more ridiculous, Clem. You're not your father, as I'm not my mother."

"I don't want it."

"Nor do I," he countered.

I sighed, weary of arguing with him. "Will you do it for me, Phelan? For Olivette and Nura? For the people whose nightmares you once fought, for those who are lost and displaced and yet dream of the mountains? Who dream of home?"

He closed his eyes, and I knew my words had stirred something in him. I waited, and when he looked at me again, my worry and my fear began to slip away.

"I will do this, Clem, but only if you are there beside me."

"Where else would I be?" I teased with a smile.

He reached out and traced my face, and I knew that he would do this for me. I knew that he was the one to bring life back to these mountains.

Mazarine stepped aside and Phelan turned to the throne. He began to close the distance between himself and the chair. I watched at first, eager to see this curse come to its end. But then I felt a prickling at the nape of my neck. A warning that someone was staring at me, which seemed absurd, as everyone in the hall was beholding this moment. But the past two nights, I had been attacked from behind. I had not guarded my back.

I spun to study the hall.

Everyone was just as they had been—Imonie held Emrys, my parents sat on the floor beside a puddle of blood, Nura and Olivette and Mr. Wolfe stood three tables away transfixed, the countess lay unconscious on a tabletop with Lennox at her side, and Mazarine remained close with her crossbow.

And then I realized I was missing someone.

The duke. The master of coin.

I had not seen him since the beginning of the night.

The fires in the hearth continued to cast light, but there were endless pools of shadows. And from one of those shadows the master of coin stepped forward, a crossbow braced against his chest, aimed at the throne.

His avarice was so keen that he had no qualms in killing his own "investment." *The countess is right,* I thought. The master of coin didn't want to see this curse broken. It would ruin the life he had built for himself in Endellion. All the money that dreams brought into his hands.

He let the arrow fly. It sang in the air.

I only had a breath to react. I was the only one who saw him, my eyes trained upon the arrow's path. All my spells disintegrated in my memory. I couldn't summon a single shield.

And so I didn't think. I merely reacted—I let my body respond—and I stepped between Phelan and the master of coin. I took the arrow in my chest, hoping it would find the stone of my heart.

The arrow met me with startling force, blowing me off my feet. I slid along the floor and then came to a stop, gasping. I gazed down at myself like this body belonged to someone else, with this shaft of wood that protruded from my chest and the blood that began to spill like wine. The pain surged when I tried to breathe, when I felt the sting of my wound.

And then the screams rose. My mother's. Olivette's. Imonie's. My father's.

Phelan gathered me in his arms and together we sat at the footstool of the throne. He was saying my name, over and over—*Clem, Clem, Clem*—like it was a prayer, like it was an answer. Like he didn't know what to do without me.

"Phelan," I managed to say, and I must have sounded like my old self, because it calmed him.

He quieted, caressing my face. Fear burned in his eyes like embers. I tried to breathe and felt the excruciating pinch in my lungs again. A pressure sat on my chest, and pain crackled between my ribs.

My parents hovered, as did Mazarine. They were frantically speaking; their words rushed over me like a river. I wanted to tell them to *be quiet*, and I closed my eyes. Clenched my teeth. Ordered myself to keep drawing breath even though it was agonizing. And then the silence came, and it was beautiful and cold and calm, like resting underwater. I knew why the words had faded, because a shiver raced across my skin, and I began to change.

I opened my eyes. My guise started to crack along my arms, up my neck, across the planes of my face like ice.

Phelan continued to hold me against his chest. His warmth seeped into me, and I could hear his heart pounding, humming-bird swift in his breast. I watched the wonder in his face. It eclipsed the terror, the agony.

And I breathed and I broke and I transformed in his arms.

Mazarine's ancient magic relinquished me. I watched Anna Neven crumble and fall away, and she lay in fragments around me, like pieces of stained glass.

My hair was long copper waves once more. My two inches of height and my full lips and the dimples in my cheeks and my brown eyes all came back to me, just as I remembered them. And yet I could not explain why I felt like a different girl.

Until I breathed again and felt my heart struggle to beat.

The arrow had not broken the stone within me. A wound had not ushered my breaking. It had been my decision to take an arrow for Phelan. For I couldn't imagine a world with him gone.

And the last stone of my heart turned into dust.

"Mazarine," my father said in a ragged voice. I felt his hand touch my hair. "Mazarine, can you do something?"

Mazarine gazed down at me. I saw that her guise had started to crack as well. Half of her face was human, and half of her face was troll. She was breaking, and I wondered why. Wondered until she laid her hand upon my chest, as if sensing the state of my heart. And I knew she had come to care for me.

"Her heart is weakening," she said. When she drew her hand back, her fingers were drenched in my blood. "And the curse still stands. Perhaps . . ."

She had no chance to finish her statement.

Phelan rose with me in his arms.

I wanted to ask him, *What are you doing?* But my voice . . . I couldn't find it. Yet he seemed to know my thoughts, because he said, "I don't want to do this without you."

I released a tremulous breath—*all right, as you wish*—and he walked us to the throne.

He claimed the sovereignty with me in his arms. We sat together, as one, and the curse came undone.

A wind tore through the hall. It was violent at first, the makings of a storm, and it extinguished the fires and made the shadows twine and dance. The windows shattered one by one, raining glass and lead. The snow swept in. I thought that we would all be torn apart, blown into pieces.

But sometimes things must break before they can be made whole again, so that they can be forged into something stronger.

The wind died, escaping out the open windows, and the snow gathered on the floor.

It was a quiet, peaceful night. A night for dreams. And magic teemed, thick and cold, in the air.

I looked at Phelan only to discover he was already gazing at me.

The pain in my chest was relentless. I couldn't draw breath, and I made a sad, gurgling sound. Blood filled my mouth, and I knew I had reached the end of myself. And yet I wasn't afraid.

I began to let go. It was a sweet surrender, to not have to hold on to things so fiercely as I had before. To open my hands and my heart and be who I wanted to be.

"Clem," Phelan whispered.

It was the last thing I heard.

Mazarine suddenly appeared before us. In one swift stroke, she yanked the arrow from my heart.

I closed my eyes and surrendered to the rush of darkness.

43

One does not expect to wake after their heart has stopped beating, after they have slipped into the cold, quiet dark. One also does not expect to return to the light only to be greeted by a troll.

Mazarine sat beside me, her human form gone, shed like scales. She was just as I remembered from that fateful September day months ago: a jagged face like rocks, teeth overlapping her lips, stained with old blood. Coarse hair that shone silver, threaded with leaves and sticks and thorny vines. Her twin horns gleamed like bones.

She noticed my stirring and smiled, which roused a tiny flame of fear in me.

"My mortal girl awakens," she said. "Sit forward and drink."

I didn't tell her I felt weak and shaky, and that my chest smoldered with pain. I didn't think it wise to oppose her, even if her love for me had made her disguise break, and she helped me sit forward in my bed.

I blinked against the streams of sunlight that flooded in through the balcony doors. I didn't recognize this room. It was far grander than the one I had originally chosen for myself, and I frowned, rubbing the ache in my temples.

"Mazarine . . . where am I?"

"The fortress in the clouds," she answered, lifting a wooden cup of cold water to my lips. "The Duchy of Seren. The realm of Azenor. Drink, Clementine."

I sighed, exasperated by her replies, but began to sip the water. It washed through me, trickling into the parched places of my soul, and I felt refreshed.

And then Mazarine added, "My duchess."

I promptly choked on the water.

"What did you call me?" I rasped, coughing. The pain flared in my chest, and I groaned, laying my hand over my heart. I could feel linen bandages wrapped snugly around me, beneath my chemise. But my wound was still bright and tender. I wondered how long it would take before I could breathe without feeling that pinch of pain.

"I called you duchess," the troll replied.

"Why? I'm not your duchess."

She cocked her gnarled brow at me. "You do not remember, Clementine?"

I traced through my memories. Bloodstains, darkness, wind, shattering glass. Breaking and breathing and arrows and dreams and the rhythm of Phelan's heart against my cheek.

"I remember, but Phelan is the one who claimed the throne," I said.

"You both did. You sat as one; you broke the curse as one." Mazarine paused, watching the emotions ripple across my face. "You are not pleased, child?"

"I . . . I didn't *want* this!"

"Nor did he. Which means the two of you are perfect for this task."

"So he is duke?"

"Aye."

"And I am duchess?"

"That's what I said, wasn't it?"

I swallowed a hysterical laugh. "But . . . how can you call us that? We aren't married."

Mazarine shrugged, utterly unperturbed. "You and Phelan are still bound by commitment and magic of your own making. You are partners."

I was quiet, overwhelmed.

"The two of you are like iron, sharpening the other," Mazarine said. "I sense that he could not do this without you, and you would not want to do it without him. Together you are stronger, a balance. You will both lead the duchy into a new era."

I groaned again and covered my face with my hands. But I couldn't deny that I felt a small thrill when I imagined this new path before me.

The door opened.

I glanced up to see it was Imonie, and my heart lifted at the sight of her.

The lines on her face eased when she beheld me awake and sitting in bed. But then she looked at Mazarine, and her scowl returned with vengeance.

"You've upset her," Imonie stated.

"I have kept this extraordinary yet fragile mortal alive," Mazarine replied smoothly. "I believe gratitude is in order?"

Imonie huffed, but she nodded. "You have my eternal gratitude, Brin of Stonefall."

Mazarine made a smug noise. But she set down my water cup and rose. "I will be just outside the door if you need me, Your Grace."

It took me a moment to realize she was addressing *me*, and I cleared my throat and nodded. "Thank you, Mazarine. *Brin*."

The troll left, shutting the door behind her.

Imonie quietly took her place, her eyes never leaving my face.

"How are you feeling, Clementine?" she asked.

"I've been better. How long have I been asleep?"

"For a week."

"A *week*?"

Imonie nodded. "Your parents and I have been worried sick, but that troll would only let us visit you once a day." She reached forward to take my hand, a rare display of affection from her.

I smiled and squeezed her fingers with what strength I could find, which was still faint.

"Can I get you anything, Clementine? Water, tea, food?"

My stomach was indeed empty, but I wasn't hungry for food. I leaned back into my array of pillows and said, "Will you tell me a story?"

A flicker of surprise passed over Imonie's face. But then she smiled and smoothed the wrinkles from my blankets.

And my grandmother told me the stories of the mountains.

My parents visited not long after Imonie departed. Papa brought in a tray of soup, soft bread, and tea, and my mother acted like she was going to feed it to me until I took the spoon.

They perched on either side of my bed, watching me eat.

"I'm going to be fine," I said, seeking to reassure them. But my hand trembled as I lifted the spoon to my lips. I knew I still had many weeks of recovery before me, and I wondered where Phelan was, but I was too proud to ask after him.

"Where is the countess?" I asked instead.

"She's recovering," Papa replied. "She plans to leave the mountains and return to Endellion once she is able to travel. Lennox will accompany her. She'll be under house arrest for a while, per Phelan's wishes."

"And what of the duke? The master of coin?"

My parents were silent, provoking me to look up from my soup.

"He fled the hall after he shot you," Mama said. "And after Mazarine removed the arrow and tended to you, she hunted him down. He was hiding in one of the lower levels of the fortress."

"Is he dead?" I asked.

My father nodded.

I didn't pity the master of coin, not after seeing the extent of his greed. But I would certainly need to speak to Mazarine about how I wanted to dole out punishment in the days to come.

"Mazarine has taken up her service to you with unfaltering allegiance," my mother stated, as if she had read the trail of my thoughts. "I believe she has appointed herself as your guard."

"And let her remain that way, Clem," my father pleaded. "She is stubborn and frightening, but she will protect you."

"Yes, I think I'll keep her." I set down my soup, feeling nauseated. After a week of being asleep, I had filled my stomach too swiftly. I reached for the teapot but my father beat me to it, pouring me a cup. He even knew how much cream and honey to stir into it. And then I realized there was tea, when there had not been before, and I whispered, "Where did the tea come from?"

"Phelan has opened the fortress," Papa replied. "He has been busy while you slept, traveling and gathering resources and people. This place has returned to life."

I fell quiet, listening. And while the walls around me were thick . . . I caught a faint trace of laughter. A rumble of furniture being shifted. The clang of something like pots. Doors opening and closing.

My unworthiness rose. My fears and worries nipped at my thoughts and I suddenly felt very small and very unprepared.

I looked at my parents and said, "Will you both help me? Will you both stay with me? I don't know what I'm doing."

Papa made a sound, and I think he was swallowing his tears. He leaned close to me and dropped a kiss on my brow, and I knew he would walk beside me, that he would be with me for the hard days as well as the good days.

My mother took my hand in hers, a hand full of magic and love and gentleness. "We will help you, Clementine. Whatever you need, we will be here for you."

She exchanged a glance with my father, one that made my breath catch.

I thought about the different paths we had each taken—vengeance and fear and anger and solitude and pain—and yet how all three of us had ended up here, in this strange moment of new beginnings.

I'd once believed that magic and secrets and beliefs had torn us apart. But in the end, I think it wove us back together with stronger threads.

The next day, Mazarine said it was time for me to get up and walk. I bathed and dressed with her assistance, and then I stood beside the hearth, holding on to the back of a chair. My head swam, and my legs felt like pudding, but I was not about to say such things to the troll.

"I think . . . I think I need a cane," I said.

"Will we do?"

I glanced up to see Nura and Olivette enter my chamber. I hadn't dared to hope that they had remained in the fortress after the curse's breaking. I hadn't dared to hope that they would want to see me, speak with me.

But here they were. Olivette was broadly grinning, her face flushed and ribbons braided into her blond hair. Nura was far more reserved, dressed in a sleek black dress, and I still sensed her pain over my deceit. But her eyes were gentle when they met mine. An invitation to make things right between us.

They each offered me an arm, and I walked between them, through the winding corridors of the fortress.

We passed people I had never seen before, people who were carrying crates and bags of produce and stacks of linens, working to transform this place into home. All of them paused to curtsy or bow to me, and I thought I might die from the embarrassment.

"Here," Nura suggested, guiding us to the courtyard doors. "Let's walk the gardens. You need fresh air."

We stepped outside. The snow was ankle deep on the ground, hiding the plants in white, but the sky was cloudless and ached a vibrant blue. We walked a stone path that had been cleared, through icy rosebushes and a trellis of vines. I soon grew sore for breath, and my friends guided me to a stone bench that overlooked the city of Ulla.

The three of us sat, their legs close to mine, and I swallowed the lump in my throat. I had hurt them, and I hated myself for it.

"How are you feeling, Ann—I mean, Clem," Olivette asked, flustered. "I should probably call you *Your Grace*, actually, shouldn't I?"

"Don't be silly," I said, and nudged her. "Call me Clem."

An awkward lull encompassed us.

"What comes next for the two of you?"

Nura glanced at Olivette. "Should we tell her, Oli?"

"Tell me what?" I demanded.

"We should," Olivette agreed with a wily grin. "Phelan asked us to be part of your new court."

The news was a pleasant surprise, one that buoyed my spirits, but Olivette gave me no time to respond.

"I'm not sure what we will be yet," she continued. "Perhaps your advisor?"

"Or your spymistress?" Nura added.

"Or even the mistress of coin?"

"Or your guard?"

"All of this to say . . . we want to join you in the restoration," Olivette concluded. "If you will have us."

I laughed, which drummed up the ache in my chest, and slipped my arms around them. "You can both be whatever you desire. I'm thrilled you're staying." I fell silent for a moment, and then added, "And I'm sorry, for deceiving you both for so long."

"We have questions," Nura said. "We want to know why and how you did what you did."

I let out a shaky breath. "Ah, where do I even begin?"

Olivette leaned closer to me. "Begin at the beginning."

My mind wandered back to that moment in Hereswith when I sat in Mazarine's library, drawing her twelfth portrait by candle-light.

And so that was where I began.

It took me most of the day to tell them the story. We shared a pot of tea and a tray of cold cuts and cheese and fruit in the afternoon before Mazarine called me back to rest in bed.

I heeded her, because only a fool wouldn't.

472

My slumber was deep, full of flashes of dreams that I struggled to remember when I woke. My room was dark, lit by the fire in my hearth and a few candles. I slipped from my bed and gingerly reached for a robe and my boots, walking to the door.

Mazarine was in the corridor, on guard. But she allowed me to walk, and she followed me to the courtyard doors. She stood watch as I walked the gardens alone, savoring the quiet splendor of night, how the snow crunched beneath my steps, how the world looked different beneath the moon and stars.

I found a bench and sat, shivering and cold and feeling more alive than I ever had before.

I don't know how long I was there before he came. But I soon heard his quiet tread on the snow, and I felt his presence draw near.

"Her Grace looks well rested," said Phelan.

I glanced over my shoulder to see him standing beneath the trellis of glittering vines. He wore simple clothes—just his boots and trousers and a white shirt—and his hair was loose, dark as raven wings. A woolen cloak was fastened at his neck.

"And His Grace looks the same," I said wryly, and he joined me on the bench.

"How are you, truly, Clem?" he asked, and then noticed what I was wearing—a thin robe. "And why aren't you wearing a cloak, for gods' sake!" He unbuckled his and draped it over my shoulders.

I sank into the cloak's warmth, hiding a smile. "I grow stronger every day. And you? I hear you've been busy."

"To the uttermost. But it's given me something to do while I waited for you to wake."

We fell quiet, content to simply sit beside each other.

Phelan whispered, "May I hold you?"

My heart stirred, beating a heady song within my blood. But I said, "Someone might see us." Which was ridiculous, as I could only dimly discern him in the dark.

Phelan laughed. "I really don't care."

Once, he had been afraid of what others thought of him. Once, I had been bent by revenge and coldness and believed myself stronger alone.

I shifted toward him and he drew me onto his lap. Our fingers entwined and I rested in his embrace. We sat like that for a moment, admiring the starlit sky, until I turned to face him.

"What do you dream of, Phelan?" I asked.

"What do I dream of?" he countered, amused. "By night or by day?"

Of course, I wanted to know the things he beheld at night, the dreams that rose from his darkest places. But more than that . . . I wanted to know what he wanted.

"By day," I said.

He glanced beyond me, where the mountains rested in the moonlight, glazed in ice. "I used to dream of being someone worthy, and so I became a magician. And then I dreamt of finding somewhere I belonged, where I could use my magic for the good of others. I never thought I would find it in Seren, but the past couple of days have proven to me that purpose can be found in unexpected places." He paused, his gaze tracing me. "What about you, Clem? What do you dream of by day?"

I closed my eyes, as if I could see my desire, resting just beyond my reach. "I dream of finding a new home. Of bringing something broken back together, and not just with magic but with stories and friendship and good food."

When I looked at Phelan again, I caught a glimmer in his eyes, as if he dreamt the same things as me. I leaned closer to him until our lips met, polite and cautious and then hungry and familiar, and my heart was suddenly racing. But for the first time in months, there was no pain.

"I have something for you," he said with a smile, drawing away from me.

Intrigued, I listened as he reached for something in his pocket, how it crinkled in his hands like parchment.

"What is it?" I asked warily.

He set something long and square in my palms, hidden beneath paper and twine. There was a hint of joy in his voice when he told me, "Open it later."

44

I opened it later that night, when I was alone in my bedchamber. I pulled away the parchment and twine, and for a moment I merely stared at what rested within. And then I touched it, hesitantly, as if it might bring me pain to remember.

A sketchbook full of empty pages. Three sticks of sharpened charcoal.

I slowly began to draw again.

It didn't take long until I craved to draw a portrait of myself. My skill was raw, nothing as it had once been when I'd surrendered it for a stone heart, but whenever I had a spare moment, I was in my room, drawing. Eager to regain what I had lost.

Eventually, I had a mirror brought into my bedchamber.

I arranged myself before it, sketchbook open to a fresh page, charcoal ready in hand, the window drapes parted to welcome winter sunshine.

I studied my face in the mirror and began to render it on paper. But with each glance from the paper to the glass . . . I realized that I was drawing someone I didn't recognize. A girl with gleaming teeth and fallen stars in her long, red hair. A girl with cold, determined eyes.

My hand shook.

I stopped and set down the charcoal, staring at my reflection. Mazarine's words rose to memory. *Your true reflection will always shine brightly upon a mirror.*

Perhaps one day I would draw what was reflected. Perhaps one day, I'd be ready to acknowledge what truly dwelled on the other side of the glass. What I was becoming. But it was not that day, and I closed my sketchbook with a snap.

I rose and turned away from the mirror.

ACKNOWLEDGMENTS

It's December 31 and I'm finally sitting down to write the acknowledgments for this fourth (how is that even possible?!) book of mine. I wanted to save this moment for the last day of 2020, a year that all of us will vividly remember. A year that brought immense challenges and heartache and a new way of life. It would be remiss of me if I did not mention working on this book all through the chaos of 2020, and to illuminate the people who made this book its best version, even as they were called to stay home and suddenly had to balance work and family and feelings of isolation and worry and fatigue and illness. I had moments when it felt difficult to open my manuscript and focus on what I had created, but I also think so many of us found peace and joy and wonder in books this year—writing them, revising them, and reading them—and my words now will never be enough to express my gratitude to the people who joined me on this journey and carried me through 2020.

To Suzie Townsend, agent extraordinaire. Thank you for making one of my greatest dreams a reality, for loving my stories and finding them the best homes, and for always being there for me. You are the best. To Dani Segelbaum, who helps me with vital behind-the-scenes things . . . I truly couldn't do this without your assistance and insight, and I'm so thankful for you. To Mia Roman, Veronica Grijalva, and Victoria Hendersen, who all have been instrumental in my foreign rights and sales—thank you for working so endlessly and finding a home for my stories overseas. To the New Leaf Dream Team—I'm so honored to be one of your authors. Thank you for investing in me and my books.

To Karen Chaplin, my editor. Thank you for continuing to fearlessly step into the convoluted and verbose worlds I create and helping me find the threads to bring together to make a stronger story. It's been an honor to work on four novels with you. To Rosemary Brosnan, I'm so delighted to be published by your inimitable team at Quill Tree Books. Thank you for loving my stories and giving them a place on the shelf. To my publicist, Lauren Levite, who brought so many wonderful opportunities my way despite the strangeness of 2020—thank you. To Bria Ragin, who has been with me and my stories since my debut year . . . thank you for all your notes and lovely emails. To my copy editor (I'm truly in awe of you!) who will forever be changing my greys into grays—thank you for polishing this manuscript. To my proofreaders, who help catch errors and ensure I'm making sense—thank you. To the production team, the marketing team, the sales team, the design team . . . y'all are simply amazing and I am eternally thankful for you and your expertise. To Molly Fehr and your absolutely gorgeous design ideas—I'm so happy that I got to have you for two book covers! To Annie Stegg Gerard, who illustrated the cover of my dreams—I'm in love with how beautiful it is. To Virginia Allyn, who illustrated the gorgeous map. I was thrilled to discover you were going to create another map for my book!

To my wonderful critique partner, Isabel Ibañez, who made this year so much better with your stories and phone talk walks and insights into my messy first drafts—thank you, sweet friend.

To Ciannon Smart, thank you for reading an early copy. You inspire me in countless ways and I'm excited to see your books take flight.

To my readers, in the United States and abroad, who are so lovely and have encouraged me on the days when I felt like giving up. Thank you. I would not be where I am today without you. If there is a dream in your heart, one you're secretly holding on to, I hope this is the year when you begin to see it come true.

To Mom and Dad, for always believing in me and my writing, even when I didn't. You taught me all the magic I ever needed to know, and this book is for you. To my siblings—Caleb, Gabriel, Ruth, Mary, and Luke. Our D&D campaign has been one of the highlights of this year for me, and I love each of you fiercely. To my family—my grandparents and aunts and uncles and cousins and in-laws—and my friends, thank you for always supporting this dream of mine.

To Sierra, who *loved* the quarantine because it meant we were home with you all the time. I have yet to write a story where a dog fails to appear, all because of you.

To Ben, my other half. At the beginning of this year, you told me, "2015 Becca would be very proud of 2020 Becca." And that image has stayed with me, all through the ups and downs. To see how much I've grown and changed in the last five years—to realize how much I've accomplished. I can't help but look forward to all the good things yet to come. Thank you for dreaming alongside me, always.

And to my Heavenly Father, for taking this small dream of mine and turning it into paper and ink. *Soli Deo Gloria.*